P B N

LEAVING PIMLICO

WATERMILL CLASSICS

P B NORTH

PB North was born in Stockton-on-Tees, England. He studied at the University of Cambridge where he received an MA in English and won the Latham Prize for English Literature. He later went on to take a post graduate degree at Edinburgh University.

He has lived most of his life in Scotland, where he has worked in various roles as a government official, writing many thousands of words for public reports. He is currently based in East Lothian where he lives with his Norwegian wife, his cat and his rescue Staffie/dachshund cross. When he is not writing, he tries to grow things, plays golf badly and goes out in his boat.

Leaving Pimlico is his first novel, which draws extensively on his time spent in Norway, Scotland and the north of England. It is his first excursion into long fiction which he regards as a lot more enjoyable to do than government reports. His second novel is planned to appear later this year.

pb_north@btinternet.com

This novel is entirely a work of fiction. The names, characters and incidents portrayed in it are the work of the author's imagination. Any resemblance to actual persons, living or dead, is entirely coincidental. Parts of the novel are set against a general historical background which the author does not claim is accurate in detail.

P B North © 2014

Acknowledgements

To Inger, for enticing me to Norway in the first instance and then advising on all things Scandinavian in the book; and to THB at Watermill Classics for all his work on the cover design and production.

Prologue

York Psychiatric Hospital, June, 1999

We were reaching the end of the session.

'OK, Peter. Tell me how it's been these last few weeks.'

'Better, yes, much better.'

'No morbid thoughts?'

'No. Not really. But I still have these vivid dreams, mostly at night, but sometimes daydreams too.'

'And they're about the usual?'

'Same thing as always. I told you about them. It's the story I read ten years ago. It's as if it had really happened to me. I can feel the horror of the man holding a gun to his head, in that dark cold chapel in the forest. I can hear the scream when the light goes out and the gun fires, just once. And then I come to. Same every time. But it's not me. It's someone else.'

'It might as well be you though. That will pass, in time.'

'How much time? That's the point.'

'I can't tell you. It's up to you.'

'I know, live in the present, not the past. That's what I'm trying to do.'

'You got it. Do you want to see me next week?'

'Do you think I should?'

'See how you feel. You can phone me any time. You're almost there.'

That was yesterday. This is my present. I'm sitting at my desk in the window, moors stretching away into the blue distance, blank screen in front of me, and Tom barges into the room. He's ten years old, skinny as a rake, with brown curly hair, brown eyes and a wide smile.

'You busy Dad?' he shouts from the doorway.

'Trying to be busy, Tom, but nothing's coming. What do you want?'

'Will you bowl at me?'

He's mad about cricket and we have a flat patch of grass at the back of the farm with a fruit cage for a net.

'I need to get going on this, Tom,' I reply. 'What about Katie? What's she doing?'

Katie is his fifteen year old half-sister, who used to be good at cricket, until she developed the usual teenage girl interests. There's a long groan from the doorway. I know I have no option.

'OK. Just a minute. Let me write one sentence and then I know I can start.'

This is my writer's trick. It's seen me through six novels: write a sentence – anything – when you can't write a thing. Then come back and edit it later. It gets you off the hook and the panic and things start to flow. Tom sidles up to my desk, bat in hand.

'What's this Dad?' he asks, picking up a small velvet box from the top of a pile of papers.

'That, Tom, is a Norwegian War Cross.'

'What's that?'

'It's a medal given by the king of Norway to people who have done brave things in the war.'

I took it from its box and held it up, a simple ribbon in the colours of the Norwegian flag, and suspended from it a Nordic cross, with the royal coat of arms at the centre.

'You've seen it before. It's been on my desk for a long time.'

'Yes... I think so, but I've never really looked at it. How did you get it, Dad?

'I didn't. It was your grandmother and grandfather. They were so brave, the king of Norway decided to give them a medal.'

'You mean Angelina and Andrew?'

'No, my parents. Your other grandparents. They died before you were born. I went to Norway to collect it from the King.'

Tom doesn't ask for more. It's time for cricket. I put the medal back in the box on my desk and we go outside to pretend we're playing in a test match at Headingley.

'I'll be Gower and you can be Botham,' he says.

And so I bowl away in the sunshine, not thinking so much about the strange divinity that shapes my destiny and has brought me at this particular time to this still point of the turning world. I'm content to let it happen, in the knowledge that it will anyway.

PART ONE: THE SEARCH

Chapter 1

Stockton, November 1988

I was sitting in a train, travelling north, in the dead time of the year. It wasn't a trip I wanted to make. And I was far from clear why I had been summoned. I took the letter from my inside pocket and read it once more. It was brief and to the point but offered no explanation:

Dear Mr Kingsmill

I would be grateful if you would make an appointment to meet me in my office at your convenience in connection with the winding-up of your mother's estate.

There followed the name of the firm – Guest and Wedderburn – and the signature of the partner, John Skene LLB, with an address in the old part of town between the High Street and the river. That was three days earlier and now I found myself heading north again, after a lifetime away.

The train slowed as it approached the town, a straight half-mile of track; time to gather bags and make for the carriage door. Despite the years, memory did not fail me. Out of the window I recognised the familiar sights, rows of small Victorian villas at right angles to the railway line, wrought iron park gates, the trellised footbridge across the web of lines and then the vaulted glass roof of the station. I had made this trip many times in my long-gone student days when youthful energy prevailed over faded optimism.

The train slowed to a halt and I stepped down on to an empty platform. The November wind scurried in sharp bursts. It was four o'clock and the grey sky hung heavy with clouds. I walked through the underpass, skipping pools of standing water, and stood in the station forecourt. No taxis in the taxi rank; so no change there. I thought of trudging into the High Street, where a taxi might be more likely, when I saw a grubby phone in a dusty booth with a sign that read "Guthrie's Taxis. Lift handset to call". A voice answered in a broad north-east accent: 'It'll be five minutes.' It felt much longer, with the cold wind whipping through the red-brick station yard, but at last the taxi appeared. The driver nodded towards me.

'Queen's Hotel please,' I said.

He seemed keen to start a conversation.

'Come far?' he asked, over his shoulder.

'London,' I replied, not looking to start a dialogue.

'Up here on business then? No other reason to come here, is there? I mean, when you look round, they've made a right mess of town.' He nodded right and left to cut-price stores and boarded-up windows.

'So I see,' I said. 'I used to live near here, years ago. It's changed.'

'Aye, you'll notice a difference alright. Used to be a great street this, widest high street in England,' the driver said, as we pulled up at the traffic lights by the town hall. 'It's all bingo and pound-saver shops now. No quality at all.'

I was relieved to reach the hotel. I didn't need a further injection of gloom to add to my low spirits. The desk clerk confirmed the booking and handed me a plastic swipe card. Two flights up, I looked out of my window. I remembered how it used to look: the slow oily waters of the river of my childhood; and the derricks and the shabby coasters cluttering the waterfront of the old port. Plastic motor cruisers and yachts now lay at their moorings in clear, fresh water. Across the river, modern office buildings stood on the loop of land that used to be a waste patch. I felt an unexpected wave of nostalgia. I regretted the passing of an old dirty town, as if a part of my identity had been lost in a new landscape that had no place for me. Still, I had deserted it years ago and blanked it out; I could hardly blame it for forgetting me.

I looked at my watch: it was nearing six and I had to fill

the void of an evening in an unwelcoming hotel. It was already dark outside so a walk was not inviting. Immersed in my introspective gloom, I made my way to the bar for a drink before dinner. Looking back, I often wonder if my life would have taken the course it did, if instead I had flopped on the bed and watched the television news.

The lounge was rich in fake luxury: heavily-lined velvet curtains and deep upholstered armchairs with white and gold painted woodwork. It was heaving with middle-aged men in grey suits. I found a table in a corner, the only one free, and ordered a whisky. I was depressed, deep in thoughts of nothing in particular, when I realised a young woman was speaking to me.

'Is this seat taken?' she asked, pointing to one of the three empty chairs.

'No..... please,' I replied, half standing. 'Do join me.'
She was pretty, dark-haired and no more than twenty-five; the only woman in the room as far as I could see.

'Not much room tonight is there? This seems to be the only free table,' she said.

'Yes, quite a gang. Looks like Rotary night.'

'Not quite. It's the local Chamber of Commerce. They're about to meet the boss of a Japanese chemical company. They're setting up a plant here, you know. Chemical capital of the world Teesside, or used to be.'

'You seem very well informed,' I said.

'I should be. I've just done an interview with him for the local paper. They won't find him a bundle of laughs. His English is awful and my Japanese non-existent, so we exchanged comments through one of those diminutive little Japanese women who seem to accompany big-wigs on trips abroad. The conversation got very anaemic and very official. Still, I should be able to cobble something together.'

'It sounds like you need a drink,' I said.

'Not half,' she replied with a laugh. I felt myself warming to this confident young woman.

'What will you have?'

'Whatever you're drinking? I'll have one of those.'

I called the waiter across and ordered two whiskies.

'And what about you?' she asked. 'What brings you here?'

'Oh, something very dull I'm afraid – the final bits of my mother's estate. I'm seeing the family solicitor tomorrow. I haven't set foot in this town for years. I must say it brings back a lot of memories, most of which I'm not too keen to dig up again. You know, family stuff, brothers not speaking to each other, and not being able to remember why.'

'Most families seem to be like that. Not that I have personal experience. No brothers and sisters to argue with, thank God!'

'It certainly makes life simpler that way.'

She took a long swig at her drink.

'I needed that. It's been a long dry day. Not my favourite subject, chemistry.'

We talked for a while, entirely trivial, but within that I became aware of her sharp intelligence coming through. She had a sense of humour. Her eyes had a playfulness about them, as if she were looking for the fun in a situation. Then she abruptly finished her drink and stood up.

'Well, I'd better be off,' she said. 'Got to get this copy in tonight. Thanks for the drink. Hope everything goes well tomorrow. It's been nice talking to you.'

And with that she vanished through the jungle of suited businessmen. Later, under her empty glass on the table I noticed a card – *Alexi Truman, Investigative Journalist*. I thought little of it at first and then I began to wonder if it was more than accidental, but why would a bright young woman be interested in me? Self-delusion, an older man out of practice, I said to myself. But my gloom of the afternoon seemed to have lifted a little. I picked up the card and put it in my pocket, not quite knowing what I was going to do with it.

Chapter 2

The offices of Guest and Wedderburn were in Finkle Street, between the High Street and the river, in the Georgian part of the town, a warren of ancient alleys and passages which in my childhood were no-go areas. Now they were restored and gentrified. The Green Dragon pub served gastro meals and real ale and was no longer a spit and sawdust dive. As I walked along the riverside promenade in the light morning sunshine, I thought of the chance meeting the night before. After all, when you have been on your own for as long as I had, you become sensitive to the possibility of making a fool of yourself. This didn't stop me, however, from thinking about the young woman I had met, even if I dismissed it as meaningless.

After a few minutes walking, I turned left up a cobbled sloping street where in former times horse-drawn carts hauled cargoes from the docks. On my right was a row of red-brick buildings with small square window panes. On a doorpost on one of these a brass plate marked the offices of Guest and Wedderburn. On the second floor, in a Dickensian oak-lined vestibule, I found a receptionist behind a desk. She asked me to wait for a few minutes and then her intercom buzzed.

'Mr Skene will see you now. If you would like to come this way.'

I followed her along the corridor to the office at the end. Skene was a slight, elderly man with thinning mousy hair. His mannerisms and style of speech struck me as somewhat courtly, a man from an older world. He rose from his desk to greet me.

'Mr Kingsmill, do sit down. Thank you so much for coming up so quickly. I trust you had a good journey. Did you fly up this morning?'

'By train yesterday. I stayed overnight in the Queen's.'

'Ah, not what it used to be I regret to say. There was a time when the dining room there was as good as most you would find in the north. Nowadays people seem to want country house hotels or travel lodges. Dreadful things. The old civic hotel seems to have disappeared.'

I had an image, as he spoke, of waitresses in black-and-white uniforms and heavy silver service in the dining room.

'No, not what they used to be,' I agreed.

'Well, I expect you will be wondering why I requested your presence in person regarding this matter. Normally it would have been dealt with quite adequately by correspondence but in this case I felt it better to have the opportunity to discuss the matter with you.'

'I appreciate that, but I am intrigued. Is there a problem?' I asked.

'Not a problem as such, but an intrigue certainly. Let me explain. Your mother, as you know, inherited a large sum of money several years ago on the death of your father. This sum has remained more or less intact in her estate and, with sound investment, you consequently now stand to inherit a very great amount. Eight years ago your mother changed her will to make you sole beneficiary and excluded your late brother completely, although I did point out to her that this settlement could be challenged in the courts. However, as you are now the sole surviving heir, that possibility has been removed.'

I was familiar with all of this information but Skene was clearly in his element, as if he were the lawyer at the start of a detective novel. I let him continue without pressing him. He liked long sentences.

'A week ago the will was granted probate and I was on the point of contacting you to make the necessary financial arrangements when I received a rather unusual communication by letter. I have it here.'

He fished a small sheet of notepaper from the file on his desk, rather yellowing at the edges, and handed it to me. It read:

For Peter Kingsmill

I have followed your life from afar. I offer you this in the hope that the truth can no longer hurt you.

The writing was spidery and frail, as if the work of an old person, and the language archaic and strange. Skene looked at me.

'Do you have any idea what this means, Mr Kingsmill?'

'None at all. Is that all there is?'

'Just this,' he replied.

He handed me a small envelope containing black-and-white photographs, old and faded. The first showed two young women, dressed in summer clothes, standing side by side in an orchard full of blossom and the grass long about their feet. In front of them were two little girls in summer dresses with dark hair in plaits tied with ribbons. They looked about four or five years old and were so similar they could have passed for sisters. The four were smiling, looking happy and relaxed in the bright early summer sunshine. In the background was the verandah of a wooden chalet, painted in a dark colour with rails picked out in white. I turned the photograph over. On the back was the date 1939 and the word Oslo.

'I have never seen this before,' I said, 'but I can tell you that one of the women is my mother. I have no idea about the others in the picture. Nor do I understand the message at all. How did you get this?'

'At your request, as you will recall, we placed a notice of your mother's death in the newspaper. This was after the funeral, which was a private affair. Shortly afterwards, the newspaper received a letter containing this note and the photographs with a request for it to be forwarded to the person placing the death notice. That's how it came to us. I felt that I should personally tell you this as I have never before come across such an odd communication. In legal terms, the letter has no bearing on the settlement of your mother's estate, of course, but it does coincide with your receipt of a large inherited sum, which makes the circumstances somewhat singular. It also seems to have been triggered by the death of your mother, as if someone had been waiting for this moment before contacting you.'

'That seems more than likely. I appreciate your contacting me about this. May I take the letter away? I need to think about this, I guess. A bit of a puzzle. You don't think there can be anything sinister about it, do you?'

'I doubt it. Could be the work of a crank. You have a public life, haven't you, picture in the papers and television and so on?'

'Yes, I suppose I do.'

I looked briefly through the other photographs. There was one of my mother with a young British officer in front of a large villa surrounded by trees and another of a girl in her twenties, with the name Marta on the back. She was holding a small baby and smiling. All in all, they meant nothing to me. I put the letter and the photographs back in the envelope. There was some paperwork to be completed concerning the will and with that our business was concluded. We shook hands.

'Let me know if I can be of any further assistance, Mr Kingsmill, and safe journey back to London.'

I had booked into the hotel for a second night on the off chance that I needed to spend more time here. As it turned out, it was not necessary, but I decided to let the booking stand. The sun was shining; I was away from Whitehall for the first time in a long while; and I had plenty to think about. Who was it who had followed my life, and why? How could I now be beyond hurt by learning the truth about what? And what was I supposed to understand from the faded photographs I had been sent? If I had known then where these questions would lead me, or how the journey would change the assumptions which had underpinned my forty-odd years of life, would I have pursued them? I needed to think it all through and I decided I would do my thinking while walking.

It was an unseasonably mild late November day when I set off from the hotel. I walked down the High Street past the Dutch town hall and the shambles. After half a mile I turned left along Dovecot Street and walked on until the town centre turned to residential housing and then to fields and lanes. I had walked this way many times as a boy, often with my brother, along country lanes lined by horse chestnut, sycamore, oak and ash. Now the foliage was golden in the sunlight and deep drifts of fallen leaves gathered in the hedge bottoms. Despite the industry all around, the place still had the character of a market town, and farmland and market gardens still encircled the newer housing that had grown up over the years.

Yesterday I had made the journey north in low spirits. For a year I had been alone, since Lucy's sudden death. Although my career in Whitehall had taken me quickly to a senior level, and continued to thrust me into demanding and challenging work, it was as if something had died inside me in the last year. I had buried myself in work, taken no holiday, and hoped I would emerge into daylight with the old ambition and drive. It had not proved to be so. The familiar round of ministerial briefings, policy work and political scrambles, which before inspired such energy, now fell flat. My mother's recent death had slid into this grey period, almost unnoticed. And it was in this mood that I had returned to my home town.

As I walked further into the countryside I realised that the events of the last twenty-fours hours were beginning to fascinate me in a way I had not experienced for many months. The writer of the letter clearly did not wish to contact me personally but wanted me to begin to piece together a trail, which somehow or other would lead me to a hidden truth, and a truth that apparently would be painful. The question was where to begin? There were precious few clues. And was it worth the effort?

My walk had taken me far into the countryside to the north of the town. I passed through the village of Carlton, with its red-brick houses and cottages, church and pub, and steered my way back to town through Redmarshal. When I reached the hotel I reckoned I must have walked about eight miles but I felt refreshed and energised by the country air and the change from my London routine. It was late afternoon and copies of the *Evening Gazette* lay on the hotel desk. I picked one up. The banner headline read: "Japanese chemical giant in pollution scandal". There followed a news item about the visit of the general manager of the Fuji Coal and Chemical company to negotiate the terms of a new chemical plant to be built on a derelict industrial site on Teesside. Then the revelation that the Japanese provincial Government had jailed its environment minister and senior managers for corruption in covering up a history of environmental disasters caused by the company's operations. The article concluded: "Is this the kind of company we wish to welcome to Teesside?" A footnote indicated a full article could be found on page four. I turned the pages and there inside was a double spread, "by our special reporter Alexi Truman", and in the top right corner I recognised the smiling face of the young woman I had met the previous evening.

'Well, well,' I thought, 'so much for her claim to have no interest in chemistry.' Her interview with the general manager must have been pretty incisive. Not only that, towards the end of the article was a quotation from a Department of Trade and Industry spokesman, which meant she had aired the text in advance with the DTI press office, who were attempting to take the heat out of the situation. She was by no means a local hack. She knew the ropes and doubtless the story would run on the local and national TV news programmes that night.

Back in my room, I turned on the television to catch the six o'clock news. The chemical plant item came up third, after the European Monetary System and a train derailment in Cumbria. The TV journalist delivered the punchlines against a landscape of old industrial plant with some low hills in the background. Then the camera cut to Alexi Truman for a thirty second slot where she demanded a Government investigation into the ethics of the Fuji Coal and Chemical company. The item was rounded off from the DTI building in London by a junior minister from the department blowing on about the stiff regulatory standards that would be applied to the plant under EEC law. The Government had been clearly caught off balance and needed a quick fix. The main point though was whether Japanese honour had been wounded and whether they would walk away from what the Government had been selling as a done deal.

This was a situation I knew well. I imagined the early morning call from the press office for a line-to-take to fend off the early-bird journalists and TV stations who had spotted the embargoed article from the Teesside paper. Then a quickfire demand from the divisional head at the DTI for a ministerial statement and a question-and-answer brief from down the line. No doubt the local MPs would be tabling written and oral parliamentary questions right now. In other words, Alexi Truman's piece of work would have derailed the DTI programme completely, while junior civil servants scrabbled about trying to piece together coherent paragraphs that said little and promised less. The main point as always would be to placate, defuse and plug gaps. It would run and run, until something else unforeseen hit home. From a distance I could appreciate the subtle human comedy of Government in a democracy. Tomorrow I would be back in the thick of it and, close-up, it would be less amusing.

Chapter 3

Next day I took an early train from Darlington and was at King's Cross by mid-morning. A few stops on the tube and I was at Westminster, a short walk from my office in Whitehall. I threw my overnight bag in the corner and sat down to switch on my computer but before I could log in, my secretary, Jenny, put her head round the door:

'Welcome back, Peter. Sir Gerald wants to see you.'

Sir Gerald was the Permanent Secretary.

'What, now? Is he free?'

'Judy said his diary was clear all morning, so I guess so.'

I walked a few yards down the carpeted corridor to his ante-room where Judy was clicking away at her keyboard.

'Go straight in,' she said.

I knocked and entered.

Gerald was a tall silver-haired man in his late fifties, just a couple of years to go before he could call it a day and land a few consultancies and the odd city chairman's job to top up his ample pension. He was very well preserved, immaculately turned out, and always in control of the situation. He had done the rounds of Whitehall and seen ministers come and go with unfailing regularity.

'Ah Peter. Good to see you. I trust your trip was a success. Come in. I need a hand from you.'

I entered the hushed calm of the Permanent Secretary's office and sat down facing his spacious mahogany desk. He began:

'Minister of State is very keen to ensure this afternoon's press conference on his health reforms gets off to a flier. Doesn't want negative stuff in the papers and then have to react. Retaliation first is the by-word. Dickson has called in sick this morning and I need you to hold the Minister's hand, help him spot googlies.'

Sir Gerald was a member of the MCC and was always keen to deploy cricketing metaphors. Dickson was the head of division sponsoring the reforms and normally he would be guiding his Minister through the political minefield of quotable press conferences.

'Walker knows all the facts and figures and can field the details. I need you to watch out for the bigger stuff.'

Walker was head of branch and had a close knowledge of the proposals but little front-of-house experience.

'He has all the briefing papers for you. Scheduled for two o'clock. Minister has to be off to Brussels straight after so it should be brief. Pop in afterwards and let me know how it went. Everything go well in the north?'

'Fine, thank you, Gerald.'

The press conference was a low-key affair. The usual faces from the major nationals appeared, together with a collection of lesser known journalists from the provincials. One never knew who would turn up but I never ceased to be surprised by the boredom levels which seasoned journalists could endure, and the passivity with which they accepted the anodyne prose which was offered to them in the press releases and notes for editors which civil servants were so skilled at producing. The Minister churned through his set paragraphs, referred skilfully to his prepared answers to predicted questions, and scarcely had to resort to the "if pressed" column of briefing paragraphs. After half an hour the whole thing was over, the Minister was whisked off to the airport, accompanied by Walker, and the room slowly emptied of journalists. I made my way on to the conference room floor to say hello to a few old friends from the newspaper and television world, whose careers in print and picture had curiously paralleled mine in the Service. We had in common the talent of sounding knowledgeable in areas as diverse as foreign affairs and health reforms, depending on what our current deployment demanded. The British tradition of the all-rounder was, after all, engrained in Whitehall and the media, a characteristic which our French cousins, with their constipated obsession with professionalism, could never quite come to terms with. As the room cleared, I recognised a face that only recently had quietly slipped into my world. She advanced towards me, hand extended:

'Mr Kingsmill, how nice to see you again.'

She had learned my identity from the name plates on the top table.

'Miss Truman, I wasn't expecting to see you here. I hope you found that informative.'

She showed no surprise that I knew her name, remembered from the card left on the hotel table only thirty-six hours earlier.

'Very,' she replied in an unconvincing tone. 'I had no idea this was your way of earning a living.'

'I've spent the last twenty years on this,' I said. 'A senior colleague of mine in my early days called it lying for money, but that is far too cynical,' I added with a smile.

'Would you mind if I asked you a few more questions?' she asked.

'Against the rules, I'm afraid. We would have to clear it with Press Office but' – and I have no idea why I suddenly said this – 'as compensation, I can offer you a coffee in the inner sanctum if you like. Not many of your lot get that far.'

'OK,' she said.

The walk from the conference room to mine was brief. I signed her in at the security desk and she received her visitor badge. My office was four floors up in the lift, the logic being that less traffic reached successive floors and therefore the select top management could think their great thoughts in relative peace. Jenny was at her desk: 'Coffee for two?'

'Please,' I said.

My office window pointed away from Whitehall and from the back of the building I had a spectacular view over Horse Guards Parade. The afternoon sun shone crisply on the perfectly tended gravel expanse.

'This is splendid,' said Alexi. 'I always forget how beautiful a city London can be.'

The coffee arrived and we sat together in the easy chairs

by the window.

'Are you staying here long?' I asked. 'I didn't expect to bump into you again down here of all places.'

'Well, I'm freelance. I finished my Japanese piece yesterday and I'm hoping to work up a new piece in this area, which I could sell to the weeklies here or abroad. I saw the notice on the wires yesterday and got down this morning.'

'It must be hard work to get established I suppose but, if you want to avoid flower shows and gymkhanas, you have to aim for the big stuff as soon as possible.'

'And I've done some of that,' she said, 'straight out of college.'

'Well, your Japanese piece got good coverage. I saw you on the TV bulletins last night, local and national. Well done.'

'Thanks. You're very generous.'

There was a pause while we looked across the parade ground to watch a troop of horses trot across, black and shiny and perfectly groomed. Alexi turned towards me, with her deep brown smiling eyes.

'You must have important things to do. Thanks for the coffee. I should be letting you get on.'

'You're welcome and very nice to see you again. I wish you all the best in your work.'

I took her down in the lift and walked out into the watery afternoon sunshine on Whitehall.

'Are you staying in London tonight, or heading off?'

'Oh, I have a cheap little hotel for the night between Victoria Street and Pimlico. Not exactly the Ritz but I can afford it – just about. It's called the Elizabethan, in Elizabeth Street.'

I turned and looked at her. I had to overcome my default position that had prevailed for more than a year now in order to ask the question:

'Would you join me for dinner tonight? There's a little Italian restaurant not far from you, nothing special, but good food and no glitter. I could pick you up if you like.'

She paused, then said:

'OK….yes…that would be great. What time?'

'About seven-thirty.'

'Great. See you then.'

'And by the way, call me Peter.'

'And I'm Alexi.'

'I know. I've got your card, remember.'

She looked at me for a moment and then swung her long dark hair round and set off down Whitehall towards Westminster.

Back in the office, I shuffled a few papers, with no real appetite for doing anything. The last couple of days had brought back a lot of the past and shaken me out of the year I had spent insulated from real life since Lucy had died. Being back in my home town was such a contrast with my London existence, not so much in terms of so-called life-style, as in the sharp painful memories of childhood which I could never explain away. Then the strange meeting with the solicitor and the photographs and cryptic message. And Alexi Truman was the last thing I had expected to encounter, a lively young woman, full of confidence and on the way up. And I had asked her to dinner in a way that was not my usual style. I suddenly remembered that Gerald had asked for a word about the conference. Along the corridor Judy still manned the barricade to his office but she waved me in. Gerald was in the process of putting on his overcoat and scarf.

'Peter, come in. I'm off early this afternoon, calling in at Cabinet Office on the way. Henry wants a word about the business programme before next week's Cabinet.'

'You wanted to know about the conference. Totally uneventful. I guess there'll be a lot of factual stuff around tomorrow. There didn't seem much appetite for a dog-fight yet. Minister did well.'

'Good, but I suspect we shall hear more when the media bounces the Government proposals off the Opposition. We'll see. By the way, Peter, I wanted to say something to you. You've been hard at it this last year. I don't suppose you've taken any leave since your wife died and it's been a very busy programme. Christmas recess isn't far away and you haven't anything going through the House before then. So why don't you take off until the New Year. You need a break. If we need you in a hurry, we can always track you down.'

'The truth is, Gerald, that work stops me from thinking, if you can follow that logic. This way I don't have to make decisions that mean anything to me. There is a comforting anaesthetic in what we do I suppose.'

'I know exactly what you mean, but do give some thought to what I have said, won't you.'

I said that I would and with that he disappeared down the corridor to see the Cabinet Secretary.

I was sitting at my desk when I heard Big Ben strike four. I suddenly realised that I was very tired and that nothing useful would be achieved by hanging about any longer. I grabbed my bag, put my head round the door, told Jenny I was going home and to call me there if she needed me.

Chapter 4

I had a flat in Winchester Street, within walking distance of my office, albeit a sprightly walk, in a part of the city lying behind Millbank, a curiously quiet area of white-painted Victorian terraced houses converted into apartments. Every corner shop seemed to be a bistro, or delicatessen, or wine bar. There was little through traffic and during the day it felt almost entirely depopulated as the professional singles and couples who lived there worked their long hours in the city, only returning in the evening to fill up the bistros and wine bars. I had lived there for eight years with Lucy without really knowing anyone. Our friends were all sourced from work and professional contacts. I remember thinking, when I first moved to the city, how unusual that was when I compared it with my younger days in the north. Now, the anonymity of city life seemed normality; to say good morning to a neighbour, quite abnormal. For the last year of my self-imposed isolation, I had been grateful for the privacy this gave me. The long hours in Whitehall, the frequent evening sessions working on papers, and weekends spent alone drinking coffee and studying the sundays, left little time for meditating on the meaning of it all.

After Lucy died, our friends kept up their links with me, for a while. But, as they became accustomed to the fact that I was no longer part of an attractive couple to invite to their smart-but-casual supper evenings, and as I became less likely to accept, the flow of invitations ebbed and finally died. I did not regret this. True friendship is only revealed under the harshest of lights and I had little tolerance for pretence. Consequently, I valued the honesty of relationships with working colleagues, where each gave to each on a utilitarian basis, above the shallow contacts which I had in the past taken for friendship.

Back home I poured myself a whisky, put my feet up on the coffee table, and fell asleep on the sofa. The next thing I knew, it was seven o'clock. I showered, threw on some casual clothes, and went down to the street. Lucy's weakness was cars, and together with her salary as a city lawyer, and mine as a senior civil servant, we had splashed out on a 1986 Aston Martin in British racing green. It rarely moved in the city but at weekends we explored the countryside south of London. It had hardly moved for a year but here I was, about to pick up a beautiful girl, in a car that young men would have died for. My life had suddenly taken a direction that I could not have predicted two days ago, and I was excited.

The Elizabethan was typical of many London hotels which had sprung up since the war, town houses on three or four floors, often in stylish squares, too expensive for family homes. The lounge was to the left of the entrance hall at the top of a flight of steps, with a vestibule sectioned off for reception. The upper floors consisted of small bedrooms, while the breakfast room was below stairs at the front, but at garden level at the rear. There was no dining room and guests were required to eat out in the evening. A general air of mediocrity and poor taste pervaded, the cheap English hotel still largely unchanged by the years of union with the continent.

I parked the Aston and climbed the steps into the hotel. Alexi was sitting in the front lounge reading a magazine. She was strikingly pretty and I suddenly felt as gauche as a schoolboy. I was definitely out of practice. English politeness came to the rescue and I made some innocuous remark.

'Hi, how are you? Hope you settled in alright. I've got the car outside,' I said.

'Great. Are we going far?'

We descended the steps. I could see that Alexi was impressed.

'Peter, that's beautiful,' she said, 'whatever it is!'

'Do you really want to know, or will it do to say that it's a ridiculously expensive and wasteful leftover from a bygone age?'

'I guess it will do then.'

The restaurant was quiet and we took a table in a corner away from the door. A young couple were drinking red wine out of balloon glasses in the other corner and a single man in a slightly grubby suit was laying into pasta at a table for two. Lucy and I had been regulars here once or twice a week over the years. The owner and the waiters knew me and in the last year recognised my need for privacy. Tonight was different. For the first time in ages I was not alone and Francesco was more than usually attentive. He presented the menus with flamboyant Italian panache, despite the fact that he knew I could almost recite them by heart.

'Signor Kingsmill, how nice to see you again. Would you like a drink?'

'Yes, of course, Francesco. Alexi, is dry white wine OK for you?'

'Perfect,' she said.

We drank, we ordered and we talked. The starters arrived and we talked more. It was easy and relaxed. We seemed to fit together perfectly.

'Alexi is an interesting name. Where did it come from?' I asked.

'Well, my mother is Italian. She came to England in the late forties as a young girl and married my father, who is a solid Yorkshireman, as you might guess with a name like Truman. Yorkshire bitter and fast bowlers. I suppose I'm a combination of Italian hot-bloodedness and Yorkshire grit.'

'Not a bad combination in your line of business,' I said.

'And what about you?'

'Well, my father was a German-speaking Pole from Danzig – Jewish of course – who came to England as a refugee in 1939 with the Polish air force. His name was Reichsmüller, which he changed, for obvious reasons. Hence Kingsmill. Would you believe it, he married a Polish Catholic and I was sent to a Catholic public school. How many contradictions can you cram into a life, I wonder?'

'And do you have a family still?'

'Not one. My parents are dead, my brother died some years ago, and my wife died last year. We have no children. So it's only me I'm afraid.'

'That is so sad. You must feel very alone.'

'You know, I suppose I must, but for the last year I've developed a strategy which revolves around not thinking, just doing. I don't pause for thought. To be honest with you, my wife and I had drifted into no-man's-land before she was diagnosed. She had her law and I had my career. We had an unwritten agreement, I suppose, that nothing would disrupt our comfortable professional regime. In fact, we lived together by habit. It wasn't until she died that I realised what an emptiness we had shared. But this is a very heavy conversation to burden you with. We should be enjoying the evening.'

At which point our main course arrived. The restaurant had been quiet all evening and by ten-thirty the other diners had left. We detected the tell-tale sounds of waiters beginning to stack glasses and move furniture, a signal that we should be on the move. I paid the bill and shook hands with Francesco.

'Good night, Signor Kingsmill, Signorina.'

In the car I turned to Alexi.

'One thing I did want to ask, Alexi, was why you left your card on my table the other night.'

She looked at me, a playful smile on her lips. Then she said:

'Peter, you don't know much about women do you? They sometimes just do things for fun. Men on the other hand follow plans. When I saw you I thought: "He looks kind and thoughtful and a bit lost" and I behaved like a fourth form girl meeting the head boy from the sixth.' She laughed. 'But I never thought I would bump into you again. That rather blew my cover.'

'I'm glad you did,' I said.

'So am I.'

We drove back to the hotel and I turned off the engine. I put my arm round Alexi and we kissed, briefly and gently. It was as if a burden of anxiety was lifting from my shoulders.

For the first time for many years I began to feel the world was perhaps not such a puzzling place. I might not be so alone after all. Out of the blue I said:

'Alexi, tomorrow I'm driving back to Yorkshire. I have some thinking to do and I'm taking leave from Whitehall. Will you come with me? I can explain what it's all about tomorrow.'

'That would be good. I was planning to catch the train but the Aston beats that. Thanks for tonight. I enjoyed it.'

She kissed me on the cheek and jumped out of the car. Through the open door I shouted, 'I'll pick you up tomorrow.' She waved and was gone up the steps and into the hotel. My decision to take the leave that Gerald had encouraged me to take was no more than five minutes in the making but it was clear-cut and final. I would phone Jenny in the morning. Tonight I would sleep soundly. And tomorrow I needed to begin to think through the mystery of the letter and the photographs; and to trust that my new view of life was not a mirage.

A November Friday morning in Pimlico is not the most romantic of settings but I awoke early to see the light shafting through the gap in the curtains. I could not remember the last time I actually felt happy to get out of bed. And then I thought: was last night all a stupid fantasy? I phoned the office about eight-thirty when I knew Jenny would be in and drinking her coffee. I told her I was taking off until the New Year and could she tell Gerald.

'Good for you,' she said. 'You need a break.'

'You can contact me on the mobile or on my landline in Yorkshire if you need me.'

'I think the country will avoid civil war in your absence. I'll tell Sir Gerald.'

By ten I had packed my bag and driven to the Elizabethan Hotel. A slight uneasiness lurked inside me as I mounted the steps. Was I about to be stood up? But in the lounge I saw Alexi waiting with her holdall and felt a surge of relief. She was in conversation with another resident. In the car she said:

'That chap I was talking to just now was in the restaurant

last night.'

'Yes, I thought I vaguely recognised him. Small world I guess.'

I started the car and we set off through the city. The morning light played on the white buildings, the yellowing plane trees caught the sun and a gentle breeze ruffled the river as we headed across town to the Great North Road. At Stamford we turned off the A1.

'Coffee,' I said.

We drove through the narrow medieval sandstone streets and pulled up opposite The George Hotel. We sat by the open fire in easy chairs, with a pot of good coffee and a plate of sandwiches.

'Alexi, you remember when I told you I had been called back to Stockton to settle family business? Well, it turned out to be rather more complicated than that.'

I handed her the envelope containing the note and the photographs. She carefully studied them.

'What do you make of that?'

'I'm not sure. What does "hurt" refer to? And what does the collection of photos mean? "From afar" is a strange expression, really archaic English.'

'I've been thinking about this. I've come to the conclusion that the photos are a trail, a set of clues, and that the writer of the note has a special reason far wanting to tell me something without disclosing his or her identity. I haven't got further than that. The family lawyer handed me this lot when we met the other day.'

'"The truth can no longer hurt you". Do you have any idea what that can mean?'

'None at all, but I mean to find out. Would you help me? My mother is in the first photograph but I don't know who the other woman is. I've never been to Norway and I have no idea of the significance of the "Oslo 1939" note on the back. The other photos are a complete mystery.'

'You told me your father was a Polish Jew who came to England to escape the Nazis. Don't you think that's where we should start? There must be records concerning him that might explain how Norway in 1939 figures in the story.'

'You're right, but where do we start?'

'He fought in the war, didn't he?'

'Yes, RAF. There were Polish squadrons, as you probably know. He flew a Hurricane and was based near Lincoln. In fact, it could have been not far from this very spot. He must have taken British citizenship very soon after reaching Britain.'

'I think we have a starting point at least with his war record and there must be some Home Office information relating to his immigration.'

Alexi was warming to the quest. Her investigative instincts were becoming active. We finished our coffee and set off north. In the car, I said to Alexi:

'Two days ago you didn't even know me and now you're investigating the story of my life. Are you sure you want to get involved in this?'

'Too late now. I shouldn't have left my card at your table I suppose.'

She looked at me with a playful smile and squeezed my hand on the gear lever. I knew she was happy, and so was I.

The Great North Road was its usual clutter of heavy goods vehicles and road works. But we made good time and soon reached Dishforth. We turned off on the A168 to Thirsk and then on to the A19. Across to my right the low blue Hambleton Hills rose up and I remembered the times I returned home from Cambridge as a student, looking out from the carriage window to the familiar slopes, so different from the flat expanses of East Anglia. At Clack Lane End we turned off the main road and drove for a mile up a steady climb to the village of Osmotherley, nestling in the northern slopes of the Cleveland Hills overlooking the valley of the Tees. Yorkshire sandstone cottages, a village cross, a primitive Methodist chapel and the Queen Catherine Arms. At the tee-junction in the centre I turned right on the Thimbleby road and drew to a halt at the roadside. Alexi, who had fallen asleep, woke with a start and said:

'Where are we?'

'I'm about to show you my country residence,' I said. 'Come on.'

We crossed the broad grass verge by the roadside and I led Alexi up a narrow alleyway of sandstone pavings between the terraced cottages. This opened out into a garden and a simple cottage front at right angles to the main street.

'Here we are. Don't expect too much. It's not Brideshead.'

I forced open the front door which was swollen and stuck. We stepped straight into a tiny hallway. To the right lay a small living room with a kitchen behind it, and straight in front a steep flight of wooden stairs climbing to a landing with two bedrooms and a bathroom.

'This is where I spent most of my holidays as a schoolboy,' I said.

'It's lovely.'

'It's freezing! I'll get a fire going.'

There was a log pile at the back door and soon I had a bright fire burning in the living room. I found a bottle of wine in the cupboard and we toasted each other in the firelight as the day faded. After a while Alexi said:

'Peter, I was supposed to be going home.'

'Were you really? Well you'd better phone home and say you're not,' I said, surprised at my own forthrightness.

Alexi paused and we looked at each other.

'OK,' she said after a while, 'but I don't need to let anybody know, so I won't.'

'Where is home anyway?'

'Home is a moveable feast. I have a room in a flat in York with two girlfriends from university days. Not the most bijou of residences. But I often spend the weekends with my parents in the country. As you see, I'm not really very settled at all. I haven't quite worked out yet where I want to be.'

'That will come soon enough. Enjoy your unsettled state while you have it.'

'But you're settled in a top career and you have freedom, haven't you?'

'I suppose so, but freedom often comes in strange ways. A year ago I wouldn't have described my state as free. Now I think it may be getting that way.'

'Sorry. That was a stupid remark. You must have had a very tough year.'

'That's alright. Don't worry about it. Here, have another glass of wine and then I think we should stagger across to the Queen Catherine for a bit of supper. You must be hungry. It's been a long day.'

'That sounds a great idea.'

I handed Alexi a glass of wine and she put her arms round me. I buried my head in her hair. It was soft and smelled good. I could feel the tension draining from my shoulders.

'I'm so glad you came with me today,' I said.

'So am I.'

'And I'm glad you're staying.'

Friday night in the Queen Catherine was busy. In the public bar a scrum of locals, mostly farm workers and local tradesmen, celebrated the end of the working week. In the lounge the more sedate members of the community were tucking into bar meals, together with a few people who had driven out from the town for the evening. We found a table and I went to the bar for menus and a couple of drinks. The landlord, Bill Maxwell, was serving. He knew me pretty well as I had used the cottage from time to time when Lucy was alive. He was a bluff friendly Yorkshireman, red in the face and broad in the beam.

'Hello sir. How are you? Up for the weekend? What can I get you?'

'Bit longer this time Bill. I'm taking a couple of weeks' leave from London. A pint of Pedigree and a glass of dry white wine please. And a couple of bar menus.'

'Coming up.'

We ordered and paid for scampi and chips and a steak and ale pie, which arrived on large plates piled high. Appetites always seemed to expand the further from London you travelled. Halfway through, Alexi said to me:

'Look through there,' nodding towards the horseshoe counter which separated the lounge from the public bar, 'that's the chap who was in my hotel this morning. You know, the one who was at Francesco's the night before.'

Sure enough, in the public bar, seated in the corner, I recognised the face of the middle-aged man from London. Three sightings in twenty-four hours was not a coincidence.

'He's following us, and doing a bad job of it,' I said. 'I'm going to find out.'

'Wait, I'm coming too.'

As I stood up to go into the public bar, the man saw me, moved quickly to the door and went outside. I followed and grabbed his sleeve. He was surprisingly feeble and timid.

'OK, what are you up to following us?' I shouted, pushing him against the pub wall.

'Nothing. I don't know what you're talking about,' he stammered.

'Come off it! You were in the restaurant last night and this morning I saw you in the hotel in London. And now you're here. You expect me to believe that's all a coincidence?'

'OK, OK. Let me go and I'll tell you.'

In my anger I had almost lifted him off his feet so, as my grip relaxed, he slid several inches down the wall. He was very small and scrawny and clearly frightened as I towered above him. He spoke with a strange lisp. By this time Alexi was standing at my elbow and he knew he was cornered.

'I work for an agency. I've been told to trail you. Don't ask me why. It's not a divorce case as far as I can make out. I just put in a few lines every month.'

'About what?'

'Where you go. Who you meet. That sort of thing. Been pretty easy mostly – till you decided to come up here, that is. Had a hell of a job keeping up with you today in that flash car of yours.'

'Who pays you?'

'Dunno. Cheque in the post every month. No questions. Boss said it was a London law firm but that's all I can say. You won't get more than that out of him, and I wouldn't advise you to push him. It can get pretty dirty in this line of business.'

'If I were you, I'd get out of here back to London as quick

as you can. And if I ever see you again, you'll regret it.'

'Don't worry mate. I'm going now. Sorry to have bothered you and the young lady.'

He scuttled off down the village street, jumped into a car and drove off at speed.

'What was that all about?' Alexi asked.

'I'm pretty sure it's very much to do with the letter,' I said. 'Somebody's been keeping tabs on me, but for how long, and why, I've no idea.'

Alexi put her arm through mine:

'Come on. Let's get back to the cottage. You look shaken to bits.'

'I am. It's the most exciting thing I've done for years – being a tough guy.'

'You're not a tough guy, Peter, you're a nice guy.'

The embers of the fire were still glowing and the cottage was warmed through when we returned. There were a couple of glasses of wine left in the bottle and I poured them out. As we sat by the fireplace, I said to Alexi:

'There's something we need to discuss.'

'Oh, yes, and what would that be?'

'Where we're sleeping tonight.'

'Why do you need to discuss that? Let's just see what happens.'

'I suppose it's because I read English under the influence of Leavis. It all had to have a serious moral purpose which was deeply embedded in the text.'

'Well I read English at a red-brick and literature can mean what you want it to mean if you're a structuralist.'

And that was that. We shared the double bed in the front bedroom. I didn't care to remember how long it had been but it felt right, and that was all that mattered. Once or twice that night I looked across at Alexi, breathing quietly, so slender as to be almost lost in the hollow of the mattress. I hoped it would last; that my loneliness might be over.

Chapter 5

During the night the temperature must have plummeted. In the morning the hills were blanketed in snow. As I came to the surface, I realised I was alone in the bed and I had to work hard to persuade myself that last night had really happened. This was ultimately confirmed by the clatter from downstairs in the kitchen. I clambered down the steep staircase and into the living room. In the kitchen, Alexi was frying bacon, wearing a ridiculously long pullover of mine, which she must have found in the wardrobe, with a woollen hat on her head. A kettle was coming to the boil on the stove.

'Tea?'

'Please. Where did you get this lot?'

'Been up for hours. Village shop has everything. Bacon, fresh rolls and milk. What more do we need, apart from heat?'

'Yes, it's bloody cold. I'll drink my tea and then get a fire going. I think we have some electric heaters somewhere knocking about as well.'

Ten minutes later we had a fire burning and an electric radiator going in the kitchen. We sat at the table by the window in the living room eating bacon rolls.

'Alexi, this is my happiest day for as long as I can remember,' I said.

'I'm glad,' she replied. 'Pass me the HP sauce.'

'Have you no romance in your soul?'

'Sure, but that comes after bacon rolls and keeping warm.'

'You really are a structuralist.'

I was falling in love with this odd, clever girl and I had no desire to catch myself on the way down.

By late morning the snow had begun to fall again. Alexi sat on the floor by the fire, cross-legged, looking at articles on her laptop. Later I noticed that she was working on a document, which I assumed must be her piece on the health reforms. I recognised my department's publications and consultation documents spread around her on the floor.

'How's it going?' I asked.

'Fine thanks. Don't worry, I'm not going to ask you to break the Official Secrets Act – not unless I have to, that is.'

I was suddenly aware of how rash my behaviour could appear, if Alexi's piece hammered the Government policy, and our relationship – if that word was not premature – became public. The odd thing was, I didn't really care, which was a measure of how far I had shifted in the last few days. I was becoming reckless, which was quite a liberating feeling.

I sat at the table by the window and watched the snow falling. In this weather there would be no way down the hill today and I was pleased we would be marooned in the cottage for another night. I began to think about the events of last night outside the pub. It was clear that the little grey man I had pinned to the wall was not a professional thug. If he had been, he could have finished me off many times over. His story was no doubt true – he was a pretty useless spy with the job of reporting back to his paymaster on the life of an ordinary man. And who would be interested in that, unless it was a personal interest? This took me straight to the letter: someone out there was interested in me. The photographs were an invitation to follow a trail.

I laid them out on the table and shuffled them about: the picture of my mother in the orchard in Oslo in 1939; the young British officer in front of the large villa; and the picture of Marta holding a baby. Whoever sent them to me thought there was enough information for me to piece together a story. I thought about the first picture. Nineteen-thirty-nine was an important year for my family. It was the year my father had fled Germany, where he had been working, with my mother-to-be. It seemed now that this must be the start of the trail. What I didn't understand was the significance of Norway; and what I didn't know, when I came to think of it, was how my father had got to England. He never spoke about it and I suppose I had respected his wishes by not asking him too many questions, except about Spitfires, Hurricanes and Lancaster bombers.

'Alexi, how would you find out about the life of someone who is dead?'

She thought for a moment and then said:

'Read his letters.'

'Never found any.'

'OK, ask his relatives.'

'I'm the only one.'

'Ask someone who knew him, from private life, workplace or wherever.'

My mind then clicked three things together – Hurricanes, workplace and comrades. Perhaps there was someone from his wartime career still alive, who flew with him and lived with him, with whom he had shared his story.

'Alexi, you're brilliant.'

'I know. Now will you let me finish this paragraph about your health reforms. Then you can read it and tell me what you think. I won't spill the beans to Sir Gerald.'

I went to the back door and fetched a couple of logs for the fire. I now had a plan of action, which Alexi would of course regard as a typical male weakness. I needed to track my father through RAF records and then find a living witness from that time. My father had survived the war but it was possible that those in whom he had confided had died in combat, or those who had survived with him had died later in life. I knew it was a long shot but I would give it a go.

Through the window I watched the heavy snowflakes fall. It was a silent world of white. The fire burned happily and Alexi clicked away at her keyboard.

'Finished,' she said, and tapped shut the laptop lid.

'Don't you want me to read it?'

'Yep, but I'd rather get you in a compromising position first, so that I can blackmail you into revealing all.'

I was not used to this kind of thing on a Saturday morning in Pimlico but, after all, this was Yorkshire, the snow was falling, and there wasn't much else to do.

At two o'clock we ventured out, clad in ancient wellies

which we found in the back porch. The snow was six inches deep on the road and there were few tyre tracks to be seen. The local bus hadn't made it up the hill and the pub car park was empty. No doubt later in the afternoon the council snow plough would appear. I had told Alexi my plan and she approved. In the meantime I wanted to ask Bill Maxwell in the Queen Catherine if he knew the identity of the little man from the night before. In my rush of bravado I had missed out on the simple fact of asking him his name.

The pub was almost completely deserted. Bill was behind the bar looking bored. A couple of locals sat in a corner reading the paper and discussing football.

'Mr Kingsmill, how are you sir? You're the third person to get here today. What can I get you?'

'Hello Bill. A pint and a glass of white wine please. Any food on the menu today?'

'Not much, I'm afraid. Chef didn't get up the hill today. We can do you a sandwich.'

'That sounds fine. Anything you like.'

Bill shouted through the back and then poured a glass of wine for Alexi and topped up my pint.

'Do you remember that little chap with glasses in the bar last night. Left when we did. You don't by any chance know his name do you?'

'Not off-hand I don't. But come to think of it, he paid by credit card, so I should have a counterfoil here somewhere.'

Bill opened the till and lifted the lid on the vouchers box. After leafing through a few receipts, he pulled one out.

'This is it. Steak and chips and a pint. Funny chap. Didn't speak to anyone. Paid up front, then scarpered double-quick. Never seen him before. Not a local. Signed his name here: "J. Spurling".'

'That's it. Thought I'd seen him before' – I was feigning of course – 'down in London. Just couldn't remember his name.'

'Not your type I should say, Mr Kingsmill. Looked a bit shifty to me.'

At this point a plate of sandwiches appeared on the bar

and we headed off to a bench in the corner to consume them.

'What was all that about?' Alexi asked.

'I had this thought that if I could track down the spook, it might short circuit the hunt for whoever is tracking me. Finding a Spurling in London might not be that easy, of course, and then who's to say I can persuade him to spill the beans, assuming he knows anything.'

'You're becoming quite a sleuth, Peter. You should become a journalist.'

'Well, assuming we can get out of here tomorrow, I'm going to see what I can find out from RAF records and if Spurling can be traced.'

We ate our sandwiches and drank our drinks. A little later we ventured out into the village. It had stopped snowing and the flashing orange lights of the council snow plough suddenly appeared over the crest of the hill. The village was re-connected to the outside world.

'I always regret returning to normality,' I said. 'The Famous Five could always survive as long as there were packets of biscuits and tins of sardines in the larder.'

'Well, I'm back to normality tomorrow too,' said Alexi. 'I've got to get back to York to sort out my things and get this article polished off.'

'But you're coming back,' I said hastily, as I felt a sudden cold dread of the old life returning.

'Yes, I'm coming back,' she said. 'Got stuff to do, but I'm coming back.'

'Alexi, do you know how I feel about you?'

'Peter, not so fast. You hardly know me. A mature senior civil servant like you should behave more circumspectly.'

She was making gentle fun of me.

'That's been my bloody problem all my life,' I said, 'and I'm damned if I'm putting up with it any longer.'

Chapter 6

We woke late on Sunday morning. The road into the village was clear and I drove Alexi into York. I dropped her outside a three-storey terrace house in an area of faded family houses, sub-divided into apartments and student bed-sits.

'Shall I come up,' I asked, lifting her bag out of the boot.

'No thanks Peter. You don't want to be exposed to the squalor of how women live when men are not around. Call me.'

We kissed goodbye and I drove on south. I had read her think-piece the night before and was impressed. She seemed pleased.

'Good luck with your article,' I said.

I was surprised to find myself on the road back to London so soon after my escape on Friday but this time I knew what I wanted to achieve, which filled me with some of the old energy. But at the same time I was conscious that Alexi and I had only known each other for five days and what had blossomed so quickly could as easily wither.

I got back to Pimlico in the late afternoon. As usual for a Sunday, the streets were deserted. I parked the car in the underground space I rented for a small fortune and came in by the back staircase. I suddenly felt how empty my apartment was and I realised I had been denying my loneliness for years. Whatever happened between Alexi and me, I knew I could not go back to this way of living. I thought of phoning her but decided to give her some space. Ten minutes later the phone rang. It was Alexi.

'Hi, just wanted to check you got back alright.'

'I did, to my empty flat. Wish you were here.'

'Wish my flat was empty,' she said. 'Too many females clattering about here. I long for a snow-bound cottage in north

Yorkshire with a sensitive male to keep me in check.'

I imagined the twinkle in her eye as she said this.

'If all goes well tomorrow I plan to be back in the cottage on Tuesday. Shall I collect you from York on the way?'

I hoped to God she would say yes.

'That would be great but can you collect me from Helmsley? I'm going there tonight. Dad's coming for me in a few minutes. They live in Rievaulx Cottage, two doors up from the Black Swan in the square.'

'OK, I'll be there by midday.'

'Gotta go now. Do you miss me?'

'What do you think?' I replied, and the phone went dead. Being twenty-five seemed to make life so much easier.

That evening I strolled round to Francesco's. It was early so the restaurant was quiet.

'Mr Kingsmill, welcome. No signorina this evening sir?'

'No, Francesco, all on my own.'

'Pity. Well your usual table is ready for you I and will bring you a glass of red wine, on the house.'

Early next morning I walked to Victoria undergound station and took the District Line to Kew. The National Archives were housed in a modern glass-fronted building overlooking the Thames. The RAF records I needed to consult were mainstream and therefore easily accessible on-line once I had checked in with the front desk. I was allocated a computer in the main reading room and I sat down to see what I could discover. I typed in "RAF" to the search box on the home page and then clicked on "RAF officers" from the menu that appeared. The computer then asked me for a specific name and I typed in "Stanislaw Reichsmüller". After a little while the search was completed and two pages of information appeared. I read through the material and then stopped to take it all in. I could not believe that my father had led such a life and never spoken about it. I read through the records line by line. He had fought with the famous 303 Polish Fighter Squadron, the highest scoring squadron in the Battle of Britain, formed in August 1940 and disbanded in December 1946. From 1941 to 1944 he had flown Hurricanes in the Fortress Europe campaign and in 1945 flew missions over Holland. His last operation was in April 1945 escorting Lancaster bombers on a raid on Berchtesgaden. It was as if he had been another person.

I switched off the computer and sat quietly for a few minutes. For the first time I saw my father through the eyes of an outsider, not those of a son, and I was saddened to realise that I had never had the chance to show my pride in him nor to say how much I valued his friendship. I was too busy with the business of growing up and getting on to recognise the courage and commitment of the human being I should have known best of all. I felt my eyes welling up, a reaction I had failed to predict. I looked around me in the silence of the reading room and wondered how many of those earnest researchers had felt such emotion.

I realised quickly that if I was to take this search forward I needed to know who had served with my father in 303 Squadron. The most likely to know him well were his fellow pilots. I switched the computer on again and put out a search for "Pilots of 303 Squadron". The machine ground on and in a few seconds a page appeared listing 64 pilots of 303. Of these, 26 were listed as killed in action which meant that 38 pilots had survived the war and may have known my father well. I needed to find out how many of this number were still alive and where they were living. I was confident that all would have been offered British citizenship in 1945 and probably were living in Britain, as a return to their native Poland under Soviet control was not a viable option. The only way I could track them down would be through the Home Office, where applications for citizenship were processed, and then through name changes by way of deed poll. Only then would I have a solid basis for identifying and locating my father's surviving comrades. My heart sank at the complexity of the challenge that faced me.

I had been around Whitehall for years and had moved between departments on my way up the ladder. Contemporaries' paths crossed like the railway lines at London Bridge station. Back in my flat I looked up my Civil

Service List for the telephone number of an old contact I knew was now senior in the Home Office. He had been a year above me at Trinity Hall and we had played cricket together in the college team. I rang the number and got his secretary.

'Peter Kingsmill speaking, Health department. Is Ken Brandon available please?'

'Yes he is. May I ask you what it is about before I put you through?'

'Technical question about immigration records.'

The line went quiet and then a familiar voice sounded:

'Peter, how are you? It's been a long time. How are you getting on?'

I knew he meant since Lucy died.

'OK Ken, thanks. How's life in the Home Office?'

'Chaotic as usual, still trying to count immigrants – and failing. What can I do for you?'

'It's a personal thing. I need a bit of technical advice from an old friend. Difficult to explain over the phone. Let's meet for a drink. How about the Oxford and Cambridge Club tonight at six?'

'Sounds fine. Staying in town tonight anyway. Got a third reading going through the House before ten and I won't be able to face the slog to Sevenoaks after that. Most of the members who can be bothered to turn up will be half-cut by then so I may as well follow their example.'

'You haven't changed. See you at six.'

The Oxford and Cambridge Club occupied a stately Victorian building in Pall Mall, a ten minute walk from Whitehall. I had been a member since my earliest days in the Service when, during postings away from London, I could use it for overnight stays on official business at rates well below hotel prices. The club had the hushed, slightly shabby feel of the senior common room of an Oxbridge college, and at breakfast you could encounter ancient dons stooping over their scrambled eggs just as they would over a medieval text in the University Library. But I preferred it to the other London clubs I had experienced, where suits were sharper and political ambitions better honed.

That evening I was already ensconced in the reading room when Ken appeared, wearing his Whitehall suit with tie out of centre, looking like an overgrown schoolboy late for the bus.

'Peter, so sorry I'm late. Got nabbed by PS/S of S on exit, in a flap about a deal over a Lords amendment to tonight's bill. Thought PM might be having reservations about easing immigration numbers. Had to contact Number Ten to explode the myth. Total red herring. Need a stiff one.'

Ken had always affected this woosterish style as a cover for his sharp intelligence. I ordered a couple of whiskies from the steward.

'Good to see you Ken. Sorry I've been a missing person for so long. I've been out of circulation for a year or so. I'm actually on leave at the moment and trying to tie up some family business.'

I explained what I needed to do and the scale of the operation. Ken mulled over the matter, aided by the whisky.

'Well, you're right to assume that almost all of the 38 pilots would have become British citizens in 1945. As far as I recall, as early as 1943 the War Cabinet agreed a policy on this in recognition of the fight the Polish airmen were putting up in support of the British. None would have returned to Poland, which was up in flames. A few might have gone to the States, I suppose.

'Changes of name might be a problem as quite a few might have gone for anglicisations but that could be tracked through deed poll records. The General Register Office will have records of registered deaths. Between the two, you should be able to arrive at the list of surviving pilots who may still be resident in the UK. Addresses could be tracked by electoral registers. The whole thing is labour intensive but it can be done.'

'How long do you think it would take?'

'If you knew what you were doing, two or three days, a week at most.'

'But I don't know what I'm doing, that's the problem.'

'Peter, I can do you a favour, as long as it's just between

you and me. We have an investigation unit in the Home Office, mostly dedicated to tracking false documentation in relation to immigration permits. You know, relatives already in the country and so on. If you like, I could get one of the juniors on to this job. It's pretty simple: either the records exist, or they don't. Not a lot of judgements to be made. Have you a list of names?'

I pulled out the handwritten sheet of 38 Polish names I had compiled that morning in Kew and handed them over. Ken folded the paper and put it in his inside pocket.

'Leave it with me. Where can I contact you?'

'I'm going up to Yorkshire tomorrow. Here's my address and telephone number. I owe you one, Ken,' I said

'You certainly do. I'll have a ten-year-old McAllan,' he grinned.

I ordered a couple more whiskies, which we downed, and then set off into the London night, Ken in a black cab to his gloomy late night session in the House, and I on foot to Winchester Street. It was a clear sky and the air felt cold. The city lights swamped the stars and I longed to see the night sky again from the empty northern countryside.

I was pleased that I had set the ball rolling but I still needed to find out more about the shady Mr Spurling. Later that evening I looked through the London telephone directories in my flat. There were three "J. Spurling" entries. My telephone was ex-directory so I could safely phone without leaving a number. I reckoned I could recognise the lisping voice of J. Spurling without actually having to say anything. I tried the first two numbers but drew a blank: the first was a plummy Hampstead voice and the second sounded Caribbean. The third could definitely be him, south London tones with a clear lisp. I put the receiver down without speaking. I noted the Camden Town address for future reference.

Chapter 7

I was glad to escape London. I could not wait to see Alexi again, with her challenging, uncomplicated view of how life could be lived. But it was more than that. It was like leaving a house you have lived in for years, which you once thought was the place you wanted to be. Then one day something unexpected happens and the house you once cherished, you decide to sell. You can leave what you once valued so much, without a trace of regret. That was how my London existence had died; life had moved on for me and I began to see the shallowness of how I had lived for so long. I wished I had known my father for what he was and my ignorance of the life he had lived filled me with pain. As I drove out of London I tried to recall my memories of him and found I could not remember a single conversation between us which had meant anything. I could visualise him, a small figure, always well-dressed, standing on the touchline at school matches or on the boundary of the cricket field and being pleased at what I had achieved. I remember him buying me a pint of beer when I was eighteen and smoking a cigarette with him. But what he thought and what he felt he never stated, and nor did I. He died too early for me to know him and I became a man too late for him to be my friend. I felt now I was on a journey to discover a person I thought I already knew and in the process might learn something about myself.

The road north flashed by, my mind filled with the upheavals of the last few days. I reached Helmsley earlier than expected and pulled up in front of the Black Swan. Rievaulx Cottage was easy to find. Its Yorkshire stone front, covered in dormant wisteria, clematis and climbing roses, faced directly on to the town square. A wooden gate opened on to a narrow front garden. Alexi was already closing the front door behind her, holdall over her shoulder. She looked tired.

'Hello,' I said, aware of being too formal, suddenly feeling awkward, as if we were meeting for the first time. Alexi, true to form, defused the situation by reaching up and kissing me.

'Come on Peter, let's go.'

'You're in a hurry,' I said, and then noticed that a cloud seemed to be hanging over her. 'Are you OK? You look a bit down. Has something happened?'

'No, I'm fine, really. I just need a change of scenery.'

I loaded her bag in the boot and we drove off up the hill out of the square. We sat in silence for a while. After a few minutes she said:

'Pull over. Let's walk.'

I drove into the first stopping place I could find, which turned out to be the entrance to The Rievaulx Terrace, a swathe of curved lawn with views slicing through the woodland to the valley below and the ruins of the Cistercian abbey. A thin layer of snow covered the ground but the air was warm. We walked slowly along the terrace, her arm in mine.

'Peter, I know you think I'm a carefree young spirit but you don't know me yet. And there are things about my life that I'm not ready to share with you. But I'm just asking you to be patient.'

'I have no right to expect anything of you,' I replied, 'but I just want you to know that I am in love with you. So if you want to finish this now, please tell me.'

'No, I don't want to, so don't think that at all. Please.'

She put both arms round me and held her head against my chest and we stood there like statues for a minute.

Finally I said:

'I've been talking about myself for the last few days. I'm sorry. I can't assume that other people have any less baggage to carry.'

'We're fine together, you and me. Now let's get on.'

A mile or two further on we turned off on to the Hawnby road which rolled and twisted up the valley and across the moors into Osmotherley. That night in the cottage Alexi told me about her latest work. Her article was to appear in *The Guardian* society supplement that week and we drank a toast to that. I brought her up to date with my search and my meeting with Ken Brandon. It was a fine feeling to know that we had a few days of escape together.

Three days later a brown envelope landed on the doormat. I recognised the Home Office livery. Inside was a scribbled covering note from Ken and a list of twelve names, ten of them Polish. At the bottom, Ken had written: "PS. Did you know there's a Polish Airmen's Association in London? Polish consulate should be able to help." There followed a telephone number. Later that morning I phoned the number and got a receptionist on the line.

'Polish Airmen's Association? Yes, I think we have details of that organisation. One moment please.'

The line went quiet for a few moments. Then the voice returned:

'You understand that we cannot give out personal details but we can give you contact details for the secretary, who would be able to forward any message to one of his members. His name is Tadeusz Ratomski. If you want to call him I can give you his number.'

As I wrote it down, the area code appeared familiar and I hoped it might be a northern exchange. I punched in the numbers and heard the ringing tones at the end of the line. After what seemed an age the receiver was lifted and an elderly voice answered.

'Hello, this is Tadeusz Ratomski speaking.'

The accent was strongly Polish but the English was fluent.

'Good morning. My name is Peter Kingsmill. I'm calling in connection with my father who flew with the Polish Squadron 303 in the war. His name was Stanislaw Reichsmüller. I wondered if there was anyone in your association who might have known him.'

There was a long pause. Then:

'Peter Kingsmill you say.... Stanislaw.... Yes, yes, Stan. Of course I knew him. Everybody knew him. Flew the whole war. Not all were that lucky. What exactly did you want to know?'

'I wondered if it would be possible to contact one of his comrades who knew him well. I have lots of questions I need to answer. I have a list of surviving pilots who are living in Britain but I don't know who was close to him,' I said.

'You have been doing your homework I see,' he replied, 'but you need to go no further. I escaped from Poland with your father in 1939. It would a pleasure for me to meet you. We had many experiences together. At my age, the past gets larger, you understand, because the future becomes so much smaller and less inviting.'

'Thank you so much Mr Ratomski. I would like that. Where can I find you? Your telephone number looks north country.'

'I live in a little town in Northumberland called Alnmouth. Have you heard of it? I suppose not.'

'Of course, I know it from childhood visits. Would it be possible to visit you tomorrow and I have a friend who might come with me?' I replied.

'I would be delighted my boy. Come in the afternoon about two. I will have played my nine holes and taken the dog for a walk by then. You see how dangerously I live now!' He laughed. 'I am looking forward to meeting you and your friend, a young lady I hope.'

'Her name is Alexi, ' I added.

'Wonderful. I look forward to meeting you both tomorrow. It will be good to tell you about old times. I think I have bored all my friends to death.'

Alexi was in the kitchen making coffee. I shouted through the open door:

'Do you fancy a trip to Northumberland tomorrow to meet a charming old Polish officer called Tadeusz Ratomski?'

'Sure. That's the best offer I've had all week.' She laughed. 'Coffee?'

We set off the next day at noon. It was only a two-hour drive north, through Durham and round Newcastle. The rusting arms of the Angel of the North, standing high on its hilltop, signalled our arrival on the Tyne and once we had cleared the city the country opened its rolling landscape and silver sea.

Tadeusz Ratomski lived in a three-storey house on a headland overlooking the North Sea. Below, the sweep of sands and dunes curved round into a shallow harbour bounded by breakwaters, into which flowed a shallow river. To the north lay the flat grey shapes of the distant Farne Islands, with the spike that is Lindisfarne castle rock rising steeply from the sea. To the south lay an expanse of shimmering water stretching as far as the eye could see to the mouth of the Tyne.

A man in his mid-seventies greeted us at the door. His red cheeks suggested robust health and a love of fresh air. A pair of blue eyes looked out below a crop of sandy grey hair. He was smartly dressed in a tweed jacket and checked flannel shirt. I could see that he was wearing a tie with a round design in the centre bearing the number 303 against a red and white striped background, which I took to be his and my father's squadron insignia, no doubt brought out in honour of our visit. A friendly black-and-white Staffordshire bull terrier fussed around his feet, wagging its tail.

'Mr Kingsmill, how very good of you to come and visit me. You are most welcome. And this is, of course, Alexi. Welcome to you both.'

He shook my hand vigorously and bowed, then took Alexi's hand and kissed it in a formal, courtly way.

'I have looked forward to this so much since you called yesterday. It is such a pleasure to meet Stan's son,' he continued. 'Please call me Tadeusz and I shall call you Peter and Alexi, alright?'

He spoke in a fluent, correct English and a strong Polish accent with Geordie undertones.

'Alright,' I said smiling.

'Now, if you follow me up the stairs I will take you to my look-out station.'

We clambered up two flights of stairs with the dog hopping from step to step around our feet. The house was at the end of a terrace and had a small corner room, almost like a turret, with bay windows looking out to sea on two sides. In the centre of one stood a tripod supporting a large white telescope.

'You see I have everything I need here to view the world. I watch Tornados from Leuchars and Jaguars from Coningsby practising low flying over the sea. Wonderful to be a pilot in one of those I think. Your father and I were based near Coningsby you know. I also watch shipping.'

'You're obviously an expert,' I said.

'Not an expert. But I still love the RAF and I love the British too. I married what I think you call "a Geordie lass". Sadly she is no longer with me. Please, sit down, and tell me how I can help you.'

Alexi and I sat on a slightly tattered sofa and immediately were joined by the bull terrier, which put its head on Alexi's knee and promptly fell asleep. I thought it was time I came to the point but in doing so I avoided referring to the cryptic letter. I told Tadeusz about my mother's death and the discovery of some photographs and a reference to Norway before the war.

'I suddenly realised that I actually knew very little about my father so I have started on a journey of discovery. I know now about his wartime service with 303 Squadron but that's it. I hoped you could tell me more.'

Tadeusz took a deep breath, as if about to embark on a long, well-rehearsed tale.

'I knew Stan from before the war but I saw him only once after we disbanded in 1946. It seemed he did not wish to keep in touch, as if some memory he wanted to bury was triggered by contact with his old life. But that is beside the point. Let me start at the beginning.

'Stan and I joined the Polish air force in 1938. I was 22 years old and I think Stan was a little younger. But he was the brains. He had top grades from school and had started studying engineering in Kraców. I was a motor mechanic but I drove very fast motorbikes at the weekends for fun. I think we both knew the war was coming sooner or later, like all Poles, and we wanted to get into the action. We were very young and reckless. Learning to fly for us was like...a duck taking to water, I think you could say.

'In 1938 we were flying Polish fighters – P11s – out of Posnán. Good planes but not so fast, top speed 240 miles an hour. We were just waiting for the Germans to invade but when they did we were overwhelmed by the speed of it all. First day, September first, they destroyed one fifth of our air force on the ground. We retreated eastwards but the Russians invaded from the east and in two weeks we had nowhere to go with our planes. Orders came down that we should escape through Hungary but Stan had a different idea. "Tadeusz, you come with me. We fly to Sweden." "Why Sweden?" I said. "Because Sweden is a neutral country and from there we can get to England and fight Germans with the British. Besides I have a beautiful girl waiting for me in Oslo. We can go to England together from Norway. Hitler is not interested in Norway, small country, not important." I said, "I hope you're right Stan".'

'Who was this girl in Oslo, do you know?' asked Alexi. 'Would you recognise her from a photograph?'

'Very beautiful dark-haired girl, brown eyes, just like you Alexi. But I only met her once. Do you have a photograph?'

I passed him the faded picture of the two young women in the orchard with the children. He studied it carefully through his reading glasses.

'Yes, I am ninety per cent sure she is here but I cannot tell for certain which one. They are so similar. Stan told me later they were sisters and his girl was staying with her sister to get out of Poland before the trouble started. I think she had connections with the Polish Embassy in Oslo.'

'Tadeusz, we got side-tracked. How did you get to Norway?' I asked.

'You must remember, it was total chaos in Poland at the time. We had retreated to a grass airfield in the south. Most of our comrades had gone and Stan and I took a two-seater trainer and flew north across the Baltic. We had to wait till nightfall. In daylight the German fighters would have blasted us out of the sky, we were so slow. We also wanted to reach the Swedish coast at first light or we would have to land in the dark. We took off about three in the morning and we were clear of the Polish coast at sunrise. Then we ran out of fuel and had to ditch near the island of Bornholm. Stan took the plane down on a slow glide – he was very skilful – but when we hit the water a wave flipped us over. The next thing I knew, we were hanging upside down from our straps in freezing cold salt water. Luckily the cockpit cover had blown off so we could loose our harnesses and drop down under the fuselage and climb on to the wings. The Baltic is not warm in late September and I did not expect to survive but after an hour or so a Swedish air force S17 seaplane flew over. Shortly after, a Swedish naval patrol appeared and picked us up. We spent that night in Ystad in southern Sweden. The Swedes were very good to us and gave us meatballs, beer and lots of blankets. We were not the only Poles to arrive out of the blue.

'The Swedish military debriefed us about the situation in Poland. We had our papers and identity tags. After forty-eight hours we were issued with military rail passes and were escorted on a train to Gothenburg and on to Oslo. At the Norwegian border the train stopped and a Norwegian escort took over. He told us there was a mustering station in Oslo for Polish servicemen wishing to proceed to England. When we arrived at Østbane station, I remember Stan phoned a number and a black limousine arrived with a Polish flag and CD plates and took us to the embassy. That was when I met his beautiful girlfriend. I could not believe our luck. We slept in clean beds with white linen and woke to a great breakfast of yellow cheese, sausage and rye bread with excellent coffee. It was heaven.'

Tadeusz paused for breath. He was in his element, telling his story to willing listeners, and he was gathering strength as he continued.

'We spent a couple of days there and, to be honest, I didn't know what was being arranged. Then one morning Stan came to me and told me to pack up and be ready to move. We were to travel across Norway to Bergen, where we would be collected by a Royal Navy vessel, along with other Polish servicemen, and taken to Scotland. We travelled by truck and it was damned uncomfortable. The road was pot-holed and seemed to wind in and out of interminable fjords. But we made it eventually. I did not ask Stan about his girlfriend but I assumed she was staying in Oslo for the time being.

'We were damned hungry too. In Bergen we were billeted with a few other Poles in what seemed to be an army camp. We ate boiled potatoes and steamed cod – very dull but welcome nonetheless. After I forget how long, we shipped out aboard a Royal Navy destroyer to Rosyth in the Forth. The crossing was very rough and we were all sick. I spent most of the voyage on deck looking at the grey waves and wondering why I had given up on motor mechanics.'

Tadeusz paused and I could see his pale blue eyes were tearful.

'Please excuse me – we lost so many good friends in the years that followed. We thought we would die; we never expected to come through it. I think of these boys every day of my life.'

'I wonder, Tadeusz, if you know these two people,' I asked.

He looked at the two remaining photographs, one of the young girl with a baby, and the other of the British army officer.

'I am afraid they mean nothing to me Peter. I'm sorry I can't help you more.'

'You have been a great help to us,' said Alexi. 'Thank you so much for giving us your time.'

'My dear Alexi, time is what I have plenty of. It has been a pleasure to meet you and Peter. Look after each other. True friendship is something that is more valuable than most things in life but perhaps you only learn this when it is lost. I think you may be more than friends perhaps. But you must have some tea before you go. I am afraid we have to go all the way down again.'

We followed him slowly downstairs to the ground floor, the dog lolloping from step to step behind us. The kitchen was warm from the Aga stove, in front of which lay a large tabby cat curled up on a cushion. Tadeusz put the kettle on the hot plate and took a cake out of one of the kitchen cupboards.

'You are in luck. Mrs Yardley does for me on Thursdays and she always brings me a cake for my afternoon tea. You see I love your English customs.'

So we sat for a half-hour with Tadeusz, in his kitchen in Northumberland, drinking English tea and eating chocolate cake. Then we took our leave. Alexi gave him a hug and I shook his hand.

'It has been so good to talk to you,' he said. 'It is important that one remembers the past. I am happy to have met Stan's son and you especially Alexi.'

The light was fading as we drove south. I turned to Alexi and said:

'Thanks for coming with me. I hope that wasn't too boring for you.'

'Boring? The opposite. I loved him. I bet he had a few girls in tow during the war. What a charmer.'

'Was he right when he said he thought we were more than friends, Alexi? My cards are already on the table.'

She thought for a moment and then said:

'Yes, I think we are.'

We drove on in silence. After forty minutes or so I pulled off the motorway at the Durham services.

'I'll be back in a minute,' I said, then walked across the car park into a WH Smith store and bought *The Guardian*. In her politeness to me, Alexi had put aside thoughts of her own work and I didn't want her to miss out. I could see her article was in the banner across the top of the front page where inside features were listed. Back at the car I handed her the paper.

'Congratulations. You've hit the heights again Ms Truman. Look inside.'

'God, I'd forgotten all about this coming out today.'

Her eyes lit up as she rifled through the pages to the section on society.

'Well, is it good?' I asked.

'It's more than good. It's bloody great!'

She was so pleased and I was delighted for her. I pondered how my life had changed since I first set eyes on her in that shabby Teesside hotel.

'Alexi, I want you to promise me that you won't let my rambling investigations get in the way of what you want to do in your career.'

'I promise, but I should tell you I've already been offered a series of six more fortnightly pieces with *The Guardian*.'

'But that's marvellous,' I cried.

'Terrifying, I should say. I haven't a clue what I'm going to write about,' she replied.

We arrived back at the cottage late and walked across to the Queen Catherine for a bar meal and a drink. It was quiet inside and Bill was busying himself re-arranging glasses on the shelves. We ordered and were taking our drinks when Bill leaned across and said quietly:

'I should tell you that fella's been back again Mr Kingsmill. T'other night. In't bar.'

'Spurling?'

'Aye, that's him. Didn't say owt, but I thought you'd want to know.'

'Thanks Bill.'

I told Alexi what Bill had said and that I had decided, albeit on the spur of the moment, that I couldn't tolerate being followed around the kingdom by a third-rate spook.

'So what do you propose to do about it?' she asked.

'I didn't tell you but I have his London address. I mean to track him down and really sort him out this time.'

'OK, Peter, but for God's sake don't get hurt,' she replied. She sipped her wine, then said: 'I've been thinking. That photograph taken in 1939, what strikes you about it?'

'Not a lot. What are your thoughts?'

'Well, blossom appears on apple trees in May or June. So your mother must have been in Oslo months before your father arrived, since the photo shows lots of blossom. Then, somebody – a third party – was behind the camera, and that person was the one who had the children, who will be adults by now. So what we need to do is track down through records exactly what your aunt's role was in the embassy. This might help us get closer to Marta – whoever she was – and the British officer, because I am sure this will take us closer to the answer that your mysterious correspondent wants us to find.'

'I'm sure you're right,' I said. 'I think I may have to take a trip to Norway, sooner or later.'

'Peter, I would love to come with you, but I need to think about what I'm going to offer *The Guardian* next time round and I've two weeks to do it.'

'Don't worry. How about a feature on immigration? My chum Ken at the Home Office will give you an interview, I'm sure, and while you're fixing that, I can try to sort out Spurling. Anyway, it's time I showed you my etchings in Pimlico, don't you think?'

'I've been waiting to hear you say that. What else would a girl desire?'

We crossed the road to the freezing cottage, drank a double scotch each, and fell into bed, hoping that the heat of passion would dispel the chill of the Yorkshire winter.

Chapter 8

The following day Alexi announced that she needed to get to Helmsley for the weekend. I could see she was uncomfortable about this so I didn't question her reasons. I knew there were things about her life that she was not ready to share with me and I had confidence in her. But I remembered the cloud which had hung over her at the start of the week. I could not escape a nagging question in my head about why these weekends away were so important, and a lurking depression about being alone again, if only for a couple of days.

We drove the short distance to Helmsley over the snow-covered hills. Tough black-faced sheep huddled below hedgerows and a wintry sun, already at its zenith for the day, cast long shadows across the fields. I dropped Alexi at Rievaulx Cottage and said goodbye. I saw with some relief that she carried little with her, indicating the Osmotherley cottage was beginning to accumulate her things, which I had already started to notice. It reminded me of living with Lucy, constantly encountering drying clothes on bathroom rails, nail varnish on the kitchen table, and half empty pots of low-fat yoghurt in the fridge. It was the kind of clutter that women seemed to collect as a simple by-product of daily life, comforting but slightly irritating.

I had made a detour via Northallerton station and bought Alexi a first class rail ticket from York to King's Cross, which she planned to use on Monday. Her father could drop her off in Northallerton for the commuter train to York. I knew she was short of cash and I had more than I could use. As I drove south my mind drifted over the search that I had embarked upon. I realised I really wanted to discover who I was, and what had happened those years ago, instead of being parcelled up in job and career and getting on.

I had no desire to spend a lonely weekend in Pimlico but no clear idea of what I should do instead. By the time I reached Doncaster I was weary of the motorway so I turned off into Lincolnshire and followed the A15 south towards Lincoln. The road was dead straight for miles. On my right the sun was almost set and a red glow illuminated the fields. I stopped in a lay-by to stretch and breath cold air. A straggle of low brick buildings stretched away from me and a weed-strewn expanse of decaying concrete headed straight into the setting sun. I was looking down the runway of a wartime airfield. It was as if I could hear the low drone of piston engines and see the dark shapes of aircraft taking off into the night, crews of young men and boys, not knowing if they would return on their shields. Or in the sunny afternoons of 1940, brash and confident, young Britons, Czechs, Canadians, Anzacs and Poles, united in their fresh energy and their fear, taking off into a war they neither sought nor fully understood. I felt the breath of my father amongst them and a pride I had never before considered possible. If only I had had this knowledge earlier, how much better would I have understood.

I stayed the night in Cambridge. Late November in the fens was always a dreary time. Bare trees overhung the river and the Backs shimmered in the freezing night air. Late students headed across Queens' Road, back to college from the University Library and outlying faculty buildings. The University Arms was busy with that unique transient population of visiting academics, media types, researchers at the science park and rich parents visiting their children, that always seemed to flow through this ancient university town. Regent Street and Hills Road were clogged with a slow-moving tide of cyclists, heading out to digs near the station, on a black Friday night. In a week or two the city would subside into a winter torpor as the Michaelmas Term ground to a close.

I sat in the cavernous oak-lined bar of the hotel, feeling lonely. I missed Alexi, with her soft brown eyes and wide smile, and felt a million miles away from the world I wanted to inhabit. Around me were smartly dressed young men and women, clicking on laptops, talking on mobiles, pushing the world a little further round on its axis and never questioning its meaning or its value, wrapping up the day's business and heading off to smart restaurants to celebrate another good week's work. How well I remembered all of that; how little I regretted it. I was halfway through my over-priced pint of beer, served at my table by the articulate American barman, no doubt earning some weekend cash to finish off his doctorate, when a face I recognised hove into view, round, boyish with a flop of hair across the brow.

'Peter, hello. How are you? What brings you to Cambridge?'

'A mistake I think,' was the reply.

It was Douglas Bold, an undergraduate acquaintance from the sixties, known in my group as "Ubiquitous Bold" from his amazing ability to pop up everywhere in university life as part of his plan to construct a great career through forging the right contacts. He had spoken at the Union in his first weeks in Cambridge, reported on trivia for the Varsity newspaper in his first year, ending up its editor, eaten dinners in all sorts of subterranean dining clubs, and clocked up the requisite number of attendances at Lincoln's Inn in case he chose to go for the Bar. He knew everybody and everybody knew him. He now sat on more committees of charities and quasi-governmental bodies than I could count and was destined ultimately for a knighthood.

'What are you doing up here Douglas? I thought you rarely left the city these days.'

'Speaking at a charity do this evening,' he said. 'Hell of a bore really but my name seems to be on several lists these days. Thought I would stay over instead of motoring back tonight. As a matter of fact, I'm dining at High Table in hall tomorrow night. Why don't you join me? Bound to be a motley collection of old faces on a Saturday night. Anybody with anything better to do would be out of town. But could be fun in a sadistic way. Why don't I let the steward know you're coming?'

'You haven't changed at all, Douglas. You can sell

anybody anything, as always.'

'Fine then. I'll book you in. Senior Common Room for sherry at seven-thirty tomorrow. Look forward to it. I'd better be off.'

And his slightly rotund shape scuttled off into the night. I immediately regretted agreeing to go but at least it stopped me thinking about what to do this weekend.

I made a late start next morning. The University Arms served one of the best breakfasts in Cambridge in its stately Edwardian dining room. I had a table by the window with a view of Parker's Piece and a plate of prime sausages, scrambled eggs and crispy bacon. With a day to spend I wasn't going to rush breakfast. I took out the photographs and looked at them again. By this time I was convinced that my past was far more intriguing than I had ever considered possible. I had always seen myself as straight down the middle: English public school, Cambridge, Civil Service. Nothing exciting had ever happened to me and, without the events of the last couple of weeks, I wondered if I would ever have peered over the top of the trench to see a wider world unfold. Spurling added a sinister if slightly comic dimension, to know that I was being tracked.

The photograph of the young army officer had puzzled me for some time. I looked at it carefully and slowly. It gradually dawned on me that there were a number of clues in the picture that I could use in the search I was embarking upon. First, the building – a large white-painted wooden villa – was distinctly Scandinavian. But that was a fair guess anyway, since we had already been given the Oslo clue. It was also on a grand scale, not the kind of villa that was a family home. Second, I thought it a certainty that the picture was taken after the war as it was unlikely a British officer in uniform would have any reason to be in Oslo until the surrender of the Nazis, when the Allies arrived to clear up the country. As I studied the picture more closely, something I hadn't noticed before caught my eye. In the window of the villa I could see a reflection, albeit very faint, which the camera had caught: it was the Union Flag, flying from a mast in the garden. This meant that the white villa must have been an official British residence of some sort, perhaps a consulate or embassy or British army HQ. And then the officer's uniform itself showed a hat badge of a regiment, his epaulettes and sleeves showed more, and his rows of medals revealed his service and the campaigns in which he had served. It was not beyond the wisdom of man to use these defining factors to identify exactly who he might be. And if he were still alive, as seemed a reasonable surmise, I might be able to piece together the jigsaw which had been presented to me. I was feeling more positive than ever as I tucked into the excellent Lincolnshire sausages. But I needed a military insignia nerd to help me interpret the data the photograph provided.

Fate provided me with such a person that evening. At seven o'clock, after a day spent partly strolling along familiar paths along the Backs and through the colleges, and partly in the reading room of the University Library, I changed into a collar and tie suitable for dining at the High Table in Trinity Hall. I escaped the need for a gown as I was only a college member and not a fellow. The prospect of an evening spent with aged classics dons and earnest geophysics fellows, eating a four course meal in an eighteenth century dining hall, under the eyes of portraits of former masters, did not fill me with enthusiasm. The only saving grace might be the cellar, which was well endowed with vintage French wines. However, having nothing better to do that evening, I set off relatively optimistically down Regent Street, along Petty Cury, across the market square, and down Senate House Passage to the front gates of Trinity Hall. I presented my name at the porter's lodge and was courteously directed through the archway at the end of Front Court and into the Senior Common Room.

My heart sank as I entered the room. It was sparsely populated but I spotted Bold by the bar, sherry glass in hand, engaged in earnest conversation with a grey-haired don. A small knot of other motley academics were gathered by the fireplace. In all we numbered around eight, which as I remembered was about par for a Saturday night hall. We were destined to form a tragic little coterie at one end of the long oak table and there was no escape.

'Peter, you must remember Professor Crawford. Professor, this is Peter Kingsmill, came up in sixty-five to read English. You may remember him,' said Bold.

'Ah, Kingsmill, yes, yes, rowed in the first boat I remember.'

He clearly had no idea who I was so I seized the pedigree sherry the college servant offered me and carried on with the conversation as best I could. At eight o'clock precisely we trooped into the main dining hall and stood by our seats at the High Table. Before us, at right angles, and slightly below our dais, stretched three long oak tables, at which a small number of undergraduates stood. A scholar intoned the brief Latin grace and we all sat down. I found myself wedged between the Bursar and an ancient history don who sucked his soup through his teeth and had difficulty remembering my name. At various times I was Kingsmead, or Kingston or Kingswood. And then, half way through the savoury course, the most remarkable transformation occurred. This decaying memory became a vibrant encyclopaedic database of specialist information.

'How is your collection coming along Wotherspoon?' the Bursar asked from my right side.

There was a pause, during which I imagined he was referring to some esoteric collection of medieval Mesopotamian shards.

'Well, Bursar,' Wotherspoon eventually began, 'as it happens, I came across a rare specimen only last week. A World War II Dutch army artillery hat badge in brass. Very fine condition.'

My ears pricked up. I could hardly believe that I was sitting next to a collector of military memorabilia in, of all places, the dining hall of a Cambridge college.

'That is very interesting,' I said. 'I'm in the process of trying to identify military insignia from a photograph of a British army officer from the last war. It's a personal, family matter. I wonder if you could help me?'

'My dear Kingsley, I could certainly try. Do you have the photograph with you by any chance?'

I searched in my jacket pockets, found the small bundle of photos and handed over the slightly dog-eared picture.

'Yes, the light here is not good,' said Wotherspoon. The table was in fact lit only by candles. 'But let's wait until after hall. You could come up to my rooms. I have magnifying equipment there.'

I could see his eyes were lighting up with enthusiasm.

'That would be very good of you,' I replied.

Dinner ground on. The savoury course disappeared to be followed by roast quail, accompanied by a fine Bordeaux; then an English pud with a sticky dessert wine. At last the cheese arrived and the port decanter. At this point the meal formally ended; the scholar said grace and the undergraduates trooped out. High Table stayed put for a little longer while the port went its rounds. Then we staggered back into the common room, on unsteady legs, for coffee. Wotherspoon grabbed my arm.

'Let's escape now,' he said.

I bade a hasty farewell to Bold and headed out into the cold night air. Soft lights from students' rooms shone on to the winter lawns leading down to the river as I followed Wotherspoon towards Q staircase. Two floors up, beyond a Victorian oak door, he led me into his rooms. Three out of four walls were lined with books, a two-bar electric fire sat in the fireplace, and a vast knee-hole desk occupied the fourth wall, alongside a dark mahogany map chest with wide shallow drawers, perhaps a dozen in all. The floor was covered with piles of books and unopened correspondence. We threaded our way precariously between the high-rise blocks of printed matter, across Persian carpets, towards a side table, where Wotherspoon switched on a lamp, which shone directly down through a square magnifying glass.

'Your photograph Mr Kingsmead,' he said.

He placed the small print under the glass and studied it for many minutes. Then he spoke.

'Ah yes,' he said, 'this is a maroon beret with a cap badge

showing parachute wings with the King's Crown. There are what I assume must be two light blue strips on the uniform, one parachutist badge, and two Pegasus badges, that is silver on a red background. Without doubt this is a photograph of a captain in the 1st Airborne Division, aptly dubbed the "Red Devils" by Rommel after the 1942 North Africa campaign.'

'Your knowledge is amazing,' I said. 'I don't suppose you can tell me if this soldier might have served in Norway during the war?'

'At the very last stages of the war, yes. The 1st Airborne Division were sent to Norway in spring 1945 to oversee the hand-over of power from the German occupying force after the Nazi surrender. There were by some accounts around 350,000 German soldiers in Norway at that time but they handed over their weapons without demur to no more than 6,000 British soldiers. So I can see exactly why your captain might have been in Norway at that time. The biggest challenge was probably the chaos that reigned in the civilian population after five years of suppression by Nazi forces. The 1st Airborne must have been, in effect, the equivalent of a civil police force.'

I congratulated him on his knowledge. He shrugged his shoulders.

'You know, your challenge was really very simple for me. I lost two brothers in the 1st Airborne at Arnhem, so I knew the insignia very well. But come over here.'

He led me across to the map chest and pulled out the top draw. On a sheet of green baize lay row after symmetrical row of cap badges from all armed forces imaginable.

'You see, it was not too difficult for me.'

Professor Wotherspoon, despite his apparent decrepitude, still possessed the sharpest of minds. His knowledge of modern military history was encyclopaedic, although he professed to be a medievalist. He poured us both a large brandy and opened up his box of Havana cigars. We chatted the evening away in his ghastly leather armchairs each side of the two-bar electric fire, and smoked in the comfort that only men together can enjoy.

'May I ask you what is your interest in this officer?' he said.

'I suspect he knew my parents in the war,' I replied. 'I hoped I could track him down. There are things I want to ask him.'

'Your father fought in the war?'

'He flew Hurricanes in 303 Squadron from start right through to finish,' I replied.

'A Polish pilot. They were special. You must be very proud of him.'

'I am,' I said without thinking. And then I realised this was the first time in my life I was able to say that.

At eleven I made my adieu and ventured out into the still Cambridge air. I knew what I needed to do next. Strolling past the Senate House I switched on my mobile phone and saw there was a message from Alexi: "Hi Peter. Hope all goes well with you. I'll be at King's Cross eleven-twenty on Monday. I miss you. All my Love." Had she ever used the word "love" before? I thought not. It was too late to call her back but I felt good and light-headed. Life, after all, might not be so bad, I thought. I was entering new territory.

Chapter 9

I was back in Pimlico by midday. There was a message on my machine from Ken Brandon: "Peter, Ken Brandon here. Wondered how you got on with the names we sent you. Lost your Yorkshire number but if you get this, why don't you pop down tonight for supper? Just Sue and me. If we don't hear, no problem. All the best".

A month earlier, I would have found some excuse to turn down the invitation. But this time I decided to accept. I phoned Ken's number and got Sue on the line. We had not spoken since Lucy had died.

'Hi Peter, how are you? Haven't seen you for ages.'

Her voice displayed the confident tones of the mature well-bred Englishwoman, capably organising house and home, with two children at prep school and walking the dogs every morning, while Ken worked all the hours in London. How different from Alexi, I thought.

'Good, you're coming down. Just Ken and me, in the kitchen. The boys are away at school. It'll be good to see you again.'

The house in Sevenoaks was exactly what a senior English civil servant should inhabit: five bedroom detached, mock Tudor top half, conservatory at the side and a back garden that adjoined the golf course. A VW Golf and a Range Rover were parked outside, in front of the double garage. This comfortable and predictable world seemed quite alien to me now. But Sue and Ken were good friends and good people and I would not distance myself from them just because my perspectives had changed. I had already neglected them enough in the last year.

We ate at the kitchen table in front of the Aga, pasta and salad with plenty of red wine. I told Ken that the list of names had come up trumps and that the meeting with Tadeusz had been a great success.

'I now need to track down an officer from the 1st Airborne Division,' I said. 'I have a photo of him.'

Sue looked at me questioningly:

'What exactly are you looking for?'

Ken had obviously told her nothing of our conversation at the Oxford and Cambridge Club.

'You know, Sue, I'm not exactly sure. All I can say is that something has happened which has made me look hard and square at my life, at where I came from and what I should be valuing in this labyrinth we call the world. I realise I've been sleepwalking since Lucy died, and for years before that too, and I want to wake up. I'm pretty sure I don't want to go back to my old way of life. And all this is hopelessly tangled up with the fact that I've met someone and I hope it's going to last.'

I could see Sue and Ken were suddenly coming to life, wondering what had happened to steady, respectable Peter.

'I know, I know, I shouldn't be rushing anything, should I? I might get hurt, yes?'

'May we know who she is?' asked Sue.

'A girl seventeen years younger than me, clever, funny and beautiful. She's trying to make her way as a freelance features journalist. Her work is very good. As a matter of fact, Ken, I was hoping you might see her. She's working on something in your field. Last week she did a piece for *The Guardian* on health reforms. I suppose you could say that's just about how we met.'

I could see what Ken was thinking: "Poor old Peter, on the rebound, giving away the crown jewels through pillow talk". But he covered up pretty well.

'I hope things go well for you Peter,' he said, 'and yes, I guess I can meet her. Why don't you ring me in the office next week sometime. In the meantime, good luck with your hunt. I hope you find what you're looking for.'

The evening trailed away. I was glad to have seen Sue and Ken again but I knew there was a fissure between us, now that Lucy had gone, and that might grow into a chasm. We were thinking along diverging lines.

The next morning I took the underground to King's Cross. The station forecourt was alive with travellers and long queues stretched back from the barrier. It was a grey Monday morning. People pushed and jostled, with little sense of bonhomie. I was beginning to loathe London. The human maelstrom seemed increasingly irrelevant.

Alexi's train pulled in a little late and, just when I thought she would not appear, she passed through the barrier clutching her familiar holdall. She beamed when she saw me and I felt as if the racket and the hassle of the city had faded away.

'Good trip?'

'Fine. Complimentary coffee and nobody sitting next to me. I could soon become accustomed to this life. How about you?' she asked.

'Busy week ahead for us both. I met Ken Brandon last night – Permanent Secretary at the Home Office – he'll see you if you're still interested. And I've got to track down an army officer – got chapter and verse from an aged don in Cambridge on Saturday – as well as confront the esteemed Spurling.'

'Thanks Peter. I do want to run with the article but I need to wrap it up this week,' she replied.

'That should be possible,' I said. 'Let's get out of here.'

We took a taxi to the Pimlico flat. Although it was just midday, I poured a couple of large glasses of wine and we stretched out on the sofa.

'How was your weekend?' I asked.

'Oh, tiring,' she said.

I wanted to ask why, but refrained. We would get there eventually. She fell asleep, her head on my shoulder. When she awoke I told her what I had been up to over the weekend. She was impressed:

'You really are getting on. What happens next?'

'Meet the army officer, if I can find him, and then a trip to Norway. Do you fancy a few days in the Nordic snow?'

'Sounds interesting. I'd better get my stuff written first

though. Maybe I should contact Ken Brandon,' she suggested.

'I'll phone him this afternoon. We'll arrange a time when I can introduce you. Bear in mind he'll only be prepared to explain policies. He won't get into the politics that lie behind it all. That's for ministers,' I said.

'This is quite a coup for me, Peter. Thanks so much for setting it up,' and she gave me a kiss on the forehead.

I spoke to Ken that afternoon and arranged to take Alexi round at eleven the next morning. The floor of the living room was strewn with official reports from the Home Office as Alexi got her head around the questions she wanted to put. It was very unusual for a permanent secretary to offer an interview to a relatively unknown journalist and I knew Ken was doing me a big favour. I hoped it wouldn't backfire. Ken was also putting his neck on the block, as he would have to deal with the usual negative reactions from the Press Office to any contacts with the media that they hadn't set up themselves. But Ken was going right to the top; he was already a rung above me on the ladder, although we were almost exactly the same age. I had to trust his judgement.

The next morning the phone rang at about nine o'clock. To my surprise it was my secretary, Jenny.

'Morning Peter. Sorry to bother you when you're on leave. I tried your Yorkshire number but there was no answer so I called Pimlico on the off chance I would find you. There's a parcel here for you marked "Personal". Would you like me to send it round by the courier? And by the way, are you having a good break?'

I was wandering around the kitchen with a cup of coffee in my hand, scarcely awake, but I quickly assumed the voice of reason.

'Jenny, hello. I'm fine thank you. As it happens, I'm calling in to see Ken Brandon at the Home Office this morning. I'll pop in and collect it. Any idea what it is?'

'No idea. It's a cardboard tube. Could be a map or a scroll of some sort. Postmark Cambridge,' she replied.

'Intriguing. Are you surviving without me? ' I asked jokingly

'Just about. Sir Gerald's hair is a little more grey but apart from that we're unscathed.'

'Good. I'll see you about eleven,' and I put the phone down.

'What was that?' asked Alexi, who was drifting around the apartment, cup in hand, looking for odd papers that had lain strewn on the floor overnight.

'Strange,' I replied. 'That was Jenny, my secretary. Parcel from Cambridge. No idea what that's about. In the meantime, come here.'

Alexi strolled across to me, looking dishevelled but rested. I held her against me. Her slim young body felt so small in my grasp. I wanted to protect her from everything the world could throw at her. Then the spell was broken.

'Not now Peter. We both have work to do today,' she said, and broke away from me with a laugh. I doubt if I would have been so relaxed and self-confident at that age, meeting a permanent secretary for the first time. She certainly had talent and determination.

It was a fine morning in London. December sunlight filtered through a patchy cover of white cloud so we decided to walk to Marsham Street, where Ken's office was located. This lay halfway between Horseferry Road and Victoria Street and we could get there by zig-zagging right and left for about a mile. I left Alexi at the front door and headed on to Whitehall to my office. She promised to call me when she was finished.

Whitehall was its usual stately self: wide pavements, gaggles of Japanese school groups heading down to the Houses of Parliament, civil servants with laptops in their shoulder bags, and helmeted policemen on the gates at Downing Street. Later that day a cavalcade of highly polished cars would speed down to the House for PM's question time, a farcical exchange between the most powerful woman in the world and the verbose aspirant to her office. Neither would emerge with credit. Thirty minutes later, she would be back in Number Ten. I dared not calculate how many hours I had spent over the years, crafting answers to members' questions that should never have been asked and those that had no chance of ever reaching the top of the list. The mother of parliaments certainly had unique ways of combining high seriousness with bathos.

I waved my pass at reception and took the lift to the fourth floor. Jenny was in her office and I quietly slid in.

'Don't tell anyone I'm here,' I said. 'I'm just going to be in my office for a while but I don't want a quizzing from Gerald.'

'OK,' said Jenny. 'Here's your parcel. You're looking well. You must be enjoying your break.'

'Northern air. Very bracing.'

The corridor was empty so a sidled along to my office and closed the door behind me. My conference table was neatly covered with sets of papers which Jenny had tagged and dated. These had been copied up the line by my heads of division to get me up to speed on business matters when I returned. I shuddered to think of the hours I would have to spend wading through this lot if I ever returned. On my desk, Jenny had placed the cardboard tube which had arrived from Cambridge. Inside was a roll of paper held in a rubber band. Placed inside the rubber band was a sheet of notepaper. It was from Professor Wotherspoon at Trinity Hall and addressed to Kingsmill – he had got my name right at last. It read:

My dear Kingsmill,

I very much enjoyed meeting you at hall recently. After you had left, I realised that I had a vague memory of some military photographs which my sister-in-law had kept. You will recall I mentioned that I had two brothers who served with the 1st Airborne. Although they died in the war, the army passed on to relatives the photographs taken at the disbanding of the Division after the war. I have forwarded these to you in the hope that they may help you to identify the officer whose photograph you showed to me.

I found your address from the visitors' book in the Porter's Lodge.

With kindest regards

Cecil Wotherspoon

P.S Perhaps you would be good enough to return the

photographs in due course.

I unrolled the papers and spread them on my desk. There were three in all, each stretching to about three feet in length. In faded black-and-white were row upon row of soldiers, men and officers, the front row seated, with four rows behind on a stepped dais, rather like a vast whole-school photograph from the old days. Some were smiling, others deadly serious, perhaps reflecting on the lost comrades of the war years. I took out my single photograph and began to search the group picture in the hope of finding a match but realised very quickly that this was going to be a long and tedious task, requiring both patience and a very strong magnifying glass. I rolled up the photographs very carefully, aware of their fragile state, and replaced them in the cardboard tube. This was a job for home and lots of coffee. Just then the mobile beeped twice. It was a message from Alexi: "All done. Where shall we meet?". I called her: "Pick you up in fifteen minutes". I slipped out of the room and down the corridor, hoping to God no one would intercept me, and poked my head round Jenny's door to tell her I was leaving. Down on the street there was a regular flow of black cabs. I hailed one and set off to Marsham Street. Alexi was standing on the pavement looking pleased with herself.

'How did it go?' I asked as we drove off again.

'It went well. I think I can make something out of this. In fact, I think I have enough for two articles, the topic is so complex. Ken was very old-school and charming. What did you tell him about me?'

'Oh, a few things... such as... you are clever and talented...and beautiful...and will go far,' I replied with a grin.

'Talking of which, where are we going now?' she asked.

'To the most famous stamp shop in the world, Stanley Gibbons on the Strand.'

'Don't tell me you collect stamps as well as run the country!'

'I do the latter in my spare time,' I said.

The taxi dropped us at Stanley Gibbons. Alexi clearly had expected to find a dusty old shop full of shabby little men sorting through heaps of stamps of the world, or schoolboys in short trousers doing swaps. Instead, it was as smart and polished as a Bond Street jewellery store.

'Don't worry,' I said, 'I'm not trying to buy the Swedish Blue, only a good magnifying glass. Then I'll tell you what I'm up to over lunch.'

'Sounds good.'

By three o'clock we were back in the Pimlico apartment. I was at the dining table poring over the photograph scrolls with my new illuminated magnifying glass while Alexi was at her keyboard, surrounded by notes and documents. She was making the more rapid progress. After an hour I felt as if my eyeballs were bursting. I had had a few close calls, times when I thought I had found the face I was searching for, only to have second thoughts. If only my officer had sported a moustache, or large ears, or a prominent nose. But no such luck; he was a fresh-faced young Englishman, albeit no doubt battle-hardened. I picked up my glass and struggled on. After another hour, hopes had faded. It seemed I was out of luck.

'How's it going?' Alexi asked, looking up from her paperwork.

'Badly,' I replied. 'I think I've drawn a blank.'

'Show me where you've got to,' she said as she came across to the table and stood behind me. I pointed.

'OK. Let me take over. I need to do something brainless. You go and make some tea.'

I did as I was told and went into the kitchen. The kettle was coming to the boil when Alexi called from the living room.

'Peter, come and look at this. I think I've found him.'

I looked through the glass at the face she had singled out, checked it against the photograph, looked again and checked again.

'Yes! I think you've found him,' I cried. 'Yes, I'm certain that's him. You are brilliant, as usual.'

'Well, so you keep telling me,' she said smugly.

The bottom one-third of the group photographs consisted of names, arranged in rows and columns matching the men shown above, so that it was a simple enough task to match the face to the name. Our man was Captain J.A.F. McAlister. All we had to hope for now was that he was still alive and that we could find him. We sat down with our mugs of tea to plan our next move. Alexi needed another half day to finish her article, which I could spend tracking down McAlister. I hadn't forgotten my vow to have another go at Spurling.

'Do you fancy a bit of sleuthing this evening? I mean to see if I can affront that fellow Spurling again,' I said. 'I really need to know if he's still on my tail.'

'Do I need to bring a blunt instrument with me?' she asked.

'If he's anything like last time, a handbag should do,' I replied.

Spurling's address turned out to be a block of council flats in Camden. We took the Aston since it was a cold wet night and our enthusiasm for detective work did not extend as far as getting wet. We forgot, until we were parked outside the building, that an Aston Martin was not the most anonymous of vehicles for mounting a stake-out. Spurling's flat was on the third floor, according to the entry phone at the main door. After ten minutes or so the temperature started to drop and our wait became less and less comfortable.

'Why not just ring his door bell?' asked Alexi, with utmost simplicity.

'You've got a point,' I replied. 'We aren't any more professional than Spurling, are we? You wait here,' I said in a put-on manly tone.

'Not likely. I'm not sitting here while you have all the fun.'

It was not until we were standing outside Spurling's door on the third landing that I realised I had no idea what I was going to say. Too late, Alexi had rung the bell and the sounds of footsteps approached from inside. The door opened and the thin grey face of J Spurling appeared.

'Yes,' he began, then he stopped as he recognised my face. 'Oh, it's you. What do you want?'

'That's exactly what I would like to ask you, Spurling. You were seen following me again in Yorkshire a week ago,' I said firmly.

'How d'you know my name, eh?' he asked, looking very nervous.

'Never you mind,' I said, adopting the tone of a TV detective. 'Why were you in the Queen Catherine pub a week ago, tell me that?'

'Oh my God,' he groaned, 'what a cock-up! You'd better come in, I suppose.'

He led the way into a small living room, switched the TV off and beckoned to us to sit down.

'The truth is,' he began, 'you gave me a real shake-up last time we met. I scarpered double-quick. The trouble was when I got to the bottom of that hill out of the village, my car blew a gasket. Whole load of bloody steam came out the back and the engine over-heated. Christ, I thought, what do I do now? Broken down in Yorkshire with a nutter trying to kill me. As it turned out there was a petrol station just on the main road with a workshop attached. So I left my car there for the mechanic to look at the following day. Meanwhile I got a bus into York. A few days later he phoned me here to say it was fixed – cost me £150 – so I went back up to fetch it. That's when I called into the pub for a meal. I hoped I wouldn't bump into you again. Honest, mate, I told my boss I was out of this kind of work for good, after being pinned to the bloody wall! Didn't get no expenses, neither.'

There was a pause. Throughout his speech it slowly dawned on me that Spurling was as much a victim as I and I actually began to feel sorry for the chap. I could feel the ambiguity of the situation: should I laugh or preserve my gravity? Alexi must have felt the same.

'I think we should go,' she said.

And we left as gracefully as we could, aware of the comedy of the situation. Outside, in the cold night air, we collapsed in laughter.

'What a farce,' I said. 'Let's get the hell out of here.'

Back in the flat, I cooked one of my specials, largely consisting of eggs, and we sat on the sofa eating and drinking wine, with our feet on the coffee table. I was as content as I had felt in years.

'Alexi, thank you for making me happy,' I said. 'You are something special.'

'I think you are too – in your cramped over-educated way, that is! No, you've made me happy too, especially with these eggs.'

'That's great then. We must both be happy,' I said.

Chapter 10

I left Alexi asleep in bed the next morning. I knew she wanted to finish her writing and I wanted to get to Kew as early as possible to look up the army records. I left a note on her pillow: "Gone to Kew. Back as soon as possible. I love you. Peter". I knew I was behaving like a besotted teenager but I was enjoying my escape from high seriousness.

I grabbed a sandwich at the top of the underground steps and ate it as I lurched towards Kew on the District Line. This time I knew my way round the National Archives. There was a heap of information about the formation of the 1st Airborne Division and operations in France, Holland, Norway and Italy. It was clear that the Division never recovered its strength after the casualties suffered at Arnhem and that the policing role in Norway in 1945 was the correct deployment of an understrength force. I searched a number of databases until I found what I was looking for. Captain J.A.F McAlister had certainly served as a diplomatic liaison officer with the British Embassy in Oslo in 1945. Later army lists showed that he had stayed on with the British Army until 1959 when he retired with the rank of colonel and a host of military service medals. At this point I felt I had hit a brick wall. Where did I go next?

I wandered back in the direction of the cafe in the basement for a cup of coffee. I had set off in the morning without pausing and I now felt the need of a caffeine shot to get the brain moving. My route took me through the general reference library and I could not help noticing the yards of red-covered volumes with gold letters – "Who's Who 1962" and so on. The penny dropped like a brick. If Colonel J.A.F. McAlister was still alive, with his distinguished army career, he would doubtless be listed in the latest volume – 1987. I skimmed along the shelves. Right at the end, in the shiniest covers, was the 1987 edition. I took it down and searched the alphabetical entries. There were certainly plenty of McAlisters but only one J.A.F. And, without a doubt, this was he. "Colonel J.A.F. McAlister MC, CBE, conservative local councillor, and leader of Norfolk County Council". There it was, in a nutshell. He was still alive. All I had to do was make an appointment to see him and I would be half way through my journey of discovery.

I gulped down a coffee in the cafe before heading back to the main reading room to sit in front of a computer. I typed in a search for "Norfolk County Council", clicked on a menu item "Where you can meet your councillor" and discovered that Councillor McAlister represented the Feltwell Division of the council. There was a list of his surgeries: tonight he would be in attendance at St Peter's church hall in Hockhold-cum-Wilton between the hours of seven and eight in the evening. I had never heard of Feltwell, let alone Hockhold-cum-Wilton. In fact my only experience of Norfolk had been a school cricket match against Norwich School on a blistering Saturday some twenty-five years earlier. Undeterred I set off back to the Winchester Street flat, stopping off at the Pimlico public library on the way. In the general reference section I looked up Hockhold-cum-Wilton in *Encyclopaedia Britannica*: it was a village of twelve hundred souls, ten miles west of Thetford, with two churches. It had been burnt to the ground in the fourteenth century at the time of the Black Death. Nothing else of significance seemed to have happened. I wondered how Alexi would take to joining me on a trip into the middle of nowhere.

Back at the flat I found Alexi sitting at the dining table with her laptop open.

'How's it going?' I asked.

'Just finishing off. I'm calling it part one. I hope the editor will buy the idea of a sequel. I need a bit of breathing space before I leap into another topic.'

'I'm sure he will. In my experience, papers are always looking for good copy. Don't worry.'

'And how did you fare? Any further forward?' she asked.

'Yep. I've tracked him down. He's alive. He's a local politician in Norfolk. How would you like a trip to Hockhold-cum-Wilton this evening? I'll bribe you with sweetmeats and the finest wines. How about that?'

'Funnily enough, I've always fancied a trip to Hopley-cum-Wallop, or whatever it's called. Just let me finish this and send it off. I take it we're escaping the smoke?'

'Sure thing. I'll pack my stuff and see if I can find somewhere for us to stay tonight.'

By three o'clock we were driving out of London and heading towards the M11. Alexi had faxed her article to the newspaper and was relaxed and happy. I was glad to be leaving the city although I was not sure what the evening's confrontation might bring. City turned to suburb and suburb to countryside as the December sun slid below the western horizon. A great orange glow lit up the bowl of the East Anglian sky, reflecting on ditches and drains, casting shadows beyond the dykes, and a magical light over the oldest English landscape of all, of fens and bogs and eerie marshlands. The motorway ended, the traffic thinned and we turned off to Brandon House Hotel, an eighteenth century red-brick manor house boasting two AA stars and a restaurant called "The Conifers". I apologised to Alexi in advance.

'I have no idea what this place is like but I was hard pressed to find anything in the area. Just drink plenty and the pain will be lessened.'

'I'll take your advice,' she replied.

We checked in at five and were pleasantly surprised. The room was spacious, the hotel charming, and a log fire burned within a stone fireplace in the hall. The furniture was suitably sagging and English, with floral loose covers in abundance. Copies of *Country Life* lay on side tables and small paintings of horses and hounds hung everywhere on the uneven walls.

I left Alexi with a glass of wine by the fireside and set off at about six thirty into the pitch black to find Hockhold-cum-Wilton. The desk clerk had given me directions and assured me I could not get lost. The road wound its way round field after field, following the ancient pattern of medieval strip farming, at one moment the headlights illuminating a white five-barred gate dead ahead, at another a low grey cottage, only for the road each time to turn at right angles down another dark passageway. At last a church tower appeared out of the gloom and a road sign indicated my miraculous arrival at Hockhold-cum-Wilton.

The church hall was easy to find, being the largest building in the village, apart from the two churches. I was five minutes early and the low stone building was lost in darkness. Not a soul could be seen. The only signs of life were yellow lights behind the odd window here and there. I rejoiced at the triumph of the British democracy that had built its glorious edifice on such humble foundations. At seven o'clock precisely a car pulled up outside the hall and a figure got out. At the same moment the door of the adjoining cottage opened and a woman appeared, crossed to the hall and I heard the sound of a key turning in a heavy lock. Lights were switched on. Colonel McAlister had arrived. I felt unsure about what I was about to do: I did not know how the Colonel would respond to my presence; moreover, I had no right to be taking up his time as he discharged his council duty to his constituents.

I pushed open the door and found myself in what appeared to be a medieval hall. At one end there was a large open fireplace, the floor was dark wooden boards, and around the sides what looked like old church pews provided the only seating. Colonel McAlister had stationed himself in a far corner, as near as possible to an archaic electric wall heater. The hall was bitterly cold, a definite disincentive to lengthy audiences. I approached the Colonel, my footsteps echoing round the empty building.

'Colonel McAlister, good evening. My name is Peter Kingsmill. I should point out that I am here to see you on a personal matter. I'm not one of your constituents.'

'Perhaps you should explain, Mr Kingsmill,' he replied, with a look of slight unease.

I embarked on my story, providing McAlister with the bare facts needed to understand my visit. I handed him the photographs one by one, first his own, to which he responded with a wry smile. He did not react to the picture of the two women in the orchard but when I handed him the picture of Marta, he held it for a long time, but said nothing. I could tell, however, by his rapt attention, that the photograph had meaning for him.

'Well Mr Kingsmill, what can I tell you? I knew this girl a long, long time ago, in another time and another country. I'm not sure I wish to revisit it.'

'It would help me enormously if you could,' I said. 'I realise it may be painful but I need to know.'

At that moment I heard the hall door open and a man appeared, holding some papers, clearly a constituent with a question. The Colonel looked up briefly. I could see he was deeply moved. Then he spoke.

'I understand your request and I would like to help you but, as you will appreciate, it is a long story, and not entirely suitable for a freezing church hall, with a constituent waiting to see me. Can you see me tomorrow, at my house? Let's say ten-thirty.'

And he handed me his card. I thanked him, we shook hands, and I set off back to Brandon along the black, winding lanes of East Anglia. When I reached the hotel, I found it as quiet as before. Alexi was in the residents' lounge, reading a paper.

'Thank God you're back. I'm starving. How did it go?'

'McAlister knows a lot, I think. My guess is that he was tied up with the girl Marta in some way but whether he will come clean on this is another matter. There is probably very little gain for him in revealing much about his past and possibly a lot of pain. Why should a man in his position reveal anything to a total stranger who pops up out of the blue? But I think he was very moved when he saw her picture. I felt quite guilty at springing that on him. He promised to see me tomorrow morning at his house. We'll just have to see how things turn out. How are things with you?'

'Great. Guess what. I got an call from the editor a while ago. My piece is going out on Thursday and they've agreed to do a two-parter as I suggested. Now I can relax.'

'But that's wonderful. We must celebrate,' I said.

And celebrate we did. I did not fall short on my promise of sweetmeats and the finest wines. The Conifers did us proud. By ten o'clock we had collapsed into our antique bed, which had that pleasing habit of old beds of throwing their occupants together in a warm hollow, while the wind and rain of the Norfolk night rattled the slates and shook the windows in their frame.

At breakfast the next morning I suggested to Alexi that she should stay in the hotel until I got back from meeting McAlister. If he were to have reservations about speaking to me about an episode in his past, they would be doubled if he found he had an audience. Moreover, Alexi was keen to make a start on planning her next article and was happy to hide away in a corner of the residents' lounge for the morning.

Inside the car, I took McAlister's card out of my wallet to find his address: Stableford House, Great Cressingham, Norfolk, which I discovered was only a few miles up the road. I should be there in twenty minutes or so, which gave me ample time. I assumed that Stableford House would be known to the locals. I had not expected it to be quite as imposing as it turned out. The village itself was tiny but, as always in Norfolk, graced by a handsome Norman church. I asked for directions in the post office-cum-village shop and was furnished with ample information in the round rolling accent of the fens. A little beyond the village I was to turn right up a tree-lined drive and I would find the house past the paddock.

The drive itself was a thing of beauty. It must have been half a mile long with mature beech and ash on either side, their leafless branches forming a cathedral roof over the road. At the end of the drive the road swung round, following the perimeter of the paddock which was enclosed in traditional iron rail fencing. Two horses grazed, heads into the wind, among mature oaks and chestnuts. The house itself stood at the top of a slight rise, facing south, the clean Norfolk stone shining white in the morning light. Either side of the entrance porch were three tall sash windows. To the right of the house a round archway led into the stable yard and the coach house; to the left a single-storey wing, which probably housed kitchens, scullery and domestic quarters. A slightly battered bottle-green Land Rover was parked by the door. Colonel McAlister was clearly a man of substance. No doubt business success had furnished him with his Englishman's castle as well as his prominent position in the county. As the Aston crunched to a halt on the gravel drive, I felt increasing unease at my intrusion into this enclosed world.

The housekeeper answered the door and took me into a fine panelled library. Three of the walls were covered in books, many of them in Latin and Greek. The fourth displayed a number of black-and-white photographs of groups of soldiers wearing the Pegasus badge of the 1st Airborne Division.

'The Colonel is expecting you. Please make yourself comfortable. Would you like some coffee?'

A few minutes later McAlister entered the room followed by a black labrador. In the cold and gloom of the previous night I had scarcely registered his appearance but now I saw what an imposing figure he made: tall and straight, grey haired, with the healthy skin tones of the outdoors and good claret. He wore the casual uniform of the well-to-do countryman at home, brogues, strawberry-coloured corduroy trousers, and a heavy checked shirt under a navy pullover. The housekeeper followed him into the room with a tray holding a coffee pot and two cups.

'Mr Kingsmill, I have been thinking about your request. I am not sure exactly how I can help you,' he said defensively.

'If you can tell me what you know about Marta, that would be a great help. You see, I am trying to piece together the story of my parents. I know so little about them. It is a personal matter,' I replied.

McAlister sat in silence for a minute or two.

'Very well, I can tell you what I know, which may not be a great deal, you understand.'

'I am grateful to you, Colonel McAlister.'

'My acquaintance with Marta began sometime in 1945.

1st Airborne Division took a hammering in Holland and never got back up to strength again. When the war ended we were sent to Norway on Operation Doomsday to police the country until the civilian authorities could take over. You can imagine the situation. The country had over three hundred thousand German troops; we numbered not much more than six thousand. Furthermore, thousands of Norwegians were returning from across the border in Sweden. We had to disarm the Germans and hold them securely, as well as feed them. And there were reprisals. Those who had collaborated were frequently disposed of summarily and we had to maintain order. Most depressing of all was the treatment of Norwegian women who had had liaisons with the Germans and particularly the large number of women who had borne children to them. These were outcasts and treated cruelly. For a young man like myself this was a most challenging experience.

'And then there were the concentration camp prisoners. Jews, intellectuals, left-wing politicians, and every type of citizen who may not have fitted the Nazi mould, suddenly free to roam, homeless, penniless, often in appalling physical condition. What were we to do? It was a matter of living from day to day, planning for each contingency, in the hope that life would get better. I still relive the horrors of those times today.

'I was assigned to the British Embassy in Oslo with responsibility for overseeing the issuing of visas to travel to Britain. Marta was a young Norwegian girl working in the department. She said she had come down to Oslo from the valleys, as so many did, seeking work and a place to live. We gave her a job and quarters. She was young, blonde-haired, very pretty and very naïve. But was good at her job.'

Here McAlister paused and considered.

'To be frank with you Mr Kingsmill, at twenty-five I was lonely and vulnerable. To be sure I had fought and killed and in that sense I was hardened. But my days were full of tales of human misery. And I fell in love with Marta as a kind of escape, I suppose. And I too was naïve. I had come down from Oxford with as much experience of life as reading

Greats could provide, which was very little, and then plunged into the obsessive life of a paratrooper. I had had ambitions to spend my life in academe. A man to the outside world, but a boy inside.'

I realised that seeing the photograph of Marta had triggered a flood of painful memories for Colonel McAlister, which surprised me. I felt I should say something.

'I had no idea that you would be so affected by seeing the photograph of Marta. I am sorry if this has been difficult for you,' I said.

'Not difficult, Mr Kingsmill. Scarcely a day passes but I think of the past, of the people I knew and the friends I had. Marta is one of those, but I think of her always with a sense of loss and betrayal. When my duties took me back to England, I promised to return to fetch her. I never did. I fell into the smothering world that our backgrounds determine for us. The army took me away to other worlds and as time passed the thought of Marta became no more than a painful sense of guilt, and it was easier to ignore it than correct it. And then my business life took over, I married twice, unhappily, and now I am a pillar of the community, as you see. If I can give you any advice, do what you must and never postpone it, and that is why I have told you what I have today, because I see you are following a journey to find where you belong in this world. Never finding that place is the most painful of failures. I hope I have helped you.'

I did not know how to respond to this. His revelations were completely unexpected. But I was grateful to him.

'You have helped me enormously,' I said, but there was more I wanted to know. 'Do you have any idea who took the photographs of you and Marta and the baby?'

'I have a vague memory of a sunny day and perhaps an older woman friend of Marta's was there. Perhaps it was she who took the photographs. As to the baby, it was not Marta's, and I was not the father, if that is what you may have thought.'

'I don't suppose you know where Marta might be today and what her name is?' I asked.

'No, I don't. Her maiden name was Pettersen. I presume she forgot about me and got married and now has grandchildren and is called something else. Perhaps she went back to her home in western Norway. I think she came from a small town. Røldal rings a bell, but I can't be sure. Now may I ask you a question?' he said.

'Of course, you have every right to do so,' I replied, grateful for the surprising frankness which he had shown me.

'I find it difficult to believe that you are simply trying to fill in your family background. Is there not more to it than that?'

'To be honest, I must admit there is. I'm not just filling in the family tree. A while ago a message from the past reached me which made me reassess everything. I realised I had blanked out so much in my drive for success, academically and professionally, that I no longer knew why I was living or where I was going. My father, I learned, was a war hero, and I had never known it till now, and never really known him; my mother was a mystery, a shadowy memory until now, but perhaps in the process of becoming more vivid. You said one should never put off what one must do in life: I think that's exactly what I am setting about, but you have defined it for me in a way I had not considered before. I thank you, Colonel.'

It seemed our conversation had reached its natural conclusion. We finished our coffee and I rose to leave. McAlister shook me by the hand and said:

'Mr Kingsmill, may I ask one great favour of you but, before I do, be clear that you are under no obligation to me?'

'Of course.'

'If you find Marta, as I think you mean to, perhaps you would offer her an account of me that is true to what I have told you? And you would be welcome to return here. I would be happy to know that she may have found her happiness more easily than I.'

As I motored back down the drive I thought about the morning's conversation and I was deeply moved, not only by McAlister's sad tale, but more about the moral lesson he had offered me, drawn from his own failure. And then I thought back to Tadeusz and his lesson of true friendship. How had I lived this long without knowing these things? But I was stronger in my commitment to finding the truth that had been promised me, whether painful or not.

I cut a sorry figure when I arrived at Brandon to collect Alexi and she noticed my silence immediately.

'Whatever is the matter, Peter?' she asked.

She herself was breezy to the point of annoyance. Her work was obviously going very well.

'I feel exhausted,' I replied, 'mentally, not physically, that is. McAlister is where I would have ended up in life. I've missed it by the skin of my teeth.'

'I'm not sure I understand what you mean,' she replied.

'Alexi, you don't have to, but you are part of my salvation,' I said.

'Now, you're making fun of me,' she said.

'No. Far from it. Why would I make fun of the best thing that has happened to me, ever?'

'Peter, you are the strangest, most elusive person I have ever known, which may be why I think I love you, despite my better judgement. Come on, it's time we moved.'

Chapter 11

We were heading back to the peace of the north Yorkshire hills. Having decided to take a month's leave from Whitehall, it was ironic that I had made so many visits to London and that the Aston had covered more miles in three weeks than it had in the previous year. But then nothing surprised me any more since my life had been turned upside down.

It was a joy to turn off the main road and head up the long hill into Osmotherley. Daylight was fading rapidly and I looked forward to the simple task of lighting the log fire and relaxing with Alexi, this time in the knowledge that a visit from Spurling would not be likely. Lights were already on in the Queen Catherine and it seemed that all was well with the world. It was strange how my trip north was now so welcome when three weeks before I had viewed it with a kind of dread.

Dawn came bright and sunny. We were on our second cup of coffee when the letterbox rattled and a heavy envelope thudded on to the hall mat. It was a letter from Skene at Guest and Wedderburn. Before I quit London a lifetime ago, as it seemed, I had redirected my mail to Yorkshire. I opened the letter in the hall and read it.

Dear Mr Kingsmill
Estate of Theresa Kingsmill
I am pleased to inform you that the winding-up of your mother's estate is now complete. I enclose a Note of Account, showing our fee and expenses. These have been deducted from the settlement figure and the closing balance has been transferred to your bank account as agreed at our last meeting.
I should draw to your attention the continuing employment of the housekeeper at Worsall House, Yarm and you will see that her salary has been paid from the estate of the deceased

up until 31 December 1988. You may wish to give your attention to this matter at your earliest convenience.

Yours sincerely
John Skene LLB

I looked at the enclosed note of account. The figure at the bottom was eight digits long. I knew of course that the settlement was for a very large sum but had no idea the estate would run to this amount. For a moment I stood rooted to the spot.

'Bad news?' asked Alexi, with a mouth full of buttered toast, when I returned to the living room.

'No...No...Just quite breathtaking. Look at that.'

I handed her the letter.

'Good God!'

'Exactly. I think I'd better call in at Worsall House today to see Mrs Cuthbert. She's been our housekeeper for years. She must be wondering what's happening. Do you want to come? You can see where I passed my mis-spent youth.'

'That would be interesting. I might start to understand what goes on in your head,' she replied. 'I take it Worsall House is yours?'

'The family home, although I only stayed there during the school holidays. My father bought it in 1956, when I was ten years old. After the war he started up an engineering business on Teesside. He must have been exceptionally astute. He very quickly expanded and won contracts to build bridges all over the world. Kingsmill became a famous name in civil engineering. He sold the business just before he died. He must have made a fortune, judging by the amount of money he left.'

'I get the impression you didn't enjoy your childhood.'

'You probably find this hard to believe, Alexi, but my brother and I looked forward to the school term so that we could get away, have friends and play games. Cold baths and cross-country runs bore no threats for us. Home was empty. My father worked all the time; my mother was a remote figure when I was young. I never really got to know her. Maybe this explains something. I remember she was very religious, always saying the rosary, and having priests round for tea. God knows what my father made of it all. George and I spent more time with Mrs Cuthbert in her kitchen, or on her husband's lawnmower, than with our parents. George was my brother.'

'What happened to him? I remember you told me he had died.'

'The official story was a car accident in 1976 when he was twenty-five, but it's not the whole truth,' I said.

'Will you tell me the whole truth?' she asked.

'I will, but not right now. Let's get across to Worsall House and I'll introduce you to Mrs Cuthbert. She'll like you, I know.'

From Osmotherley to Yarm was a very short drive, to start with through the rolling fields of the Tees valley and then the outskirts of the town. The road crossed the river and swung round into Yarm with its cobbled eighteenth century High Street and Georgian houses, many of them shop fronts and pubs. The village of Low Worsall was a mile or two further on in a loop in the river and above that, on a hill with a river view, stood Worsall House, a red-brick Victorian sprawl tacked on to a simpler, earlier farmhouse. There were lawns, a paddock and a walled garden, with greenhouses and a few outbuildings. The house had character but no style and no architect would have gained in reputation from its construction.

'This is it,' I said, as I pulled up at the side of the house, outside the kitchen door.

I showed Alexi in. The kitchen was empty but I could hear a vacuum cleaner somewhere in the house. I stood at the bottom of the staircase in the hall and shouted Mrs Cuthbert's name. After several attempts at making myself heard, the noise stopped, followed by the sounds of footsteps on the stairs.

'Well, Mr Peter. What a surprise to see you. You should have told me you were coming,' she said in a broad north-east accent.

Mrs Cuthbert was in her mid-sixties. She was five feet two inches tall, about the same round the middle, and her weight was distributed in the proportions of a cottage loaf. She was warm, kind and very hard-working. She had worked as housekeeper, cook and cleaner at Worsall since 1956, when my father bought the house. My mother had recruited her from the congregation of the local Catholic church, together with her husband, and they had been with the family for thirty-two years. They lived in a cottage in the village but spent five days each week at Worsall House. They knew more about the Kingsmills than any of us in the family.

'I wanted to surprise you, Mrs Cuthbert. If you'd known in advance, you would have made a cake.'

'But I have a cake,' she said, in total seriousness.

'Mrs Cuthbert, I would like you to meet Alexi.'

'Lovely to meet you pet,' she said, as she shook Alexi by the hand. 'Now you will have a piece of cake won't you, and some tea?'

'That would be very nice, Mrs Cuthbert,' Alexi replied, showing true diplomacy. So we sat down at the kitchen table while tea was made and a cake produced.

'You've not been here for a long time, Mr Peter. It'll be a couple of years, I suppose. You must be busy in London I guess. It's very quiet here since Mrs Kingsmill passed away but Bert and me try to keep the place going as best we can. In case the family want to use it.'

By the word "family", she had to mean me.

'You've done a wonderful job Mrs Cuthbert, you and Bert.'

I detected she was worried about the future, with two state pensions and nothing else to look forward to. Without thinking for a moment I said:

'I wanted to have a word with you about that. The lawyer told me that you had been paid until the end of the year. I'd like you and Bert to carry on indefinitely. Is that alright with you? I'm planning to spend more time here next year.'

Alexi was looking sideways at me, surprised at my assumed tone of certainty.

'Of course that's alright, Mr Peter. Bert and me would be more than happy to carry on,' she said.

89

'Well that's fine then. Now, I'm going to show Alexi round, and then we'll be off,' I said.

I took Alexi on a tour of the ground floor. I showed her the dining room with the long mahogany table and twelve Sheraton chairs, a carver at each end. In the drawing room she stopped to look at the photographs on the grand piano – my mother in evening dress, tall and elegant; my father in dinner jacket, with a cigar in his hand.

'She was very beautiful,' she said, 'and your father, so handsome.'

'They were a Hollywood couple I suppose. Invited to every civic do; entertaining foreign businessmen at their table. My mother shone at that. But she had little time for her children. We stood by and watched and then were sent off to boarding school.'

'And this must be you and George.'

Alexi had picked up a silver-framed photograph of two boys. I looked about fourteen, dressed in senior school blazer for Ampleforth, and George in his garish prep school outfit, brown curly hair and smiling morning face.

'Peter, looking very earnest, as always, and little brother George, looking like an angel. You were going to tell me about him,' she said.

'I want to show you something first,' I replied.

I took Alexi up to the first floor and along the corridor, past half a dozen closed bedroom doors. A smaller staircase curved up to the second floor, narrower and less grand than the first. On the top landing there were four small bedrooms, formerly servants' rooms, but in our day the children's rooms. I opened one and led the way in. I could see that Alexi was stunned.

'This was George's room. He left home in 1969 to train for the priesthood in an enclosed order. After he died my mother allowed no one in here. Mrs Cuthbert was not allowed to clear his things away or disturb anything. It has been like this for more than ten years.'

The room was a shrine. Above the single bed hung a wooden crucifix, the contorted body of Christ in bronze. On the bedside table there was a Roman missal, with rosewood covers, carved with the initials "IHS". A set of ivory rosary beads hung from the bedpost and on the wall at each side of the dressing table were fixed plaster statues of the Virgin Mary and St Joseph. On another was the "Sacred Heart" painting and the Holman Hunt depiction of Christ as the Light of the World. A small bookcase stood in the corner holding Newman's *Apologia*, the writings of Aquinas, a copy of *The Imitation of Christ*, Donne's sermons and the collected poems of Gerald Manley Hopkins. A palm cross pinned to the curtains recalled some Palm Sunday service of years ago. On a side table there was a large photograph of George, in priestly garb, with a cleric in bishop's attire and my mother dressed as the mother-of-the-bride. The inscription read: "On the occasion of the ordination of George Kingsmill by the Bishop of Hexham and Newcastle, Ushaw College, Durham, 1975."

'You see what happened, Alexi?' I asked.

'I think I am beginning to,' she replied. 'Your mother sounds like Lady Marchmain.'

'And you're right, there was a touch of Sebastian Flyte about George, I suppose. Looking back on it all, it seems to me that when George hit the teens he suffered a storm of religious fervour. The romantic view of Catholicism forced on him by his mother, coupled with being starved of emotional contact with her, threw him into a religious obsession. Sebastian started drinking; George started praying. The religious order was his way of escaping.'

'What happened next? He can't have been a priest for long before he died.'

'What happened next was inevitable. Religion was a cover-up for his homosexuality. All those years of fervour and devotion to Christ were his way of avoiding the real question he should have been asking himself. The lid blew off less than a year after he joined the order.'

'But surely gay priests and monks are par for the course,' said Alexi. 'The order wouldn't throw him out for that.'

'They didn't. But I can only surmise that when George

realised that his real nature was defined by the Church as unnatural and a mortal sin, his whole world imploded. He left the order and landed back home with one very small suitcase. The reason I never spoke to my mother again was that she slammed the door in his face, almost literally. He was a failed priest, a pervert, a disgrace in the eyes of God. And she cut him out of her will.'

'What did he do then?' she asked. 'Where did he go?'

'In seventy-six I was living in London, not married. I had a tiny flat in Finchley. He turned up and slept on the sofa for a few days. We talked a bit but he was in a bad way. One evening I returned late. We'd had a bit of a flap in the office. George had gone. I was worried sick about him. Two days later the police telephoned me and asked me to come down to the station. They wanted to question me about something. I feared the worst of course. I had given George my number and the police had found it on his body. They hoped that I would be able to identify him.'

'That must have been terrible.'

'It was. He was found downstream in the Thames. The car accident was the story my mother gave to the Cuthberts and the rest of the world. Nobody questioned it. The inquest wasn't reported in the press so the truth never came out. But I knew he had killed himself. The worst thing was that, for a Catholic, suicide is the greatest of mortal sins, the sin of despair, that you have no hope or belief in salvation, that you have destroyed the gift of life that God has given you to cherish. Can you imagine the mental horrors he must have gone through? I should have done more for him.'

I paused, unable to string any more words together in my anguish. Alexi put her arms around me. She could see I was near tears.

'That is a terrible burden to bear, Peter. Thanks for sharing it with me,' she said.

'I'm sorry for all this Alexi. I shouldn't be lumbering you with my problems. I want you to be happy with me, not to get weighed down by all this family garbage.'

'I am happy with you, Peter. I think I know you better

now and I want to know you more. Isn't that a good thing?' she said, smiling up at me.

'Yes, yes it is, of course,' I replied.

'You know what I think you should do now? Get Mrs Cuthbert to put all this religious stuff in a cardboard box and put it in the attic. Then get in here with a duster and clean the room. This is a shrine your mother created out of her world; it's not yours, and you shouldn't have to live with it.'

This was the first time I had seen Alexi angry but I knew she was right. Like most other things in my life, I had been running away from this for years. I needed to wake up and she had given me that jolt.

'You're absolutely right,' I said. 'I'll tell Mrs Cuthbert before we leave.'

And I did. Mrs Cuthbert's reaction should not have surprised me.

'I didn't like to say anything, Mr Peter, but you're right. It's time to move on – that's what our Bert thinks and I agree. Mrs Kingsmill won't know 'owt about it, where she is. And you should get yerself a nice young wife,' she added as an afterthought.

'I hope so, one day,' I replied.

I was happy to be leaving that house of dismal memories. But I wanted to draw a line under all this and there was one more thing for me to do. We drove down into Yarm and parked outside the Catholic church. There was a wooden gate into the churchyard and I led Alexi in. Twenty yards down a gravel footpath we stopped in front of a simple white gravestone marked "George Kingsmill Died February 25 1976 Aged 25 Rest in Peace". We stood for a minute or two in silence.

'I won't be coming here again, Alexi,' I said.

She put her arm through mine.

'Come on. Let's go,' she said.

As we drove back to Osmotherley, Alexi sat deep in thought. Then she said:

'You know, it's as if she didn't want to know you – your mother, that is. She thought she owned George, that he was her creature, and that is why she rejected him when he failed to pass her test. But you were allowed to escape, weren't you?'

'I suppose I was,' I agreed.

'Why do you think that was?'

'I've never thought of it as owning or escaping but perhaps you're right. Maybe I realised she never wanted me and leapt for my freedom when I did.'

But I myself had now been plunged into deep thought.

We spent the rest of the week quietly. Alexi had her work to do and she made good progress. I read her draft as she produced it, section by section, and was impressed by her grasp of the topic and the incisive style of her writing. My fears that she might compromise my professional relationship with Ken Brandon were completely unfounded. She handled the sensitive topic of immigration policy with balance and insight, without losing the critical edge that good journalism demands. Her article appeared on the Thursday morning and I received a call from Ken that day: "Your girl has done well. Give her my best wishes." Typical old-school patronisation, I thought to myself, but I knew that he was well intentioned. I passed on the part of the message that I thought would be well received but missed out "my girl". I was amused to watch Alexi, in other ways so wordly-wise and sophisticated, blushing as if she were a school girl receiving a good mark for her essay. Perhaps she was not quite so sure of herself as I had thought.

That afternoon the snow began to fall again in large white flakes. The temperature had sunk rapidly and the ground was soon covered, sounds of traffic disappeared, and the world drifted into a silent winter dream. The row of conifers at the bottom of the tiny garden started to bend under their white load. Alexi was busy with her writing but I could not settle to anything. Our visit to Worsall House had raised so many memories that I felt I needed to stop the world until I could make sense of it all. I had not thought of George for years and yet explaining his story to Alexi had shown me that the wounds had not healed. I had merely concealed them. I needed to make sense of why my mother had possessed

George so powerfully that he had felt there was only one way to escape his failure; and why I had been so peripheral to her demands. I began to feel that my search for what my past held was the only way in which I could ever move forward. And on top of everything, I knew that the weekend was approaching. I feared that Alexi would perform her disappearing act again and I would be left to question the meaning of it all, too polite to force the issue. I was beginning to feel trapped by events.

At two-thirty I decided I needed fresh air. Although the snow was falling, the air was still and there was an hour or more before the December light faded. I wanted to be alone, to think things through, so was relieved when Alexi declined a walk in order to finish her work. I put on boots and a warm coat and set off with no real idea where I was going.

I knew from childhood explorations in the area that there was a footpath from the top of the village leading down the hillside to the ruins of Mount Grace Priory. It was not generally known, except to the locals. So I set off up the village street on the Swainby road. There was no traffic and not a soul about. A couple of hundred yards further on, a rickety wooden gate opened through the hawthorn hedge into a snow-covered field of rough grass and dead bracken and what looked like a sheep track wound its way among the undulations down the hillside. The thin layer of untouched snow crunched under my boots. After twenty minutes I reached the fence running along the back of the ruined priory and it was a simple matter to clamber over it into the medieval cloisters. The honey-coloured stones had gathered dustings of snow; it seemed to be the most peaceful place in the world. Although the ruins were now closed and the main gate locked I felt no sense of trespass. The monks' ruined cells stood open to the weather. I entered one and sat down on a stone ledge, warm enough from my walk not to feel the cold.

The Carthusian monk who sat here six hundred years before me was a hermit. Perhaps his name was Nicholas or Robert or Henry. He prayed alone and ate alone. He lived and died within the confines of his cell, in silence. His universe was the stone of his cell walls, the blue of the sky through the narrow window and the voice of God in his head, if his prayers were answered. I began to understand why George had died. The fabric upon which he had built his life, and the purpose which justified his existence, had been destroyed in the most brutal fashion. The life blood of his soul had been stopped at source and there was nothing a living person could have done to help him at the end. And I thought of McAlister's advice: do what you must do, and never leave it undone. Every one of us who had known George was guilty of doing nothing, until the clock stood at one minute to midnight. When the chimes struck, it was too late.

I had lost track of time. The snow had ceased but the light was beginning to fade. It was time to get back to Alexi in the cottage. The climb up the hill was harder than the descent. The snow was thicker, the light was poor, the bracken seemed to grab my boots and more than once I slid sideways off the path, such as it was. Finally I reached the road and wandered back down the hill into the village. Lights in cottage windows shone on to the snowy grass verges, the village shop was drawing down its blinds, and Bill in the Queen Catherine was contemplating another night with only pedestrians for customers.

When I got back to the cottage, Alexi was in the kitchen making preparations for supper later that night. There was an impression of onions being chopped and tomatoes sliced, in a frenzy of culinary enthusiasm, but little apparent overall plan.

'You look as if you're finished,' I said. 'Happy with it?'

'Yep, I think so. Take a look and let me know what you think,' she replied. She carried on chopping, wielding the kitchen knife with gay abandon.

'Later,' I said. 'I need to talk to you.'

'About what?'

'About us,' I replied.

She put down the knife and waited.

'Alexi, would you say you know a lot about me?' I asked, as a kind of prelude.

'Don't tell me you're a serial killer!' she said.

'Seriously, please. Answer the question.'

'Well, taken all in all, I have learned about you and your family, and mostly your problems and uncertainties. So, yes, I know quite a lot about you,' she agreed.

'I know nothing about you – and I need to know,' I said. 'I know you told me last week that there were things you were not ready to share with me, but I feel that times have changed. After all, we're living together, more or less. I've told you that I love you – and I think you feel the same, don't you? And yet, you're holding back. I'm waiting for you to tell me you're disappearing again this weekend. What are you keeping from me? Can't you tell me?'

Alexi put the knife down and walked across the kitchen towards me. I was sitting on a kitchen chair and she perched on my knee, her arms round my neck.

'Everything you say is true,' she said. 'But I'm afraid Peter. I shouldn't be, but I am. You are the kindest, most sensitive, most delightfully honest man I have ever met. And I should have faith in you. But I am afraid, nevertheless.'

'What are you so frightened of?'

She fell silent for a minute. I could see her eyes were shining, but she struggled at last to speak.

'I'm afraid of losing you, that's it. I love you, Peter, and I know you love me, but I am afraid that if you knew all about me, you would drift away and I would lose you. I've been in a hopeless state of paralysis these last couple of weeks, wondering what I should do.'

'The only thing you can do – tell me,' I said.

She buried her head in my shoulder and I held her firmly.

'Trust me Alexi – please! If there's one thing I've learned these last few weeks it's the importance of sharing the truth. Do you think there is anything you can tell me that will overturn my feelings for you?'

'The truth is – I don't know, and neither do you, I suspect,' she replied.

'Try me!' I said.

'Alright, I will. But I need a drink.'

We went through to the living room where the log fire

was glowing steadily. I took a bottle of Glenmorangie from the cupboard, poured a couple of glasses and we settled down on the sofa. I had no idea what to expect when Alexi started to speak.

'Four years ago, when I was very young, an impoverished student but full of myself, I fell in love – or so I thought at the time – with an older man. Almost as old as you, in fact,' she added, with a smile. 'You see, I have a weakness for older men. He was clever and handsome – just like you. I wonder sometimes if I'm not reliving my life on a kind of video loop. I got pregnant and he left, back to his wife and kids, as I found out later. He was a visiting professor from Turkey, very smooth, and very much aware of the pickings that might be had among naïve young female students, like me. It turned out I wasn't the only one, of course. I suppose it's a story that could be told a hundred times across university campuses everywhere. But can you imagine the glamour of an affair with a well paid academic, no ties, weekends in hotels and dinners out, while your friends are hanging around in the students' union and getting drunk on designer cocktails in cut-price happy hours? Then crash! It all goes wrong. His sabbatical finishes and off he goes, back to Istanbul, while I am left high and dry.'

'Did you try to contact him?' I asked.

'Of course, but the university authorities could only release his personal details, they said, if I took legal action against him. That was impossible. It would mean a court case, expense, and what would I achieve? A petty financial settlement, which would be impossible to enforce in a country like Turkey. No, I cut my losses, and told myself it was all part of an education!'

'What did you do?'

'I did nothing at first, just lived from day to day, went to lectures, wrote essays and attended tutorials. Funnily enough, my work improved. I got top marks for everything. I think it was because I suddenly grew up. Staying in and working seemed more rewarding than trogging around with overgrown teenagers. But, of course, I had to make a decision sooner or later. You know what I mean, don't you?'

'And what did you decide?' I asked.

She hesitated, then grasped my hand.

'I was in uncharted waters. I was completely unprepared for the emotional turmoil I would feel. On the one hand, being pregnant was just a bloody nuisance; but on the other, I felt a totally unexpected surge of happiness, a kind of magical wonder that my body could perform such a miracle as to create new life. My brave new world was full of miracles.

'Of course I took advice. But I found it full of impersonal check-lists: things you should consider in having a baby; or things to bear in mind if you wish a termination. Oh, yes, there was all the measured counselling you could ask for but nobody other than me to make the decision.

'I left it and left it. In a sense I think this was the decision already made. But I knew the complications of my life in the future, of the worry I would cause my parents. I never want to go through those weeks again alone, unable to talk about it. Peter, I have a child.'

I was silent, my mind in turmoil. This was the last thing I had expected. I realised what a naïve fool I had been to be suspicious of her weekends away. I was ashamed at my lack of trust in Alexi and I was sorry that she had struggled to be open with me.

'Peter, say something, please.'

I had drifted off into a reverie but was brought back abruptly.

'What can I say – except that it's fine with me. No it's more than fine – it's great with me! Isn't it great with you too?'

'It's great with me too!' she cried. 'I'm so happy that you feel that way.'

'How old is your child?'

'She's four. Her name is Katerina. She has brown eyes and dark hair and a lot of attitude,' Alexi said.

'Just like her mother, then,' I said.

'Do you want to see her picture?'

'Of course.'

And Alexi produced a small photograph from the voluminous canvas bag that held her bits and pieces. Katerina was the prettiest of things, dressed in blue dungarees, with two short pony tails sticking out sideways from her head. She was sitting on a wall in a garden, legs hanging down, wearing flowery trainers that said "right" and "left". She wore a pair of national health glasses hooked behind her ears.

'She is delightful, Alexi. You must miss her during the week. She has glasses?'

'A squint in one eye. The eye hospital says it will be OK in six months. Yes, I miss her. Mum and Dad are fantastic with her. She lives with them in Helmsley. I've been travelling around these last few months, doing odd journalism jobs, trying to earn a living. That's why I disappear at weekends. To give my parents a break and spend time with Katerina.'

'I see that now,' I said. 'I'm sorry I pushed you for an explanation. I thought all the wrong things.'

'No, Peter, I'm glad you did. I had to be straight with you but I was running away from it all the time. Now you know about me and I know about you. It's much better that way.'

'Enough of this self-analysis!' I said. 'We should be celebrating the arrival on the scene of Katerina, Alexi's baby! And I insist on meeting her and your Mum and Dad this weekend.'

'You're mad, Peter. Are you sure you know what you're letting yourself in for?' she asked, with a broad smile on her face.

'The answer to that is a resounding "no",' I said, 'but quite frankly, my dear, I don't give a damn. I'm happy!' I poured two more large whiskies and we clinked the glasses together.

'To Katerina and Alexi...and me,' I said.

It was one of those moments in life when black thoughts seemed impossible, banished to the outer regions by the simple joy of sharing. We sat on the sofa together, watching the logs burn down, each of us knowing there was now a bond between us that had been forged that afternoon. After a little while Alexi stood up to go into the kitchen.

'The chopped onions and sliced tomatoes are calling for

their culinary partners,' she said. 'They have been sorely neglected.'

'Do you have a grand design for this meal?' I asked, fearing the worst. 'If not, I suggest we try the Queen Catherine tonight.'

There was little opposition to be overcome. Over the road, through the thickening snow which had began to fall again, Bill was twiddling his thumbs behind the bar.

'Any food tonight, Bill?' I asked.

'Plenty. The chef can't get down the road this time,' he replied with a wicked grin, 'so you can enjoy the gastronomic delights of our full menu! It's a Marston's and a white wine, is it?'

I nodded and he handed us two bar menus while he poured our drinks.

When we finally staggered back across the road to the cottage, we were tired but happy. The combination of emotional peace and alcohol proved a deadly combination. We fell into bed and made love in a way we had not done before. It was as if the physical act of sex was spiritual, corny as that may sound. For me, to feel the warmth of Alexi's body next to mine was like the lifting of a great weight from my shoulders. I had no need to worry any longer and I could not explain why. I felt she knew me and trusted me and that I had no reason to struggle any more. And we were expressing that through the way our bodies moved together. I had never experienced that with Lucy when we were first married and in later years we showed each other only absolute kindness and respect, a substitute for love. Her illness made me emotionally numb; her death left me strained and tense. Alexi was the antidote that chased away the years of emptiness. Her long dark hair lay across the pillow while she slept and I stroked it while I listened to the slight rise and fall of her breathing. I wanted to look after this woman for ever.

Chapter 12

In the early hours of Friday morning a snow plough trundled up the hill, orange lights flashing, and swathes of grit fanning out from the spreader. The noise of the engine woke me as the driver performed a three-point turn in the main street, before heading back down the hill to the A19. Osmotherley rejoined the outside world but the minor roads to Swainby and Hawnby remained blocked.

After breakfast Alexi faxed her article for next week's society supplement, which put her comfortably ahead of schedule. She had told me she was going to try to get to Helmsley that afternoon as she needed to prepare the way with her parents and Katerina.

'I can't just spring you on them,' she said.

'You sound like John the Baptist.'

'And who does that make you then?'

At that point I was silenced, deciding it best to toe the line and do as I was told. I was to be in Helmsley for lunch on Sunday. I realised though that my appearance at Rievaulx Cottage was, for Alexi, a bigger deal than I had thought. After all, she was bringing home a man she had known for only a few weeks and who was seventeen years her elder. This was an uncanny parallel with the visiting Turkish professor and the fact would not go unnoticed by Alexi's parents, who naturally would fear that history was repeating itself. That was why she wanted time and space on her own with them and Katerina.

There was only one way to Helmsley since the minor roads were closed. I would have to drive south to Thirsk and then hope I could get up Sutton Bank and on to the Helmsley road. The Aston was a powerful car but, with its rear-wheel drive, totally unsuited for winter conditions. I was not looking forward to the journey. The thought of sliding sideways down the hill on the compacted snow was not appealing, nor the challenge of climbing Sutton Bank. But I was determined to get Alexi home so that she could deal with things in her own way.

I went to the front door to see what the weather was doing. Along the passageway to the main road I caught a glimpse of Bill with a shovel, clearing a route to the entrance to his hotel. Parked at the front of the Queen Catherine I recognised the front grille of his green Land Rover sticking out from under a thick white blanket of snow. I had an idea. I put on my boots and trotted across to him.

'Morning Bill,' I said. 'Does your Land Rover have winter tyres, by any chance?'

'Aye, it does Mr Kingsmill. You need them here all right. Why do you ask?'

'I've got a problem. I have to get Alexi home to Helmsley – you've met Alexi – and I don't think my ridiculous car would make it in these conditions. Do you think I could hire your Land Rover for an hour?'

'Hire? No lad, don't be daft! You can have it. Floor's full of holes, the tailgate leaks, and the back box is about to fall off, but it'll get yer there alright. Put new tyres on just a while back. Tell your lass she's welcome but better wrap up. Heater's knackered.'

I felt like giving Bill a hug but remembered that north country men didn't behave like Chelsea footballers. So I just said:

'Thanks Bill. That's really good of you. Keep some of that steak and kidney pie for me tonight. I'll be on my own.'

'Will do Mr Kingsmill. Have a safe trip and say hello to Alexi. She's a right bonny lass that one. You did well for yourself there,' he said laughing. 'Well, better get on, though I doubt if many folk'll venture out today,' and he returned to his shovelling.

When I returned to the cottage I found Alexi had packed a few things and was just about ready to leave.

'Do you think we'll manage in your car?' she asked, looking very dubious.

'No, I don't. That's why we're going in a Land Rover. Bill's lent us his. He says hello, and you're a bonny lass, but wrap up well because there's no heater. Wellie boots with thick socks would do.'

A few minutes later we walked across to the Queen Catherine. Bill had kindly swept the snow from the roof and bonnet of the Land Rover. The keys were in the ignition but he came to the door to see us off.

'Bill, this is Alexi. It's time you had a formal introduction,' I said.

'Hello, Bill. It's very kind of you to lend us your car,' Alexi said. 'I don't think we would manage it without a four-wheel drive.'

'No problem at all. Just mind how you go at the top of Sutton Bank. Those bends are pretty bad in this weather,' he replied.

We climbed in and turned the ignition. After a slow churning of the thick engine oil the Land Rover chugged into life, a large black cloud of diesel smoke pouring from the exhaust. I could see chinks of white snow between my feet where the floor pan had rusted through.

'How on earth this passed the MOT I've no idea,' I said.

'He probably knows someone in the business,' said Alexi.

I shoved the car into gear and released the clutch. The car slowly moved forward through the low wall of snow pushed up by the plough, crunching and juddering its way on to the road. I pushed it into second, keeping my foot off the brakes, relying on the gearbox to keep our speed down and the wheels turning. In this manner we trundled down the hill to the main road. A few slow-moving vehicles headed each way so the inside lanes of the dual carriageway were passable. Bill was right about the heater and we could feel shafts of cold air coming from every direction – window seals, rattling doors and holes in the floor.

'This is it,' I said, 'total motoring!'

We turned off at Thirsk and on to the Helmsley road. I

was worried that, even with winter tyres and four-wheel-drive, we might run into difficulties getting up Sutton Bank. The Gods were with us. There were no other cars in front of us so I could put her into second gear and keep a steady pace all the way up. At the top all the winter beauty of the Hambleton Hills hit us, trees laden with drapes of snow, the rolling hills deep in drifts, fence posts half concealed. The only sign of life was a tractor crossing a field leaving a trail of hay for the black-faced sheep, which followed in a bustling flock.

'Where else would you rather be?' I said, musing aloud. Then, before Alexi had a chance to reply, I added, 'Don't answer that!'

By the time we reached Helmsley I was chilled to the bone. I knew Alexi wanted to avoid family introductions until Sunday so I pulled up a little way from the cottage.

'How will you explain you got here?' I asked.

'Oh, dropped off by one of my flatmates in York, on her way to Pickering. That should do it,' she answered.

She gave me a frozen kiss, the tip of her nose feeling like ice.

'See you on Sunday, Peter, and thanks. Mind how you go on the way back.'

I watched her plod off up the road through the snow, in her oversized boots from the cottage. She looked so small and alone, off to face the difficult explanations and persuasions that were bound to follow. I wished I was with her but I knew she had decided on her course of action. I admired her bravery. It was as if all the courage in the world were rolled up in that fragile frame and she had never doubted herself. I thought of my own privileged life, the ease with which I had sailed through it. But I had been ignorant, until now, of the fibre of people around me. I realised I had never had to face a challenge in my life, never even had the courage to say to Lucy that it was all over. I had never really done the sums, to calculate what my life was worth, until this very moment. I swung the Land Rover round and set off back to Osmotherley. I parked the car in front of the pub and went round the back to give Bill the keys.

'Everything alright?' he asked.

'Fine Bill and thanks. I put some diesel in for you.'

'You shouldn't have bothered,' he said.

The cottage felt cold and very empty but I knew it would soon be Sunday. I lit the fire and brought in a couple of armfuls of logs. I made a pot of tea and picked up my battered copy of *Bleak House*. It had been a habit of mine for years, when I ran out of the trendy stuff that might have made the Booker shortlist, to revisit Dickens. The plots were complex and the characters numerous so that it always felt like a fresh start, trying to piece things together with half of it forgotten. Moreover, it was a simple pleasure to read a book with a beginning, a middle and an end, and usually in that order, even if it took forever to get there. The mysteries of the past were now also part of my stock-in-trade, like a Dickensian plot, and despite the turn my life had taken since meeting Alexi, I still felt a burning desire to piece the jigsaw together. Everything pointed towards a chapter of events in Norway at the close of the war and I wanted to get to the bottom of why someone should feel it worthwhile to follow me from a distance, but simultaneously to remain anonymous. There was only one thing that I could do next and that was to try to find Marta Pettersen, which meant a trip to Norway.

Over my steak and kidney pie that evening, in the almost empty bar of the Queen Catherine, I decided on a course of action. Alexi had enough on her plate with her burgeoning journalistic career, and finding time to look after her child. She did not need a trip to a frozen Norway in December, on what might turn out to be a wild goose chase. But she needed a proper place to live, and a car. The first was simple: she could have the cottage, to use whenever she wanted; the second was even simpler: I would drive into York the next day and buy her a car. Not only that, I would ditch London for good, forget about the pettiness of politicians who came and went with the fragility of an English summer's day. If I ever had to waste my life with that again, I would rather put a gun to my head. My spirits lifted like a hot-air balloon, with no effort, floating like gossamer. I went across to the bar.

'Bill,' I said, 'you're a wonderful chap. Let me buy you a drink to thank you for all your help today. What will you have?'

'You're very happy, Mr Kingsmill. Won the pools?'

'Call me Peter, please,' I interrupted.

'Well, Peter.... I'll have a brandy. And you?'

'I'll have one too.'

Bill poured the two brandies and we clinked glasses. The other locals in the bar looked at us with faint amusement.

'To the most beautiful girl in the world – Alexi,' I said.

'To Alexi,' said Bill, 'and good luck to you both.'

And that is how Bill and I became blood brothers.

On Saturday morning I drove into York. The roads were clear and the Aston behaved itself admirably. I stopped at the Land Rover dealership and found a well-dressed car salesman called Gary, clearly surprised that anyone would wish to buy a car in the depths of a British winter with Christmas approaching.

'I want a Land Rover 90, diesel, with winter tyres, preferably green,' I said. 'What have you got?'

'Well, there's a six month waiting list for a new one,' he said, 'but we do have a two-year old low mileage one in the forecourt. And it's green. Do you want to have a look at it?

'Not particularly, as long as it's in good nick,' I replied.

'It's in very good nick and it comes with one year manufacturer's warranty. Eight thousand pounds.'

'That will be fine,' I said.

It was the quickest car sale in his career, I had no doubt.

'Now, what I want you to do is have this car ready for me to take away today. I'll pay by cheque and leave my car as a deposit. If you will lend me your phone I can switch the insurance cover right now. Is that OK?'

Gary looked dumbfounded. He had never come across such a deal in his short career.

'And your car is the Aston Martin?' he asked.

'Correct. Should be worth fifty thousand I would think. Here are the keys. The log book's in the glove compartment to prove I own the car. Once the cheque for the Land Rover is cleared, I'll come back for the Aston.'

'I'll have to call my boss to clear this deal,' he said. 'This is pretty unusual.'

'Not quite done yet,' I said. 'I also need a Range Rover to pick up next week when I come back for the Aston. What have you got?'

'I've got a one-year-old, twenty-five grand, automatic, two-year warranty. How's that?'

'Perfect. I'll write you a cheque now for thirty-three thousand pounds. Give me a ring at this number when its cleared, to let me know I can pick up the Range Rover.'

I wrote the cheque there and then. Gary seemed delighted, thinking of the commission that was coming his way and the kudos he would gain when he told his boss on Monday that he had sold two cars in five minutes.

'I don't think I need to phone the boss after all,' he said.

'Quite right,' I said. 'May I borrow your phone?'

'Certainly, Mr Kingsmill, and would you like a coffee?'

Ten minutes later I was driving out of the garage in the Land Rover, slightly shocked but amused at living dangerously. Quite out of character, I thought. But then, what was my character these days?

I drove into the centre of York and parked the car in a multi-storey. I had shopping to do for a four-year-old girl. I wandered around aimlessly with no clear notion of what I was looking for. Eventually, down one of the city's medieval streets where the houses on either side reached out to each other, I found a small shop with a bow window and bottle-glass window panes, through which I could see an array of dolls, toy rabbits with floppy ears and puppies with scrunched-up noses. Inside a young girl sat behind the counter.

'If you were a four-year-old girl, what would you most desire in this shop?' I asked.

She laughed and pointed straight to a long-legged patchwork doll with flaxen pig-tails and a checked apron.

'I think this is delightful,' she said, 'but it is rather

expensive. In fact, it's the most expensive thing we have. But it is lovely, don't you think? She's called Pippa.'

'I'll take her. Have you got a nice big box with a ribbon round it?'

'Of course. I'll just wrap it for you.' And she disappeared into the back room with the doll.

On the way back to Osmotherley, I turned off into Northallerton to a country outfitters and bought myself a Barbour, a pair of cords, a thick pullover and a couple of lumberjack shirts. If I really was ditching my life as a city dweller, I might as well dress for it. Next I went to the florists and bought a large bouquet for Alexi's mother.

I was back in Osmotherley by one o'clock and slightly at a loose end. Buying cars, dolls and flowers had set my pulse racing but I now needed to fill in the hours until my requisite appearance at Rievaulx Cottage the next day. The weather was fine and cold, the air clear. I had a wardrobe of countryman's clothes and nothing to do for the rest of the day. So I put on my walking boots and my new Barbour, made a cheese sandwich and a flask of coffee, and set off on the track that led from the village along the edge of the Cleveland Hills to the sea. I had walked this way as a boy many times before, to escape on my own during holidays with my mother. My memory always seemed to recall my mother, never my father and, as I thought about it, I had no recollection of his ever spending holidays with us. It was as if I remembered them only as separate figures, unrelated, never together as a married couple.

As I trudged along in the sharp winter light, unaware of my surroundings, it became increasingly clear to me that not only was my father's life until recently a closed book, but I knew little about my mother. It is true I had felt distanced from her but were there also reasons for her to feel alienated from me? While she had devoured George with her avaricious religious zeal, she had allowed me to drift freely away. This was another piece which I needed to complete the jigsaw.

After an hour I took a break for coffee and my humble cheese sandwich, sitting on a stone at the car park by the reservoir on the Swainby road. Then I cut up the track and headed south to Chequers before dropping down the valley and back to Osmotherley from the lower road. The year was heading towards its winter solstice and the afternoon light was fading fast. Once back at the cottage, I telephoned Worsall House, hoping to catch Mrs Cuthbert before she locked up. After a few rings I heard the receiver lifted and Mrs Cuthbert's voice.

'Mrs Cuthbert, it's Peter Kingsmill here,' I said.

'Ah, Mr Peter, how are you? I was just thinking about you. I've been doing a lot of clearing out and I wondered if you wanted to keep some of the stuff. You should come and look at it before I do anything,' she said.

'That's exactly why I was calling. Have you found any papers belonging to my mother by any chance?' I asked.

'Yes I have, not a lot mind you. She was always good at clearing out rubbish herself. I've got a lot of things out of Mr George's room, as you asked.'

'That's very good, Mrs Cuthbert. Thank you. Why don't I come over on Monday and take a look at it all? Say about eleven?'

'That will be fine and will you be bringing your young lady with you again, Mr Peter? She's a lovely lass. I'll have a cake ready for your coffee.'

'That would be very nice, Mrs Cuthbert. Thank you.'

I put the phone down. I had no idea what I was looking for among the papers that my mother had left but my instinct told me that the story, if there was one, would be complicated.

That evening the Queen Catherine was busy. Bill was behind the bar and his wife was in the kitchen, organising the part-time staff. As I was on my own, I went into the bar and ordered a pint.

'Now then, Peter. I see you've bought a posh new Land Rover,' Bill said. 'Mine not good enough for you, eh?' he laughed.

'On the contrary, Bill, I fell in love with yours so I had to go out and buy myself one. Not new actually – two years old. You don't want to buy the Aston Martin do you?' I asked jokingly.

'Not likely. The Boro could get a new striker for that price. No Alexi this evening, Peter?'

'She's at home with her parents tonight but I am formally invited to meet them for lunch tomorrow,' I replied.

'Well, now. That's sounds a bit alarming.'

'To tell you the truth, I haven't felt this nervous for years. Alexi went ahead to prepare the way, and I can't help wondering what they are expecting.'

'Well, lad, just be yerself and remember, as my mother used to say, when you're married son, a tuppenny pie costs fourpence. Let that be a warning, eh!'

Bill grinned all over his broad Yorkshire face.

Chapter 13

I didn't know why I should feel nervous but I did. I suppose I felt I was about to be looked over, with all the close scrutiny that a Yorkshire father and an Italian mother could muster between them. I was painfully conscious of what they might see as my failings: I was too old; I had been to what they might think of as a posh school and university; I was too well-off for them; and I had never had a proper job. My life in London for the last twenty years had been spent within the narrow confines of a social group who ate out during the week, drank in wine bars, and looked the same, whether they voted Labour or Conservative. My return to the north had thrown my subtle shades of grey into the sharpness of black and white. North Yorkshire was not London and the people were as different as the landscape. I suppose, at the bottom of it all, I feared that Alexi's parents might not trust me to be good for their daughter. When I thought back to my early days with Lucy, I could now see how unthinkingly she and I had slipped into our relationship. We thought the same, we wanted the same and eventually our sameness snuffed out the spark with polite boredom.

I parked the Land Rover outside Rievaulx Cottage. As I unloaded my gifts, Alexi came down the garden path, followed by a border collie with a wagging tail, and opened the gate.

'Hi Peter,' she said, and put her arms round me, as I struggled with both hands full. 'You seem to be overloaded. Come on in.'

And she led me into the cottage. I stepped into a low-beamed entrance hall, at the end of which I could see the kitchen. To the right a door opened into the living room and Alexi led me in by the arm. A coal fire burned in the open hearth.

'Dad, this is Peter,' she said.

'Hello, Peter. I am very pleased to meet you. I've heard a lot about you.' And we shook hands.

'I'm pleased to meet you too, Mr Truman,' I replied.

'Call me Andrew, please. Now come on in and have a drink,' he said, pointing to a fireside chair. Andrew was a man of around sixty years, of medium height, with the complexion of a countryman and thinning grey hair combed back.

'Not yet Dad. Peter needs to meet Mum first,' and Alexi shot off into the kitchen. She returned a moment later with her mother.

'Mum, this is Peter.' And again we shook hands.

'Very pleased to meet you Mrs Truman,' I said.

I handed her the bouquet of flowers which she took and held to her face.

'Thank you. They are beautiful. Angelina, please, Peter. You are very welcome. Alexi has told us so much about you. It is a pleasure to meet you.'

She had the soft dark eyes of her daughter and the same strong hair, albeit slightly greying at the temples. She spoke with a musical Italian accent laced with flat Yorkshire vowels. I felt the warmth of their welcome.

'Now, let's have a drink,' said Andrew. 'What will you have Peter? Beer or a glass of wine?'

'Oh, whatever is going,' I said.

'Well, I'm having a beer and the girls will have a glass of white wine, I'm sure. I've got a bottle of something Italian here.'

'A beer then.'

Andrew poured the drinks and we stood in a small circle in front of the fire and touched our glasses. Alexi put her arm through mine.

'Here's to Peter, and welcome to our house,' said Andrew. He had taken on the formal style of the Englishman married to a foreigner, his words seeming to echo those of a signor welcoming a guest to his house in Italy.

'Thank you so much,' I said, 'I am pleased to be here.'

At that moment there was a clattering like clogs on a wooden floor. The living room door burst open and a small girl tumbled into the room.

'This must be Katerina,' I said.

'Katie, come and say hello to Peter,' said Alexi, taking her by the hand.

Katerina advanced towards me and grudgingly said hello but her eyes had fallen on the pink ribbon bow around the large box I had placed on the sofa.

'What's in the box, Mummy?' she asked.

'Why don't you open it?' I said.

Within seconds the ribbon had been removed and the tissue paper wrapping the doll lay strewn on the floor. Pippa made her gangling entrance, much to the delight of her new owner.

'Now, Katie, you must thank Peter for the present,' said Alexi.

I went down on my haunches and Katerina staggered towards me clutching the doll.

'Thank you, Peter,' she said, and planted a formal kiss on my cheek.

'I'm glad you like her. She's called Pippa.'

Katerina disappeared up the stairs with Pippa, as noisily as she had entered. Andrew topped up our glasses. We chatted easily about trivial things, the weather or the roads. Then Andrew raised the stakes.

'That was a very kind thing to do, Peter, bringing a present for Katerina,' he said. 'You've made Alexi very happy. She was worried you might not like children.'

'Oh, Dad,' Alexi sighed, with the resignation that girls often show towards their well-meaning but tactless fathers. I saw her glance towards her mother.

'Peter, you must be hungry. Come and eat,' interrupted Angelina, deftly changing the subject.

The kitchen ran the length of the cottage and in the centre stood a heavy rectangular pine kitchen table, laid for five people. The centre piece was a display of winter foliage and red berries. Andrew took his place at the head of the table with Alexi on his right. Katerina was summoned from her room and clattered down the staircase, clutching Pippa, both of whom took up precarious residence alongside Alexi. I was shown pride of place on Angelina's right hand.

'I hope you like Italian food, Peter,' she said. 'I have prepared a meal from my home in Tuscany for you.'

'I love Italian food, Angelina. Alexi will tell you I used to eat every week at Francesco's in Pimlico but I think your food will be better,' I replied.

'I hope so,' she said, ladling out bowls of thick soup from the tureen in front of her. 'This is what we call ribollita, which means yesterday's cabbage and bean soup reheated. But it's better than it sounds.'

Andrew filled our glasses with red wine and we drank a toast. The soup was delicious, salty and robust. I had never felt such sense of belonging. Everybody was happy, talking too much, interrupting each other, and making plenty of noise. After the soup came bistecca alla fiorentina – large grilled t-bone steaks, with an accompaniment of white beans, followed by more wine. Then something called zuccotto which seemed to be a sponge cake covered in chocolate, cream, fruit and nuts. At last, good strong coffee in small cups. Throughout the meal, not only the conversation, but the wine flowed freely. I was enchanted by it all. I had not believed that a family meal could be so. Eventually, we reclined in satisfaction.

'Angelina, that was the most delicious meal I have had in years,' I said. 'Thank you for inviting me. It has been such a pleasure to meet you and Andrew and, of course, Katerina.'

By this time Katerina had been given permission to leave the table and had vanished into her private domain.

'Why don't you and Andrew go into the living room and Alexi and I can clear away here?' she said.

This was clearly part of the strategy and I knew what was coming. Andrew and I took our places either side of the fireplace and I waited for the conversation to start. There was some small talk before Andrew managed to edge towards the real issue he wished to raise. And then he began.

'Peter, I want you to know what a difficult time Alexi has

had in the last few years. Angelina and I are very proud of the way she stuck in and got her degree and now she seems to be doing well in the journalism line.'

'She's doing extremely well,' I said. 'She's very clever and determined.'

'I suppose you know she was badly let down by an older man some time ago. Probably a good thing really. It would never have lasted, I think. But I want you to know that I don't want Alexi hurt again like that. I think you're a good man but that may not be enough since there is a child involved. That complicates matters.'

He paused. He was not a man used to making speeches but this had been his duty as a father.

'I understand entirely your concerns,' I said. 'Meeting Alexi has been the best thing that has happened to me in my life, and that is no exaggeration. Meeting Katerina has been a joy. It's very early days but I hope that Alexi, Katerina and I can make our lives together. You see, I have never experienced the joy of having a family that you experience every day of your life. Today has been special for me. What else can I say?'

'You don't need to say more, Peter. I'm a good judge of character. Alexi is her own woman, even though she's still my little girl, and she is capable of making her own decisions. But I worry for her nevertheless.'

'Please don't worry. I mean to take care of her for the rest of my life – if she'll have me!'

'I think she'll have you,' he replied, smiling.

We fell into conversation less poignant. Andrew told me about himself. He had been a tenant farmer with a thousand acres of sheep grazing on the moors, following in his father's footsteps. Fifteen years ago the landowner had decided there was more money in grouse moors for London stockbrokers and the lease on the sheep farm had been ended. Sheep and grouse did not sit easily together. He had enough in the bank to buy Rievaulx Cottage and got himself seasonal jobs with other sheep farmers in the district, supplemented by a part-time job at the college of agriculture, training students in sheep husbandry.

'So Alexi was ten when you had to leave the farm?' I said.

'Aye, ten. She missed it a lot. Used to come out with me and Bonnie on the hill in all weathers. Bonnie was my border collie. Fine dog. Nothing can replace that, even if life is easier now.'

'How did you meet Angelina?'

'I was very lucky. Thirty years ago I was at a YFC dance down in Northallerton. Got dragged along by some old mates. Not really my scene. She came over to learn English and had a job in a hotel in Thirsk. She'd come along with someone else. Obviously, not her cup of tea. We got chatting. She was a real beauty, as you might imagine. Still is. She must have fancied my tractor. Can't imagine what else she saw in me.'

I warmed to Andrew. He was intelligent and perceptive. Just then Alexi and Angelina came into the room, no doubt having judged enough time had elapsed for the men's business to be completed.

'Why don't you two young people go for a stroll?' said Angelina. 'It's a fine afternoon.'

She had decided we needed some time alone.

'Let's walk up to Rievaulx,' Alexi suggested.

'OK,' I said.

When we got outside, I pointed to the Land Rover, which Alexi had not noticed I was driving when I arrived.

'Do you like it?' I asked.

'I do. Is it yours?'

'Not exactly. Can you drive?' I asked.

'Of course. I used to drive Dad's tractor across the field when I was ten. Why do you ask?'

'Because it's yours. Here are the keys.'

And I handed Alexi a set of car keys.

'You need transport, and this is the best I could do in a hurry. Now let's drive up the road to Rievaulx. I put you on the insurance cover yesterday over the phone. Made up the details so I hope you've not been banned.'

'Peter, what's going on? Explain yourself, please.'

'Let's drive while we talk,' I said.

We got in the car, Alexi behind the wheel. She was pretty smooth with the gears, as befitted a farmer's daughter with a history of driving tractors. I could see she was enjoying herself.

'OK, this is what I think,' I began. 'I'm selling the Aston Martin. It's a stupid car for me now – in fact, it probably always was. I've bought myself a Range Rover. I'm giving up London – it's not for me any more. But I've got stuff to do and you need to be independent. I want you to move into the cottage, where you can have the space and quiet to do your work, but if you have transport it means you can see Katerina and your parents whenever you want to. Every day if need be. What do you think?'

'That would be great, Peter. But my funds are low. I'm only getting fees at the moment. I'm not salaried to anybody and, to tell you the truth, I prefer to stay freelance.'

'Don't worry about that. I've added your name to my current account. You'll be getting a bank card through the post soon. Put all your expenses on that.'

'You certainly don't mess about. Am I to be a kept woman?' she asked laughing.

'You most certainly are. I want to keep you forever, if you'll have me.'

'Is that what I think it is?'

'It is. What do you say?'

There was a long silence as she drove, then a smile, then a laugh. Then a whole chorus.

'What are you laughing at?' I asked.

'I never thought I would be wooed by the offer of a Barclay's bank card and a second-hand Land Rover. You are the only man I have ever met who would think of such an approach. That's why I love you, I suppose.'

'Are you ever going to answer the question?' I asked.

'Yes, it's yes.'

We reached the turn-off to Rievaulx and she stopped the car. She reached across to me, doing battle with the gear lever, and we embraced for a long time.

'How did you get on with Dad?' she asked.

'I think I passed the test. I told him you were the best thing that has ever happened to me. I think that did it,' I said.

'Poor Peter, having to be checked out at your age. Dad's so protective. He still thinks I'm six years old. I don't suppose fathers ever stop feeling that way, do they?'

'I suppose not,' I replied. 'Let's walk.'

The Rievaulx Terrace was flooded in late afternoon sun, sparkling on the crystallised snow that crunched like sugar. The dark trees threw long shadows that fell like the bars of a grille across the crescent of grass. I had always loved this place but now it was magical. I remembered the last time Alexi and I had stood here, when I knew she was holding back from me and I was full of doubts. Now the sky was clear, there were no clouds. We walked on in silence. Then Alexi spoke.

'Peter, you said you had stuff to do. What does that mean? Are you going away?'

'I'm not sure where to start. This last month has changed my life. I feel as if I've surfaced from a kind of subterranean existence. I was living in the dark. I couldn't find the controls to stop the machine. Two things have happened. I've seen what real life can be, through you. Today could have been a tableau from Merrie England, everybody talking at once, loving each other, looking out for each other. I've never had that, you know. I was brought up in a fridge. I want to kick the door down and live in the warmth. The second thing is curiously connected, in a way. If I can ever slam that fridge door closed for good, I have to find out about myself. There is more to this mystery of who was watching me. I'm determined to find out the truth. I don't know who I am or where I came from. My mother is a lurking shadow, my father someone I never knew. That's why I'm going away for a short time to follow up the leads I have.'

'You mean the photographs? They still haunt you?'

'Yes, they do, but I have a few ideas I need to pursue. I'm going to Norway next week and I hope I'll come back knowing a lot more. Then we can think about our lives together I hope. That's why I've done what I've done. You understand?'

'I do. Completely.'

By this time we had completed the length of the terrace and turned back towards the car.

'Alexi, you know I want Katerina to be part of our life together, don't you?' I said.

'I was hoping that,' she replied.

We drove back to Rievaulx Cottage. It was getting dark. Yellow lights shone from the windows and a smell of wood smoke hung on the air.

'Are we going to tell them anything?' I asked.

'Not yet. Leave it to me. I'll stay here tonight with Katie and see you tomorrow. You'll need the Land Rover till you get your new car,' she said.

I told her I needed to go across to Worsall House in the morning and she said she would come with me. All that remained was to say goodbye to the Truman family. This took longer than expected but eventually I dragged myself away. Alexi and Katerina followed me to the gate to wave me off. At the last moment, Katerina held out a crumpled piece of paper and said;

'For you.'

It was a crayon drawing of a house with a smoking chimney, a garden with flowers as high as the house, and in front a man and a woman with a little girl between them.

'That's you, that's Mummy and that's me,' she said, pointing to the figures.

'That's beautiful, Katie, thank you,' I said, a lump forming in my throat. They stood at the gate and waved as I drove off back to Osmotherley.

The next morning I collected Alexi from Helmsley and drove across to Worsall House. Mrs Cuthbert force-fed us on cherry cake and coffee before we could escape. She handed me a manila cardboard wallet with my mother's papers.

'All tidied up now, Mr Peter,' she said. 'Mr George's stuff is in a box in the loft.'

I thanked her and we took our leave. On the way back Alexi's mobile rang and there ensued a lengthy conversation, only parts of which I caught.

'That was *The Guardian*,' she said. 'They want me to cover a press conference in Bradford on Wednesday. Apparently a Home Office minister is launching a Government initiative in the Asian community. They want me to do some interviews with community leaders as a surround. They've already set them up for me.'

'Sounds good. They obviously like your stuff. You'll need to go down on Tuesday night. Make sure you book a decent hotel,' I said.

'What will you do?' she asked.

'Well, with luck I'll have my car by Wednesday. I'm going to London, I think. I need to speak to Sir Gerald, tell him I'm packing it in. It's the only decent thing to do. He's been good to me. Then I need to sort out my Norwegian trip.'

'This will be our last night together then, for a while. Let's spend it at the cottage in Osmotherley.'

We drove back there straightaway. Alexi spent the afternoon researching the Wednesday press conference via the Home Office documents and gathering background material on the Bradford community groups. I settled down to look at the file of papers Mrs Cuthbert had collected for me. I spread them out on the dining table. They included a faded document in Polish, which I took to be a birth certificate, and a British certificate recording the marriage of Stanislaw Kingsmill to Theresa Bienkowska, dated June 1946. I noted that my father had already anglicised his surname. To my surprise, I calculated that my mother must have been pregnant before she married. Why surprise? I suppose because my image of my parents had ruled this out in my mind for the last forty-two years. The rest of the papers were family trivia, newspaper cuttings, and so on. But on leafing through them I came across a black-and-white photograph of a young woman. It was familiar. I looked at it more closely and recognised immediately the same woman who had stood next to my mother in the photograph from the orchard in Oslo, the one Tadeusz Ratomski had said was her sister. Towards the bottom of the pile of papers I found a manila envelope with a short typed letter inside, addressed to Theresa Bienkowska. It was from a Major General Colin Gribbon and the letter heading read "Special Operations Executive, 64 Baker Street, London." The letter was dated 10 January 1946. It read:

Dear Miss Bienkowska

The Special Operations Executive will be dissolved with effect from 15 January 1946 following a decision by His Majesty's Government. From this date you will cease to act as an agent for this organisation. It is my duty as Commanding Officer to thank you for the bravery and dedication you have shown in your years of service to the Executive.

Yours sincerely

Major General Colin Gribbon

It was brief and impersonal but it shook me to the core.

'My God!' I exclaimed.

'What is it?' asked Alexi, looking up from her note-making.

'Read this,' I said, handing her the letter. She read it slowly. Then said:

'Who's Miss Bienkowska?'

'My mother,' I replied. 'She was a British agent! I can't believe it! All these years, and she never spoke about it.'

'That's not really so surprising. She must have had bad memories of the ghastly things that happened. She probably just wanted to forget.'

'Of course, you're right. I'm beginning to piece things together. My mother went to stay with her sister, who worked at the Polish Embassy in Oslo. Tadeusz told us that. She must have been recruited there by the British to work as an agent in Norway,' I said.

'But Norway wasn't in the war then, was it?'

'No, but the British knew it would be very soon, since the Germans were desperate to get hold of North Sea ports and Swedish iron ore that passed through Narvik. They needed to have agents in place before the invasion started, I suppose. That's why she stayed on in Norway while Stanislaw went to Britain. When the SOE was set up she must have transferred to it. So they both were fighting their wars but in different ways. They must have trusted they would come through it and meet afterwards. Can you imagine what that must have felt like?'

'OK, so Theresa survives the war and comes to England to marry Stanislaw. What happens to her sister? Why doesn't she come to England with the Polish Embassy staff before the invasion? They would have been evacuated, wouldn't they, or would they have been interned by the Nazis?'

'Maybe the two sisters stayed there together. Maybe both were agents,' I said. 'At any rate, this is all pointing to Marta Petterson — you remember, the girl with the baby in the photograph, who worked with McAlister. I think she's the key to the story.'

I put the photograph of my mother into the envelope containing the other pictures. I could feel my search coming alive and the tension was mounting inside my head. I sat and thought for a while. Then Alexi snapped her laptop closed and swept up her papers.

'That should do for now,' she said. 'I can do more on this tomorrow night. And you should stop thinking your deep thoughts, Peter. You are yourself, whatever the past turns out to be.'

'Where did you learn your philosophy?' I said, knowing she was right. 'I wish I had your ability to keep your feet firmly on the ground. Where would I be without you?'

She put her arms round my waist and rested her head on my chest.

'Sitting on top of your ivory tower, contemplating the meaning of life, I suspect,' she replied, smiling. 'There are much better things to do, you know.'

'I can't imagine what they can be,' I said.

Later that afternoon we drove down to Helmsley so see the Truman family. Alexi wanted them to know she would be away for a few days and to spend some time with Katerina. I had booked Alexi into a good hotel in Bradford and paid the hotel bill in advance over the phone. She could afford to pay bits and pieces herself but I made sure the car was full of diesel so she wouldn't have to fill up. We had talked about the immediate future. It made sense for Alexi to move into the Osmotherley cottage, where she had room to work in peace, and for Katerina to come and live with us there after Christmas, when my travels would be over and I would be a free agent. But for the moment we kept this to ourselves, waiting for the right moment to inform Angelina and Andrew. As before, they gave me a warm welcome. Angelina could read the runes and knew that Alexi and I were a fixture but, with the good sense of a mother, was leaving her daughter to come clean about it. I was just happy to go along with everything: Andrew and I had made things clear between us and the atmosphere was easy. Katerina was her usual bustling self. She ran to meet us at the gate and grabbed both of us by the hand. We had tea in the kitchen while Alexi told her parents about her trip to Bradford.

We left around six. Katerina came with us to the gate. She gave Alexi a farewell hug and then turned to me.

'Are you going to marry Mummy?' she asked.

For a moment I was lost for words. Then I said:

'Can you keep a secret, Katie?'

'Yes,' was the reply.

'Then I'll tell you,' I said. 'Yes, I am, but it's not going to happen till after Christmas.'

'When's Christmas?' was the next question, at which point Alexi stepped in.

'Now Katie, that's enough. You run in to Grandma. It's getting cold standing out here. Bye now.'

And the little girl trotted off into the cottage.

'Do you think our secret is safe?' I asked.

'No chance,' Alexi replied. 'She'll be drawing pictures of brides and bridesmaids before she goes to bed.'

It was a clear night with a bright moon and no wind. Away from the city, the night sky was pitch black and a million points of light shone down. During my years in London, I had forgotten the miracle of the northern night sky.

'I think we need a change tonight,' I said. 'Let's drive across to the coast and find somewhere to eat. Any ideas?'

'Well, there's a great little seafood restaurant in Staithes, down near the harbour. We went there last year on Mum and Dad's anniversary. It's Monday night, so we shouldn't have to book.'

We set off in the dark along the winding road climbing up to Chop Gate. Alexi was driving along the roads she knew so well and we made good progress. Just before Great Broughton she turned off along a tiny country lane which seemed to lead nowhere. The road was no wider than a cart track. On each side the rolling hills disappeared into the night, mile after mile of rough grass, bracken and heather. The occasional sheep stood near the roadside as we approached, before bolting off into the darkness.

'Where the hell are we going?' I asked.

'Short cut. Trust me,' came the reply.

A few miles after Commondale, we cut across the main road, dropping down to the coast and soon we were at the top of the steep hill leading down to the tiny harbour of Staithes.

'Better leave the car here,' she said. 'No space at the bottom.'

We walked hand-in-hand down the narrow street lined with artists' and fishermen's cottages until we reached the small bay, with a breakwater and a row of fishing cobles drawn up on the stony beach. A full autumn moon had risen in the east and hung low over the sea, its light reflecting in restless, endless shards of silver in the water, and the white walls of the cottages glowed in the dark.

'This is beautiful,' I said.

'Have you never been here?' Alexi asked.

'I don't think I have,' I replied.

'You know, there is so much I want to show you, Peter. Not the expensive, exclusive things that people usually covet, but ordinary, everyday life. The sea and the sky, growing things, happiness that comes naturally, of its own accord.'

'But you need to be at peace with yourself even to notice the sky is blue. Otherwise it's just grey. You're right of course and that's where I'm trying to go,' I said.

Alexi put her arm through mine and said:

'Don't worry, you'll get there. I know you will.'

Then she led the way to our restaurant, hidden away in the muddle of cottages clustered around the bay beneath the towering cliffs. We drank champagne and ate lobsters; unoriginal but it's what people do when they fall in love and believe that the world belongs to them alone in all its unsullied freshness.

Alexi left Osmotherley in the middle of the following morning, wanting to check in early and settle down to more preparations for Wednesday's programme. She promised to phone me later. I thought I would be without a car for the whole day until the phone rang. It was Gary from the Land Rover dealer in York to say that the payment was confirmed and I could pick up the Range Rover.

'I tell you what, Gary. I'm a bit stuck for transport up here. Do you think you could deliver it for me?' I asked.

'Sure thing Mr Kingsmill. I'll get one of the lads to take it up this afternoon. He lives in Northallerton. Do you think you could drop him off near a bus?'

'No, I'll take him home,' I said, 'and by the way, I'm leaving the Aston with you till I get back from London next week. Ask your boss if he wants to make me an offer for it. I'm selling.'

'Will do, Mr Kingsmill. Give us a ring when you get back and we'll see what we can do for you.'

I put the telephone down and returned to my thoughts about my mother and the SOE. I was amazed that she had the nerve to take on such dangerous work. Then I thought about her clinical determination and single-mindedness in her later life. After all, bravery was nothing to do with the physical; it was all in the head. I decided to telephone Colonel McAlister to see if he could furnish more information. His housekeeper answered the telephone and, to my surprise, he was at home.

'This is Peter Kingsmill speaking. You may remember I came to see you a couple of weeks ago,' I said. There was a pause, as if the listener were taken by surprise and needed to recover his calm, the unhappy memory of my last visit no doubt resurfacing.

'Oh, yes, yes. Of course. How can I help you?' he asked.

'I was wondering if you might be able to give me some information about the SOE in Norway. You see, after I came to see you I received some papers and discovered that my mother was a British agent during the war. I found a letter from Major General Gribbon thanking her for her work at the time of the disbanding of the SOE in 1946.'

'Yes, Gribbon was the last CO. Well, if she was an agent she was most likely a radio operator or a courier. There were about sixty operators and a host of couriers, mostly women. Of course, a very high percentage were caught and executed or sent to concentration camps. We processed a lot of them after the war to get them back to Britain.'

'Did you deal with many Poles?' I asked.

'As a matter of fact, there was a surprising number of Poles operating in Norway. The SOE recruited from everywhere and from every group. The Poles had a particular grudge against the Germans and many were recruited as refugees in Britain and sent to Norway. After the war they were given British citizenship and most of them had nowhere else to go.'

'I don't suppose you remember the name Theresa Bienkowska?' I asked.

'Can't say that I do. It's a very long time ago. We had a special unit to deal with agents who were aliens wishing to enter Britain. She could have been dealt with by someone there,' he explained.

There was a pause.

'You were planning to go to Norway, weren't you, to see Marta Pettersen?'

'Yes, leaving in a couple of days actually.'

'Well, you might ask Marta about that name, if you find her. She had friends in all the departments. She might be able to help you more than I. Oh, and by the way, after you left here I remembered she had a cousin in Oslo. Same age, pretty girl. I met her once. I think her father ran a grocery store somewhere around Majorstuen. Same name – Pettersen. It might still be there. They might help you track her down. Good luck anyway.'

127

'That's very helpful, Colonel. Thank you.'

'One thing, Kingsmill. If you do find Marta, get in touch when you get back, won't you.'

'Of course.'

I could hear the sadness in his voice. My appearance out of the blue had resurrected long-buried regrets.

I decided I had no reason to stay in the empty cottage that night so I began to pack my things. At around three o'clock there was a knock on the door. It was the driver from York, a young man called Derek. I grabbed my bag, locked up the cottage and jumped into the Range Rover, Derek in the passenger seat.

'Where to Derek?' I asked.

'Oh, anywhere in the centre of Northallerton will do fine, thanks.'

As we drove, Derek chatted away in his broad north Yorkshire accent.

'That's a smashing car you've got there, Mr Kingsmill. We don't see many Astons around here. Bit of a come-down the Range Rover, eh?'

'Not at all, Derek. It's time I grew up. Aston Martins are for young lads like you,' I replied.

'No chance. It takes me all me time keeping the Escort on the road. Getting married next year, me and our lass. Then it'll be kids and a bigger 'ouse,' he said.

'Derek, you're a very fortunate young man to have it all sorted out so quickly. Don't take it for granted.'

'No, suppose yer right. Me Mam'll be pleased to 'ave shot of me anyway. This is it. You can drop me anywhere 'ere.'

I pulled up by the bus stop and let him out.

'Thanks, Mr Kingsmill,' he said.

'Good luck to you and your lass,' I shouted, as he crossed the road, skipping between traffic. When I was his age, I thought, I was deciphering middle English alliterative verse and life was a mystery, but I stopped myself before drifting off into the noble savage fallacy.

I was in the Pimlico flat by eleven that night. I had phoned Alexi on the way to wish her well for the next day. I had enough energy to park the car in the underground car park and fall into bed. The flat was cold, empty and depressing, and it no longer felt as if it belonged to me. But I had a busy day to come. I needed to see Sir Gerald, talk to Ken Brandon, and then get a flight to Oslo. I fell into a deep sleep, in the knowledge that I was on the brink of something completely unknown.

Chapter 14

I listened to the roar of the jet engines as the plane accelerated down the runway. Then the nose lifted into the air and the undercarriage effortlessly left the ground. I sat back in my seat as we climbed above the murky Heathrow night. I had before me a couple of hours disconnected from the world, in that strange limbo that modern flight creates between departing and arriving, interrupted only by the bizarre ritual of onboard dining from plastic containers, sitting wedged in bucket seats between complete strangers.

I had spent an hour that morning with Sir Gerald. I told him of my decision to resign from the Service and my reasons, stressing my new-found economic independence, as well as my altered world view, as I might pretentiously term it. I made no mention of Alexi, of my new family, and my total disillusionment with my glittering career. Gerald accepted it without demur.

'I won't try to dissuade you,' he said, 'but you must realise that you have an excellent chance of succeeding me in two years' time. That is high office for a man of your age. And beyond that, you have a chance of competing for the top prize.'

'I know that, Gerald,' I replied, 'but it is not something I value any longer. I know you must find this difficult to believe but I have come to the view that I want to spend my one time on earth doing something different, something creative, something with blood flowing through its veins.'

'And what do you suppose that would be?' he asked.

'I think perhaps I shall write,' I said, aware that this must sound naïve. 'How many thousand words of mine have been published in the last twenty years of service, without my name attached, in reports and every shade of Government paper? And what is the total impact of my output? How many times can one put forward the case for dismantling the NHS and then, when the Government changes, for supporting it?'

'But that is what makes us professionals, Peter. We don't have feelings. We are non-committal. We are distanced from emotional judgements. We express the rational. And then we move on. And you are very good at it.'

'Precisely, and that is why I'm going. I want to leave a footprint in the snow, so that people will know I've been here. I want to leave a thumbprint on the page, however smudged it may be. I have learned that emotions are as valuable as reasons.'

'I'm not quite sure I understand exactly what you are saying, Peter, but I respect the honesty with which you express your position and I wish you well. Please remember that if I can be of any help, you must get in touch with me,' he said.

Gerald was signalling the end of the conversation and I knew it was time for me to go. We shook hands warmly and parted. I knew that I could not leave the office without seeing Jenny, who had been with me for years. I told her briefly that I was resigning with immediate effect. She wasn't surprised. Instead of wishing me good luck for the future, she said:

'I hope you have found the happiness you deserve, Peter.'

As I descended the stairs for the last time, I realised that she must have known about Alexi in order to make the statement she had made. And then I remembered that she had shared an office with Ken Brandon's secretary when we both were assistant secretaries in defence. They had stayed friends and no doubt my confidence to Ken that Sunday night in Sevenoaks had leaked into the Whitehall plumbing system very effectively. As to my sudden decision to become a writer, I had no idea why I had said that. But then, as I thought about it, I knew that it was exactly what I wanted to do. Alexi could show me the world; I would take pleasure in describing it.

The fresh cold air of the London December hit me when I stepped out into Whitehall. I remember distinctly what I thought:

'Now that it's over, what was all that about?'

Not the parting conversations, but the twenty years of ambition, of scrabbling to get on, to make it to the top. What was it really all about? It amounted to very little indeed.

I had phoned Ken the night before to fill him in. He was my only real friend in Whitehall and I owed it to him not to ride off into the sunset without saying farewell. He was not shocked. He knew the rules had changed for me.

'Let me buy you lunch tomorrow,' he had said. 'Savoy Grill, twelve thirty. How about that?'

'Fine,' I replied.

It was a mystery how Ken always managed to get a booking at the best restaurants at the shortest notice. I looked at my watch. It was twelve o'clock. I had time to walk to the Savoy at a stroll. It was a pleasure to wander up Whitehall, through Trafalgar Square and along the Strand. I can only attribute the feeling to a sense of escape, of relief to be leaving London. It was invigorating not knowing what the future would hold for me.

The Savoy front hall was a peaceful escape from the traffic on the Strand. The chess board marble floor shone like polished glass under the subdued light of the lamps on each side table. I was a little early for Ken so I made for a corner cluster of chairs. Out of nowhere I heard my name called out.

'Peter, what a surprise!'

My heart sank. It was Douglas Bold.

'Are you lunching?' he asked.

'I am, Douglas, with Ken Brandon.'

'Ken, my goodness, haven't seen him for a while. How's he doing these days?'

'Climbing the greasy pole right to the top,' I said.

'Yes, he would, wouldn't he. Too bloody clever by half. I tell you what, why don't I join you? We can have a good chat about old times.'

And before I could invent a good reason for saying no, Ken appeared and Douglas presented him with a *fait accompli*. What I had hoped might be a gentle exodus for me, became a meaningless gallop through Bold's memories of days gone by. From time to time I detected a pained look on Ken's face as Bold droned on. As soon as it was possible to escape without breaching the laws of good manners, I made my excuses. Ken walked me to the door.

'Sorry about that, Peter. Truly painful. I did hope we could have had a quiet farewell. I don't think I shall be seeing much of you from now on, shall I?'

'I don't think so Ken. But I shall watch your progress right to the top,' I replied. 'Say hello to Sue, won't you. Thanks for lunch.'

We shook hands and I went out through the revolving doors. When I looked back, Ken had already returned to his table and Douglas Bold. I felt as if I were leaving a world of aliens, never to return.

Just then the pilot's voice came over the public address system to inform us we were cruising at thirty-thousand feet and had just crossed the coast of Norway. We would begin our descent to Oslo Gardermoen airport in fifteen minutes. I was back to reality. A little later, turbulence indicated we were descending through the cloud layer. As I looked out of the cabin window I could make out white pools of light where street lamps shone down on the snow-covered roads of small towns. It was a white frozen landscape broken by vast swathes of dark pine forests. Then the airport lights loomed into view and we bounced on to the runway, the engines reversed thrust and we slowed to taxi to the terminal.

I had booked a room at the Hotel Continental in the city centre. After checking in, I sat in the lobby and consulted the Oslo telephone directory. The name Pettersen filled a full page. Finding Marta by this method, if she was indeed still called Pettersen, would require an army of staff. So I decided on the other lead I had, the information from McAlister that Marta had a cousin in the retail grocery business in the city. I went over to the hotel reception desk.

'I know this may sound a strange question to ask, but is there a grocery store in Oslo called Pettersen's?' I asked.

'Oh, yes, there is, sir,' replied the receptionist without hesitation. It has been here for many years. You will find it at

133

Majorstuen.'

'And how can I get there?'

'Well, the tram over the road at the National Theatre will take you there. Numbers eleven, twelve and nineteen,' she replied.

So that was my plan for the morning. Not exactly carefully worked out but I would give it a go. Just then my mobile rang. It was a call from Alexi. She told me everything had gone well. |She was back in the cottage and writing all day tomorrow. I felt a sudden surge of loneliness but I replied bravely: "Hot on trail. Miss you very much".

The next morning I realised I was under-dressed for the climate. It was minus ten degrees with a grey sky and a sharp wind off the sea. I went into a sports shop and bought a huge ski jacket, a hat, a scarf and a pair of gloves, leaving my London gear in my hotel room. Thus clad, I blended well into the crowd of Norwegians waiting at the tram stop outside the National Theatre. A tram soon arrived and in fifteen minutes or so I heard the automated voice announce Majorstuen. We had stopped in a small square. On one side was a suburban railway station. About five roads spread out in all directions and I had no idea which way to go to find Pettersen's shop. The pavements were crisp with ice. People trudged along in heavy footwear, wrapped up against the bitter cold, but I intercepted a middle-aged woman carrying a shopping basket.

'Ah, you mean Smør Pettersen. Of course, in Norwegian that means "butter Pettersen". The shop is just across the square on the corner of Bogstadveien,' and she pointed over the road.

I thanked her and headed towards the pedestrian crossing.

Smør Pettersen's was an exclusive and expensive delicatessen. As I entered I realised the oddity of the situation. I looked around for some kind of counter where I could ask a question, without having to stand in a queue to buy a lump of Jarlsberg or a tub of marinated herring. A young assistant was arranging goods on a stand by the shop window so I intercepted her.

'Excuse me, I wonder if it would be possible to speak to

Mr Pettersen?' I asked.

She looked at me in surprise. Then said:

'There is no Herr Pettersen here. But I can fetch the manager.'

The manager eventually came out of a back room. He was a tall man with a good English accent.

'Hello, how can I help you?' he asked.

'I'm looking for Mr Pettersen,' I said, with a sinking feeling that perhaps I really was entirely losing the trail.

'Herr Pettersen has retired some time ago,' he said. 'If it is a business matter, I can help you.'

'It's not business, it's personal. It's to do with his cousin, Marta.'

I knew this was a shot in the dark but it seemed to hit the target.

'Herr Pettersen still owns the business. I can telephone him, if you like. Who shall I say is asking?'

'He won't know my name, but it's Peter Kingsmill. Please ask if I can see him, on a personal matter to do with Marta.'

'Very well, Herr Kingsmill. If you would like to come through to my office, I shall try to telephone him now.'

He showed me through to the back of the shop and I waited while he spoke on the telephone. I didn't understand a word of the conversation, which seemed to continue for ever. Then the manager put the telephone down.

'Herr Pettersen will see you. He suggests you meet at Frognerseteren. His house is nearby, just a short walk away. Do you know Frognerseteren?'

'No, I'm afraid I don't.'

'Well, it is very simple. If you cross over the square at Majorstuen to the station you can take the wonderful mountain railway, Holmenkollbanen, to the last stop, which is Frognerseteren restaurant. You can't miss it. It is a very beautiful ride, only thirty minutes. You will enjoy the scenery.'

'When will Mr Pettersen be there?' I asked.

'He said about two-thirty this afternoon.'

I was making progress. I was getting near to Marta and the story which lay behind everything. I just hoped she was still alive and could tell me what I needed to know. I thanked the manager for his help and left the shop. I looked at my watch: it was a quarter past one.

I crossed the square to the station and bought a ticket to Frognerseteren. As I waited on the platform, I began to feel like a character from a spy novel set during the Cold War. Was I being set up with a phoney rendezvous, only to be captured by forces of the evil empire and tortured to reveal my secrets? Or was I being followed, as I had been in England, by some seedy shadow, sending back information about my movements? Then I remembered I was simply Peter Kingsmill, retired civil servant, here in Norway to research his family history. I waited in the freezing cold for fifteen minutes with my feet beginning to turn to ice. At last an electric train marked "Frognerseteren" arrived and I got in.

The train made its slow progress through the city suburbs, constantly ascending the mountain that overlooked Oslo and the head of the fjord. As it gained height, the houses became grander and more sparsely distributed. Every few minutes or so the train stopped at a tiny halt, the mountain side becoming rocky and wild. After Holmenkollen, we entered a dense blanket of fog and visibility fell to a few yards. And then we stopped and I read on the station sign that I had arrived at the end of the line. I was the only passenger left on the train, emerging into an eerie world of fog, snow and rocks. A few feet below the station I could make out the lights of a building, which I took to be the restaurant. A narrow path led down to a gravelled car park surrounding a large old villa, built entirely of logs, with wooden arches and porticoes in traditional carved designs. It could have been the hall of The Mountain King himself. I stepped inside to a large salon, darkened by the ancient wooden walls. I chose a table to the side which allowed me to study the few faces in the room and of any new arrival. None showed any interest in me. My watch said only quarter past two so I settled down to await the arrival of Pettersen. The waitress came and I ordered a beer, which arrived clear and ice cold. A few people came and went, cross-country skiers on their way home from the tracks in the forests of Nordmarka, and the occasional fur-clad middle-aged Oslo couples who had driven up from the city for a coffee and a roast beef sandwich. I began to wonder if my appointment would be kept as the clock passed the two-thirty mark. At twenty to three I became nervous and then the door opened and an elderly man entered. He was dressed entirely in black, with a fur collar to his overcoat, and a homburg hat. His skin was ivory white and thin like parchment, which made his lips seem luridly carmine. I knew at once it was Pettersen. I rose to my feet and he looked across the room towards me.

'Herr Pettersen,' I said. 'I'm Peter Kingsmill.'

He looked at me through the thick lenses of his glasses.

'Please, let us sit down,' he said. There was a lengthy silence and then he said, to my surprise, 'Let us order the eplekake. It is the speciality of the house.'

He waved his hand to the waitress who came over and took his order for two eplekaker and coffee.

'Herr Kingsmill, I do not understand why you are here. Please explain.'

The eplekaker and coffee arrived, apple pie coated in thick whipped cream and dark black coffee, steaming in the cups.

I began. I told him of the photographs I had received so mysteriously. I showed him the picture of Marta, his cousin, with the baby. I told him of my meeting with Colonel McAlister and of my mother's links with Norway through the SOE. As I spoke I was aware of the unlikely nature of my story and the flimsiness of my explanations. When I had finished, he picked up the photograph of Marta and studied it silently. Then he spoke.

'Marta was greatly hurt, you know. The English officer, he never returned. She suffered so badly. I thought she would take her own life. But she rallied, eventually, and time passed.' He paused. 'Tell me, Herr Kingsmill, why I should remind her of all this?'

'So she is still alive?'

'Alive, yes, certainly.'

'Herr Pettersen, I have no right to ask you to expose Marta to the pain of the past. I can only say to you that I too have suffered, and I believe that Marta can help me understand what has happened in my life. You see, and I have never said this to a living soul before, I do not think I have ever known my mother. Can you imagine the pain of that? I think Marta can help me.'

There it was. I had said my piece. My case rested in Pettersen's hands. He sipped his coffee. There was an interminable silence.

'Very well. I will call Marta this evening and ask her if she is willing to meet you. I can guarantee nothing, you understand.'

'Of course,' I replied.

'Where are you staying, so that I can reach you?' he asked.

'At the Continental. I shall be in this evening,' I said. 'Herr Pettersen, thank you. This means so much to me.'

Pettersen rose unsteadily to his feet, waved his hand in a gesture as if to dismiss my thanks, turned and walked slowly away. I watched him through the steamed-up window get into a chauffeur-driven Mercedes that had drawn up to the entrance. He had the air of a godfather, even though he had earned his money as a grocer. He looked as if he had never known happiness, nor cared much to have done so.

There was nothing for me but to finish my coffee and pay the bill. The December afternoon light was almost gone and the fog seemed denser than ever. I climbed the rocky path back up to the tiny station. The cold came down like a clamp. Luckily, the two-carriage train was waiting to descend the mountain. I sat looking out of the window as the lights of the city came closer. I was lonely and I longed for the warm company of Alexi at home. But I knew I was on a journey and had to see it through.

That evening in the hotel I ordered room service and waited for the telephone to ring. The time passed painfully slowly. At last, around nine o'clock, reception called to say there was an outside call for me.

'Herr Kingsmill, Pettersen here. I have spoken to Marta. What I told her came as a shock but she will see you tomorrow at eleven. She has an apartment on the west side of the city, at number six Gamle Madserud Allé, not far from you. I will spell that for you.'

I hastily found paper and pen and wrote down the address, letter by letter.

'She is a widow. Her name is Andersen.'

Before I could speak, I heard the telephone go dead.

Chapter 15

The morning broke clear and bright. I decided to walk the mile or so to Marta's flat. I had studied a street map and worked out that I needed to walk the length of a boulevard called Bygdøy Allé and then turn right for a short distance along Drammensveien. Bygdøy Allé was a handsome street lined with chestnut trees and dotted with stylish boutiques and restaurants. Radiating from it were quiet roads of expensive-looking apartments, from a stately era in the last century, with fine wrought iron balconies and cream-painted walls. I recognised the flags of several countries flying from embassies and consulates along the way. I welcomed the walk in the fresh air as I needed the time to prepare myself for my meeting with Marta Pettersen, as I still regarded her, despite her married name.

After twenty minutes or so the road joined Drammensveien. I turned right and walked for about a quarter of a mile to a narrow road, almost a country lane, leading up a hill on the right. The sign read Gamle Madserud Allé. At the top was a block of 1930s flats with a number six on the communal door. I scanned the names on the metal plate, found "Andersen" and pressed the bell. After a while a woman's voice answered through the intercom.

'This is Peter Kingsmill,' I said.

The door buzzed and the lock slid open. I pushed open the door and entered. On the second landing of the curved staircase I met Marta waiting for me outside her front door.

'Good morning, Herr Kingsmill. Oskar told me you wanted to see me. Please come in.'

She was a woman in her mid-sixties, with fine blonde-grey hair, and strong features. I recognised immediately the pretty young girl of the photograph, aged by the years. The apartment was furnished like a set from an Ibsen play, with dark furniture, heavy curtains, and oil paintings on the walls. The floors were highly-polished hardwood, with Persian rugs scattered here and there. Yards of bookshelves lined the central room in which we stood, holding leather-bound volumes in Norwegian, Swedish, English and German. At each end of the room there were double doors opening to a formal dining room on the right and a drawing room on the left.

'I see you are admiring my apartment,' she said. 'All my late husband's work. He collected expensive things wherever he went. He had exquisite taste.'

'I can see that,' I said.

'Please, sit down. I have some coffee ready.'

She poured me a cup of coffee and then said:

'I was reluctant to meet you, you know, but Oskar said it was important for you. What is it you say in English – "the past is another country"? I did not wish to revisit it. You know Oskar lost his parents during the war, sent to a concentration camp as reprisal for his activities. He was a resistance fighter. Most of his friends died. He never recovered from that. You may have noticed. He lives now like a recluse. I think he understood something of your problems.'

'I am grateful to you,' I said. 'Perhaps you can help me with my search.'

'You must explain,' she said.

I laid out the photographs on the coffee table. The effect was immediate. Her eyes began to fill and her hand went to her mouth as if to hold back a sob. She passed from picture to picture in silence.

'These photographs were sent to me through the post. The sender was anonymous. But I am certain he or she expected me to follow the clues they afforded. I received them after my mother had died. I think that is significant. Perhaps I should say that I met James McAlister.'

'James, yes, of course. He was so young – we both were. He was very handsome and gallant, a typical English officer. I remember the sunny day when this photograph was taken. I was very much in love with him. But he left and never came back. Perhaps I should have realised that he would not return.'

'You were indeed very young, Marta. May I call you Marta?'

She nodded.

'And I can tell you that James has regretted his actions all his life,' I said.

'You have met him? How is he?' she asked.

'I would say he is a very sad and lonely man. He has achieved high office in the army and in local politics but his life is very empty. He wanted you to know he thinks of you still and hopes you may remember him kindly.'

'What right do you think he has to ask that? But strangely enough, as the years have gone by, the pain has passed. I do remember him with fondness now. For years I buried myself in my family, my husband and my children, while all the time I knew that my life ought to have moved in a totally different direction, a different country. I was bitter for a long time.'

I slid the photograph of Marta and the baby towards her.

'Tell me Marta, do you know whose baby that was, and what is the connection with James McAlister?'

Marta was silent, struggling to clear her mind and overcome her emotions. After a while she began to speak.

'James was a young officer, stationed at the British Embassy in Oslo. Diplomatic staff were beginning to return to their posts after the war had ended but the administrative burden of handling the large number of people wishing to enter Britain was very heavy. It seems strange now that this task should fall to an airborne division, the toughest fighters of the war. But this was a chaotic situation that needed tough policing as well as sensitive administration. Norwegian authorities were not yet in place to handle the thousands of returning refugees from Sweden and Britain. Peace had to be maintained and the huge number of German PoWs had to be controlled. You can imagine how many forms and passes were signed, lost or forged in those times. James was responsible for authorising visas to Britain for those who were entitled to them and I worked in his office. Foreign agents working for the SOE were given the right to British citizenship but they had to apply through his office.

'Before the war I became a friend of two Polish sisters. Here is the photograph I took of them in 1939.'

She pointed to the third photograph.

'We were in the garden at the back of the embassy. It was a sunny day, before the war had started.'

'Yes, I recognised my mother in the picture,' I interrupted.

'Yes, and the two children are the Ambassador's twin daughters. I often had the job of looking after them in the afternoon. You see I was a clerk at the embassy until it was closed just before the occupation.'

'Do you know why the two sisters came to Norway?' I asked.

'Nothing was ever said at the time. But it was just before Poland was invaded. We all assumed they were recruited as agents by the British, before the German invasion, and placed in Norway in anticipation of the invasion there. The British knew very well what was going to happen in Europe, even if the people did not. They spent time training in England and they spoke Norwegian almost like a native after a short time in Oslo. You know it is difficult for a German to recognise a foreigner speaking Norwegian, so their cover was good. We knew them in the embassy as the Bienkowska sisters – Theresa and Maria – but of course during the war they had cover names. I was one of the few in Norway who knew their real names, after the embassy staff were evacuated in 1940. I stayed on, of course.'

'And did you have contact with them during the war?' I asked.

'From time to time. I ran a safe house where agents could stay. I saw them occasionally, mostly Theresa. She miraculously managed to operate throughout the war and returned to England very quickly. I believe she married there.'

'She married my father, Stanislaw. He was with 303 Squadron in the RAF. And the other sister, Maria?'

'She was arrested in 1943 and it was assumed she was sent to a concentration camp.'

Tears filled her eyes and she could not go on.

'Excuse me, Peter. She was such a beautiful girl. I learned to love her. We were all desolate when we heard she had been arrested by the Gestapo. Some time afterwards, a whole ring of agents were arrested. The only one who escaped was Theresa.'

'Did you ever see Maria again?'

'I heard nothing about her for over two years. Then, when the war ended, one day I received a letter sent to my address at the safe house. She used her real name, not her code name, and she asked me to meet her. I was so happy to hear she was still alive. The address she gave me was in the eastern part of Oslo, a very poor district. I thought it odd that she did not come to the safe house, or return to the embassy. When I got there I was appalled by the way she was living. It was a slum and she seemed afraid to go out. I asked her why she had not sought help from the authorities. She said: "Who would help someone like me?" I remember that very clearly. At first I did not understand and then I realised what had happened. She was not alone – she had a child. And when I saw the child, it was a baby boy, she told me who the father was. It was a German officer, she said, and he had been recalled to Germany before the end of the war. So she was alone and pregnant. Do you know what we did to women who slept with the enemy? And what future the child of a German soldier could have in this country? She told me that she had gone to a hospital when her time had come but the nurses refused to help her. She was left alone in a corridor and almost died. Both mother and child were made outcasts. There was no future for the child in this country as far as she could see.'

'But what did she think you could do for her?' I asked.

'She must have known I had gone back to working with the British Embassy, at this time under the administration of the British army of course. She asked me to see if I could arrange to take the child to England, so I said I would try.'

I lifted my coffee cup to my lips. Marta had stopped, as if afraid to continue. At last I broke the silence.

'Please go on, Marta,' I said.

'I spoke to James about it. At first he was reluctant but at last he came around, after a lot of persuasion. The plan was that I should travel to England on a temporary visa, taking the baby with me as my own. He signed the papers himself. An infant so young could travel on my papers. I would then return without the baby and no one would see from my visa that I had not travelled alone from the outset. It was a simple arrangement and it worked.'

I felt I knew the answer to my next question but I still asked it.

'And where did you take the child?'

'I took it to Theresa and Stanislaw. They had married and were living somewhere in the north of England. Stanislaw was just about to leave the RAF and I think they had married quarters near his base. I told them Maria's story and they took the baby as their own. I never saw them or the child again. When I got back I went to tell Maria what had happened. She was destroyed to have given her child away but knew that it was the best thing she could have done.'

I felt a sudden panic and a cold shudder passed through my whole body. The story was moving towards an inevitable conclusion, like the unfolding of a Greek tragedy.

'And the child?'

She paused and looked at me. I knew what was coming.

'The child was you, of course, Peter.'

She reached out and took my hand. There were tears in her eyes. I felt like a small boy who has felt a great hurt and needs comfort from his mother. I had no words to describe the total confusion of that instant. I rose to my feet and for a few moments I paced the room, speechless. I remember noticing from the window a flight of bullfinches perched on the black bare branches of a sycamore tree, and hearing the crescendo of the trams on the main road at the bottom of the hill. Such trivial observations seemed to squeeze out the shattering magnitude of the truth I had just learned, as if the mind could not bear too much reality. At length Marta walked across to stand by me at the window. I turned and spoke to her.

'I find this very difficult to understand. Everything I took to be fact is now denied by what you have told me.'

'I know this must be very hard for you, isn't it,' she said, 'but it is the truth. Maria is your mother, not Theresa. Nor was Stanislaw your father. What will you do, Peter?' she asked.

'What can I do? I have been living another life all these years. I now have to come to terms with a new one.'

'I know it is a new one, but remember what Maria did was done out of love for you. Never forget that,' she said.

'Yes, I see that. I need to spend some time alone thinking this through. But thank you. No one should be burdened with carrying the truth as you have been. Tell me though, do you know where Maria is now?'

'Are you sure you want to contact her? It is a big decision to make in such a hurry.'

'I am sure. The photographs must have been sent to me by her. She wants me to contact her. She expects me to find her. She has chosen her moment carefully. But why has she sent me on this chase? Why not just write to me?' I said.

'Think Peter. Would you have believed her story if, out of the blue, a woman you never knew existed, made claims like that. No, this way you have discovered the evidence yourself and you know it to be true. You have discovered her story, and your own into the bargain. But most of all, you have the choice to say yes or no. That is the point, is it not? She used her skills as a secret agent to make a trail she knew you would follow but, at the end, she has given you the freedom to make your own decisions. She did not want to force you into anything.'

'You're right. And I have decided. Will you give me her address?' I asked.

'Of course,' she replied. She walked across to a desk in the drawing room and wrote on a piece of paper, folded it, and handed it to me.

'I visit her every month. She is not strong. I know you will be kind to her. She has had a difficult life. You are a kind person, I can tell. You will be happy again, Peter. Believe me. Will you be meeting James again? If so, remember me to him – kindly.'

'I promised to be in touch when I got back. I'll give him your message,' I replied, sadly.

'Thank you. Goodbye, I don't suppose our paths will cross again. It has been good to meet you.'

She held out her hand but I leaned across and kissed her cheek. She smiled, and the face of the pretty young girl in the photograph came alive again, echoing down the years.

I said goodbye and set off to walk into the city. My mind was racing; I was disorientated. At the bottom of Gamle Madserud Allé, I reached the main road and turned left. My feet crunched on the frozen snow and I drifted along with no idea of my progress. I must have taken a turn to the left too soon for, instead of retracing my steps up Bygdøy Allé, I found myself walking along the side of a park. Soon I reached the gates, a massive portico of black wrought iron set out in geometrical shapes, squares and rectangles, topped by white lights set in glass cubes. Through the gates a straight drive led across an artificial lake to a piazza with a massive fountain in the centre, the bowl held upright by heavy naked bronze figures of men and women. Beyond, grey granite steps rose towards a central point, a vast minaret of interwoven granite bodies, locked in constant motion. The whole effect was overwhelming, the dark bronze figures set against the snow; the grey granite sculptures – men, women and children – sparkling with frost, in what seemed a never-ending dance of life and death. Amidst it all, children played on toboggans or threw bread to the ducks, old ladies walked their dogs and young mothers pushed prams. Real life went on in its unstoppable daily round amidst the frozen stone figures. And I had no choice but to do the same, come what may. I turned and caught a taxi to the Continental. I longed to hold Alexi in my arms again, to listen to Katerina's chatter, and to sit in Angelina's kitchen in Helmsley. But it felt a lifetime away from the harsh reality that faced me now. In the back of the taxi, I called Alexi's mobile: "Everything going well. Back soon". In the hotel I picked up the overseas copy of *The Guardian*. I turned to the society section and there was Alexi's article in pride of place: "Integration not segregation: the story of Bradford's community".

I spent the evening in my hotel room in a kind of desolation, not knowing which way to turn. I drank a lot, finishing off the miniatures from the mini bar. I ate nothing. Out of this fog some solid shapes slowly materialised. I began to see how my relationship with Theresa had been predetermined by my history. I was not her child. Perhaps she even resented my very existence. I could see now why George had been smothered by her religious zeal and why I had been ignored. She bore no responsibility for me and so I had grown up in the vacuum of her emotions. Stanislaw had been distant too, treating me with fairness but little warmth, a father figure who never felt like one. I began to understand how it all fitted together. I was after all the illegitimate child of the hated enemy in the eyes of my erstwhile parents. And Maria, what could I blame her for? She had sent me away to give me a life she could not provide and in that she had succeeded. Should I carry with me the sins of the fathers, like an Ibsen character seeking to escape from the shadow of his past into the sunlight? As I pondered this question my mobile rang. It was Alexi: "Sorry it's late. Missing you a lot. Come home soon. I love you. Alexi. Katie sends you a big kiss". I suddenly felt so tired and very drunk but I knew where my sunlight was to be found and I was never going to let it go. I had a way out of this mess after all. I was who I was; I had to set the rules for myself. I had somewhere real to return to now.

I fell asleep on the sofa, waking at three in the morning, only to stumble into the hotel bed. I awoke at eight, took a shower and ordered breakfast in my room. As I drank my strong coffee I remembered something that Marta had said: that after Maria had been arrested, a whole ring of agents had been rounded up, and presumably executed. But Theresa had miraculously escaped. Were these events connected? And Maria had survived too, to have an affair with a German officer. The thought began to form in my mind that Maria had saved Theresa, but had betrayed the other agents; that in fact she had gone over to the enemy; she had done a deal with them to save herself. Could this be true? Could this be the conclusion that Theresa had drawn, that her sister had turned traitor?

I finished my coffee and pulled out the piece of paper bearing Maria's address. It seemed to be a home of some sort, as far as my limited Norwegian could determine, and I remembered that Marta had said Maria was not strong and that she visited her every month. I had a telephone number. I think I sat on the bed and looked at it for at least five minutes, trying to build up courage to call. What do you say to a mother you have never consciously met, who discarded you as a child? "Good morning, this is Peter Kingsmill, your long lost son?" Or do you say nothing, letting the silence speak for itself? Should I love her or should I hate her? Should I feel anything at all? Should I close the book and go back to the world I knew, to Alexi and her family, my family now? Why was I seeking out this pain when I could so easily have denied it all? But that was the point. It was there, dragging me like some magnetic force, undeniable. I had no choice but to confront it. I dialled the number and waited. The telephone rang for a long time and then the receiver was lifted and the quiet voice of a woman answered.

'Hello. Maria Bienkowska.'

'My name is Peter Kingsmill.'

There was a long pause. I could hear an intake of breath.

'Peter.'

'I spoke to Marta. She gave me your number,' I said.

'Marta phoned me last night. I was expecting you to call.'

Again a long pause. Then I spoke.

'I would like to see you,' I said.

Another pause.

'Marta said you wanted to meet me,' she said.

'I have your address. May I come now?' I asked.

'Yes,' she replied, after a while.

Then the phone went dead.

I threw on my outdoor clothes and went down to the lobby. The doorman called me a taxi. The address was Ansgar Sorlies Vei, number twenty-two. I had no idea where we were going, except that it was in the east of the city. We drove through the heavy morning traffic towards the harbour and the City Hall, through a multi-lane underpass and out into the morning light again, amid factories and office blocks. After a little while we turned off a busy main road into a quiet residential street and stopped. I handed over a few kroner notes and took the change. We had stopped outside a red-brick terrace of flats, with communal entrances at intervals along the frontage. At the end of the block was a small children's playground, snow-covered, with bundled-up toddlers playing on swings and slides. Number twenty-two was the last entrance in the terrace. When I rang the bell it was answered by a janitor who signed me in to a visitors' book in his office. It was clearly a sheltered housing complex. I said I wanted to visit Maria Bienkowska and that she was expecting me. He telephoned a number and directed me to the first floor.

When I reached the small landing on the first floor the front door to Maria's apartment was already open. I knocked and went in. It was a small living room with a sleeping alcove off to the side. An emergency bell pull hung from the ceiling with an intercom speaker fixed to the wall beside it. The room felt overheated and airless, the room of an old person. An old woman sat in an armchair by the window, walking sticks by her side. She was very thin, almost emaciated, and looked ill. Behind the aged face I could recognise the young woman in the photograph. I stood silently and she looked at me.

'Peter, I am glad you have found me at last,' she said. 'I knew you would find a way. Thank you for coming. Let me look at you. So handsome, just like your photographs in the newspapers. You see, I know all about you. I was sorry when your wife died but I think you have a new life beginning now. I am happy for you.'

I found myself short of words. I looked at her face. She was old beyond her years, and I remembered Marta saying she had had a hard life. It showed. She beckoned me to sit down on the sofa beside her. We sat side by side in silence for some time. Then she turned to me.

'You will wonder why I chose this way to contact you,'

she said. 'I thought it best to leave you undisturbed. I had no right to interfere after all. I gave you away and at the same moment I gave away any rights I had over you.'

'You did it for me,' I said at last.

'Do you understand that, Peter?' she asked.

'I do.'

'I could not contact you while you were growing up anyway, even if I had thought it good for you. Theresa prevented everything. We never spoke again after the war. I tried to write but my letters were returned unopened. I felt like a dead person. Then when I heard from the lawyer in London that Theresa had died I began to think you should have the choice of knowing the truth about yourself.'

I wondered how she could have afforded a lawyer in London. There was little sign of wealth around her. Then I realised it must be Marta who had helped her. She had married well and saw Maria regularly.

'But why such a tortuous way to go about it?' I asked.

She hesitated a while before she spoke.

'How could I hope to explain to you all that you now know for yourself? And how could I impose myself on you, from nowhere, out of the blue? What right did I have to force the truth upon you? I let you find it out for yourself.'

'I'm glad you did,' I said.

'Are you Peter, are you? I wonder if that is the case. I cannot be a mother to you now. You do not need one. It is too late. But I want to leave this world knowing that you have understood why I did what I did. That will be my peace, of a sort.'

She paused, becoming breathless.

'I'm beginning to understand, but there are lots of questions still to ask,' I said.

'Of course, but not now. I am very tired. I need to rest.'

She stood up shakily and I helped her walk towards the sofa where she lay down. I felt her thin hand grip mine tight. I stroked her head and she looked at me kindly, in a way Theresa had never done. I knew it was too late but also that what she had done was done out of love for me. That was all that mattered. We sat in silence for several minutes. This was no triumphant reunion; merely a recognition that we were what we were and that nothing could change that. At last she seemed to arouse herself and spoke.

'Come back tomorrow Peter. I have something I want to give you,' she said.

'I will,' I said, and kissed her on the forehead.

I closed the door behind me as I left. On my way out I asked the janitor if she would have a visitor today.

'She has a home help each morning and evening,' he said. 'She brings the shopping and prepares a meal. I'm on call here if she needs any help.'

'Thanks. I'm coming back tomorrow,' I said.

I needed air, so I walked back to the city centre, not knowing exactly where I was, except that I needed to go west towards the harbour. I followed my nose, and in the process discovered the hidden corners of the city, the old town and the botanical gardens, frozen solid by the northern winter. I saw the spire of the cathedral in the distance and headed for that, knowing that would bring me near to the parliament building at the top of Carl Johan Gate. It took me an hour.

My mind was strangely calm. Maria had been right. It was good that I should know the truth about my past and that I should have control of the process of discovering it. She was right too, that she could not be a mother to me. I had answered the question of how I should feel. My feelings at meeting her were not those of love. Too many years of ignorance had seen to that. But I felt a strong sympathy for her and compassion for the suffering she had endured. I could not create a new relationship with her and found I had no desire to do so. After all, she had deliberately chosen not to contact me in my adult life. But I felt a huge surge of relief that the business was over and I could begin to enjoy a new existence without the mill stone of an unknown past hanging round my neck. I would see her tomorrow and say goodbye. She could not expect me to do anything other than that and I knew she would already have recognised that. All she had wanted to achieve, she had done, by careful calculation and judgement. But she didn't want me to stay.

As I weighed these thoughts I realised I had walked the length of Carl Johan. I stopped at the Theatre Cafe, in the corner of the Continental Hotel building, suddenly feeling the need for food. I ordered a roast beef sandwich and a beer, the roast beef pink to perfection with a creamy remoulade dressing and a slice of gherkin. Even though it was only midday, the cafe was busy with the cosmopolitan mix of the city. It had an almost Parisian atmosphere, of actors, writers and their hangers-on, with a discernible variety of sexual orientation. For the first time since I had arrived in Norway I could enjoy the vibrancy of my surroundings; the world seemed to have lost its monochrome. I called Alexi: "I'm flying back tomorrow. The business is completed. I'll phone from London. I love you". I finished my beer and went back to the hotel. I telephoned the SAS desk at Gardermoen and booked a seat on the afternoon flight to Heathrow. I could not wait to get back.

Chapter 16

The next morning around eleven I took a taxi to Ansgar Sorlies Vei. As we turned into the street I saw a police car and an ambulance parked down the road. When we approached, I realised they were outside number twenty-two. I paid off the taxi and rushed up to the main door. The janitor opened and recognised me.

'What's happened?' I asked.

'Herr Kingsmill isn't it? I'm afraid there's been a death. Frøken Bienkowska was found this morning by the home help.'

'My God, how did it happen? Did she fall?'

'No, nothing like that. The home help found some pills by her bedside. That's all I know,' he replied. 'The police are there now, if you wish to speak to them. Are you family?'

It took me only a second to decide on my answer.

'No,' I said, 'I only met her for the first time yesterday. I'm not family. She doesn't have any. She said she was going to give me something today. That's why I came back.'

The janitor took a brown paper parcel off a shelf in his office and handed it to me.

'She phoned down last night,' he said, 'and asked me to give you this today when you arrived.'

I took the parcel and left. I did not belong there. So this was the final piece of the plan. Maria could not have signalled any more clearly than this that she wanted me to draw a line under the whole affair. In the most categorical way open to her she had concluded our relationship. I had found the truth for myself but was not bound by the consequences. I was staggered by the clinical logic of her strategy.

I walked slowly back down the street in a state of shock. At the main road I caught a tram into the centre and walked along Carl Johan Gate to my hotel to collect my bags from the porter. I sat in the corner of the lobby and telephoned Marta on my mobile. She answered immediately.

'This is Peter Kingsmill. I've just come back from Maria's flat. She's dead. She took an overdose, apparently.'

'I know,' she replied, 'she telephoned me last night and told me what she planned to do.'

'You knew, and did nothing?'

'That's right, I knew. You should know Peter, she was dying of cancer and had only a few weeks to live. Her one hope was that she would see you before she died and when you came she had no reason to live any longer. I always knew that this was her plan. Her training as an agent meant that such things were not unknown to her.'

'I see. She left me a parcel. Do you know about that too?'

'I do. It's what she called her book. I helped her put it together. Read it when you get home. I avoided mentioning it to you yesterday. That was Maria's request that you should see it only now. It will tell you everything.'

'Everything about what?' I asked.

'About her life, and why she did what she did. Nothing is as simple as it seems. She wrote it for you, Peter. Now it's time you went back to your new family. You have a lot ahead of you.'

I heard the telephone go dead. I sat for a while, then looked at my watch. I had an hour to get to Gardermoen and check in for my flight. I could pick up the airport train at the underground station across the square if I hurried. Minutes later, as I sat in the high-speed airport link, I found it difficult to believe I was in the real world. The events of the last twenty-four hours seemed truly incredible. I had travelled to Oslo with one identity; I was returning with a different one; and the person who had provided my new identity was dead, by her own hand.

I opened my bag and took out the brown paper parcel Maria had left for me. Inside was a file with a thick wad of typed sheets, a hundred pages or so. There was also a hand-written note:

My Dear Peter

By the time you read this note, it will all be over. You are a free man, with only the responsibilities you accepted of your own free will. If you think of me at all, I ask you to do so with compassion, but do not think you owe me anything. What I have done with my life, is my decision. I have given you these pages so that you may understand that. You must live your life to the full and have no regrets. Goodbye and farewell.
Maria

I put the parcel back into my bag. I could not begin to read the document now. I would let time settle my mind in the hope I could view the contents dispassionately. I looked out of the train window as it raced silently through the white landscape, the afternoon light already fading, although my watch showed only two-thirty. I was glad to be leaving this frozen country. After this morning, I could see no reason ever to return.

We slid into the airport terminal and I followed the signs along moving escalators to the Departures desks. The process of air travel took over and I followed the routine as an automaton. In no time I was checked in and heading towards my gate, then boarding, then airborne. I was utterly exhausted and leaned back in my seat, my eyes closing and a semi-sleep taking over. Before I knew it, we were on the descent to Heathrow and the stewardesses were checking the seat belts. By six o'clock I was on the underground heading into central London and by seven-thirty I was in my flat in Pimlico. I telephoned Alexi.

'You sound exhausted, Peter. How did it go?' she said.

'I'll tell you tomorrow,' I replied, 'at least some of it. But it's over, thank God.'

'Come to the cottage,' she said. 'I'm here with Katie. The school Christmas holidays have begun, so she's staying here with me.'

'Christmas? I'd totally forgotten that. It will be wonderful to see you both again.'

'You've only been away a few days, Peter.'

'Feels like a lifetime. I love you, Alexi.'

'I love you too.'

That evening I strolled round to Francesco's. He welcomed me like a long lost friend.

'Signor Kingsmill, welcome. We have not seen you for so long. How are you?'

'I'm well Francesco, and very happy to be back,' I said.

'We are very happy to have you back. Your glass of red wine?' he asked.

I looked around the restaurant. It was almost empty.

'Francesco, have a glass of champagne with me, won't you. I want to celebrate something.'

His lively eyes glinted and he smiled with pleasure.

'No Signor Kingsmill, you take a glass with me!'

He fetched two champagne glasses and a chilled bottle from the cabinet.

'Now you must tell me what we are celebrating,' he said, as we sat down at my usual table.

'I'm getting married,' I said.

'Ah, of course, the beautiful signorina. My very best wishes to you both,' and we clinked glasses. 'I hope you will bring her with you next time.'

'I will, but not for a long time,' I said. 'I'm leaving London tomorrow. A new start in the country.'

'To a new start, then,' he said, and we drank again.

Before I left Pimlico the next morning, I called at the estate agent's office round the corner. I gave them a set of keys and asked them to get a cleaner in and put the apartment on the market. I wanted to close the door on it for good. They were delighted to oblige as the flat would sell quickly for a high price and with little trouble to them. As I drove out of London I thought of Maria and marvelled at her single-mindedness: to devise such a plan and then to carry it out with cold unflinching calculation. I began to wonder if the accusations of her treachery could hold up in the light of her courage and determination at the end. The miles flew by and soon I was able to see the familiar blue of the Hambleton Hills. In a few more minutes I would be home, away from all unknowns, able to rebuild my life with the certainties I now possessed. I turned off the main road and drove quickly up the hill to the village. It was a pitch black winter evening and the yellow lights of the cottages shone out invitingly. I parked the car and strode up the alleyway to the cottage, to begin life again.

Christmas came with the excitement that only a small child can bring. Katie made us alive. We bought a Christmas tree together and put it up on Christmas Eve, decorating it with red and green ornaments and white lights. We wrapped our parcels and laid them out for the morning. Alexi and I propped ourselves up in front of the fire and drank a whisky together before shambling off to bed, only to be summoned at an unearthly hour by the sound of Katie impatiently waiting for us to awake. We drove to Helmsley for lunch with Andrew and Angelina.

'Shall we tell them?' asked Alexi.
'Tell them what?' I replied.
'That we're going to get married, of course.'
I could hear Katerina's ears rustling in the back seat.
'Why not?' I said.

In the days between Christmas and New Year I told Alexi what had happened in Norway. I was slowly coming to terms with my new past but I could not yet bring myself to open the folder that Maria had given me. Alexi understood and was calm and undemanding in not seeking to know more than I was ready to give. I began to think of Stanislaw and Theresa in a new light, with more understanding of their treatment of me, while still not able to justify their coldness. I wondered if Mrs Cuthbert had been aware of the facts, or had the secrets been held under lock and key? One morning I drove across to Worsall House. It was a grey wet day in that fag end of the year before the world turns on its axis and a new year begins. I found Mrs Cuthbert, as usual, in the kitchen. I felt down and it must have showed.

'Why, Mr Peter, whatever's the matter? You don't look well at all,' she said, putting on the kettle.

'Oh, just mid-winter blues,' I lied. 'Alexi and I are going to get married next month,' I added, more for something to say than to share the news.

'Well, that's wonderful news. You should be happy, not sad.'

'Of course, I'm happy,' I said.

She poured the coffee and we sat at the kitchen table together.

'It's not that at all. I was in Norway before Christmas. Did you know Theresa had a sister, Mrs Cuthbert? She was called Maria and she lived in Oslo.'

'That comes as a surprise to me. All the years I worked here, I never heard mention of that,' she replied.

I could hear she was covering up and I had put her on the spot.

'They both worked as British agents there during the war. Maria was captured by the Germans but Theresa saw the war out. I learned that on my trip to Oslo.'

'Well, I never. Who would have thought that? And what became of Maria?' she asked.

'She died – last week. She killed herself – the day after I first met her.'

'Good heavens, why would she do that, at her age?'

'I think you know why, don't you? You know who Maria really was, to me that is?'

There was a long pause before she spoke.

'I'm sorry Mr Peter. Yes, I knew. Theresa confided in me years ago but I was sworn to silence. It came out in one of those black moods she used to have – you won't remember them – you were only a small child. That was before she had Mr George and became religious. I knew they were not your parents and that your mother was her sister called Maria. But I was told Maria died when the war ended and you were brought here to live.'

'Not true. She survived the war. I spoke to her last week. She killed herself, I think, because her life was over. She wanted to free me by telling me the truth about my life, which she did.'

Mrs Cuthbert took out a handkerchief from her apron and blew her nose. She was near to tears.

'All those years I watched you growing up, Mr Peter. I could see you were lonely and I wanted to do something. But what could I do? You were always my favourite. Then you went off to school and university and it was too late. I always felt she treated you coldly. Not Stanislaw, he was always too busy working and earning money. But you know all that, don't you?' she said.

'Please don't blame yourself for anything, Mrs Cuthbert. You were the best thing about this house, the only person that made school holidays bearable for me. But I have to tell you I won't be coming back here to Worsall House. It has no happy memories for me and I need to start afresh. I'm selling the house next year. You and Mr Cuthbert must stay on until then and I'll see if the new owners will take you on. If not, I'll see what I can do for you financially. I'm sorry if this comes as a shock.'

'I would be lying if I said it didn't but you must do what you have to,' she said. 'I never thought you would come back here to live and you and Miss Alexi will need to make your own way. Give her my best wishes, please.'

'I will, and you will come to our wedding, won't you?'

'Of course we will, Mr Peter,' she said.

I left Worsall without regret. When I got back to the cottage I opened the brown paper parcel and began to read. Alexi came in from the kitchen.

'You're starting?' she said.

'Yes, I'm starting,' I replied. 'It's time I heard Maria's story.'

PART TWO: BETRAYAL

Chapter 1

Kracόw, October 1938

My dear Peter, I wondered where I should begin my story. Should it be in my childhood memories of Poland as a small girl, the long hot summers, the dusty roads lined with wild flowers? I had hope and innocence in those years. But my story is one of hopes dashed by the complexities and compromises of living, of innocence lost in the violent stream of my life.

My father was professor of applied mathematics at Kracόw University. My sister and I were bred for the same pursuit. We were put through our paces everyday. At the dinner table we were solving mathematical puzzles while we ate. By the time we were eighteen we were the stars of our school and we took our places at the university as a matter of course. Theresa was a year younger than I and followed in my footsteps. I matriculated in 1937.

I remember one October afternoon in 1938. Lectures had finished for the day and I was walking alone along the sunny street towards the city. A young man came alongside me, wearing glasses and carrying books and papers in a battered leather portfolio. I had seen him before many times across the lecture hall but we had never spoken.

'Maria Bienkowska, isn't it?' he said.

I nodded.

'My name is Stefan. I've seen you in my class. Would you like to have a coffee with me?'

He was very polite and very shy. So I said yes.

There was a coffee shop frequented by students in a

cobbled square in the old town. The weather was fine and warm and we sat outside. I waited for him to speak.

'I think your father is the most brilliant man in the university,' he suddenly said, out of the blue. 'I just wish I could understand his lectures. I suppose you do.'

'I've heard most of it before,' I said, 'so I guess I have an advantage.'

'It's a pity all this will be destroyed.'

'How do you mean, destroyed?' I asked.

'When the Germans move in,' he answered.

'You think that will happen?'

'Certainly,' he replied. 'How do you feel about that?'

'I think it would be a tragedy for Poland,' I said.

'I do too.'

And then he suddenly changed the topic of conversation. We talked a little about the lecture we had attended that afternoon. When it was time to leave he said to me:

'I'm meeting some friends tonight. Will you come? We drink a little beer and talk politics.'

'OK.'

'We meet at the White Eagle bar, near the cathedral. About seven. See you then,' he said.

I walked home without thinking more about it. Just after seven I took a tram to the cathedral square. I had heard of the White Eagle but had never set foot in it. I led a sheltered life, I suppose, and had never had a boyfriend. The bar was down some dark steps into a cellar. I could hear the noise of voices and smelled tobacco smoke long before I reached the door. Inside was a crowd of young people, mostly students, and across the room I caught sight of Stefan. He waved and came across to meet me.

'Come and meet my friends,' he said, taking my arm. 'This is Anton Szwarczynski, Maria.'

A tall young man with small round spectacles stood up and shook my hand.

'Very pleased to meet you, Maria,' he said. 'This is my friend Stanislaw Reichsmüller.'

Another young man, very athletic in appearance, got to

his feet and bowed. He was dark and Jewish-looking.

'Call me Stan,' he said.

'Now, you must have a drink,' Stefan said, and went across to the crude wooden bar.

I sat down with these three young men and took a sip of the light beer Stefan had brought me. It tasted bitter to my innocent palate.

'Tell me Maria,' said Stanislaw, 'will you leave Poland, or will you stay?'

'I'm not sure I understand. Leave when?' I replied.

'When the Germans invade from the west and the Russians from the east,' he replied.

'I've never thought about it,' I said.

'Well, you should,' said Stanislaw, taking a long draught of his beer. 'You see, I'm a Jew, and if either side gets to me, I'm done for. Look at what Herr Hitler has done for Jews in Germany. Do you think I will receive better treatment here in Poland?'

'No, I don't expect you will. What will you do?' I asked.

'He's done it,' interrupted Stefan. 'He's off to do his air force training next week. He's going to fight the Hun!'

'Here's to Stan,' said Anton, raising his glass. And we all drank to Stan. As the evening wore on, we drank more and talked of the German problem. At ten o'clock I said I must be going.

'Let me walk you home,' said Stefan.

We walked through the quiet streets of Kraców, up the tree-lined avenues, full of solid villas, until we reached the corner of my street.

'Your friends are very political,' I said.

'Not political, just patriotic,' he replied. 'We want to do something for Poland. We have friends abroad who can help us. Do you want to help us?' he asked.

'I think I do but I don't know what it all means,' I said.

'I'll see you at lectures tomorrow,' he said. 'Good night.'

I shared a bedroom with my sister Theresa. When I got home she was already in bed reading.

'You smell of beer and cigarettes,' she said. 'Where have

you been?'

I told her who I had met.

'Stanislaw Reichsmüller? He's in my year, doing engineering I think. Always involved with political meetings. Very good looking though.'

'Why don't you come with me next time?' I said. 'I'll introduce you to Stanislaw.'

The next day Stefan met me at the university.

'I hope you enjoyed yourself last night,' he said.

'It was interesting,' I replied, giving little away.

'Come tonight,' he said. 'There's an anti-Nazi meeting at the cellar. Rumak's addressing it.'

'Who's he?' I asked.

'Only the leader of the Polish Communist Party,' he answered with a grin.

'OK. Is it alright if I bring my sister?'

'Sure, the more the merrier,' he said. 'Usual time.'

That evening Theresa and I together took the tram to the cathedral square. Outside the White Eagle a crowd had gathered, mostly students but with a smattering of older people. Stefan met us.

'The Jewish League and the Liberal Party have come tonight,' he said. 'Should be a big affair.'

He was right. The crowd gradually increased and by eight o'clock had reached a couple of hundred. Stanislaw came to join us and I introduced him to Theresa. They seemed to hit it off immediately. Just after eight Rumak began to speak, on the threat facing Poland's Jews and Liberals with the growth of German fascism. He spoke of the need to protect our independence and to reject extremism. The crowd listened quietly. At that moment, the audience suddenly seemed to swell in numbers. There was a wave of shouting and jostling and before I realised what was happening a gang of Nazi sympathisers, wearing swastika armbands, rushed through the crowd. I could see Rumak jump down from the platform, defended by Anton Szwarczynski, as the fists flew in. Suddenly there was a scream and the crowd opened. On the cobbled ground I saw the body of a man, with blood swelling from the wound in his chest. There was a frantic dash away from the scene as a police car screeched to a halt in the square.

A few minutes later Theresa and I found ourselves in a side street. Stanislaw was with us.

'What happened?' I asked.

'Bloody Nazis,' he replied. 'They're biding their time, until the Germans invade. This is what the streets will be like then.'

Just then Stefan came running towards us. He had blood on his shirt and was out of breath. His face was white.

'Anton's dead,' he said. 'The fucking bastards stabbed him. He was trying to defend Rumak. Come on, let's get out of here.'

He led us down the street and through a warren of tiny alleys to his flat above a butcher's shop. He made coffee and poured glasses of vodka for us. We sat in silence for a while, shocked by what had happened. Then Stefan said to me:

'Do you want to help, Maria?'

'Yes, but why me? I'm no good in a fight,' I said.

'There's a different fight. A much tougher fight. Do you want to know about it?' he replied. I thought of Anton's bleeding body on the ground and then said:

'Yes,' not knowing what else I could say.

Throughout, Theresa said nothing. She seemed stunned by the events of the evening. We spoke little of it as we travelled home that night.

The next day the university campus was subdued. Anton had been a popular figure, known to many through his political activities. I suddenly realised that the introspective academic life I had led so far had kept me in ignorance of what was happening all around me. I met Stefan in the afternoon. He was sombre.

'Stan's gone,' he said. 'Walked out. He's going to air force training school at Posnán next week. He asked me to give you this letter for Theresa.'

I took the letter and put it in my bag.

'What will you do, Stefan?' I asked.

'I have my job to do,' he replied cryptically. 'You said you wanted to help. Go to this address at five o'clock today,' he said, handing me a small piece of paper.

I looked at it. It was a room number in the languages department of the university. And so, partly against my better judgement, and partly out of unquenchable curiosity, at five o'clock I climbed the stairs to the third floor of the languages building in the centre of the university campus. The room number was all I knew. It was a blank door with no name and when I knocked it was opened by a middle-aged man in an untidy suit.

'Stefan sent me,' I said.

'Miss Bienkowska I assume. Do come in.'

It was a barely furnished room, a table with two chairs behind it and one placed in front. It felt like an interview for a job.

'My name is Doctor Storey and this is Andrew Leadbetter,' the middle-aged man said, indicating the young man seated on the other side of the table.

He wore an English pin-striped suit with a club tie. He didn't speak and hardly reacted.

'Do have a seat, Maria,' Doctor Storey began. 'Stefan told us your name, of course. I'm professor of medieval European languages here and Andrew is from the British Embassy in Warsaw.'

'Stefan has told us a lot about you,' Leadbetter began. 'I understand you would like to help us. Why would that be?'

'I saw a student murdered on the streets yesterday by fascists. I would like to help stop that,' I said, knowing I was sounding hopelessly naïve.

'Yes, of course you would, and so would we,' said Doctor Storey.

'You see, Maria,' said Leadbetter, 'we need clever young people like you, if we are going to outwit the Germans. But we need them to work in secret. The German invasion will certainly come and we want to be prepared, to help Poland you understand. Do you think you could do that, to work in secret, to use your brains to defeat the enemy? Is that something you would be prepared to do?'

'I think so,' I said, and I saw Dr Storey and Leadbetter look at each other as I said this.

There was a pause.

'Good, Maria. Well we think you can help us very well,' Doctor Storey said.

'What shall I say to my parents?' I asked.

'Nothing at all. I have already spoken to your father, you see, Maria. He knows you are here today,' said Doctor Storey with a smile.

Then Leadbetter took out an envelope from his breast pocket and pushed it across the table towards me.

'This is a first class ticket to Warsaw tomorrow. The embassy car will meet you at the station. Pack an overnight bag.'

And so I was recruited to British Intelligence.

Chapter 2

The train to Warsaw pulled slowly across the flat landscape all day. We stopped at tiny stations, mere halts, where the only sounds were those of the engine wheezing and the whistle of the guard. Occasionally, travellers alighted in what seemed the middle of nowhere. At last, as evening closed in, we crawled under the high arches of Warsaw central station. The train came to a halt and exhaled; the voice of the guard announced our final destination had been reached. I was a young girl. I had travelled little and I was nervous of the strange city, with its crowds of rushing people. At the exit I hesitated, not knowing what to look for. Then a young man in a chauffeur's uniform came out of nowhere.

'Miss Bienkowska?'

I nodded.

'Please come with me.'

He led me towards a shiny black car parked in the station forecourt and opened the rear door for me as if I were a VIP. For all the care I took, he could have been my abductor. But I suppose I was simply taking it all in and too star-struck to think straight. We drove quickly through the city and, as the light faded and the street lamps began to shine, I saw we were in a residential area full of detached houses and tree-lined avenues. The car swept into a driveway and stopped before high wrought iron gates. The driver pressed the horn once and a guard appeared, to let us enter. As we pulled up before the house, the door opened and a woman descended the steps to meet me.

'Good evening, Miss Bienkowska. I'm Mrs McIntyre, the housekeeper here.' She spoke in refined English. 'Do let me take your bag. Follow me please. I hope you had a pleasant journey. I'll show you straight to your room. Mr Leadbetter will see you in the morning but tonight you will be dining with the resident staff here. Dinner is at seven-thirty so you just have time to freshen up.'

I had no chance to speak. We climbed two flights of stately stairs to a long corridor with at least eight doors opening off, one of which was mine.

'The dining room is on the ground floor. I look forward to seeing you then. If there's anything you need, call zero on the telephone in your room. By the way, do not speak to any of the staff this evening about your meeting with Mr Leadbetter.'

And with that she departed. I suddenly became aware that my life was entering a new and daunting phase. I looked out of my window over gardens and rooftops. I felt a million miles away from quiet Kraców.

After breakfast the next morning, Mrs McIntyre escorted me to the first floor. We walked on deep-piled burgundy carpets past white-painted doors marked "HM Ambassador" and then "First Secretary". A corridor turned off at right angles, closed-off by what looked like an old-fashioned lift gate, with a uniformed security guard sitting at a desk. Mrs McIntyre spoke to him in Polish and he unlocked the trellised gate and showed me into a small waiting room. We were in the secure part of the embassy. After a few minutes Andrew Leadbetter appeared. He was as smartly dressed as before with his black hair sleeked down.

'Good morning Miss Bienkowska. Please come this way.'

We walked past a telephonists' room, where young women sat in a row wearing headphones and making notes in shorthand. Then a room with a wall full of clocks showing the time in the capitals of the world – Washington, London, Berlin, Tokyo, Moscow; then Leadbetter's office, with a mahogany desk clear of clutter, and a single telephone. He placed a piece of paper in front of me with the heading "Declaration: The Official Secrets Act (1911)".

'I would be grateful if you would sign this please, Miss Bienkowska. You are over twenty-one aren't you? Yes, I thought so. It does not affect your rights under the law but it is a requirement of service with the British Government where secret information may come your way.'

I signed.

'And this please. This is a waiver of any rights for claims for loss or damage while in the service of the British Government.'

'What do you mean – loss or damage?' I asked.

'It is a formality, but there may be times when your personal safety is at risk,' he replied.

I looked at his face and saw his eyes staring coldly back at me.

'You must realise that, if you proceed with this employment, you may be asked to place yourself at risk, don't you?'

Again, I signed and handed the paper back to him.

'Doctor Storey spoke highly of you. Your reputation in the university is high,' he said.

'I never met Doctor Storey until two days ago. How does he know anything about me?' I asked.

Leadbetter smiled.

'You have a friend called Stefan, don't you? He is one of ours. We have been watching you for a while, Miss Bienkowska. Now, this afternoon you will be meeting one of my colleagues who will ask you various questions about your past. Simply double-checking, you understand. If all goes well we will be sending you to London this evening by plane. You will be issued with everything you need when you get there. You will have the chance to telephone your home today but remember your call will be monitored and you should not comment on anything that we have discussed here today. Do you have any questions?'

'After my training, how will I be deployed?'

'That is for London to decide. It is quite possible, if and when Poland is invaded by Germany, that you will operate as an agent here; or you may be sent to Scandinavia to operate a courier service between Sweden and occupied Poland. These are operational matters beyond my responsibility.'

'I understand,' I said, which was the opposite of the case.

That evening I flew to London. I was met, along with two other Polish girls, by an army car and driven to a country house about an hour from the airfield. It was already late: a black night with a persistent drizzle and a sharp wind. We were given cocoa and a sandwich, army kit, and shown our quarters, a dormitory for six with iron bedsteads in a row, in a wooden army hut in the grounds. But it was a light-hearted gang of young women, and I felt glad to have arrived. I knew nothing of what the future would hold.

At Hertford House we were taught operational intelligence procedures by the most unlikely of characters, some resembling short-sighted school teachers, others matronly blue-stockings or pernickety bank clerks. Our tradecraft, as they termed it, included courier routines, codes and ciphers, radio operating and surveillance techniques, among a host of other esoteric black arts. Our class numbered about forty men and women, Czechs, Poles, British, Norwegian, French and many others, all intelligent and quick to learn.

That was the easy bit. After six weeks we were sent to the north-west coast of Scotland to an outdoor training school to toughen us up. The journey was exhausting: the night train from King's Cross to Inverness, followed by three hours in the back of an army lorry to a remote camp overlooking the sea. We learned self-defence, unarmed combat and how to kill with a single blow of the hand. They gave us Browning pistols and we learned to shoot; we ran across the moors in the dark, navigating by map and compass; we survived in the wild for days, living off what we could catch or trap. And we learned to jump from aircraft into hostile territory, buoyed only by the gossamer of parachutes.

I had become friendly with a Polish girl named Irena. We had met on that first night at Hertford House. She came from Pomerania and was therefore bilingual in Polish and German. We used to pass the evenings together in our hut, usually exhausted from the day's efforts, talking and smoking strong English cigarettes. I remember one night particularly. The day had been tragic. A trainee agent had died from an accident in the hills and activities had been suspended for the afternoon. The mood was sombre that night.

'I sometimes wonder why I go on with this,' I said. Irena looked up from the magazine she was reading, lying on her bed. 'Don't you ever wonder that?' I asked.

She put the magazine down and lay back, studying the ceiling.

'I mean, what are we being trained for? There's no war going on,' I continued. 'How do you keep going, Irena?'

'You shouldn't think that way, Maria. You're just feeling depressed at what has happened. You're young and away from home. For me, I'm getting ready to fight for my home, my house and my family.'

'What do you mean?'

'The British are not fools. They know what is coming and are preparing for it, despite their politicians' talk of peace-making. We're part of that. The time is not far away when my home town will once again be in the hands of the Germans. My uncle is a Jew – like all my family – but he lives in Dresden. He has a shop selling all kinds of things – an ironmongery, I think it is called in English. Last month his shop was set on fire by the Nazi gangs roaming the streets. The authorities did nothing. Now the Jews are forbidden to walk the streets as free Germans. Do you think my family in Poland will be any better treated when Hitler invades? That's what I'm fighting for. Don't be deceived by the fact that your family are middle class and educated. The universities will be closed and the intellectuals who oppose fascism will go the same way as the Jews.'

'I saw a young man die on the streets. That's why I started this. Now I'm not sure of anything,' I said.

Irena jumped off her bed and put her arms round me.

'Don't cry,' she said. 'You're here because you want to fight for right. That's one better than me. I just want to save my family. You're very brave but you're very young and the world is a wretched place. But it will get better, believe me. Here,' and she gave me a cigarette.

She bent down and pulled out a small bottle from the

back of her bedside locker.

'Have a swig,' she said and handed me the bottle.

I took a mouthful and coughed. It felt like fire inside me. Irena laughed:

'Scotch whisky, the best in the world. Fuck the Nazis!'

And she took a swig herself. We finished the bottle that night. I woke with a bursting head to hear the clanging bell at six in the morning. But understanding was growing inside me and got stronger as the weeks went by.

At the end of December, 1938, I was given two weeks Christmas leave and a travel pass back to Kraców. I could tell my parents nothing of my work. I still shared a bedroom with Theresa. Late one night we lay talking.

'Have you seen Stanislaw lately?' I asked.

'I see him when he gets leave. He's finished his pilot's training in Posnán. He says they are all waiting for the Germans to attack.'

'Do you love him, Theresa? Tell me the truth.'

I could feel her blush in the dark.

'Yes, I do, but don't tell father will you?' she said.

In the first week of January, 1939, I took the long train journey back to Warsaw and the plane from there to London. My parents knew my work was secret and did not press me for information. But our parting was difficult. The clouds of war had become darker still and we all knew my work would throw me into danger. Theresa was most affected: she had lost interest in her studies since Stanislaw had entered her life; and the glimpses she had of my new life appeared glamorous and exciting. At the station she had embraced me and whispered in my ear:

'I wish I was coming with you,' so quietly that father could not hear her.

Before the year was out the pieces of all our lives would be brutally thrown into the air, never to fall back into place again.

Chapter 3

Hertford House in winter was unwelcoming. Around the red-brick Victorian mansion crouched rows of dreary army huts, cold and barren. The leafless sycamores stood black and sodden against the sky. I was glad to be leaving it.

The morning after I returned from Kracόw I was summoned to meet Major Robertson, our unit commander, in his office. I had met him only once before, and that simply as a member of our squad of forty, when we were first assembled at Hertford House.

'We're sending you to the Polish Embassy in Oslo tomorrow,' he said. 'Your cover will be a secretarial job in the embassy but you will work to a line manager in the secure section of the British Embassy. He will make contact with you when you get there. This has been cleared by your Government in Poland but, in the event of any mishaps, they will of course deny any knowledge of your intelligence function. The Norwegian Government know nothing of this arrangement. Any questions?'

'Can you tell me what I will be doing, sir?' I asked.

'Needless to say, you will not be involved in secretarial work. The first thing you must achieve is fluency in Norwegian. An intensive language course is already in place for embassy staff, so there is nothing unusual about that. You will work with your handler to establish safe clandestine routes from the Baltic, via Sweden if necessary, to the North Sea coast of Norway. We also need to establish a local network of agents in Norway in anticipation of German occupation, in which case you will remain in place under cover, after the Polish Embassy is evacuated. You will be busy, Miss Bienkowska.'

'Why Norway?' I asked.

'Did you know that every German battleship currently afloat was built of steel made from Swedish iron ore exported to Germany by sea from the railhead in northern Norway? Germany has no iron ore itself. When war breaks out Germany will need to control that route. It's as simple as that. We must ensure we have reliable information coming to us from Norway. That will be your job.'

He paused and offered me a cigarette.

'You've done well here, Maria, but the real thing starts now. I wish you luck.'

He handed me an envelope.

'Don't open that now and destroy it as soon as you've read it. You will need it to verify the correct contact has been made, when you get to Oslo. Now you should go to housekeeping, to get yourself kitted out for civilian life.'

The interview was over. I went back to my quarters and found Irena had arrived that morning. She was as confident and pushy as ever.

'Well, where is it? Where are they sending you?' she asked.

'Oslo, the Polish Embassy as a cover,' I replied. 'What about you?'

'The word is we German speakers are going into the lion's den.'

'You mean Germany?' I said.

'Not just Germany, Berlin itself,' Irena replied.

'Christ.'

'Yes, Christ. I'll hear for certain this afternoon.'

I spent two hours in housekeeping getting kitted out for travel: bank account, passport, papers, civilian clothes and so on. Hardware, such as the radio, would be provided in Norway. When I got back to the hut, Irena was flat out on her bed looking at the ceiling.

'I was too bloody right,' she said. 'Day after tomorrow.'

'We should celebrate,' I said. 'You never know...'

'You mean, if we'll make it through,' she said.

That night we took the bus into Stevenage. It was a Friday and the pubs were full. There was a lot of khaki about and plenty of attention paid to two unattached young females. I was not a seasoned drinker, unlike Irena, and the evening soon became a blur. In the taxi on the way back to camp, I realised that Irena was different. I had no experience of men but I was attracted to them. Irena was immune. Back in our quarters she held me in her arms and kissed me on the lips. I felt a strange combination of pleasure and fear. I could not make sense of my emotions. But I responded.

'You've never loved anyone, have you, Maria?' she said.

'I think I love Theresa,' I replied. 'I suppose I must love my parents, although they just seem to have been always there.'

'No, real love, I mean,' Irena said.

'I think I love you, Irena,' I said.

'Maria, you don't love me. You have what the English describe as a crush on an older woman.' She laughed. 'One day, you will love a man, because that is the way you are. I can tell. And then, believe me, you will forget your ideals and promises, because love overcomes everything else, country, faith, the lot.'

There was a whisky bottle as usual in her bedside locker and we drank too much that night. I feared for Irena, for her self-destructive drive. I heard one year later that she had been shot by firing squad in Berlin. Years later, tears still came to my eyes whenever I thought of her, my Irena, the first of my loves and my losses.

I flew next day from Henley in an RAF York transport to Fornebu airfield near Oslo. The plane was unheated, noisy and very uncomfortable but the flight was not long. The approach to landing lay low over the fjord and just as we seemed to be ditching in the water, the landing strip miraculously appeared beneath our wheels and we bumped down on the hard-packed snow. The temperature was twenty below with a cutting wind off the sea. As I stepped off the plane, I realised the game was over. This was the real thing.

A British Embassy car collected me from the airfield and took me to a small flat in the outskirts of the city. I had no idea where I was. I remember the city in monochrome; white snow on the ground, leafless trees and a grey sky. The road into the city ran along the fjord where ice floes bobbed in the waves. The driver pulled up outside a concrete block and pressed a doorbell on the entry board. The main door opened and he led me up the stairs, carrying my bag. Two flights up we paused before a door and knocked. It was opened by a young man who showed me in, while the driver descended the staircase.

'I understand the weather in London is unseasonably mild,' he said.

'For the time of year, but the forecast is for snow,' I replied.

'Who the hell writes this rubbish? Welcome to Oslo, Maria. This is your *pied-à-terre* and I am Jonathan Blake.'

He held out his hand and shook mine. He was tall, slim and intensely good-looking. He could have been a star in a black-and-white movie.

'Leave your bag and let's get out of here. You must be starving after that freezing flight from London. Let's get some lunch.'

He took me downstairs and we jumped into the waiting car.

'Take us to Bagatelle, Anders, would you. Should manage to get a late lunch.'

The car whisked us off into the traffic and along a tree-lined main street. I caught a sign on a large stone building nearby, Universitets Bibliotek, and then we pulled up outside a small restaurant with a flare burning from a brazier outside.

'Best steak with bearnaise in town here,' Jonathan said, as he opened the door for me.

At the sound of Jonathan's Oxford accent, the proprietor appeared from the back of the restaurant.

'Ah, Monsieur Blake,' he said, in an exaggerated French accent, 'a table for two?'

'Thanks Jean-Pierre, not too late I hope. This is Mademoiselle Camilla. She will be a regular here in future.'

We shook hands.

'Enchanté, Mademoiselle Camilla. You will always be

most welcome.'

So that was my code name – Camilla something. I was swept along by it all, buzzing with excitement. Jonathan ordered two champagne cocktails which came in tall glasses, then scallops with dry white wine, and two rare fillet steaks with a heavy burgundy.

'Well Camilla,' he said. 'How do you like all this? Not a bad life is it, away from the smoke of London.'

'Very nice,' I replied. 'It would be helpful to know the rest of my name.'

'Time for everything, Camilla.'

He took out an envelope from his inside pocket.

'Read this tonight. It tells you all you need to know. Needless to say, dispose of it afterwards. Anders will pick you up in the morning around nine. I can tell you more then. In the meantime, let's enjoy ourselves. The office can wait.'

At four o'clock Jonathan paid the bill and called a taxi. As we sat in the back together, I felt his hand on my knee.

'You're a very pretty girl, Camilla,' he said, 'but I suppose you've been told that many times.'

'Do you say that to all your agents?'

'Only the girls,' he replied. 'Remember, I am your handler.'

Jonathan was the perfect combination of style and sleaze, of English public school and barrow boy. But, as I learned very quickly, there was not a girl in his team who was not in love with him and a man who would not go to the ends of the earth for him. When I got back to my flat, I disentangled myself from the back seat and stepped on to the pavement. Jonathan got out too.

'Your keys, Camilla,' he said. 'I'll see you tomorrow.'

The sun sets very early in Oslo in winter and it was already dark when I finally found time to unpack my case. I suddenly felt the acute pain of loneliness, even fear, as I sat in my tiny bed-sitting room. I opened the envelope Jonathan had given me. It contained my brief biography. My cover name in Norway was Camilla Andreassen, although I would be listed on the staff of the Polish Embassy as Alicja Kolubinska.

There was no cross-referencing of the two names between the embassies. Only security-cleared staff in the British Embassy would know my real name as Maria Bienkowska. My birthplace was a small town called Asker, south-east of Oslo, and I had a complete list of dates, schools and qualifications, which supported my Norwegian cover identity. I learned these by heart and then burned the papers in a tin waste paper bin. I realised that from tomorrow I would be three people: to the Polish Embassy, a junior administrator learning Norwegian; to the British Embassy intelligence staff, I would be Maria Bienkowska; and to the world outside I would be a Norwegian girl called Camilla Andreassen from Asker. Only Jonathan would know all three identities.

At nine o'clock the following morning Anders collected me and drove me to the British Embassy. I noticed that the car had tinted windows and I sat in the back seat invisible to the outside world. At the embassy the car drove into an underground garage and I was taken by lift to the third floor where Jonathan was there to meet me. He punched in a set of numbers and opened a heavy door into the intelligence section of the embassy. His office was unimpressive and impersonal, as if he rarely used it. The furniture was functional; a metal filing cabinet stood in the corner secured by a heavy deadlock.

'This is the only place where you will be known by your real name, Maria. If you are ever in trouble, you only call this number, do you understand? No others. You ask for Mr Rodgers. I will answer in a certain format so that you will know it is I. If your call is taken by the duty officer here, you will say that Camilla would like to meet Mr Rodgers at the usual place and time.'

He handed me a piece of paper with a telephone number on it; an address; and the time – seven pm.

'Is that clear, Maria?'

'How will you know it's me?' I asked.

'Because all the agents use different names for me. Rodgers is your identifier. Now, you must be wondering what we are going to ask you to do. The answer is, nothing – yet.

We will meet regularly, and you will meet other people on my behalf. Your first task is to become fluent in Norwegian. Forget about the Polish Embassy – that's only your official cover. You will be given an office there which you can use as you please but your only real work is for me. Anders will take you and Marta along there in a moment.'

He got up and opened the door and called a name. A young blonde-haired girl appeared.

'Maria, this is Marta Pettersen. She'll explain about the language classes and give you a pass to get in here. Then Marta if you get Anders to take you both along to meet the Poles? I'll say goodbye now, for the time being.'

Marta took me along the corridor.

'Watch out for Jonathan,' she said, 'he's quite a charmer.'

'I've already found that out,' I replied.

Marta showed me into her tiny office and gave me my pass. She also gave me a letter in English confirming my enrolment in the language course at the university.

'Now we'll go along and meet the Poles, as Jonathan calls them.'

Anders drove us out of the embassy with the same secrecy as my arrival. The journey was no more than half a kilometre, through the same wide streets lined with detached villas. At the Polish Embassy, Marta introduced me as Alicja Kolubinska, and one of the secretaries showed me my office which already had my name on the door.

'I hope you will feel at home here, Alicja,' he said. 'Mr Blake has explained the arrangements to me. Please use the office as much as you wish.'

This was the start of my new life. My mornings were filled with language classes and my evenings with homework. I visited the Polish Embassy most days and got to know many of the staff. Once a week I met Jonathan, at one restaurant or another in the city, and sometimes he brought with him other contacts whom he introduced to me by their code names. I assembled a growing list of telephone numbers and names which I had to commit to memory. It felt like being in a spider's web, with Jonathan at the centre and agents all around him on the ends of threads. Although I had no real work to do, I began to feel this peaceful life could not last much longer.

Winter turned to spring. Overnight the snow on the hills began to melt and the frozen streams became torrents. The birch trees threw out their lime green virgin leaves and the crocuses in Carl Johan burst through to the lightening sky. The days began to lengthen. I was walking one afternoon with Jonathan in Frogner Park. By this time we had become close, and we walked hand in hand. I suppose, looking back, that it was inevitable I would fall in love with him. Before I met him, my experience of the opposite sex was restricted to incompetent fumblings after school dances when the sisters allowed the convent girls to meet the boys from the Catholic gymnasium once a year. At university I had been regarded as a blue stocking, sexless and too clever. But Jonathan had lit a light in me. He was beautiful and, for a young girl, he had that special advantage: he knew how to do everything properly. Whether he loved me at all, I doubt; but he was kind and caring, despite his opening gambit in the back of the taxi. How many other girls he had, I never asked. I was just happy in his presence. As we were walking, he suddenly stunned me with a bolt out of the blue.

'We have your sister Theresa with us at the embassy. You must come and meet her.'

'Theresa? What on earth is she doing here?' I asked.

'She's been here a week. Sorry not to have told you, but we've been checking her out.'

'Has something happened? Is something wrong?' I asked in a panic.

'She'll tell you. We'd better go now,' he said. 'By the way, she's joining us.'

Jonathan drove us quickly down Kirkeveien towards the embassy, dodging cars and bouncing over tramlines.

'Why didn't you tell me before?' I asked.

'No point. We might have sent her back. Now that we think we can use her, she can stay,' he replied.

This was the professional Jonathan; calculating to the end, without a shred of emotion.

I met Theresa in Jonathan's office. He left us to ourselves. I hadn't seen her since Christmas but I was surprised by the change. She had grown up, from the timid first year student, to a smart young woman, confident and collected. She threw her arms round my neck when I entered the room; we both laughed and cried for joy.

'Theresa, this is the last thing I expected. How did you get here, for God's sake?'

'Ran away didn't I? God, I couldn't stand the boredom any longer. Stanislaw is flying his planes and you were working over here. I spoke to Stefan and he sent me to see Leadbetter in Warsaw, and here I am. Bit of a risk, I know, but I made it. I had a terrible row with father but I went ahead. Maria, you look so chic. And who was that handsome man?' she asked, nodding her head towards the door through which Jonathan had left.

'So you haven't met Jonathan, yet? You will. He's the head of the intelligence unit in the embassy. He knows all about you. He says you can join us.'

I looked at Theresa. She was thriving on the threat of it all; being in love with a dare-devil pilot; leaving home; and risking her life, as she saw it, in the dark world of the Secret Service. How events had changed us both.

Later that month, I think it may have been Norway's National Day – the 17th of May – Theresa and I had tea with Marta in the back garden of the embassy. Marta was looking after the Ambassador's two small daughters for the afternoon while he attended a ceremony at the City Hall. It was a glorious sunny day, the white blossom suddenly out on the apple trees in the orchard. Theresa and I stood together with the two little girls while Marta took our photograph. I kept it through the years as a reminder of that blissful summer in Oslo before the war destroyed everything. Theresa was sent to Hertford House a few days later to start her training. In less than four months Hitler invaded Poland. I was never to return to see the wild flowers growing in the dusty verges in the long Polish summer.

Chapter 4

I remember the date exactly – the 15th of September. I was in my phoney office in the Polish Embassy in the late afternoon when the telephone rang. This was an unusual event as I did no trade from my cover office. The switchboard girl was on the line.

'I have a Flight Officer Stanislaw Reichsmüller for you,' she said. I heard the switchboard connect me and a voice I recognised.

'Hello, Maria, this is Stanislaw here. We are at the Østbane railway station in Oslo. Can you pick us up?'

'What on earth are you doing here in Oslo?' I asked, bewildered at the unexpected call.

'Ditched in the Baltic a couple of days ago. The Swedes picked us up and got us here. How's Theresa?'

'Let that wait,' I said. 'Stay where you are. I'll get an embassy car to pick you up.'

I rushed down to the general office, hoping to find a chauffeur. Kristov, the Ambassador's driver, was lounging about, chatting to the girls.

'Kristov, can you do me a favour?' I asked.

'For you Alicja, it would be a pleasure,' he said, grinning and making a mock bow.

'Drive me to Østbane station to pick up a Polish airman. He's just arrived from Sweden.'

'The only car we have free at the moment is the Ambassador's,' he replied. 'I could get into bother doing that.'

'Please,' I pleaded, 'I will repay you with everlasting love.'

'In that case, the price will be worth paying,' and he put on his cap, stubbed out his cigarette, and we jumped into the Ambassador's Mercedes-Benz.

Kristov swept through the city streets, with traffic opening before him, easing our way. We pulled up in the station yard and I looked around. Then I saw two Polish airmen standing by the taxi rank, looking lost. I recognised Stanislaw as one of them.

'Maria, good to see you. I didn't expect the red carpet,' he said, eyeing the Polish flag and the CD plates. 'This is my friend Tadeusz. We escaped from Poland together. I hope you have a space for us both. I so much wanted to see Theresa. How is she?'

'She's fine Stanislaw. Get in the car and we'll get you straight back to the embassy.'

Kristov drove off at speed, anxious to return the car before anyone senior had spotted it had disappeared. I telephoned Theresa in her apartment and she came across straightaway. The housekeeper made two guest rooms available for Stanislaw and Tadeusz that night and I remember they stayed two nights before leaving for Bergen to take a British navy ship to England. They were part of a growing stream of Polish military who regrouped in England to fight the enemy of their country.

I didn't see Theresa for a couple of days and when I did she was downcast. She had finished her training in Britain and been sent to Norway to join Jonathan's team in anticipation of a German invasion. We shared my tiny flat and were known in the British Embassy as the Bienkowska sisters. I knew she was torn by the decision she had just made.

'Did you not think of going to England with Stanislaw?' I asked.

'Yes, of course I thought about it, but what would be the point? He will fly with the RAF and I might never see him. Who knows if he will survive? I can fight alongside him here just as well.'

I saw a side of my sister I had not seen before. She was made of steel and more determined than I could have imagined. Her resolution was reinforced a few weeks later when we heard through our intelligence network that our parents had been arrested by the Germans and interned for anti-fascist opinions, along with others who had protested when Jewish teachers and students were expelled from the university. They were sent to a camp for Polish intelligentsia to be "re-educated". We never saw them again.

The autumn of 1939 was a bitter-sweet time. The short Nordic summer was over but a late flourish of fine weather burned briefly before dying into the embers of autumn. We knew our days were numbered. Europe was at war: it was only a matter of time before Hitler added Norway to his list of victims, to secure his supply of iron ore and, in the process, swarm through Denmark as the advance camp for the invasion further north. And what did we do? We enjoyed life. I was in love with Jonathan, in the knowledge that soon he would be recalled to Britain, which made it all the more poignant. We danced at the Grand Hotel with groups of friends from the British diplomatic service, anxious to spend their foreign allowance before returning to food rationing back home. We stayed up all night and returned home with the first trams. Theresa and I were swept along on a swirling tide of self-delusion until our world crashed about our ears.

By Christmas, it was clear that Norway could not maintain its neutrality and by February the Norwegian navy had shown its loyalties during the Altmark incident. The country was glued to radio sets everywhere to follow the unfolding and inescapable fate awaiting it. For Theresa and me the resolution of any uncertainty about our future came with a brutality quite unexpected. One Monday morning in late March I walked to my office at the Polish Embassy. The front door to the villa was locked and the windows were shuttered. I rang the bell and after a while the janitor opened the door. He was a familiar figure, a local Norwegian, as were most of the domestic staff.

'What's going on Per? Where is everybody?' I asked.

'Packed up and gone,' he said. 'All the Polish staff left over the weekend, including the Ambassador and his family.'

'Where to?'

'London. The embassy's been evacuated. Only the Norwegian staff are left. The orders are to lock up and leave when we have to, Miss Kolubinska. I'm surprised you weren't told,' he added.

I was not surprised. Only the top people in the Polish embassy knew my real purpose and they would have expected Jonathan Blake to brief me. After all, they knew I worked for him. At this thought, I became concerned: why hadn't Jonathan been in touch? It took me ten minutes to walk along the road to the British Embassy. It was locked and silent. The metal gates around the front garden were bolted and there was no way in. I remembered my briefing: if in trouble phone Mr Rodgers; if he isn't there, say to the duty officer "Camilla would like to meet Mr Rodgers at the usual time and place". There was a telephone box at the street corner. I pulled out the piece of paper from my bag and phoned the number. Immediately a voice came on the line:

'Duty officer.'

'Camilla would like to meet Mr Rodgers at the usual time and place,' I said.

'I'll tell Mr Rodgers. Goodbye.'

'Wait, what's going on?' I snapped.

The line went dead in an instant. I felt desolate, cut-off and alone. Then I knew that my secret life had really started. This was how it was going to be. I took a taxi back to my flat. Theresa was still in bed but awake.

'Theresa, it's starting,' I said. 'The Poles have left for London. The British have closed up shop. I've activated the emergency meeting procedure for seven pm today.'

'Do you want me to come with you?' she said.

'I don't think so. I need to follow the rules.'

'Why didn't Jonathan call you?'

'I wondered that at first. Then I realised he knew I would use the emergency contact procedure. Things must be serious, Theresa. He must think there's a danger of blowing my cover.'

Monday dragged on interminably. Theresa and I sat around, drinking coffee, speculating on what was happening and listening to the radio news bulletins. As far as we knew, we were the only London-trained agents working for Jonathan, the rest being everyday civilians who had been vetted and roped into the network. That meant that only Theresa and I had direct contact with British intelligence; we would be the channel for everything the network could produce.

At six-thirty that evening I took the tram into the city centre and got off at the parliament house. From there it was a short walk to the Domkirke – the cathedral – the spire of which I could see rising above the rooftops. My instructions were to sit in the last row at the back on the left of the aisle. I arrived at five minutes to seven, just as the congregation were gathering for evensong. It made sense – the best way to conceal oneself was in a crowd in an open place.

The service started and the choir began to sing. No one had arrived and I became restless. There was a reading and then the choir began again and, before I knew it, Jonathan was sitting next to me. His hand grasped mine.

'Wait five minutes after I'm gone and then leave. Take a taxi to Theatre Cafe. I'll be there.'

I did as I was told. I found Jonathan sitting in the far corner of the dark cafe, away from the window, smoking his English cigarette, looking as debonair as ever. He kissed me.

'I'm sorry you had a fright today, Maria. I had no time to tell you. Everything points to a German invasion in a matter of days. London ordered us to pull the plug and get out. We picked up a German agent last week and the information we got suggested that our signals were being intercepted. That's why I had to trust you to use the emergency meeting procedure. You did well.'

'I suppose this means you're leaving, Jonathan,' I said, with little hope that I would be contradicted.

'Yes,' he said, 'flying out tomorrow.'

'Will I see you again?' I asked.

'I can't say, Maria. It depends how long this racket lasts. It could all be over in six months. You know what happens now, don't you?'

'We go underground, of course. Tell me, what's happened to Marta?'

'As a Norwegian she drifts back into the population.

There will be no record of her time with us but her address will be a safe house for your network to use. She is on our payroll for that. I have her address here.'

I looked at it and committed it to memory, an address in Sinsen.

He ordered a couple of drinks and we sat and smoked. There was little to say since we both knew the situation we had rehearsed so often in our heads had actually come upon us. We drank more and held hands across the table. All I could think about was the gloom of the long weeks and months without him.

'Maria, this is our last night together. I've taken a room at the Continental. I hope you don't object,' he said smiling.

'Why would I?' I replied.

The hotel was familiar to me. We had spent many nights together there since I arrived in Oslo. Jonathan knew everyone by Christian name and tipped well. I knew from their looks on my very first visit months before that I was not the first girl he had brought there. We made love and fell asleep. In the morning I woke to an empty bed and a note tucked into the mirror. I read it then put it aside. All it said was "Good luck, love, Jonathan". I doubted if I would ever see him again. But Irena was right about real love. I had felt it now for the first time myself.

Chapter 5

It was early April before the Germans arrived, leap-frogging from Denmark by air and sea. The mood in the capital was sombre as the grey uniforms of the Wehrmacht paraded through the city centre. No one knew what to expect and a whole population seemed to become silent and distrustful. Our network came alive for the first time. Theresa and I split up for security reasons and she moved into her own small flat, a short distance from mine. We were grateful for our regular secret meetings, since we both felt alone and isolated and by talking we could keep Stanislaw and Jonathan alive in our memories.

In the months of waiting before the German invasion we had established a chain of safe houses stretching from the west of Norway to the Swedish border. The traffic was two-way: going east to neutral Sweden was a steady trickle of escaping Norwegians, many to re-group after the failed defence of their country; going west to the coast was a route for downed RAF crews and couriers to Britain, crossing the sea in Royal Navy vessels. Couriers often used the route and we kept in touch with London through dead letter boxes and coded messages on the wireless. Jonathan had given me a copy of *A Pilgrim's Progress* bound in leather and the coded messages from London could be unlocked using this text. It worked well but there was always a lurking fear that a careless moment might give us all away. We had a network of agents supplying us with information on German troop movements, shipping movements in ports and through the narrow fjords, and movements of German aircraft. None of the agents knew the identity of others; they worked alone to Theresa or me. Only three people had possession of the whole picture; the third person was Jonathan.

In 1942, I think it must have been near the Norwegian midsummer, when the sun never set, Theresa and I sat on my veranda until one or two in the morning, drinking aquavit and smoking endless cigarettes. Mid June, when the sun scarcely sank over the headland at Bygdøy. The war seemed endless; the occupation numbingly pointless. We passed our information on and received new commands. But nothing seemed to change. I had tuned in my radio as usual at eight that evening and received a pattern of numbers. I turned to Bunyan and deciphered the message. It set a rendezvous next day, an unusual event to meet an unknown contact face-to-face. I looked at Theresa and saw doubts in her face. She harboured the same suspicions as I.

The rendezvous point was the Nordmarka Chapel in the woods above Oslo, the stave church nestling in the pine forests beyond Frognerseteren, visited only by skiers in the winter and walkers in the summer. I had been there once before with Jonathan, on a summer walk along the forest tracks.

'Shall I come with you?' Theresa said.

'I think not. The contact will be expecting one person, but I'll take my Browning,' I said.

Next morning I took the mountain railway to Frognerseteren. It was a brilliant June day, without a cloud in the sky or a breath of wind. The train was almost empty, the only other occupants of my carriage two off-duty German officers going up the mountain for lunch at one of their favourite venues. I was always amazed by the German soldiers' capacity to act as tourists among a population that was their bitter enemy. I was conscious of the heavy Browning pistol in my shoulder bag and tried not to focus my attention upon it for fear of arousing suspicions. As the train wound its way higher up the mountain, the fjord stretched out further to the south, a smooth shimmering lake of tiny islands and inlets reaching as far as the open sea. The Germans got off at Holmenkollen and I relaxed a little. Two stops later the train reached Frognerseteren and I stepped down and set off to walk to Tryvannstua, then on to the chapel. The tracks were dry and dusty, the forest dense and perfumed. Blueberries grew in abundance in the clearings and deep in the woods the occasional patch of cloudberries. It was an idyll only destroyed by the spectre of war.

It took me an hour to reach my destination. I criss-crossed through the woods, avoiding the main footpaths, keeping a weather eye open for any following footsteps. At last I saw the chapel through the trees, the dark wooden logs of the walls, the black roof shingles and the traditional rustic red of the window frames and doors. I felt my heart racing and my hands shaking as I traced the outline of my pistol in my bag. I saw no one near the building so I entered. It was always the case that forest lodges were never locked and this applied to the chapel. The door gave easily to my touch. I looked around in the half light afforded by the narrow windows and saw nothing but the simple stone altar and crucifix and half a dozen plain wooden pews. I sat down where I had a clear view of the rear door – my escape route if I needed one – and waited. I could hear nothing but silence. Then, from the front of the chapel, from the darkest corner, the figure of a man appeared. I froze, my hand on my gun; then my grip relaxed as the face took shape in the slanting light from a window. It was Jonathan Blake.

'Jonathan!' I whispered.

'Hello Maria,' he said. 'I don't think you were expecting me. You can forget about your pistol now.'

He stepped forward and took me in his arms and kissed me.

'It's good to see you Maria. How has it been?

'What can I say? Hard and lonely, with a lot of waiting and watching. How about you?'

'I've got a new job for you, a really big job. That's why I'm here in person. I want you to say you'll do it,' he said. 'Let's walk.'

There was a ski lodge at Tryvannstua, about a half hour away, that was open all year round and we set off along the forest track in that direction. As we walked he talked.

'The top brass back home are working out the endgame to

this bloody war. The Americans are up to their necks in it now which means we can't lose, although it doesn't appear that way sometimes. The invasion of Europe is already being planned: perhaps it will happen next summer, perhaps a year later. The Germans are struggling on the eastern front and if the Allies push from the west at the same time, Germany will be squeezed in the middle. One escape route for them may be to go north, to Scandinavia. We already have some indication they are making plans for that. We need someone inside, Maria.'

'Inside what? I don't understand,' I said.

'Inside German Command in Norway. We've had an approach, you see, from a high-ranking German officer in Norway. He wants to secure his exit when the Germans are beaten, wants to make a deal, you understand.'

'What kind of a deal?' I asked.

'Details of German military planning in return for a free passage after the war.'

'Where do I fit in?'

'He has access to top-level information but needs a means of getting it out. If you were working for him, you know the channels for getting it to London. He'll be your protector and sponsor. Plenty of Norwegians are working for the Germans. You would be no different. Except you'll be working for us. It's dangerous but will you do it?'

'And my cover?'

'Camilla Andreassen, the name you are already using, a harmless Norwegian girl, wanting to earn her living in a safe office job. There's no need to change just now.'

'And afterwards, when the war is over?'

'You'll be a national heroine for doing the most difficult job in the world.'

Jonathan had a way of putting things, a verbal sleight of hand, that could make the tawdry seem glamorous. We walked on in silence. The track reached the small lake at Tryvann and we sat at a table outside the ski lodge. Jonathan ordered coffee.

'I know this is one hell of a request to make, Maria. But if we pull this off, we could avoid a ghastly final stand by the Germans in the north. We could shorten the war by six months and save thousands of lives. There is one thing,' Jonathan added, 'it would be better for you if it appeared you had been arrested by the Germans and shipped off to some dreadful fate in a camp. In other words, you disappear, assumed executed as a spy. In fact, you would be based at Akershus in Oslo, with a new name of course. You would need to stay anonymous for the duration of the war.'

I knew that this would be the most dangerous thing I had ever done in my life but it took me no more than a minute to decide.

'OK, I'll do it,' I said. 'But one thing, Jonathan, look after Theresa, won't you. She'll be on her own.'

'Of course I will,' he said, grasping my hand across the table.

'What happens next? What happens to my network?' I asked.

'Oh, that will continue as normal. I'll arrange for you to meet your German officer this evening. Expect a telephone call to your flat. His name is Colonel Thomas Engel.'

'And you, what will you do?'

'Me, Maria? Return to my lonely apartment in Bayswater and wait for your return, trailing clouds of glory.'

'Don't play with me, Jonathan, with your literary quotations. You never loved me, did you? Did you ever love anyone, for that matter?'

He cast his eyes down and played with the coffee spoon.

'No, I didn't Maria, you're right. I don't think I know how to love.'

I never thought then that I would ever speak to Jonathan again. I parcelled him away in the drawer marked experience. He flew out of Norway from some remote little landing strip later that week, back to his scheming life in London. He was the consummate manipulator. His triumph in placing an agent inside German High Command in the north catapulted him to the top, from which dizzy heights he did not care to remember those he had left behind.

At seven that evening the telephone rang and a voice spoke in cultured German.

'Miss Andreassen, my name is Thomas Engel.'

'I was expecting you to call,' I replied.

'I hope you are free this evening. If so, my car will collect you in thirty minutes to take you to The Grand for dinner.'

'I will be ready.'

I was twenty-two, in a foreign country, waiting to be driven to the best restaurant in Oslo, to have dinner with a Colonel in the German army. I put on my best evening dress and my highest heels. I was overwhelmed by the glamour of it all. I had never really experienced the horror of war and I suppose my behaviour revealed that naivety. I thought, if this was to be my fall, I would go down brilliantly. I never for one moment entertained the idea that the whole thing could be a trap to lure a British agent into the open. At seven-thirty precisely, the doorbell rang and I opened to a young German soldier.

'Your driver, Miss Andreassen.'

He clicked his heels and bowed. He swept us through the streets of Oslo in the black Mercedes with a military flag fluttering on the bonnet. The doorman at The Grand came down the steps to open the car door and in the lobby I was met by Colonel Thomas Engel. He was forty years old, a tinge of grey at the temples, blue-eyed with a kind face that seemed to reflect the burden he was carrying inside.

'My dear Miss Andreassen, thank you so much for joining me this evening,' he said, taking my hand.

'Camilla, please,' I said.

'Yes, Camilla. Such a beautiful name for a beautiful young lady, if I may say so. And you must call me Thomas. I have reserved a table for just the two of us, but first, let us have a drink.'

He led me into a beautiful room furnished with deep armchairs and sofas. The mirrors on the walls reflected the subdued light of a hundred candles.

'This is called the Limelight Bar, I believe.'

The waiter came across and Thomas ordered champagne.

We took two corner seats and I looked around. For the first time I saw that the room was occupied only by German officers and their guests. Thomas noticed my surprise. He spoke in a low voice.

'Shocking, isn't it? What right have we got to be here while the population have so little to eat, you are thinking. I agree with you. I am ashamed of what we have done.'

'I've never before met a German who felt that way, least of all an officer in the army,' I said.

'Then you have met very few Germans I must say. There are many of us who oppose the regime but we cannot bring it down from within. Only defeat in war will achieve that and I have a duty to speed that for the sake of humanity. You are a very brave young lady to take this on, Camilla. Did you know your name means "handmaid of the priest" in ancient Latin?'

'No, I didn't know that.'

'Before I joined the army I was at Heidelberg studying Latin and Greek and then I went to Oxford for postgraduate studies. I even learned to play cricket and rugby there, very badly. That was in 1924. When I came back to Germany Hitler was just a bad joke. My father sent me to officer training school, just as he had done in his time. By the time I was commissioned it was too late; Hitler the joke was in charge. Let us drink to the end of all this.'

We raised our glasses. I could see Thomas now as a gentle classical scholar in an ancient university. But then I remembered the way my life had turned out: I should have been a mathematician. We both were lost souls seeking a kind of salvation from the wreckage of a civilisation.

We dined in the Palm restaurant in full view of what felt like half the German officer corps. Thomas had worked a clever cover for our meeting, for the room was full of officers with their girls, and I was introduced to passing comrades without any hint of embarrassment. I was exactly as expected. We dined on oysters, a Chateaubriand, and crepes suzettes, the most luxurious meal of my life at that time. After coffee, Thomas spoke to me in a serious tone.

'Tomorrow morning I will fetch you by car. To all intents

and purposes it will appear you have been arrested. I will arrange for the necessary paperwork to cover your disappearance. Trust me Camilla, as I must you. You will of course be operating under an alias, not Camilla Andreassen.'

I did not laugh openly at the thought of yet another identity but it did sum up the weird combination of the deadly serious and the low comedy of life in secret. I was not afraid. I trusted Thomas even though he wore the uniform of the enemy and I knew very little about him. He had a palpable honesty which could not be feigned. That night I hardly slept, lying awake in the half-light of a northern midsummer. I was relieved at the arrival of dawn so that I could begin yet another existence.

Looking back I question how I could behave so calmly under such potential threat. What was my motivation? I think, more likely than not, it was an attempt to find a direction to my life. I do not think it was politics, or morality, or a sense of humanity. I wanted, above all, to carve a passage which was mine, not thrust upon me. I had an exceptional mathematical brain, I know that, but I had chosen not to pursue that route, for reasons I could not articulate. My sexuality was ambiguous: had I loved Irena more than Jonathan? Did I love either? All that was certain was that I was adrift in a threatening world and I needed to impose my order upon it, be it right or wrong. This is how it seemed to me.

Chapter 6

Akershus Castle sat on a headland overlooking the harbour and the fjord. For seven centuries it had defended Oslo from foreign invasion and had never been taken by force. It was gaunt and forbidding. In 1940 the castle opened its gates to the German invaders without a struggle, thereby avoiding putting its tradition of invincibility to the test. In my early years in Oslo I used to sit by the quay in front of the City Hall to watch the fishing boats tie up; to see the English boat leave from the Vippetangen at four o'clock; and to breath in the salt air of an ancient seafaring nation. And all under the walls of the Akershus. I never thought it would be my home for three long years.

The car called for me at the appointed time. Thomas had told me to have my belongings packed, ready to leave. This time it was not the shiny black Mercedes but a blue-grey army vehicle with German markings. The watching neighbours would be in no doubt of its purpose. Two soldiers escorted me to the car and I was directed to the back seat where I found Thomas waiting. He said nothing but I caught the hint of a reassuring smile. We drove off through the city streets, around the harbour in front of the Radhus, and up the long drive which led to the gates of the castle. The gatehouse guard lifted the black-and-white barrier and waved the car through into a cobbled courtyard. Thomas led me under a stone archway into a large quadrangle, with a square lawn in the middle surrounded by borders with flowers and trees in bloom. It was serene; I could hear birdsong. It was a million miles away from the war. When we were clear of people, he spoke to me in a quiet voice:

'My quarters are over here,' he said, 'and your office will be part of my house. You will have your own quarters there too. As far as staff here are concerned, you are my new secretary, Beata, but as far as the outside world is concerned, Camilla has been arrested. The files at Gestapo headquarters at Vika Terrassen have already been falsified to that effect. There will be no questions asked. Come, I will show you around.'

We entered a low stone building on one side of the quadrangle, the door bearing the name of Colonel Engel. In a small office on the left, a young soldier sat filling in some paperwork.

'Beata, this is Heinrich, my driver. He will take you wherever you wish in the city. Please do not travel any other way. Heinrich, look after Beata well, won't you.'

'Of course, sir,' he replied, with enthusiasm that signalled his affection for his commanding officer.

I wondered if Heinrich, with his innocent boyish face, understood why he was away from his sisters and his dog in Germany, and what was the fate that awaited him. We passed further down the hall to another office. I noticed the solid lock on the door.

'This will be your office. You should keep it locked when you are not there – or doing confidential work,' he added, with a meaningful look.

It was plainly furnished with desk, typewriter and a filing cabinet.

'My office is next, over here,' he said.

The door remained closed to view.

'Now, you will need to settle in. I have a housekeeper who will show you your quarters.'

My life fell into an unexpected routine. I had not thought that the work of a senior officer of an occupying army could be so mundane and undemanding. It was so. The purpose of occupation was to ensure that as little as possible should happen; the status quo should be maintained. From time to time there were disturbances, as resistance groups attacked the occupying forces in whatever way they could and, while the army was involved, the work of counter-resistance essentially fell to the Gestapo. Almost all of the paperwork crossing Colonel Engel's desk dealt with the everyday trivia of army life; the remaining ten per cent or so was gold dust. He passed it to me and I photographed papers dealing with troop disposition, numbers and equipment. There was an unbroken flow of information, constantly updated and changing, which I recorded and passed on to London. Each week I made a drop to a dead letter box identified by London through the nightly broadcast from the BBC and decoded from Bunyan. There was a ring of these spread throughout Oslo, in parks and open spaces, galleries and museums, and it was not difficult to deceive my driver, Heinrich, on the pretext of country walks or visits to places of interest. In any case, he had the curiosity of a farm labourer when it came to the city. I learned that he was from a small village in Hanover; his father grew cabbages, turnips and white asparagus and his mother and sisters sold eggs. He knew how to plough and mend fences; he knew nothing of, and cared less for, the intricacies of warfare. He learned to drive on his father's tractor and his outings with me were a weekly pleasure to which he looked forward with childish delight. He had the blonde hair and square jaw of the Saxon. He was a sweet boy and I became very fond of him.

I spent the evenings alone in the first weeks of that early summer of 1942. My small bed-sitting room on the first floor had a view of the harbour between the protruding rooftops. I used to sit by the window after supper and watch the life of the city flow by. I did not miss people: the colleagues from the Polish Embassy had decamped to London at the time of the invasion and the Norwegian staff had melted away into the city. My only contacts in the British Embassy were Jonathan and Marta. Jonathan was in touch nightly through the cryptic news broadcasts but I thought often of Marta, who knew nothing other than the fact of my arrest and disappearance. Theresa, I assumed, was operating alone, and I felt for her in her ignorance of the truth. Jonathan would tell no one of my work for fear of betrayal, and that included Theresa. So it was not difficult to be anonymous in the city: no one would remember Camilla Andreassen for very long.

Beata the young German was my reality now and I played the role to perfection.

August came and went. The early Norwegian autumn showed itself in the yellowing trees and the morning mist over the fjord. All summer I had listened to the gramophone through Thomas' open window as he played his Verdi and Puccini recordings. One evening he knocked on my door. His tunic was open at the collar.

'I wonder, Beata, if you would care to have a glass of wine with me – to celebrate my birthday,' he said.

'Of course, I would like that,' I replied.

We went down the stone staircase to his apartment. I had not set foot in it before. The furnishings must have been as he had found them in 1940: bare sanded floorboards with woven carpets, painted eighteenth century chairs and chaises longues, a tall rococo mirror and an ormolu clock on a marble fireplace. Heavy tapestries of pseudo-classical hunting scenes hung from the walls. His books and records were scattered by his chair. He went to a sideboard, picked up a bottle of Alsace wine from an ice bucket and poured two glasses.

'Happy birthday, Thomas,' I said. And we drank his toast.

'What is your real name, Beata? I think it is time I knew that.'

'I've had several since I came here,' I replied, 'but my real name is Maria.'

'Maria, I am forty-one today. How many more birthdays will I celebrate before this war is over, I wonder?'

'I wonder that too.'

'Tell me about yourself, Maria. How did you get involved in this work, a young girl like you?'

'I was brought up in a family where freedom was important, I suppose. Then I saw a young free-thinking boy murdered on the streets by fascists and I drifted into this.'

'And your parents?' he asked.

'My father was a professor of mathematics at Kraców. He and my mother were arrested when the Germans invaded Poland. They disappeared, I suppose to a camp.'

'My God, I am so sorry.'

He walked across to his pile of records on the floor and lifted them up.

'You see, Puccini, Rossini, Verdi – no Wagner. I hate his anti-Semitic tirades and his super-hero bullshit.'

'I'm afraid I don't know opera. I spent too much time on mathematics,' I said.

'But they are the same thing, are they not? Music and mathematics express the beauty and complexity of relationships. You should learn to love opera,' he said with enthusiasm.

'I would like to very much,' I said.

'Very well, I will show you.'

And he picked up a record and placed it on his gramophone. It was the most beautiful sound I had ever heard. That was the start of it. Each evening we would sit in Thomas' beautiful simple room and he would play me a new piece from his collection. I learned to love the yearning melodies of Puccini, Mozart's intricate race of notes and the dark colours of Verdi. Then I heard Purcell and the sad cadences of *Dido and Aeneas* played on gentle English strings. It was a new life for me, the doors to a beautiful world had been flung open, in the middle of the oppression that lay all around me.

Thomas was the most gentle of men. His life as a soldier was about honour and duty, values he had inherited from his family. He rejected cruelty. I witnessed the tragedy of his position each day, chained to an evil regime by the fear that desertion would bring harsh punishment on his family in Germany.

'This is how it is, Maria, you see. The criminals who run my country will not hesitate to destroy my family if I reject their evil empire. I have nowhere to turn.'

I understood his pain but could do nothing to help him. But I became his confidante, the only person in the world to whom he could speak his mind, who knew his true feelings. I doubt even his wife in Berlin understood the tragedy of his position.

It was brought home to Thomas on an almost daily basis.

The papers that crossed his desk, the reports that he had to act upon, recorded the reprisals, the executions and the imprisonment of blameless citizens by the regime which he represented. The weary months trailed by and the war seemed eternal. We both yearned for release but saw no sign of redemption.

One day in late afternoon Heinrich had driven me to Bygdøy where I intended to make a drop. He never seemed to consider it odd that a humble secretary to his colonel should be given a chauffeur-driven car for her amusement. I had left him at the road-end to the beach, a favourite summer haunt of bathers in the summer. The footpath wound its way through the woods before reaching a low stone wall. Behind a removable stone was a cavity which we used for drops. I slipped the package into the gap and to my surprise felt resistance. Inside I felt an envelope, which I quickly removed and hid in my dress, depositing my drop quickly and turning away into the woods again. Heinrich was surprised to see me return so soon; he was leaning on the car in the sunshine smoking a cigarette.

'Take me back Heinrich please,' I said, 'I'm not feeling too good. I have a headache.'

'Sorry, to hear that miss. Just sit back and I'll get you home in no time.'

I was agitated by the unexpected letter and went straight to my room when I got back to Akershus. I tore open the envelope and inside was a note in handwriting I recognised. It read: *"My Dear Maria, Your network has been broken and all of your agents have been arrested. Theresa has escaped capture so far and gone underground. I will contact you again. My love, Jonathan".*

I slumped down on my bed in a cold sweat. My hand was shaking. I was not in danger myself since I had already been arrested but I thought of the dozen or so people in my network, rounded up, tortured no doubt, giving their information at the end as they always did, and then summarily executed. I thought of Theresa, alone somewhere, waiting for the Gestapo to follow up a lead and knock on her door at two in the morning. The thought was too painful. I crumpled, my head on my knees, and wept. I stayed like that for some time, how long I do not recall. Then I fell asleep on the bed in a state of deep depression, welcoming sleep as an escape but waking frequently to the renewed horror of it all. I must have drifted off eventually for I awoke in the semi-light of dusk to a gentle knock on my door. It was Thomas.

'Maria, are you alright? Heinrich said you were not well.'

He walked across to my bed and sat down. He put his arms around me and I rested my head on his knee. I was crying and he stroked my hair gently.

'Tell me what is wrong,' he said.

I told him the story and he listened in silence.

'I have a contact at Vika Terrassen,' he said. 'I'll find out what has happened to them. Do you have names?'

'No, I only knew them by their cover names,' I replied.

'Yes, of course. However, I'm sure I can get some information.'

'Thank you,' I said, and my hand touched his.

I felt his firm grip and I returned it. I don't know what I felt except that our relationship changed for ever that day. I knew that. Perhaps looking back it was inevitable.

In these days I learned the meaning of betrayal for the first time in my life. The irony was that Thomas and I were brought together in a totally unexpected way. The message from Jonathan came as a shockwave which blasted the peace and routine of my secret life. It sounds paradoxical, I know, but nothing exciting had happened to me since I had moved into my quarters at Akershus, except for my growing friendship with Thomas and my burgeoning love of his music. The rest was silent and predictable. I dealt with his private correspondence, kept his diary and answered his telephone. I was a familiar figure in the castle, known to all the gardeners, domestics and the garrison. I was treated with the utmost courtesy and affection by all, as the commandant's personal assistant. I suppose my German had a tinge of Polish about it, but it must have been slight, and my fluency drawn from a childhood in a house where German was the second language, and the language of cultured exchange, was complete.

The nightly coded messages; the anonymous letter boxes; and the endless waiting – these were my real tasks. In between, I spent the days in splendid isolation. Thomas was driven each day to the administrative headquarters in the city, where his official work took place. This I knew little about. He would return to his private quarters each evening; only if he carried papers did I know I had work to do, in processing them and passing them on through the courier network. The message from Jonathan was a hammer blow; it reminded me that my life hung by a thread, that the sword was poised precariously above my neck.

And yet nothing followed. The network had been wound up, certainly, but I had not been betrayed. The nightly coded messages began again and I learned that a new set of drop points was in place for the couriers, whose chain had not been broken. Three months later I learned that Theresa was back in business, with a new network. It seemed a miracle of reconstruction that was almost implausible. It was as if nothing had happened; the flow of documents to London continued uninterrupted and Theresa's network once more supplied information from the ground.

A week after the message arrived from Jonathan, Thomas knocked on my door one evening.

'I've got some information about the network,' he said. 'Apparently, it was a tip-off. Full list of names and addresses, all except for your sister, of course. Does that make sense?'

'I can understand how I escaped,' I replied, 'since I was already dead as far as the Gestapo was concerned. Any information about me would lead to a dead end, literally. But Theresa must have known the round-up was coming and escaped before her identity could be revealed. That can mean only one of two things: either she betrayed the network herself; or Jonathan did so, after alerting Theresa to the danger. Theresa would not betray her network since that would mean giving away her own identity, since one of her people, at least, was bound to crack. It all points to Jonathan. He was the only one who knew the identities of both networks.'

'What possible motivation could he have to do such a thing?' he asked.

'Only one, Thomas. He needed to give the Germans something.'

'You mean he was a double agent?'

'Yes, and his credibility was being stretched, so he sacrificed the networks to show he was still worth something to the Germans.'

'And meanwhile he protects Theresa so that he can later resurrect a new network to keep the British happy?'

'Not only that,' I said. 'He still has me in place, supplying the best material of all. And worse than everything, the world thinks I betrayed the network following my staged arrest. He has a ready-made scapegoat you see.'

Thomas paced the room, deep in thought.

'You realise what this means Maria? He can betray us to the Germans whenever he wants and that is the hold he has over us. If we try to reveal this to the British, the Gestapo will be on to us immediately.'

'But we have a hold over him too, in a way. If he betrays us, we can betray him back. It's a stalemate, and he's banking on that to keep his career on track, whichever side wins the war. We have no choice but to continue to supply him with information and let him play his game,' I said. 'Jonathan will be safe in the knowledge that we will have arrived at this conclusion. He is no fool.'

'And what about Theresa? Won't she have worked this out too?' said Thomas.

'No doubt,' I replied, 'but if she has any sense, she will be working undercover. Jonathan may be contacting her through the agreed channels, but he won't know where she is. In contrast, we are sitting ducks.'

'This is a dirty business, Maria. Don't you feel betrayed?'

'Betrayal – honour – truth? I don't think I know what these words mean any longer. We are part of a deadly game played to rules that were kept hidden from us, until it was too late to say we didn't want to play after all,' I replied. 'I once thought I was in love with him – in another life, that is. But I learned he could never love anyone but himself.'

Thomas walked across the room towards me and took my hand.

'You have been hurt,' he said. 'I'm sorry. You are too young to be alone in the world, this filthy world we live in now. I can't help thinking I got you into this. How can I help?' he said.

'We need to go on,' I said. 'There is an end to all this – somewhere.'

And so we played Jonathan's game to his rules, in the knowledge that we were serving the same cause as before. But we began to question what Jonathan's endgame would be. At the end of the war, how would he deal with our knowledge, so dangerous to him, except by disposing of us? This was the man I had trusted, the man I had thought I had loved.

I had suspected for some time that Thomas was in love with me but that his old-fashioned sense of propriety prevented him from showing it. Whether it was loyalty to his wife back home, or a fear that I might feel he was taking advantage of me, he held back, channelling his feelings into kindness. But that evening in my room, with the sense of betrayal burning into us both, he broke the spell. And it was with a surge of joy and relief that we faced each other honestly and openly.

'When I look around me, Maria, I cannot escape the horrors that have taken over my life. The cruelty, the persecution of innocent people, the immorality of my country. The war has made me a man of peace. This gun is an obscenity to me.'

'You can do no more than you have,' I replied. 'I'm here because you wanted to end the war; and so do I. What can we do other than serve out our time in the way we have chosen?'

He led me to the window and we looked out across the courtyard below. The lights of the city cast a dim glow in the sky and we could hear the rattle of the trams and the sounds of traffic moving on the city streets.

'No, there has to be more,' he said. 'We just need to find the way. We have to stop Blake before he goes further.'

'And how do you propose we do that?' I asked, gazing up into his eyes.

He bent down and kissed me; we were locked together in this, by circumstances we had not chosen, but more than that, by a deepening love that we were only just discovering within ourselves.

'Don't worry, Maria, I'll find a way out of this,' he said.

Events showed us a possibility. Christmas 1942 was approaching. It was a bleak midwinter of ice and snow and unmitigated war. I was working in my office one morning when the motorcycle courier arrived with his messages. I opened the bag and, among the usual collection of letters and communiqués, there was something different – a personal letter for Colonel Engel marked with the Swedish state crest. I placed it unopened on Thomas' desk. Later that day he returned from a visit to Frederikstad, where the German army had based a large force to defend the eastern border. He looked exhausted and depressed. The constant pretence was beginning to wear him down. I took some coffee into him and found him leafing through his mail.

'Anything useful here?' he asked.

'Not much,' I replied, 'but there is a personal letter with the Swedish crest on it. Here it is.'

I picked it out from the pile and handed it to him.

'You read it please, Maria. My eyes are seeing double at the moment.'

'His Excellency the Ambassador requests the pleasure of your company for cocktails at 6 pm on 20 December 1942. RSVP The Royal Swedish Embassy, Oslo.'

'Oh, God,' he groaned, 'another boring evening with stuffed shirts. Send an acceptance would you please, Maria, and say I will be accompanied by a lady. You don't mind do you?'

'No, it's my job, remember.'

'Not the letter – the party,' he said. 'I need someone to talk to.'

He looked over the top of his glasses at me.

'Oh,' I said somewhat confused. 'Alright, but won't it be full of high-ranking officials and their wives?'

'Exactly. That's why I want you beside me, Maria. To keep them away,' he replied smiling.

He rose to his feet and rubbed his eyes.

'Why don't you lie down?' I said. 'I'll give Ebba the night off. I'll make some supper later and we can listen to music together. You will feel better.'

We lived a strange life in those days. To the outside world we were simply what we appeared to be: a conscientious senior army officer and his personal assistant. I often thought that Ebba, the Norwegian housekeeper, must have realised our closeness to each other, Thomas and I, but Heinrich was too engrossed in polishing his car and dreaming of home to notice anything. The fact that I accompanied Thomas to dinners with other officers meant nothing, nor did the inevitable conclusion others drew that I was Colonel Engel's mistress. There was nothing unusual in this. But our real lives took place in an interior world that we created for ourselves, a world of camouflage and concealment and of an ever-deepening love for each other.

Later that evening we sat in Thomas' drawing room listening to a recording of Mozart's clarinet quintet. Other records were scattered on the floor. Suddenly Thomas spoke.

'You know Maria, I shall never return to Germany.'

'Where will you go?' I asked.

'I shall go to England I think. To my blue remembered hills. I don't suppose you know Houseman's poetry, do you? He was a classics don at Oxford and wrote poems almost entirely about a lost childhood in Shropshire.'

'What about your wife and children, Thomas?'

'Ah yes, my wife, my wife,' he mused. 'My German wife. I married the daughter of a Prussian general. We never really loved each other. We married for career and the dynasty. These months I have spent with you have shown me that. I want you to come to England with me, Maria. Europe will be in turmoil after Hitler has lost the war. England will go on for another thousand years, drinking tea and playing cricket, among its hedgerows and its spires.'

'I think you are a lost romantic, Thomas. Does a country like that still exist anywhere but in your memory?' I replied.

'Where else does anything exist but in our minds and our memories? Answer my question,' he ordered, taking my wrist firmly.

'I promise you, if we survive this, I will come with you, wherever you go. I have nothing left in Poland, even if the country survives the war.'

Our fates were sealed together from that moment.

At five-thirty pm on 22 December Heinrich pulled up in front of our quarters with the official car, resplendent in its livery. The journey to Nobels Gate took us along the harbour front and past Vika Terrassen. It was the shortest day of the year and a chill wind blew off the fjord into the black night. We were in the heart of German power in Norway and I felt a shudder as I thought of the fragility of our situation. Thomas, in his full dress uniform, sat like stone beside me, looking out of the window at the frozen city. We passed the great blank edifice of the Universitets Bibliotek and drew up in the courtyard of the Swedish Embassy. Armed Swedish soldiers were on guard.

'Why so many?' I asked Thomas.

'The deal with Germany is fragile at best,' he replied, 'not to mention the possibility of an attack by the Norwegians who think the Swedes are traitors for staying neutral.'

Inside was a glow of light. The ambassadorial drawing room was ablaze with crystal chandeliers. The Ambassador, who Thomas had told me was called Magnus Lundquist, greeted his guests at the door, wearing his sash of office above his tailcoat. He was six feet tall, upright and at ease. His butler announced our names and we stepped forward to shake hands.

'Colonel Engel, how good of you to come,' he said in perfect German.

Thomas introduced me as Beata Schmidt, his personal assistant.

'Miss Schmidt, it is a pleasure to meet you. I hope we will find time to talk later in the evening.'

And he bowed to touch his lips on my hand. I dismissed this sentiment as politeness until, half an hour later, from the mêlée of guests, I watched Lundquist steering towards me, as I stood holding my glass of champagne, feeling awkward. Thomas was engaged in conversation with two other officers a short distance away.

'Ah, Miss Schmidt, or may I call you Beata? You must tell me how it is to live in the Akershus Castle. Is it not rather bleak up there, on that rock?'

'Not bleak at all,' I replied. 'The view is wonderful across the fjord and the city. And we have a delightful garden surrounded by stone walls where the apple trees grow. I used to sit there often on summer evenings. I believe the gardener is Swedish, married to our housekeeper, Ebba. They were at the castle before the war.'

'Of course, I recall Thomas mentioned the fact, now that I come to think about it. And you, Beata, what are your interests?'

'Colonel Engel has taught me to love music,' I replied. 'We listen to music together sometimes in the evenings.'

'So that is what being a personal assistant means,' he said, with a glint in his eye. 'He is a keen admirer of the English, is he not? And so am I. Is it not a great misfortune that we have been pulled apart by events?'

He looked closely at me as I thought out my reply, as though his question were a test.

'He spent happy years in Oxford, before the war,' I said.

'And so did I,' replied Lundquist with enthusiasm. 'You know, Beata, I would very much like to talk to you and Thomas again. Perhaps we could have a little private supper together in the New Year.'

'I'm sure Thomas would enjoy that,' I said.

With that, his attention was taken by another guest and he drifted away. Thomas had returned to my side.

'It's time we went,' he said. 'Can't take any more of this. What was Lundquist on about?'

'I'll tell you in the car,' I answered.

Five minutes later we joined the general migration through the double doors to the waiting cars. As we bade our adieux to the Ambassador, he turned to Thomas and said:

'I enjoyed my talk with your assistant, Thomas. Camilla will tell you what it was about.'

I could feel Thomas stiffen at the sound of my Norwegian cover name but he hid his shock very well. In the car I closed the glass partition between us and Heinrich and turned to Thomas.

'He knows, doesn't he?'

'He certainly knows something. I should have corrected him about your name. The fact that I didn't shows I know it too. What did he talk to you about?'

'He wants to meet us in private, he said.'

Heinrich drove us back through the city to Akershus. I held Thomas' arm firmly. I was afraid. Something was about to happen and I felt I had no control over it.

Chapter 7

Christmas and New Year came and went uneventfully and the war dragged on. One morning in mid-January, a fine clear day with little wind, I was walking in the castle garden. The trees were dormant and the rose beds covered in straw against the frost. Björn was sweeping leaves from the paths, his head bowed against the cold. We had often met here, in the most beautiful corner of the castle grounds. We spoke little but Björn knew I loved his garden as much as he did and that gave us a common bond. He was a kind, gentle man, caught up in the merciless tide of the war. He bore no grudges and asked for no explanations. Life was what it was; no more, no less. I don't think he thought of me as a German. He surprised me this morning by approaching as I sat on a bench by the frozen fountain.

'Good morning, Miss Schmidt,' he began, while he searched in his pocket for something. 'I have a message for you. Here,' and he held out an envelope.

'A message for me?' I asked. 'Who gave it to you?'

'Can't answer that, Miss Schmidt. You just take it and that's my job done.'

He looked at me calmly and then walked off to resume his sweeping. I put the letter in my coat pocket and walked back along the outer wall to the quadrangle where my office was located. Heinrich was polishing the official car and he gave me a wave as I approached.

'Fine day Miss,' he said. 'Are you driving anywhere today?'

'Not sure yet, Heinrich. I'll let you know,' I said, as I turned into the corridor of our building.

I sat behind my desk and opened the letter. It was handwritten on a sheet of Swedish Embassy notepaper, with the three crowns at the top. I knew at once that it must be from Magnus Lundquist; I also realised instantly that it had come to me by way of Björn, and not via an official route, in order to avoid tracking. The message was short and in a bold, sloping hand:

My Dear Beata

I hope you were not dismayed when I last spoke to you. You will know, of course, I needed to be certain. There is something we have in common that we must address, with Thomas. Please trust Björn. He is with us.
Magnus Lundquist

It made sense now. Lundquist was asking if it was safe to contact us. I could only assume that what we had in common was the problem of Jonathan Blake. That evening I showed Thomas the letter.

'He wants us to contact him for a meeting, it is clear. But not here. This must be done outside official boundaries. I don't want to put anything in writing. Will you speak to Björn tomorrow? We need to suggest a meeting place. You're the expert, Maria. Any ideas?'

'I think I know the perfect place,' I said. 'I'll speak to Björn tomorrow.'

In my mad, early days in Norway, when I had nothing to do but play, when the sun never set in that short northern summer of thirty-nine, when I fell in love with Jonathan although I knew him to be a rogue, he took me to a summer house on an island in the fjord. It was the weekend summer retreat of the Ambassador, but never used, the perfect hideaway for him to take his succession of impressionable young women. We swam in the warm water of the fjord and made love in the flower-decked meadows. It seemed it would last forever. The irony was that it now provided the perfect location for a meeting we did not trust. Rule number one from Hertford House was to control your exits and your entrances. An island was the perfect location. No access except by boat meant that we could control who came and went. I would take my Browning and Thomas his Lugar, just in case Lundquist was not what he seemed.

The next morning I spoke to Björn. He was in his garden shed sharpening tools for the summer. His blue eyes looked out from a weather-beaten face, the face of a mariner.

'You have a message for me, Miss Schmidt?' he asked.

'Yes, Björn, I have. It's about a meeting with Lundquist,' I replied.

He put down his file, took up a stub of a pencil, and found a scrap of paper from somewhere on his bench.

'Go ahead,' he said.

'Tomorrow, twelve o'clock. Take the airport road out of town. Turn off on the Slemmestad road as far as the left turn to Konglungen. Half a mile down there's a track through the forest to a wooden jetty and a fisherman's hut at a place called Spira. I'll be there at twelve. Got that?'

'Alone?'

'No, not alone.'

He put the paper into his pocket and took up his file again. He said nothing so I turned to leave.

'Miss Schmidt, the spring will soon be with us again,' he said.

'Yes Björn. It has been an awful winter. I long for the sun.'

That evening Ebba served us in Thomas' dining room. I looked at her homely peasant face, inscrutable and passive. Did she know what Björn knew or were we simply foreign intruders to be tolerated but never welcomed? The thought of my deception brought tears to my eyes.

'What is it, Maria?' asked Thomas.

I could not formulate my emotions at first. Then it came to me.

'Oh the loss of it all,' I replied. 'Where have the years gone, Thomas?'

'This will be over one day, my love, and you can be a young girl again, believe me.'

'Perhaps, ' I said.

That night I stayed with Thomas and we made love for the first time. It had taken him that long to overcome the weight of his past. Together we had nothing to lose; our futures lay together just as we lay together that night.

The morning broke eerily grey. The mist on the fjord swirled, vanished and reappeared in the light breeze, opening vistas of the pale morning sun at one moment only to close together at the next, like a curtain swaying. We both were nervous of what the day might bring, since Lundquist remained an enigma. Thomas had given Heinrich a day's leave, which he probably would spend in a bar in the city, coming back to the castle after hours looking the worse for wear and feeling guilty in the morning. Ebba was like a mother to him and would keep him away from the Colonel's attention as long as possible. So at eleven, an hour after the winter sun rose on that January day, we set off in the official car with Thomas at the wheel.

'You'd better tell me where we're going,' Thomas said, as he steered the car through the streets down to the City Hall steps.

'We're going to an island,' I said, 'but Lundquist doesn't know that yet. That way we have control of the situation. He will meet us at a small jetty down the fjord. Take the Drammen road until the Slemmestad turn-off. I'll direct you from there.'

'How do we get to the island?'

'By boat. I know where we can find one.'

Thomas looked across at me and smiled.

'The British certainly trained you well,' he said.

The road out of Oslo skirted the shore of the fjord, passed the airfield and headed out into the countryside of grey rocks and fir trees. There was a covering of snow on the road, which deepened as we travelled further. The mist gathered and swirled around us, wreathing the still water in a mysterious light. After twenty minutes or so we turned left on to a snaking narrow road following the indentations of the fjord, with sharp rises and falls and hairpin bends. There were no other cars. A little further along we reached a hamlet called Vettre.

'Turn left here, at the sign to Konglungen,' I said.

The road became no more than a pot-holed track between fields on the left and dark woods on the right. I felt nervously in my coat pocket for the hundredth time to check I had my pistol with me. If Lundquist was going to ambush us, it was going to be here. But there was no one in sight and no tyre tracks in the snow.

'Pull in just ahead,' I said, and the car slid to a halt. I got out and walked a few yards along the edge of the wood bordering the road. I wanted to check a clearing where I had told Lundquist to take the track through the trees. It was deserted. No car was parked, nor footprints visible. I got back into the car.

'Good. We're ahead of him. Drive on down to the end of the road. We can park the car there and take the boat back round the point to the jetty. That way, if Lundquist is not alone, we can approach from an unexpected direction, and we have a way out.'

We drove on a half-mile until the winding road ended at a small harbour, surrounded by a few white-painted wooden houses. Thomas parked the car behind a ramshackle shed, out of sight.

'Where do we go from here?' he asked.

'By boat,' I replied. 'Follow me.'

I led the way out along the jetty to a small wooden clinker-built boat with a blue canvas canopy over the cockpit. I untied the painter and hauled the boat into the jetty.

'Let's go,' I said, and jumped aboard, followed by Thomas.

I primed the engine twice, turned on power to the glow plugs three times, as Jonathan had taught me, and then pressed the starter button. The engine turned over a few times and then chugged into life, pumping black diesel fumes into the air. I shoved the engine into reverse and headed out into the fjord, turned the boat around and steered round the point towards Spira. It took no more than ten minutes to reach a point from where we could see the wooden fishing hut where we expected to meet Lundquist. The mist hung low over the water and through the grey shroud I began to make out the shape of a man. I cut the engine and we slid slowly forward on the glassy water. Thomas cupped his hands and shouted

'Lundquist!' The figure turned towards the sea:

'Engel, is that you?'

'Are you alone?' shouted Thomas.

'Yes, I am.'

'Come down then. We'll pick you up.'

I steered into the jetty and Lundquist climbed aboard. He shook our hands.

'Where are we going?' he asked.

'To the island,' I said, pointing out across the water.

'I understand,' he said. 'Why should you trust me?'

I steered the prow towards the dark shape in the distance, aiming at a wooden bathing house at the base of the cliffs. A few minutes later we tied up in a tiny bay and clambered up the wooden ladder to the jetty. I led the way up a steep path through the fir trees and then across a meadow to a wooden house at the highest point of the island. Under a stone by the door I picked up a key and opened up. My mind went back to Jonathan and the blissful weekends we had spent here and I felt a burning sense of regret that it was over, that the world had grown up.

Lundquist and Thomas followed me into the house, down a hallway and into the main room. It was a simple Norwegian interior, dark wooden walls with hanging rugs and carved furniture. In a corner a white stone fireplace stood with birch logs already in place. Thomas struck a match and lit the tinder, which flared up quickly while the softwood logs caught. We drew our chairs together before the fire. Lundquist spoke first.

'I owe you an explanation,' he began. 'I'm sorry to have surprised you, but I needed to be certain. If you had corrected me I would have had doubts. This way I could be certain. I need you to help me, you see.'

'Help you in what?' Thomas asked.

Lundquist paused, then gave us a steely stare.

'Get rid of Blake, of course.'

'What do you know about Blake?' I asked.

'As it happens, Beata – or should I call you Camilla? – quite a lot. You see, I'm not just here to hold cocktail parties and shake hands. We Swedes too have our intelligence services and we work closely with the British. You could say, I have a foot in both camps. What better for them than to have helpful neutrals in the middle of the German empire? Yes, we know all about Mr Blake's exploits. We know about his placing you, Camilla, and we know about Thomas' role as well. For a while the British were happy to feed titbits to Blake in exchange for real information. Then Blake got clever and got his hands on real stuff. The second front is coming. The Allies want to stop the leaks, quickly. And sacrificing the whole network was thought to be a step too far simply to give you a cover, Beata. What's more, you want him stopped too, don't you?'

'Why do you think that?' asked Thomas.

'Obvious, Thomas. He wouldn't want you left standing when the war ends, to reveal his treachery when the Allies have won. Your fate is already sealed, and yours Beata. It's just a matter of time. I'm sure you have worked that out.'

'Of course we have,' said Thomas, 'but why don't the British just arrest him now?'

'War and politics are not far apart,' Lundquist replied. 'The British don't want to reveal a traitor at the top of the Service at this stage in the war. Bad for national morale and for credibility with the Americans. They want to kill two birds with one stone, as they say. Get him killed while on undercover duties behind enemy lines and they have a hero on their hands, at the same time as getting rid of a major threat to allied security. His death would be just another case of British heroism.'

'And where do we come in?' I asked.

'You, Beata, are the honey in the trap.'

There was a long silence. Thomas stood up and threw another log on the fire.

'We will need proof,' he said, 'before we commit to this.'

'I assumed you would.'

Lundquist took a small book from his pocket and handed it to me.

'This is my code book. You can return it to me when we

meet again. London will broadcast my code name tonight through the usual channels. The name is "Condor". Take the first letter of each word that is sent. That is my proof.'

I took the book from him. It was a leather-bound copy of the New Testament in Swedish. Lundquist looked at me and smiled.

'You can trust me, Beata.'

'I hope so,' I said. 'By the way, how did you know my cover name was Camilla?'

'One of your network was working for us, of course. We tracked you from then on.'

There was a silence. All of a sudden everything seemed paper-thin. It looked as if Lundquist was indeed the only way out for me.

'I don't suppose we have any coffee in this place, do we?' Thomas asked.

I went into the kitchen and found the remains of a packet of ground coffee, enough to make a pot, set the kettle to boil on the electric stove and found three cups.

'No milk or sugar, I'm afraid,' I announced on returning, 'but it's hot at least.'

We drank our coffee in silence.

'We need to know more about your plans to deal with Blake,' I said.

'Of course,' Lundquist replied, 'but we should keep that until you have seen my proof of identity. We must meet again. I will be in touch through Björn. We should go now.'

We retraced our steps to the mooring by the bathing house. The mist had lifted a little and the water lay like a mirror, reflecting the grey sky above. We cast off in silence, Thomas in the bow seat, Lundquist in the middle and I at the helm. At Spira, Lundquist clambered on to the jetty and stood to watch us depart. His long grey coat and homburg hat gave him a sinister air. He raised his left arm to wave to us and we retreated into the mist, only the rhythmic beat of the diesel engine breaking the silence of the eerie day.

'Do you think we can trust him?' I asked.

Thomas turned in his seat.

'We will find out tonight, but I think so,' he said. 'If not, we have little chance of finding a way out of this. By the way, how did you know about this island, the house and the boat?'

I smiled at him.

'I used to come here with Jonathan when we were lovers, in another life, that is. I'm now about to betray him. Is there anything in life that remains true?'

Thomas looked out across the fjord as we slid silently through the water.

'Not a lot, Maria, but we can at least try to make it so, you and I.'

That evening, a few minutes before eight, I tuned into the BBC broadcast with my copy of the Swedish New Testament open on my knee. The radio crackled and then the constrained English voice came over the airwaves from London. I was trained in the techniques and had no difficulty in noting down the numbers I needed, which I wrote in columns on a sheet of paper. Then I turned to the New Testament and carefully wrote down the first letter of each word I had identified. There were six letters in all; they spelt the word "condor". I breathed an audible sigh of relief. Thomas looked up from his papers.

'What is it, Maria?'

'It's alright,' I said. 'He's genuine.'

'Thank God for that.'

Chapter 8

Next morning I deliberately walked in the garden, hoping that Björn would have a message for me. I was not disappointed. It was a bright clear day. Björn was at work in an avenue of lime trees, lopping and pruning last year's growth. When he saw me approaching he laid down his saw and moved towards me. He handed me a folded piece of paper and touched his cap. I read the message. The meeting was to take place that evening at eight o'clock in a safe house run by the Swedes. The address was in the east of the city, near the old town, a collection of cobbled streets and wooden houses surviving from the eighteenth century. I nodded to Björn and he returned to his work.

Thomas was working in his office at the castle that morning. I found him in shirt sleeves, poring over a map of southern Norway with a young officer, discussing the disposition of garrisons in the area. He looked up when I entered. He seemed drawn and tired, weary of the life of concealment that he was forced to endure.

'Yes, Beata?'

'I have some papers for you to see, Colonel Engel,' I said.

'Very well. I'll come through in a moment. I think that should do it for now,' he said, turning to the lieutenant, who folded up the map, saluted and left the office.

Thomas joined me in my office and I showed him the message.

'I think we should travel separately,' he said, 'to avoid too much attention. I'll ask Heinrich to take me in the car. He can drop me at the Old Aker Church. What about you?'

'I can take the Ekeberg tram,' I said. 'I know the way.'

'Very well. Let's agree to meet there then. I wonder what Lundquist has to offer us,' he said.

A memory of Jonathan flashed before my eyes and I felt a sudden pang of regret. How I longed to be back home now, in safety, studying my mathematics in my old academic world. Despite the fact that I had taught myself not to look back, nor to expect a future, I could not hold back the tears as I thought of the waste of it all. Thomas saw it.

'What is it Maria?'

'I came into this because I thought I could save lives. Now I see that I must be involved in betrayal.'

'He betrayed you first, remember. I'm betraying my country because it has betrayed me. You have been loyal throughout. Ending Blake's betrayal is just being loyal to your country. I know this is very hard. You have a full life to live ahead of you. Just take this one step and we can be clear of this for good. Believe me.'

'I hope I can believe you,' I said.

At seven o'clock that evening I walked through the gatehouse of the castle. The guards showed a little surprise to see me, as I did not usually go out alone at night on foot. It was a cold black night with few stars and a grinding frost clamped the ground. It took ten minutes to walk to the tram stop, where a straggle of people stood huddled against the cold, waiting for the Ekeberg tram. It rattled round the bend at last, yellow interior lights shining out into the black night, and drew to a screeching halt. My journey was no more than a few stops. I watched the squares of light from the tram windows trip across the frozen snow of the pavements as we headed east. At Stenberggaten I got off and began the walk up the hill along Akersbakken. I could make out the square tower of Old Aker church on the hilltop, looking over the city as it had done for centuries, and I wondered if Heinrich had already driven Thomas there. It was dark; the street lamps threw pools of white light on the snow-covered pavement but there were shadows everywhere. I felt alone and a little afraid. I looked around to check I was not followed. Suddenly I heard my name whispered and I turned round to see Thomas emerge from a shadowy doorway.

'Thomas, thank God it's you,' I said.

'I knew you would walk this way. I hope I didn't frighten you,' he said.

'Yes, but I'm pleased to see you. I was feeling less than brave.'

I put my arm through his and we walked on up the hill.

Number twenty-four was an ordinary block of city apartments facing directly on to the pavement, with a double door opening into an inner courtyard. A list of names, each with a bell button, was fixed to the wall. We looked at each other: we had no idea where we were going. We were searching down the list of residents for a likely clue when a figure crossed the courtyard towards us.

'Colonel Engel, Miss Schmidt, good evening.'

I recognised the voice immediately.

'Björn, it's you. What are you doing here?'

'I'm not just a gardener, Miss Schmidt. Please follow me,' he replied.

He led us across the courtyard to a far corner and up three flights of narrow stairs to a small landing. He opened a door with a key and we followed him into a tiny hall and then a living room not much bigger. Behind a table, whisky glass in hand, stood Magnus Lundquist, smiling his self-possessed smile. He could have been another Jonathan Blake.

'Thomas, Beata, thank you for coming. Whisky? Björn you know. He's a specialist in these matters..... as well as gardening, of course. Do sit down.'

We took our places round the table and Björn filled our glasses, with single malt whisky from a Highland Park bottle.

'How on earth did you get this?' asked Thomas.

'It's not only agents the Shetland Bus brings,' replied Lundquist with a smile. 'You could say I have a standing order.'

I felt the whisky glow on my tongue and I could almost smell once more the hillsides of my Scottish training camp. I thought of Irena for the first time in years and felt a deep sorrow.

'OK, let's get down to business,' said Lundquist. 'Björn, if you please.'

'We have been aware of Blake's double-agent status for some time. The message from the British was to let it run – they were getting more information coming their way through Blake, than was getting through to the enemy. Only Blake knew your identity, Colonel and Miss Schmidt, but together you are a source of invaluable information that the British did not wish to lose. We began to suspect what was going on when Camilla Andreassen was apparently arrested. That was from our agent in your network, Miss Schmidt. It didn't take us long to see what Blake's plan was and your contact with the Colonel showed us where your information was coming from.'

'Do the British know our identity also?' asked Thomas.

'No, they do not at present,' answered Lundquist. 'We thought it better to complete this deal before saying anything. You understand I hope. A leak about this in London could alert Blake to our plan.'

'And what is your plan?' I asked.

'Our plan, Beata, is to capture Blake alive and de-brief him,' said Lundquist, looking me straight in the eye as if I were invisible. 'He knows a great deal about German intelligence that we and the British need to know. After capture, we will take him to Stockholm, where he will be kept until the war is over. In the meantime, the British will report his death in honourable circumstances as a hero of the war. British intelligence will join us in the Stockholm de-briefing.'

Björn rolled out a map of Oslo on the table and pointed to an area north of the city. I recognised the forest tracks of Nordmarka.

'If we can get Blake to return to Norway,' he said, 'we can expect him to use this dropping zone here at Kopperhaug. In the winter months there is a large frozen lake there. Blake has used it several times before. The resistance have maintained it throughout the war, undetected so far. It's located about six kilometres north of Tryvann. He would travel by cross-country ski from there.'

I remembered our last meeting at Nordmarka Chapel. It all made sense.

'And how do you propose to get him here?' I asked.

There was a lengthy silence. Björn turned to Lundquist, who poured himself another whisky. Then Lundquist said:

'We want you, Beata, to ask him to meet you. As simple as that.'

'It may be simple but why do you think he will fall for it?' I asked.

'Because Blake has a weakness which will eventually finish him. He cannot resist the dashing gesture, no matter how reckless, especially when it is to help a beautiful young girl in distress.'

He smiled that chilling smile once more. I was a pawn in the game that these men were playing and Lundquist was determined to triumph.

'What do you want me to do?' I asked.

Lundquist thought for a moment before he spoke.

'You must send him a request for a meeting. Use the formula you agreed with him. Say it is a matter of life and death. Suggest a meeting at Nordmarka Chapel as before. And wait for a reply. Then we act.'

'If he takes the bait,' continued Björn, 'we will be with you all the way, have no fear. We plan to travel cross-country by ski from Ullevålseter, where we will leave a car. It is only a matter of a few kilometres to the chapel along forest ski tracks. Once we have him in our hands we will transport him to Sweden on a diplomatic flight.'

'You have it all worked out very nicely. All you need is for Beata to put her head on the block,' interrupted Thomas. 'Well, I want to be there too. Beata and I are in this together.'

Lundquist turned to Thomas with a smile.

'I knew you for a man of honour, Thomas. I expected you would accompany Beata, as you have done for a while.' And he gave Thomas a knowing look. 'I think our business this evening is concluded. I await with interest the outcome of your communiqué, Beata. Björn, if you would shut up shop.'

And with that we left the building and crossed the courtyard to the street door.

'Heinrich will be waiting by the church, Maria. We can

travel together,' said Thomas.

'Do you think it's safe?' I said.

'Heinrich would die for me, if not for the Führer,' he replied.

I put my arm through his and walked on in the darkness. It felt good to be near my solid, honourable Thomas and away from the schemers of Lundquist's world. Sure enough, at the street corner, under the looming church tower, Heinrich was leaning on the car, smoking a cigarette, which he extinguished as soon as he saw us.

'Home, Colonel?' he asked.

'Yes, home Heinrich.'

The following day I woke very early after a fitful night, my mind racing through the thoughts of the evening before. Thomas was still asleep beside me and I slid out of the bed gently and tip-toed to the window overlooking the harbour. The lights of the ships shone through the black morning, a faint orange glow in the east showing that day was still far off. If only Thomas and I could step out now on to the England boat that I had watched so many times cast off from Vippetangen before the war, to sail off into the wonderful pastoral world that his memory had created. But it was as impossible as his vision was unreal. Instead we had a harsh reality to face. Today I had to send a message to Jonathan to lure him to his destruction and to deliver our salvation. I decided that it would not be enough to send out a distress call: Jonathan had already shown himself to be cold-blooded in his willingness to sacrifice others in pursuit of his great ambition. No, it had to offer him something that was so enticing that he could not resist it, even despite the obvious dangers. So I sat down and scribbled the message: "I have information of such importance and urgency for Mr Rodgers that I must deliver it in person. Camilla". Then I encrypted it and placed it in an envelope ready for transmission through the courier network. If he came back with the expected rendezvous point so much the better; if he chose another, Björn would have to plan something in a hurry; if he didn't take the bait at all, the British would have to deal with him in their own way.

After breakfast that morning I asked Heinrich to drive me into the city. We had a collection point at the north gate of Frogner Park so I asked Heinrich to drop me at the main gates on Kirkeveien, on the pretext of my taking a brisk walk round the park in the clear air. I set off at a pace over the frozen snow, past the gallery of sculptures leading to the fountain and up the flights of steps to the monolith. There were few people in the park, the trees were bare of leaves and stood out like black skeletons against the snow. Beyond the monolith lay an unvisited park of the park, where Vigeland's vision had never been completed, and behind a loose stone of the park wall I placed the letter for collection. It should be cleared later that day. I looked around to check I had not been observed and headed off to complete my walk, getting back to Heinrich fifteen minutes later.

'All set, Miss?' he said.

'All set, Heinrich. Back to the castle please.'

My calculations were that the message would reach Jonathan in two days. I did not know if he would reply by the same method or by the radio broadcasts but I guessed it would be by radio, three nights from now, if he were to respond at all. We had three nights of waiting and wondering, at best.

Back at the castle, Thomas was at work in his office. He called me in and I closed the door behind me.

'We need to move fast Maria,' he said. 'I've just had Berlin on the telephone. General Von Rosberg is flying in on Friday for a visit of several days. You'd better be around then.'

'That gives us only five days. If Blake doesn't respond quickly, the plan could fall apart.'

'We'd better let Lundquist know. Can you talk to Björn?'

Suddenly our salvation seemed to hang by a thread.

Two nights later, Ebba served us supper in Thomas' sitting room. We sat at a small antique table in the window and drank his favourite Alsace wine. We said little but we both knew that if Blake smelled a rat from my message, he might easily sell us to the Germans to protect himself. We knew that a knock on the door in the early hours was a possibility and that our days together might be numbered. It brought us closer together. After supper, Ebba cleared away. I caught a glimpse in her eye of something I had not noticed before, something between sympathy and understanding, as if she knew what we were going through. It was unspoken but almost tangible and I was moved by it.

At a few minutes to eight we turned on the radio and tuned in to the nightly broadcast from London, my *Pilgrim's Progress* on my knee. There was no signal, no coded information, merely the usual account of the wartime events of the day, from the British propaganda machine. The tension of waiting was ratcheted up a notch; we were running out of days.

The next evening we followed the same procedure, gathering round the crackling radio a few minutes before eight. The London broadcast usually lasted no more than fifteen minutes and we were ten minutes into it when I heard the familiar clearing of the announcer's throat as a signal that a message was coming. I listened for the first number, which was the identifier for the agent. It was my number: thirty-five. I got ready to write down the numbers which came thick and fast in the next few paragraphs – numbers of aircraft shot down, prisoners taken, miles progressed. Then a second clearing of the throat, to indicate the message was complete. I took the columns of numbers and opened the requisite page of my Bunyan. The numbers translated into three short words: "chapel, Thursday, seven". It was on. I breathed a sigh of relief that something was about to happen at last; at the same time feeling a growing fear of the danger in which I was about to place myself.

Thomas heard my sudden intake of breath and looked at me expectantly.

'It's Thursday night, Thomas, and where we expected it to be,' I said. 'We'd better tell Björn immediately.'

'So this is it,' he replied.

'This is it. This time tomorrow, if all goes to plan, we will be free of Blake forever and we will have a future.'

Chapter 9

The sun fell below the western horizon at three o'clock that afternoon. The clear blue northern sky gradually translated to an inky star-studded dome as the red glow of the setting sun faded. I watched from the window of my room, the minutes and hours ticking by as my fateful meeting with Jonathan approached. Once, I used to long to be with him; now I dreaded the prospect.

At five Thomas came to my room, clad in his heavy outdoor clothing. The temperature had plummeted to fifteen below.

'We are to meet Lundquist at Ullevålseter at six,' he said. 'I've given Heinrich the night off. I'll drive. They will issue us with our gear then.'

'Does that mean guns as well?' I asked.

'I suggest you take your Browning. I shall certainly be armed.'

The road to Ullevålseter was narrow and winding, leading out of the city and heading north into a forest wilderness that stretched as far as the eye could see. The road was icy and black and more than once the car skidded off into the verge. Thomas was silent but I could sense he was on edge. After a few miles our headlights swept round a bend and illuminated a snow-covered clearing within a semi-circle of log cabins. Lundquist was standing there, beside his car, waving us down.

'Thomas, Beata, welcome. Blake dropped at Kopperhaug two hours ago,' he said. 'We have it from the resistance. Are you ready for this, Beata?'

'As ready as I can be,' I replied, trying not to reveal my nerves.

'Good. We have your winter equipment here. You'd better get moving,'

Björn appeared from the darkness and took us both into one of the log cabins where we found white alpine clothes and cross-country skis and boots. In the gloom of the cabin, I picked out at least six human shapes.

'Who are these?' I asked.

'British special forces,' said Björn.

I could see they carried sub-machine guns as well as side-arms.

'They look frightening,' I said.

'They are,' he replied. 'They crossed the Swedish border this morning from their base in the mountains. They will keep you safe. We leave our vehicles here and travel to the meeting place on skis. We'll bring Blake back here and he will be over the border this evening, all being well.'

A few minutes later we set off through the pine forests to Nordmarka Chapel. The British soldiers led the way along a narrow forest ski track. They were experts; I was adequate, but no more. It was as much as I could do to hold my place in the column. Thomas, Lundquist and Björn followed. It was a clear sky and through the gaps in the tall firs above I caught glimpses of the crescent moon. We travelled in silence, only the smooth swish of the wooden skis on the dry powder snow and the sounds of breathing audible. After twenty minutes or so the skier in front of me stopped and I pulled up alongside him. The five men in his troop had vanished unnoticed into the forest.

'We should halt here, Miss Schmidt,' he said. 'We are only two hundred yards from the chapel. My men are in position around it. You need to go on alone. Remember I shall be tracking you at a distance, with Colonel Engel and Herr Lundquist. You have nothing to fear. Good luck.'

I turned and caught Thomas' eye in the darkness and a tremor of a smile. Then I set off to traverse the longest two hundred yards of my life. The darkness was oppressive and the boughs of the trees reached across the track to form a tunnel. Although I knew I was surrounded by armed guards and observed by watching eyes, I felt utterly alone and afraid.

After what seemed like an age I reached the clearing

where the chapel stood. In the winter light it seemed a haunted place, unlike the rustic building I remembered in the summer sunshine. I saw no light and heard no sound. I unclipped my skis and stepped forward to open the wooden door, pushing forward into the entrance hall. The silence was palpable. Stepping forward slowly my foot caught the end of a pew and I knew I was in the main church. As my eyes became accustomed to the light I began to make out the pale silver of the moonlight through the windows. I whispered into the darkness:

'Jonathan, are you there?'

There was no reply. Then I heard the click of a Zippo lighter and saw the flame against the cigarette end.

'Maria, my beautiful Maria. How good to see you.'

In the glow of the cigarette I made out the silhouette of Jonathan's face. He was sitting on the step in front of the simple stone altar; behind him a crucifix and two candlesticks, one of which he proceeded to light. The candle threw a gentle light across the small nave, the wooden stave walls and the simple pews.

'Let me look at you.'

I walked slowly towards him, as if in some kind of trance. His magnetic powers had not deserted him.

'As beautiful as ever, I see. You summoned me Maria, and I came. Now you must tell me your reason,' he said. 'What is this great piece of information that I must know?'

Suddenly, the whole situation seemed impossible to explain. It was a lie that had lured him here. What could I say now to explain myself, except the truth? There was nothing else.

'I think you know, Jonathan. You have betrayed Thomas and me. We are at your mercy. You can deliver us into the hands of a deadly enemy whenever you wish. You planned the murder of a dozen loyal agents simply to promote your own interests. You have no loyalty to anyone or anything except yourself. I wanted you to know that I know all this. You have made me the instrument of your downfall but you are the cause of your own destruction.'

I had not planned these words but they spoke my true feelings.

'Yes, my own destruction, you say. Do you think I am not aware of this, Maria? I have made a great career from betrayal; I am an astounding success in that field, an unrivalled performer. But I am Dorian Gray, outside a thing of beauty, immune to decay; inside, a seething mass of corruption.'

'I don't understand you. What do you mean?'

'Do you think I would have undertaken this trip if I did not wish to end it?'

'You mean, you know this is a trap?'

'Of course. I know that I am surrounded and this is the end for me. I knew as soon as I got your message that you were the bait in the trap. My treachery was known. Either the British would drag me through a ghastly trial for treason at home, ending with the noose; or I could go out in some romantic way like this, caught in a frozen distant landscape, taking my last stand against the odds. It was appealing to me as well as the British for me to go this way. I can still be a hero although we all know it is a fraud.'

'Lundquist was right,' I said. 'He said you could not resist the dramatic gesture and it would be your downfall. What will you do?' I asked.

'This,' he said, drawing a revolver from his coat pocket.

At first I thought he meant to shoot me but he turned the gun to the side of his head. I screamed and at that very moment the church was plunged in darkness as the candle fell over. A single gunshot shook the room. I saw nothing but heard the clatter of boots and felt Thomas grab me and drag me out of the nave into the freezing air. I gasped as if I were surfacing from minutes under water. Then I found my breath. I was shaking.

'Is he dead?' I asked.

'Yes,' said Thomas, 'I saw him fall. You are safe now.'

Lundquist appeared from the church door, gun in hand.

'You two get back to your car and drive back to the city. We'll take it from here,' he said.

Thomas and I quickly put on our skis and retraced our steps. Our tracks were easy to follow and in no time we reached Ullevålseter. We dumped the skis and alpine dress in the hut, jumped into Thomas' car and drove back into the city.

'Are you alright, Maria?' he asked.

'I think so. Just a bit shaky,' I replied.

'I'm not surprised. That was a brave thing to do. But he's gone from our lives now, Maria. We can begin to think about the future, when this damned war is over.'

I reached across the seat and took his arm, burying my head in the thick cloth of his greatcoat. It felt solid and warm, like Thomas himself. Suddenly I was dead tired and I think I must have passed out because the next thing I heard was the sound of the gatehouse guard checking us through the barrier.

That night I slept intermittently, waking frequently from a shallow sleep in which I saw visions of Jonathan's face in the half-light of the church. I woke in the dark, relieved that it was all over, but seeking the comfort of Thomas' arm around me as reassurance. When morning came at last, the world had changed. Our horizons were new and different and I began to feel the possibility of happiness. I was not the betrayer; I was the witness to Blake's self-destruction, no more than that. It was not until three days later that we heard of the outcome of that night's exploits.

At eight I tuned into the London broadcast. Among the various items from the world at war came the news of the heroic death of the super agent Blake, dying behind the enemy lines, after years of brilliant service to the Empire. Britain had achieved its aim of eliminating a dangerous traitor and simultaneously celebrating a hero of the cause. It was sleight of hand of the greatest subtlety. I turned off the radio and slumped back in my chair. I wondered what price my ideals now. Was this a game I had been playing all along according to somebody else's rules?

My life with Thomas returned to routine. The passage of information to London continued uninterrupted for more than a year while the Third Reich waited for the inevitable end. Thomas and I knew that the endgame was upon us and in

June of forty-four it began.

'When the surrender comes,' said Thomas, 'I will have to stay with my men, wherever it takes me. You must return to your life of freedom. But I will come back, Maria, for you.'

It came the following year. I had slipped back into the city, using my Norwegian papers and the money I had saved during the war to rent a small flat in the east of the city, and became Camilla Andreassen once more. Day by day I watched the ships set sail, taking young Germans back to their ruined homes. Three months after I said goodbye to Thomas, I found I was carrying his child and, after the birth, I waited like Madame Butterfly for his ship to sail into the harbour. But, unlike Butterfly, it never did.

Chapter 10

It was some months after the birth of my child that I received a letter from Germany. It was addressed to me as Camilla Andreassen at the address I had given to Thomas when I fled from Akershus before the final surrender. The hand was that of a girl. I opened the letter with fear. It told me that Thomas and his regiment had been deployed to the Russian sector in the east of Germany until de-mobilisation had been completed. Thomas and his officers had been executed by firing squad after a brief showcase trial held by the Russians on the charge of war crimes. In the papers he had left to his family was a note of my address and a request that I should be notified. The letter was signed "Renate Engel", whom I knew to be his eldest daughter. His wife had either refused his request or, more likely, had disowned him upon hearing of his relationship with me.

I was alone once more. For days I seemed unconscious, only staying alive by instinct and routine. As time passed it seemed that living was more pain than it was worth and the desire to escape grew more and more pressing. It was in this state that I decided I needed to clear my life in order to end it and, with methodical calculation, I set about my plans. I had become known in the poor neighbourhood in which I lived as the woman who slept with the enemy. Oslo is a small city and it was inevitable that a Norwegian serving in Akershus by compulsion would one day recognise me in the street as the intimate of the enemy colonel. And so it happened. I was an outcast, rejected and scorned. I lived only on the savings I had, with no human contact. But I had a baby who had his own life to live even if I did not value my own. Such clear thinking brought relief: I had a course to follow. I wrote to the only person I thought might help me to fulfil this plan, not

Theresa, who I later discovered had left for England, but Marta, dear understanding Marta.

My plan worked for, a few days after posting the letter to the old safe house, Marta came to see me. She did not ask if I had betrayed my people in return for safety, nor did I speak of it. She saw my state and understood. I asked her to help me and she did. She took my baby away and I never saw him again, until many years later, as you know. Marta came to see me again two weeks later and told me what had happened. My baby was in England with Theresa and Stanislaw, thanks to a British officer at the embassy. I felt a deep sense of relief, amidst the horrors of my loss, to know that my child was in another country with another life ahead of him. And this was a turning point in a way: there was something to live for after all.

I took the only work I could find and started as a cleaner in the house of a Norwegian professor in the west of the city. I took the tram across town three days a week. It was peaceful work and a civilised house. It reminded me of my family home in Kraców. There was a library full of books and a quiet garden reaching down to the sea. I was happy with the routine, which stopped me from thinking of my poor dead Thomas and my lost child. Professor Magnussen was a widower, living on his own, in a cavernous nineteenth century villa overlooking the fjord. On the three days a week I worked there, I prepared an evening meal for him before I left. One evening he asked me to join him, so we sat in his kitchen and ate our meal together.

'Tell me Camilla,' he said, 'why is a clever young woman like you cleaning my house for me?'

'What do you mean, Professor?' I replied.

'I know you have suffered in life,' he said. 'It shows on us all, but I have watched you reading my books as you dust them. That is a real clue. I have never known a cleaner who knew what books were for, except to trap dust.' He looked at me with his deep-set blue eyes. 'Tell me about yourself, if you will.'

It was the first time in months that anyone, except Marta,

had acknowledged my existence. I swallowed hard but began to cry. The Professor left his chair and put his arm around me.

'Come, my dear. I am so sorry to have upset you.'

'No, please, it is not your fault,' I managed to say. 'It's just that I felt I was talking to my father.'

'Your father? Yes, I suppose I am old enough for that,' he said with a smile. 'Tell me about him.'

It took me a while to overcome my tears. The professor poured us coffee and held out a cup to me. I took a sip of the heavy roast coffee, a luxury after the privations of the war.

'He was a professor like you, but in mathematics at the university of Kracόw. When the war came he was arrested with my mother for holding liberal views. They died in a concentration camp.'

'And you? What happened to you, Camilla?'

'I fled to Norway. It is a long story. I fell in love with a man and had his child.'

I said nothing of my secret life. What could I say? Jonathan had taken Maria Bienkowska and turned her into a spy in a foreign land. He then made me disappear into the maw of the German war machine and I was officially dead. Now the only two men who knew the whole story were also dead; Blake by his own bullet and Thomas by a Russian one. Of Lundquist I knew nothing. I felt it would be hopeless to try to prove my innocence of treachery without a living soul to support my case. And anyway, could I ever go back to my old life, without Thomas and without my child?

'And your child now? Where is it?' he asked.

'Safe in another country, with a new life,' I replied. 'With my sister and her husband.'

The professor paused.

'I think I understand,' he said slowly. 'Your child was half German?'

'Yes, the father was a German officer I worked for. He died at the hands of the Russians when he returned to Germany after the surrender. He was a kind man and a scholar. He taught me how to love music.'

'And our wonderful democracy, which we fought to save,

treats you like a traitor for falling in love with the enemy, I suppose. Loving someone can never be betrayal, my dear. You have no guilt in this. But tell me, why do you not go to this other country, to be with your child again?'

'Because my child will have a better life without me, I know that. What I have done is for his good. He has a father and a mother who will love him. I cannot offer him that.'

'You are very brave,' he said, holding my hands in his, 'very brave.'

That was a Monday, I seem to remember, and when I returned on the Wednesday of the same week, Professor Magnussen called me into his study.

'I have been thinking, Camilla, about what you told me. Tell me, did you attend university yourself in Kracòw?'

'I had started my second year there,' I replied.

'I thought so. Would you not like to start again, here in Oslo?'

'But how could I do that? I have no money, other than this small wage, and I need to pay my fees.'

He looked at me gently and smiled kindly.

'My dear Camilla, why don't you live here? This house is far too big for me. I rattle around here on my own. Nothing would give me greater pleasure and you can pay me by looking after my simple needs. Shall I speak to my colleagues tomorrow? You are a mathematician, I suppose?'

And so I became the daughter he never had and he the father I had lost. I learned to love him very much. I started at the university that autumn and my name became Maria Bienkowska once more, a citizen of the country where I had chosen to make my home. My life had come full circle. But I often thought of my child, how he was growing up, and whether I would ever see him again.

My life became simple, as simple as it had been before I left Poland on my mission to fight the evils of the world. I became modest in my expectations. I wanted no more than to learn my mathematics and to pay my debt of care to my guardian. It was a world contained within itself and I felt at ease there. My mathematics was the world in symbols and I could shape it and create new patterns as if I were its ruler. It seemed I had an instinct for it that surpassed what could be taught; my teachers called it genius. And as time marched on the real world faded and the mathematical formulae I manipulated took its place.

Once, after a couple of years, I wrote to Theresa in England, at an address which Marta had given me. The reply was curt and dismissive. All she knew of me was that I had survived the war and that my child was the son of the enemy. My treachery could not be forgiven and I had no strength to try to defend myself. A little later I wrote again but my letter was returned unopened. My only contacts with the past were my occasional meetings with Marta, to whom I eventually told my story. She said I should write it down as my testament; but it took the real endgame of life to make me do it. She told me my little boy's name was Peter Kingsmill.

I finished my degree with the top grade of my year and took up a junior research fellowship, which turned into a lectureship. I left my home with Professor Magnussen and set up in a small flat near Blindern, handy for the university. And this was how the years passed, publishing papers, attending symposia and enjoying sabbaticals. I became a treasure of the faculty, unmarried, a strange mysterious middle-aged woman, popular with students and colleagues, unfathomable. I remember Marta telling me in 1965 that Peter was studying in Cambridge; in 1972 she told me he was in London with the Foreign Office; and then in 1986 she gave me a cutting from *The Times* listing senior Civil Service appointments. I saw Peter's name and his promotion to under secretary. Six months later I was diagnosed with cancer and given twelve months to live. The desire to see him before I died became unbearable.

I told Marta over tea in Halvorsen's konditori near the parliament house.

'I'm not sad to be dying,' I said, 'but there is one thing I would want to do before I go.'

'I think I can guess what that is,' Marta said. 'You want to see Peter, don't you?'

'It has become an obsession for me,' I replied, 'but I can't just turn up out of the blue, claiming to be his long-lost real mother, when he has spent his life not knowing me. I want him to decide if he wants to see me, and I want him to discover the truth if he wants to. I never wish to place an obligation upon him.'

'I don't understand how you will do that,' Marta replied.

'But I do,' I said, with a smile. 'I've been thinking about this for a long time and I don't have much time left to me.'

And that is when I set in motion my plan and sat back to wait, in hope that my son would find me, in certainty that death would. It was a matter of timing.

PART THREE: REDEMPTION

Chapter 1

North Yorkshire, December 1988

I dropped the bundle of papers on to the floor and rested my head in my hands. The fire had burned low in the grate. I looked at my watch: it was four o'clock and the house was silent. Alexi must have gone out with Katie, no doubt to Helmsley, and I had not heard the door. Then there was the unmistakeable sound of the Land Rover drawing up at the end of the passage leading from the main street, the slamming of car doors and the rush of feet as Katie sprinted up to the front door. I could hear the knob rattle and imagined Katie reaching up on tip-toes to open it. Next the living room door pushed open and my new little girl bounced in.

'Peter, Peter, look what I've got!' she shouted, and from a very small bundle in her arms I saw poking out the tiny wet nose of a black-and-white puppy.

'Well,' I said, 'and what's this, Katie?'

'This is Rosie and she's the great granddaughter of Bess,' she replied.

'Who's Bess?'

'Grandad's sheep dog,' and I remembered the border collie I had met at Rievaulx Cottage.

Just then Alexi came in, shaking the rain off her coat. I saw her eyes go to the floor and the bundle of papers I had thrown there.

'How was it, Peter?'

And I thought, what shall I say? That it was fine, and let's forget all about it, pretend it never happened, it has nothing to do with me.

'It was grim,' I said, 'and I don't really know what to do about it.'

'That's not like you. Would you like me to read it?'

'I think you should,' I said.

Rosie slithered out of her woollen packaging and landed on the floor, rolled over and staggered to her feet, tail so active the whole back end swayed from side to side. Alexi gave me a long-suffering look.

'I had no choice, Peter. Hope you like dogs. Dad's old friend called in while we were there with three of them. I was ambushed.'

She laughed and I joined in. Happy people, I thought, go through life collecting things that make them happy, without thinking about the consequences. I thought of my neat and tidy past life and my clutter-free existence. Now, all I wanted was to let it happen, let it happen.

'Well as a matter of fact, I love dogs, Alexi,' I said, as Katie dissolved in childish laughter, rolling on the floor with Rosie, 'almost as much as I love you.'

Alexi took off her coat and hung it in the hall, while I gathered up Maria's papers.

'Do you want to read these now?' I asked.

'Why not, if you'll keep an eye on Katie and her new friend.'

'Of course.'

I built up the fire and Alexi settled down beside it. I trusted her judgement absolutely. I was weighed down by a sense of the injustice Maria had suffered. I felt I had to act but in what way? Or was it just guilt for not taking this woman to me when I had the chance? Katie and Rosie were the perfect antidote to my black thoughts. The puppy had fallen asleep on the fireside rug when her mistress came up to me with a look that said "I want something".

'Peter, I think Rosie needs some food and she hasn't got a bed to sleep in,' she said.

'Quite right, Katie. Why don't you and I go and buy her what she needs? We can leave her here while she sleeps. Come on!'

I saw the little girl's eyes light up. We bundled on our coats and jumped into the Land Rover, where the child seat was. It would take us ten minutes to get into Northallerton before the shops closed and I thought there must be a pet shop there somewhere. Sure enough, in the main street I spotted one after a drive up and down examining each side of the road. Katie chose a tartan dog bed, a blue lead and collar, with a barrel for the telephone number, and two bowls with a picture of Snoopy on one and Pluto on the other. We picked up some tins of puppy food, a bag of biscuits shaped liked bones and, for good measure, a rubber bone which squeaked. Armed with our supplies we drove back to the cottage, to find Rosie quietly chewing a chair leg while Alexi waded through the papers. She looked up as we entered.

'How are you getting on?' I asked.

'Half way through.'

'Any thoughts?' I asked.

'No, Peter, not yet. I want to hear yours first.'

She was right. I couldn't slide out of this. I was the one who had made the first decision; I had to be the one to see it through. I looked around the room, at Alexi, at Katie, at our new dog. After all the manoeuvring, all the pretence, all the competition and the striving, this is what I wanted most of all: to love and to be loved in return. I thought of Maria, who had lost everything, and my rejection of her in Oslo. It wasn't cruelty or callousness on my part; it was fear to commit, to become involved. But I was involved and I had to repay her sacrifice. My mind was made up.

'Alexi, we should get married soon,' I said.

'OK,' she said, with that turn of the head I remembered from our first meeting a lifetime ago.

'Mummy's already told Grandma that,' said Katie, and went back to coaxing Rosie into her new bed.

We didn't talk about Maria for a day or two. New Year's Eve was upon us and we were invited to Rievaulx Cottage for dinner but Maria was in my head and I thought I was going to find it difficult to break free. We drove out of the village around six o'clock. It was a clear, cold starlit night and the lights of the towns along the Tees glowed to the north.

'You're very quiet tonight, Peter,' said Alexi. 'Don't think too much, will you.'

'I've been thinking a lot these last two days,' I replied, 'but I don't think I need to any more. I know what I have to do. It's just I'm afraid to get started. When I came back from Norway, I thought it was all over. I now know it was just the beginning.'

'I came to the same conclusion a while ago,' she said, 'but I wanted you to make your own decision. I agree with you. Let me help.'

'You know what my decision is, then?'

'You want to see the truth is known about her, don't you?'

'I do, but does anybody care?'

'You do, so what else matters?' she said.

I looked across to Alexi. She was looking ahead as we drove along the narrow winding road. How could she be so balanced, have such clear vision, and so young? It was as if she could not only read my thoughts but predict what the next one would be. I smiled, then laughed quietly.

'What are you laughing about?' she asked.

'Oh, just you... and Katie... always one move ahead of me. Talk about being outnumbered.'

We had reached the main road into Helmsley and turned right down the hill. I found I was looking forward to the evening after all. Rievaulx Cottage was ablaze with light. The Christmas tree lights shone from the living room window and the front door was draped with fir branches. A brass reindeer bell clanked as we pushed it open. Christmas was clinging on before the arrival of the New Year wiped the slate clean. In the hallway Rosie and Bess wrapped themselves round everyone's feet as the young dog tried to chew the older one's ears. Andrew appeared from the living room, wearing a collar and tie. I was glad I had made the effort to smarten myself up as I had a suspicion that the tradition of dressing for New Year's Eve might apply. He shook my hand vigorously and then took Alexi's coat. For the first time in a long time I noticed how beautiful she looked. I was so used to jeans and a baggy sweater, it came as a surprise to see her in a dark navy dress, shoulders bare, with a white silk rose at her breast, and single pearl earrings. She looked beautiful in a grown-up, sophisticated way which made me feel like an awkward schoolboy again, full of doubts that this magical girl was too good for me. Katerina had sprinted into the kitchen, before long appearing gripping Angelina's hand. She caught me in a strong embrace and I could see her eyes switching from Alexi to me, as if to check that we were still the perfect couple she wanted us to be. She smiled broadly without reserve. Once more I felt myself drowning happily, bewitched by the simplicity and warmth of my new family.

At ten Katerina was persuaded into her bed and Andrew and I sat by the fire in the living room, smoking cigars. I had not smoked since my evening with Wotherspoon but I wanted to keep Andrew company. The taste was surprisingly pleasant although I took care not to breath too deeply.

'You've made Alexi very happy, Peter,' he said.

'That's good of you to say so, but I think it's probably the other way round. My life has changed beyond recognition since I met her.'

'It's good to make a new start in life,' he said wistfully.

'You must miss your farm,' I said.

'Aye, I do that, but there's no point in fretting over it. Best just get on with life. Mind you, it was a sad day for all of us when we had to leave Brock Hall Farm.'

'That was the name of the house?' I asked.

'Aye, sounds grand, doesn't it. Nevertheless, it was a fine sandstone house, albeit seen better days, with a steading round it. A thousand acres of fields and moorland. There were six cottages on the land too, all let out to workers. The Grieve's Cottage was a good size too.'

'What happened to them?'

'Cottages standing empty, the workers off to the town to find jobs in factories. There's no sentimentality in farming, Peter, not when money's involved.'

It was approaching midnight. We went into the front garden and stood under the stars waiting to see the fireworks at midnight and hear the church bell strike. A crowd had gathered by the market cross, mostly peaceful, except for a few lads, drinking from cans, who would probably not make it home before morning. At twelve the bells struck and the fireworks from a few back gardens shot up into the sky, showering coloured lights in patterns against the darkness. Alexi came up to me and put her arms round my neck.

'Happy New Year, Peter. Nineteen eighty-nine is going to be a good year for us,' she said. 'I know it.'

'I suppose we'd better do something about getting married,' I said.

'In hand. We're seeing Father Caldwell on Tuesday.'

'A Catholic priest! I'm not a Catholic any more,' I said.

'Who cares? Just make it up as you go along. Nobody will notice. Anyway, it's a beautiful church and Mum likes the idea.'

'Outnumbered, I told you!'

On Tuesday morning Alexi and I set off in the Range Rover to our appointment with Father Caldwell.

'This is all very mysterious,' I said, as I drove down the hill. 'Where are we going, exactly?'

'I want you to meet someone special. He's been a friend of the family for twenty years. But don't expect the usual,' she replied.

'Is there such a thing, when it comes to priests and vicars? I'm not at all sure about all this, Alexi.'

'Don't worry, Peter, just let it happen,' and she smiled that smile she used when she knew I was exactly where she wanted me.

'OK, you'd better be navigator when we get to the A19.'

'We're going to Richmond. You know the way?'

At the bottom of the hill we crossed the main road and headed towards Northallerton, then along a winding road through rich winter farmland with hoar frost on the hedgerows and trees. The road skirted Catterick and soon we crossed the River Swale, brown water from the hills rushing in spate from the melting snow on the Pennines, and entered the ancient market square at Richmond. We drove in silence, lost in our thoughts; Alexi's were her own but I, strangely, returned to my conversation with Andrew on New Year's Eve and I suddenly felt a desire to see Brock Hall Farm where Alexi had been born.

'Your father was telling me about Brock Hall Farm the other night. He misses it a lot. I'd like to see it,' I said.

'We can go if you like,' she replied. 'It's empty now I think, and must be bleak at this time of the year.'

'Do you mind, Alexi?'

'No. We can do it on our way back. Turn left here,' she suddenly said as we reached a tee-junction. 'His house is along this lane, I seem to remember.'

We pulled up outside a low cottage standing at the end of the lane on its own, a copse of bare ash trees behind it and a meadow leading down to the river. In the distance I could see the castle keep standing gaunt and grey in the winter light. Smoke curled from the cottage chimney and drifted in the light breeze.

'Doesn't look like a presbytery to me,' I said.

'It isn't – quite, and don't be surprised by who opens the door.'

We walked up the garden path between neat lawns and flower beds on either side. Alexi rang the bell and after a minute the door opened to reveal the face of a middle-aged woman.

'We're here to see Father Caldwell,' Alexi said.

'Ah, yes,' came the reply, 'he said he was expecting visitors. I'll show you into his study.'

We followed her down the hall and into a room at the end. Behind a desk by the window sat an elderly man, head bowed over a page of stamps, peering through a magnifying glass. He looked up and smiled and, as his face creased, recognition dawned on me.

'Father Dominic,' I said, 'I never expected to see you here.'

'Good heavens, it's Peter Kingsmill, is it not?'

Alexi looked at each of us in bewilderment.

'You two know each other?'

'Of course, my dear Alexi,' said the priest. 'Peter was the star bowler in the first eleven. I used to umpire the matches. Do you remember that game against Stonyhurst when we bowled them out for thirty-two?'

'I do indeed,' I replied, 'I think I took nine wickets, including a hat-trick.'

'Yes, and didn't you run out the tenth man with a direct hit from the boundary?' said Father Dominic excitedly.

'I think I might have.'

'Well, well, what a small world we live in. Now, you have caught me at my hobby,' he said. 'I can see you beginning to glaze over Alexi, but let me tell you the study of the Norwegian Posthorn definitives is a fascinating and complex business.'

'I'm sure it must be,' said Alexi, throwing her head back and laughing at the joke being played on her.

At that moment, the door opened and the housekeeper entered with a tray of coffee and biscuits.

'Thank you Dorothy. Now do sit down you two young people and we can have a chat.'

We looked around to find somewhere to sit: I cleared a pile of journals from a dilapidated leather chair while Alexi carefully lifted a large ginger cat from another.

'So Peter, you are going to marry my dear Alexi, are you? Well, I am very happy for you both,' said Father Dominic, munching on a Tunnock's caramel wafer.

'I'm very happy too,' I said.

'And when would you like to get married?' he asked.

I looked at Alexi and she answered.

'As soon as it can be arranged. How long will that take?'

'I can get a special licence in two weeks I think,' said Father Dominic. 'Let me see now,' and he thumbed through his desk diary, 'that makes it the 17th of January. How does that sound?'

'That sounds fine,' I said.

He turned to Alexi.

'I assume you want to get married in the church in Helmsley?'

And, as Alexi nodded in response, he added:

'I thought so. I'll get in touch with the vicar and arrange it. I see you're looking puzzled Peter. The village church is Anglican but the Reverend Paul likes a bit of Romanism too, so he's quite happy to have the other side there. Might be the odd parishioner dropping in to join in with the hymns but that shouldn't bother us.'

That was the last piece of business to be conducted. For another thirty minutes Father Dominic chatted on about Alexi's father and mother, about Ampleforth days, and the state of Yorkshire cricket. I could see Alexi becoming restless so I made a move.

'Don't you want to ask me anything about my beliefs, or bringing up children as Catholics?' I asked.

There was a silence. Then Father Dominic's face broke into a smile and he turned to me.

'My dear Peter, as always thinking ahead, and looking to find the honourable course. You haven't changed. "No", is the answer. I have seen too much of this world, and the mess that religions make of it, to know that when two good people like you and Alexi love each other, there is no need to set any rules or place silly burdens upon them. I will be happy to marry you as you are, my dear young people.'

And with that, we said goodbye. Alexi gave him a hug and I shook his hand firmly. We got in the car and drove out of Richmond.

'If that's religion, it's OK by me,' I said with a grin.

'It's not quite proper religion. His housekeeper was a boarding house matron at the college. I think they were caught *in flagrante delicto* in the back of the cricket pavilion. The Abbot couldn't put up with any more scandal so he persuaded the Bishop to give him a part-time job in the diocese. You know, standing in for absent priests, filling gaps and so on. That's how Dad got to know him. He rented one of the cottages at Brock Hall for a couple of years – with his housekeeper, of course!'

'Good old Father Dominic,' I said, 'he was a terrible teacher but a good umpire. Difficult to decide which is more important.'

We had reached the outskirts of Northallerton.

'You wanted to visit Brock Hall,' Alexi reminded me.

'Can you face it?' I asked.

'I think so. You'd better turn right here.'

We retraced our steps back to Osmotherley and drove through the village on the tiny winding road to Hawnby. After a few miles Alexi, who had been deep in thought, told me to take the next right, up the hill. It was a stony farm track, crossing fords and bottoming out in deep hollows, for what seemed miles. The track gained height and we soon reached the snow line. Black-faced sheep lingered by the track before scuttling off at the sound of the car and I was about to give up hope of getting anywhere when we took the brow of a rise and saw before us a sandstone house and a steading with an archway. The sun broke through the clouds and a shaft of bright winter light caught the stonework.

'But this is beautiful,' I said.

'I was born here,' Alexi replied, 'so I can't be objective, but I never liked anywhere so much.'

We parked the car in front of the house and got out. Close up, the signs of neglect were obvious: boarded-up windows, rotting doorposts and wild grasses growing through the gaps in the paving stones. A door in the steading hung from one hinge and the rafters were full of pigeons. But the Georgian style shone through the decay, despite the ravages of weather and time.

'This is terrible,' said Alexi. 'The farmhouse was supposed to become a shooting lodge, at least that's what the factor told us when we had to leave. That's my room up there,' she said, pointing to a window at the end of the building.

An unruly ivy hung down over the lintel, obscuring the glass. We walked around the building. I could sense Alexi's growing sadness and steered her back to the car. We descended the track once more in silence.

'I'm sorry I put you through this. It was selfish of me. I should have left it. But it's obvious the house is being left to wrack and ruin and nothing is happening with it,' I said, 'and something should be done about it.'

'And what do you propose?' Alexi asked.

I stopped the car and turned off the engine.

'Could you live there again?' I asked.

'I don't understand you. Don't play with me, Peter. Of course I could live there again. It was where I was born, for God's sake.'

'Well, what if we both lived there? How does that sound?'

'How?'

'We could buy it and you could live in Brock Hall Farm again!'

Chapter 2

Alexi and I sat in the bar of the Black Swan a week before we married, waiting for the distinctive sound of Father Dominic's motorcycle. He was late.

'Do you think he'll make it?' asked Alexi. 'The roads are icy and the forecast is for snow.'

'He'll make it alright,' I said.

At that moment I heard the sound of the Triumph engine coming closer and then dying as the rider shut it down. The door of the bar burst open and Father Dominic, resembling an overgrown Toad of Toad Hall, complete with leathers, goggles and helmet, strode in.

'My dear children,' he shouted, and a dozen silent faces turned from their glasses to see who disturbed their peace. 'So sorry I'm late. Had a bit of a slide coming over the top. Ended in a hedge but no harm done.'

'Let me get you a drink, Father,' I said.

'Thank you my boy. Most welcome. A pint of Ruddles and a double whisky should restore my confidence,' he said.

I ordered the drinks and joined Father Dominic and Alexi in our quiet corner.

'Cheers, Peter, and here's to you both. May the Good Lord look down upon you always.'

The whisky disappeared in thirty seconds, followed by half the Ruddles. Then Father Dominic spoke.

'That's better. Now, let's drink up and then we can go across to Saint Hilda's for a quick run through.'

I looked at Alexi and she looked at me, giving a shrug and a wink. We finished our drinks and walked across the market square. The wind was getting up and a fine snow was blowing across our faces.

Saint Hilda's church occupied a corner of the village

square, surrounded by the ancient gravestones of the past: merchants and farmers of the nineteenth century; weavers and millers of the eighteenth; and yeoman Catholic families of the Reformation who had witnessed the sacking of Rievaulx. The stones of Saint Hilda's told the story of England's religious history, of the melding of traditions, one into the other, of the compromising of the new ways with the old, and of the gradual drift into tolerance and ambiguity which forged its national church. The church building itself possessed the humble charm that old sandstone, Saxon doorways and Norman windows, when thrown together, still manifest in a thousand ancient places throughout the land. It had quietly filled a corner of the square for eight hundred years, give or take, and had accommodated old Catholics, new protestants, rampant evangelicals and enthusiastic liberals, with unruffled equanimity. With such a history it should not have surprised me that the Reverend Paul and Father Dominic could share the same altar and invoke the same God through different liturgies and different creeds; that a plaster statue of the Virgin Mary should stand surrounded by candles in a side chapel; that a frieze depicting the Stations of the Cross circumnavigated the walls; or that the centrepiece of the altar, in the midst of Rome, should be a plain brass cross.

We sat in the freezing nave of the church while Father Dominic rambled on about the ceremony. At last he declared himself finished and I suggested we adjourn to the Black Swan once more, to which he agreed after much unconvincing remonstration. I bought him another set of drinks and then, after twenty minutes of chat, he kissed Alexi on the cheek, shook my hand, and disappeared into the winter night.

'I hope he survives,' I said, listening to the sound of the Triumph fading as he rode up the hill.

'I'm sorry to put you through all this Peter,' Alexi said when we were alone. 'I know you would rather we got married without fuss but Mum is Italian, remember, and you will be her only son.'

'This isn't fuss, Alexi. It's just a sideshow to the real thing. You and me.'

But I did wonder what an Italian mother-in-law might be like.

The seventeenth came soon enough. It was a brilliant cold day, when the sun shone brightly without heat and the snow-covered hills threw back its light. Bill from the Queen Catherine drove me to Saint Hilda's in his leaking Land Rover. His immaculate appearance was truly touching. His suit was perfect, his hair smoothed down and he sported his buttonhole with the panache of a Durham miner on Gala Day.

'You nervous, lad?' he asked, as we entered the aisle.

'Actually, Bill, I am.'

'No need Pete. She's a lovely lass your Lexi. She'll do you proud. Enjoy the day. It might never come again.'

We sat in our places in the front row while the congregation slowly gathered and the hum of whispers gained strength. Bill kept a weather eye on proceedings at the back of the church. The foot-pumped organ kept trundling on, with the occasional missed note as the organist hit a faulty key. Then we all stood and before I knew it Alexi was standing beside me, resplendent in a cream suit with her dark hair up and her beautiful eyes smiling, with Katerina glowing with happiness in her bridesmaid's dress. I remember nothing else about the service but, in the upper room of the Queen Catherine, where Bill's wife had laid on a Yorkshire buffet, I met the truly ecumenical family of Alexi: Andrew's two spinster sisters, Molly of the Salvationist persuasion and Edna of everything else, except the Synagogue; an Italian Catholic brother of Angelina; and the methodist cousin of Andrew. Reverend Paul of the Anglo-Catholic faith turned up, alongside Father Dominic, and the two made short work of several pints of Marston's and the cold buffet. The star of the show was Angelina who made the impact of Sophia Loren, walking past a crowd of Genoese dockers, in some iconic Italian movie. Who can predict the future? Two months earlier I had been a lost soul in a dreary hotel in Stockton. I could hardly believe my good fortune. By ten-thirty we managed to escape across the road to our bijou residence in the cottage. We closed the door behind us with a sigh of relief, Alexi threw off her shoes, I got rid of my tie, and we laughed together, holding each other in our arms.

Next morning I awoke late to the sound of the telephone ringing. By the time I got to it, the answering machine was in action, and I heard a man's voice asking for Alexi Truman to call back. I had left her deep in sleep and didn't disturb her. An hour later I was in the kitchen when she came to me, still in night clothes.

'Peter, that was my newspaper. They want me to do another series for them.'

'That's great,' I said. 'What's the topic?'

'That's what I need to discuss. He mentioned something about the changing face of eastern Europe.'

'Sounds like a pretty big subject.'

'Especially since I don't know anything about it.'

'You will,' I said. 'So what's the plan?'

'I need to be in London for a couple of meetings the day after tomorrow.'

She came towards me and put her arms round my waist.

'Don't really want to leave you so soon. What will you do, all alone?'

'Alexi, you're being really naïve. You have a job to do and I have things to sort out too, like where we are going to live for a start.'

'And what you are going to do about Maria?'

'Yes, that too. I need to do some thinking.'

'Not too much, Peter.'

'I won't. For God's sake, you're only away two days.'

I drove Alexi into York the next morning for the London train.

'Where will you stay?' I asked.

'How about the Elizabethan, for old times' sake?' she replied with a laugh. 'And I could say hello to Francesco, if he remembers me.'

'He'll remember you, of course. He's a red-blooded Italian male. Phone me.'

At that point, the train pulled into the station and Alexi disappeared into her carriage. I remember feeling a strange jealousy that she should be leaving me so soon. I wanted her all to myself for ever. Then I pulled myself back into reality, waved her goodbye and set off to sort out my life. First, I called into Rievaulx Cottage on the way home. Andrew was out with his dog and Angelina was in the kitchen. Katie was at school and her puppy was asleep in front of the stove, in Bess's bed. Angelina gave me her usual overwhelming embrace and Rosie staggered to her feet wagging her tail enthusiastically.

'How nice to see you Peter,' she said. 'I take it Alexi is away now. She phoned me yesterday to tell me about it. I hope you are not too lonely so soon after your wedding.'

'Not so far,' I said, 'but I do miss her already. She keeps me sane. Where's Andrew?'

'On the hill with his dog. He goes there most days when he is not at the college. He really misses the farm, you know.'

'Yes, I can understand that. What about you?'

Angelina looked around and then said, with a wistful smile:

'Well, to be honest, I really miss my farmhouse kitchen most of all. It was so warm and busy. I had lots to do. I had a big vegetable garden with a wall around, and the hens of course. Like home in Italy, I suppose. We had a little land there when I was a girl. Alexi loved it too. She had a pony and could ride wherever she wanted. Yes, I really miss it some days. But we have Katerina to keep us busy and now her little dog too. You must have some coffee, Peter. I just made it.'

And she took a coffee pot off the stove and poured me a cup.

'Alexi took me to see Brock Hall, you know.'

'Oh, that surprises me. I didn't think she would do that.'

'It wasn't her idea. I asked her too. You see I wanted to check out an idea I've been having.'

I paused and took a sip of coffee. Angelina looked at me closely.

'You see, Angelina, I wanted to find out if she would want to go back there.'

'And does she?'

'I think so. Well, I'm certain she would. And driving across here today I began to wonder about you and Andrew too.'

'So you came here also to check us out? So what's your conclusion?'

'I think you would too. You see, I came into a lot of money last year. I'm leaving London for good and Alexi and I need to find somewhere to live and bring up Katerina. I liked Brock Hall. It was really beautiful up there. I wondered if we could start farming again, together I mean, as a family.'

Angelina had taken out her handkerchief and suddenly was crying. I didn't know what to do, except to say sorry.

'Not sorry, Peter, no. It's just me. What you have said is so very touching. But you can't know whether it will work or not.'

'No, and for that reason I didn't want to mention it to Andrew. Will you keep it secret, until I've seen if it is possible?'

'Of course,' she replied, her face beginning to smile again. 'You are such a very kind man. Alexi is so very lucky to have found you.'

'I think I'm the lucky one, Angelina. This is my only family now. One day I'll tell you the whole story and then you'll understand everything. But it's too long and complicated for the moment.'

At that point I heard the front door open and the pitter-pat of a dog's paws came down the hall, followed by Andrew's heavy boots.

'Not a word,' said Angelina, finger to her lips.

I drank another cup of coffee with Andrew and then left. I had an idea. I drove into Stockton and parked my car in the High Street. It was market day and the place was full of stalls, parked cars, shoppers with bags, and fruit boxes and paper bags blowing everywhere in the wind. I walked to Finkle Street and to the offices of Guest and Wedderburn. At the front desk I asked if by any chance Mr Skene was available and I was told he was. Skene rose to his feet when I entered his office.

'Mr Kingsmill, this is an unexpected pleasure,' he said, holding out his hand and showing me a chair.

'Unexpected for me too,' I said. 'I'd like you to look into a property for me. All I can tell you is that the name is Brock Hall Farm. It's between Osmotherley and Hawnby. Used to be a hill farm but the estate wanted to use it for shooting. It looks derelict now and I wondered if I could buy it.'

'That's sounds very precipitous,' said Skene, looking over his spectacles at me. 'Are you sure that's what you want? It can't be a good investment.'

'Probably a bad investment, Mr Skene, but there's more to life than making good investments. I think I can make a lot of people happy, myself included. That's worth more than any investment in my book.'

Skene looked at me as if I had lost my senses. He was clearly not comfortable putting a value on happiness, preferring ledgers, contracts and deeds to human emotions.

'Very well, Mr Kingsmill. I'll get in touch with the nearest surveyors – most likely in Stokesley I would imagine – and see if I can track down the owners. As soon as I hear anything, I'll be in touch. We have your number I think.'

I thanked him and made for the door. As I turned to shake his hand, he looked closely at me and said:

'Oh, by the way, did you get any further with that business of the letter?'

'Yes, as a matter of fact I did, but it turned out in one way to be a dead end; in another way life-changing.'

'I'm not sure I understand.'

'I'm not sure I do, yet,' I said.

Chapter 3

I was to be alone for two days. The cottage that night seemed eerily silent. There was no clatter from Katie nor her puppy, both of whom had stayed with Angelina and Andrew after the wedding; and I missed Alexi's questioning conversations, her warmth and enthusiasm. I caught a cold memory of the empty shell I used to be, before she came into my life. In the evening there was one chair empty by the fire; at night I could not hear her quiet breathing as she slept; and the silence seemed filled by the groaning and creaking of the rafters and the floorboards. I awoke that first morning after a poor night's sleep, punctuated by a waking dream about Maria. I knew I would not find peace until I had decided on a course of action. But what should that be?

I put on my walking boots and waterproof jacket and set off over the moors in the general direction of Brock Hall Farm. It was a clear day with a sharp frost and a blue sky. As I rose above the village, three buzzards circled high above me, calling in their gentle monotone as they searched for prey. I followed the line of a dry stone wall until it petered out, and then a sheep track that threaded a narrow route through the dry winter bracken. Soon I felt the damp spring of peat beneath my boots and I was above the snow-line, crossing the bleak moorland that reached as far as the eye could see and beyond to the grey North Sea. It was strange that since I had returned to the north I had learned to do my thinking in the open, walking under the wide open skies. In London I had never walked; perhaps I had never done much thinking either.

I had plenty to think about now. I had learned so much. I had learned why the woman I thought was my mother had rejected me so coldly; and I understood now why Stanislaw had been so distant as a father. I had learned why Maria had sacrificed her maternal love in order to give me a life; and I was angry at the betrayal she had suffered at the hands of Jonathan Blake and the cruel injustice meted out to poor Thomas Engel, my natural father. I could hear a voice inside me which told me to leave the past alone, to look forward to my new life with a bright new family. But then another voice, more powerful, which said that justice was an end in itself, even if it served no other purpose. And so I walked on over the moors with these thoughts in my mind when suddenly I saw the walls of Brock Hall before me, sheltering in the little copse of trees. I was a quarter of a mile from the house and I could pick out quite clearly its boarded-up windows and moss-covered tiles. Then I saw a movement, a single figure moving across the paddock, and then a black-and-white dog, and I recognised from a distance that it was Andrew with Bess. Angelina had said that Andrew walked the hills with his dog but she could not know that he visited the old home that had been taken from him. I stood stock still but it was too late. Andrew's keen eyes had spotted me and he waved. I waved back and walked across to the house, Bess sprinting to greet me.

'Peter, what are you up to, here in the wilds?' he asked.

'I could ask you the same Andrew, but I think I know the answer too well,' I replied.

Andrew looked at the ground and was silent.

'Angelina doesn't know I come here,' he said.

'Don't worry, I won't say anything, but I understand your feelings.'

'Look at it now! What an injustice.'

Andrew's words suddenly encapsulated my thoughts: what an injustice! My mind was made up and I began to figure out where to start. There were three people who knew at first hand the story of Maria's betrayal and her real heroism: Blake, Thomas Engel and Lundquist. I knew two to be dead; I knew nothing of the third, so I needed to start there. But as it turned out, the road I was to follow had more twists and turns to it than I could possibly have foreseen.

'Come on down to Rievaulx Cottage and have some tea,'

said Andrew. 'I can drop you off later.'

'That sounds good, especially if there's one of Angelina's cakes in the kitchen.'

'There usually is,' said Andrew with a grin.

So we whistled up Bess, who was looking down rabbit holes in the overgrown garden, and headed down the hill to Helmsley. I didn't tell Andrew my plan for Brock Hall, although I dearly wanted to.

That evening I walked across to the Queen Catherine to share a pint with my blood brother behind the bar.

'On yer tod, Pete?' he said, as I walked into the public bar. He handed me a pint of my usual. 'Grand wedding t'other day. Where's your bonny lass?'

'In London, working, Bill. Tell me, what do you know about the people who own Brock Hall, up the hill?'

'Bunch o' wankers, if you pardon the French,' came the reply. 'Came in 'ere once. Ordered dry martinis. I tell you, before steak pie and chips. There was one little fat guy, seemed to do all the talking, very cut-glass. The rest seemed to be fund managers, judging by the chat. More likely shoot each other in't foot before they could hit a pheasant. The boss asked for a receipt when he paid the bill, would you believe, no doubt for corporate entertaining!'

'Can you remember his name?'

'No, but Maggie might,' and Bill went through to the kitchen to ask his wife. A couple of minutes later he reappeared with a piece of paper in his hand.

'This is a copy of the receipt. Goes back to a year ago.'

He handed it to me. Across the top it read "Bold Enterprises" and at the bottom, against the title "Director" I saw a name I recognised: Douglas Bold, with an address somewhere near Canary Wharf.

'Good God! Ubiquitous Bold.'

'You know him then?' said Bill.

'Too well, I'm afraid.'

The next evening I collected Alexi from York station. She had not got away from London until seven and looked exhausted. I drove her back home in silence. I could tell she was thinking about something.

'How did it go?' I asked, eventually breaking the silence.

'Tiring and, to tell you the truth, I'm a bit overawed by it all. Not sure I can do it.'

'Sure you can, Alexi. I've never known you stumped by anything. What's worrying you this time?'

'It's the scale of it. They want to do a series on changing eastern Europe.'

'You mean the opening of the borders into the west and the end of the wall?'

'And the end of Communism. Everyone is sure the wall will come down. It's only a matter of time. They want me to contribute pieces on social issues.'

'You should be flattered. They obviously liked your British stuff or they wouldn't have asked you back,' I said.

We had reached the bottom of the hill leading to the village.

'What you need is a drink,' I said, 'then you'll feel better.'

'OK, but I'm worried about leaving you.....and neglecting Katie. You see, I've got to go to Bonn next week, and God knows where thereafter.'

'Don't worry about Katie,' I said, 'she's fine with Angelina and Andrew and, who knows, we might have a new home together soon. As for me, I'm just happy for you.'

I drove on up the hill and then I heard myself quietly laughing.

'OK, what's the joke?' Alexi asked.

'Oh, just thinking about you and the *Evening Gazette* only three months ago. Things have moved on. In more ways than one.'

'Precisely.'

It was good to be back in the cottage, however humble it was. I poured a couple of whiskies and we sat together by the open fire.

'You've made progress with Brock Hall Farm, I take it?' Alexi said out of the silence.

'Some,' I replied, 'but I need to hear from the lawyer before I can say much more. I met Andrew on the hill yesterday. He was at Brock Hall with his dog. He seemed ashamed when I saw him. I told him not to be.'

'You're very good, Peter. You've taken on responsibilities which you didn't have to. I know I've been preoccupied lately and I haven't asked you.'

'Asked me what?' I said.

'How you feel about your mother and her story,' she replied.

I looked into the glowing embers for a while and thought.

'I feel guilty that I left her the way I did, and I feel....I must make recompense for the betrayal she suffered in her life. I thought I might begin to find people who were involved but I'm not sure where to start.'

'Why not come to Germany with me? You have a sister there you know.'

'Renate? I had never thought of her that way. But I've no idea where she might be, or what I would say to her.'

'Don't think about it Peter, just come with me and have a break. Get away for a while. We can have a short honeymoon and drink some German wine. How does that sound?'

'It sounds wonderful, although Bonn is not the most exciting place to be. I was there for a week on a European junket, in my other life that is. But the wine was good and the asparagus market, of course.'

I found myself laughing again.

'Why do you always do this to me, Alexi? Make me happy.'

'It's a mystery to me.'

I don't know what kind of fate governs our lives, if events can ever be more than random, or whether some divine string-puller looks down upon us, twitching us towards one exit rather than another, but our trip to Bonn was the beginning of something big for me. And it was quite unexpected. We spent a week in Yorkshire, Alexi preparing madly for her visit, making phone calls to set up interviews and researching articles. I walked a lot, brought and fetched Katerina, and generally thought about the possibility of contacting Renate Engel. It seemed a long shot to me and I was not convinced it was something I wanted to do. But I went along with Alexi's suggestion anyway. I was learning not to think ahead too much. The day before we were to travel, the telephone rang. It was Skene from Guest and Wedderburn.

'Mr Kingsmill, regarding Brock Hall Farm, I've discovered the owners are a company called Bold Enterprises based in London. I spoke to their estate manager a couple of days ago and I'm afraid I've received a negative response from them.'

'You mean they don't want to sell?' I said.

'Precisely. What would you like me to do now, Mr Kingsmill?'

'Do nothing for the time being, Mr Skene. Thanks for your trouble. I'll get back to you.'

I put the telephone down. It was a blow but I didn't think the game was lost. I had known Douglas Bold for years and he was a slippery customer. There was, however, someone who could be more slippery, and that was Ken Brandon. I thought it might be time to pay him a visit. Alexi was clicking away at her keyboard but she looked up when I put the receiver down.

'Bad news about the farm?'

'Perhaps, but I have a plan. I need to talk to Ken. Let's take the train to London tomorrow and I can see him. We can overnight there before the flight to Cologne.'

We met Ken for lunch the following day at a tiny restaurant off Piccadilly. It was a place I had used often in my London days and which was handy for Ken to walk to from his office. I had telephoned him the day before and the opportunity for him to escape the office for a couple of hours proved too much to resist. He had been his usual effusive self when I had spoken to him.

'Peter, how good to hear from you. I thought we would never tempt you south again from your northern fastness. Lunch would be good. Do you want me to book something?'

Visions of the Savoy Grill flashed before my eyes and I quickly said no. So at twelve-thirty Alexi and I strolled into Ben's Oyster Bar and sat down at a small table with a red checked table cloth and chairs that creaked. A few minutes later Ken arrived in his Whitehall garb and kissed Alexi on both cheeks as if he were an old friend.

'Ken, I think you've met my wife, Alexi,' I said.

'Wife! Good God, Peter, how wonderful. You should have told us. Congratulations to you both!'

And he took the chance of giving Alexi another kiss.

'This calls for champagne!' he shouted.

It was not until we had toasted ourselves several times, and devoured oysters and lobster, with Ken insisting on footing the bill, that he finally asked me what had brought me south. I told him about Bold Enterprises and the reluctance of the company to sell.

'I take it this is important for you both?' he asked.

Alexi answered for me.

'Yes it is,' she said, 'it used to be my home.'

'And what can you do, Ken?' I asked.

'I have an idea,' he replied, but said no more than that. 'Peter, Alexi my dear, I must be going. Government must go on,' he said, rising to his feet.

He paid the bill on the way out, kissed Alexi goodbye and shook my hand.

'Peter, don't worry. I've a feeling my idea might work. I'll call you,' he said, and strode off up Piccadilly.

'You must miss this life,' said Alexi.

'I was never any good at enjoying it,' I replied, 'not like Ken. That's why he's going all the way to the top and I would never be more than an honest vice-captain. It's a game he plays for fun.'

'What do you think is his big idea?'

'He's probably going to offer Bold a knighthood, knowing Ken,' I said with a laugh. 'That should fix it!'

The next morning we flew to Cologne. As we cleared customs we passed along a small passageway. A policewoman in dark green uniform stood with an Alsatian sniffer dog on a lead. I thought of Maria's parents getting off a train in the middle of Poland to go to their terrible fate. That it was a woman holding the dog made it worse and I shuddered at the image in my mind. Did I really want to revisit this?

'You alright Peter?' Alexi said, gripping my hand.

'Yes. I'm OK.'

The airport bus took us quickly into the city and I saw the stones of the cathedral towers rising above the city square, dark and foreboding. On the other side stood central station in all its Germanic severity, thronging with passengers, and soon we were in a compartment of the Bonn train, travelling across totally flat brown fields with rows of cabbages and asparagus reaching to the horizon. Ribbons of silver lined the furrows where recent rain reflected the grey sky.

'This feels a very alien place to me, Alexi. It's so flat and brown and rectangular.'

'I know. Don't you long for the winding lanes and rolling hills to break it up? Then, it wouldn't have produced the Prussian mind would it, if it was as mixed up as Yorkshire?'

'What are you doing in Bonn?' I asked.

'Starting tomorrow, meeting officials in the interior department, and then finishing up with the minister himself. Should take two days. What are your plans Peter? I don't want you getting lost.'

'I thought I might go to the general post office and look up a name.'

'You mean "Engel" I suppose. So you've decided?'

'Yes, I've decided to follow the trail again, wherever it leads.'

'You're right. It won't go away, unless you hunt it down.'

The train was pulling in to Bonn station and the ornate buildings of the small pretend capital city rose around us.

'I could have understood Beethoven coming from Berlin, but not Bonn. Where on earth did he find his inspiration in this city of administrators?' I said. 'It's as if Germany is waiting for its moment, then Bonn will be a footnote.'

'But they have asparagus, remember,' Alexi added with a wicked grin and I knew I was being too serious again.

Chapter 4

The next day Alexi left early for the Government offices and her series of interviews with officials and then the minister. I was left to my own devices. After coffee and toast in the sparse hotel breakfast room I wandered out into the quiet clean streets of the German capital. At first all seemed orderly and peaceful but, as I walked into the city centre towards the market square, I began to notice beggars on street corners. Their numbers increased as I neared the cathedral and on the steps of the church a dark-haired leather-skinned woman waved a plastic card at me – a kind of identity card I suppose – and spoke brusquely to me in a language that I could not identify but which sounded east European. I dropped a deutschmark in her tin and entered the church, but she followed me, rattling her tin and shaking her card. I was being pursued. To my relief, a cathedral guide stepped out of a side aisle, intercepted the woman, spoke to her in sharp German, and ushered her out. Then he came across to me, recognising me as a tourist.

'I am so sorry you were bothered,' he said. 'It is becoming a great problem here in Germany.'

'Who are these people?' I asked. 'I never thought I would see beggars on the streets of the West German capital.'

'They are Czechs, Hungarians, even some East Germans. The border crossings into West Germany are being opened to relieve the pressure of the emigrants from the communist countries on the other side. We can do nothing about it any longer. The tide is too strong. The Soviet regime is crumbling and they no longer have the will to control it. The border guards are letting them through. It is only a matter of time before the East German border disappears and the wall comes down in Berlin too.'

'And Germany will be one country again, I suppose.'

'Most certainly, but the politicians will not admit it. Only we, the ordinary people see it happening all around us and, quite frankly, we are afraid. Excuse me, I must attend to my duties,' he said, with a slight bow, and moved away.

He was elderly, polite and bemused by the harsh new world that seemed to be flooding into his ordered life.

So this was why Alexi's paper was so keen to explore the east; and then I recalled that I had seen short reports in the British press about queues of cars at Czech borders, and hundreds of pedestrians in temporary makeshift camps at Hungarian crossings. Yet, in England, the truth had generally not been recognised, that western Europe was about to be reconstructed, with nobody looking.

I wandered on into the market square where row upon row of stalls were selling what looked like identical vegetables arranged symmetrically. There was not a scrap of litter in sight and I thought of Stockton market late on a Saturday with a sense of homesickness for the shambles of it all. I suppose I had a purpose in my ramble: I wanted to find out more about my German family, even though deep inside I was afraid of what I might discover. I was therefore half relieved to find no Renate Engel in the post office directories and I scurried away, happy to find something else to do for the afternoon.

At six that evening Alexi arrived back at the hotel, looking worn out.

'Do you know what's going on in this city? I was nearly mugged this morning by a Bulgarian beggar and had to be saved by an aged cathedral verger. I thought this was boring old Bonn. What are your politicians saying about all this, Alexi? Have you asked them if the wall is coming down?'

'They're in denial, for the most part, and they don't know what the west will do. The senior people don't really want to ask that question but you can ask them yourself, if you like!' she replied.

'How?'

'We're invited to a traditional German restaurant in the

square this evening. The top man in the office will be there with his wife. The car's coming for us at seven. Better get yourself smartened up. What else did you do today, Peter?' she asked, looking at me closely, so that I knew precisely what she meant.

So I told the truth.

'Dead end really,' I replied, but I knew she knew I was dodging the issue.

The Mercedes arrived for us on the stroke of seven. I had mustered a suit and a tie and Alexi wore a business-like dress. Together we looked passable for a meeting with serious German officials. The car swept us through the well-lit city streets, where the traffic seemed non-existent in comparison with London's maelstrom, to the corner of the city square I had visited already that day. Outside a baroque edifice, two braziers threw out swirling flames either side of a stone portico and we were welcomed by a porter in white gloves and green coat. Inside real chandeliers poured down yellow light on bare wooden tables, waiters in long green aprons and with protruding bellies carried plates of what looked like whole legs of pork with potatoes and cabbage, balanced three on an arm; while others rushed between tables with long glass tankards of beer in clusters. I half expected the officials to appear in leather shorts, their frauen with plaited golden hair, in this Grimm's fairytale of a place. I looked at Alexi and she looked at me:

'This could be a long night,' I said.

And it was, but not without surprise. There were formal introductions and long statements in paragraphs from civil servants too full of themselves; oily friendliness from the boss of the show; and steely courtesy from his too-well-turned-out wife. The general theme was that everything was fine in modern forward-looking West Germany. I hoped Alexi could get to the bottom of this but I knew it was not my place to push things. As the evening wore on, and the pork legs disappeared, and the Rhine wine began to flow, the formality of the gathering gradually fragmented and I fell into conversation with my neighbour, a senior official in the interior ministry, a grey-haired man of clerical appearance called Klaus Schneider.

'So Herr Kingsmill, you are enjoying your time in Bonn while your wife is working, yes?'

He smiled and fingered his wine glass.

'Very interesting, thank you.'

'And you have been to Germany before?'

And then, numbed by the wine and my groaning belly full of pork and cabbage, I let it slip:

'My father was German, actually.'

It was out before I knew it.

'Oh, really, how interesting. But you are English, are you not?'

I felt I was being interviewed but I ploughed on, revealing my private life to a complete stranger.

'Yes, I am, but my mother was Polish and my father German, a colonel in the army in fact. He died at the hands of the Russians, I am told, after I was taken to England to be brought up by my aunt.'

'I am sorry to hear about your father. There were many terrible things happening at that time in Germany.'

He paused and I expected him to go on to say "but now things are different here" in that self-satisfied way I had already become familiar with from my brief visit. But instead he looked at me sympathetically and said:

'I don't suppose you knew your father, judging by your age.'

'As a matter of fact, that's partly why I'm here, to find out what happened. I had hoped to find a half-sister here whom I have never met.'

Klaus Schneider was like a priest in the confessional, quietly extracting the truth.

'You know, Peter – I may call you that? – Germany is full of such stories of dislocated families, destroyed by the war. Perhaps I can help you. What was your father's name?'

'Colonel Thomas Engel. He was stationed in Norway during the war and recalled to Germany at the end. All I know is that a daughter from his marriage in Germany wrote to my mother after the war to say the Russians had executed him and his officers for war crimes. He was a good man and I know such charges have no basis. You see, my mother and he never married.'

'I understand. There are many cases of disappearances like this and relatives such as you, looking for the truth. Picking up the pieces, as you say in English. I think I may be able to help. Why don't you come to my office in the morning, if you have time that is.'

'I'll do that,' I said, and he raised his glass to me.

'I like England very much you know. I spent a year in Cambridge, at Darwin College, doing a postgraduate diploma in political theory in fifty-nine. I still remember it with pleasure. Summer on the river, punting up to Grantchester for tea. You know we Germans never believed you English could really live in those chocolate-box villages. But it's true!'

'Before my time, Klaus, I was at Trinity Hall in sixty-five.'

'Ah yes, Tit Hall you call it. I played centre-half against them at Cuppers I seem to remember. We won.'

Klaus was a man with a sense of humour and I warmed to him.

The evening finally ground to a halt with formal goodbyes, handshakes and bows. In the taxi travelling back I asked Alexi what she had got out of it. She looked exhausted, bored and depressed.

'Very little. They keep putting up the shutters. I need to talk to real people, not bureaucrats. There's a real story of human suffering and change here. I think my editor has it wrong: this is not about major macropolitics. It's about ordinary people wanting a better life for themselves, and to get it they have to leave the crappy bloody country they live in.'

'I know where you should start, Alexi. Go and talk to the chap at the cathedral. He'll tell you the truth. And then meet a refugee or two from the east. They're all over the place. And tell your damned editor what you just told me. This is a human interest story.'

'That's not a bad idea. And you? I saw you in conversation with Schneider.'

'He asked me to come to his office. He thinks he can help me. Don't ask me how.'

The taxi pulled up at our hotel. It was a quiet winter night and the sky was clear.

'Let's walk a while,' said Alexi, 'I need some air after this evening.'

So we walked in the cool German night along the embankment of the Rhine with the lights of the city glinting on the sliding water. Black outlines of river barges chugged past and disappeared into the darkness, the small points of their navigation lights dwindling to nothing.

'There must be somebody here who wants to tell me the truth,' said Alexi out of the blue.

'They've spent the last forty years trying to come to terms with historical truth. It's pretty tough to have to take on new stuff after that,' I said. 'No wonder they're reluctant to face up to it. I'm a bit like that too.'

'I know, Peter. It must be hard for you, with me banging on in my selfish journalistic way, while you're trying to come to terms with all that baggage.'

Next morning we breakfasted on the usual yellow cheese slices, tasteless cold meats and dry rye bread in our stainless steel and glass hotel restaurant. Coffee came out of a machine which dribbled into our cups at the press of a button. Outside, the Westphalian sky was the colour of gun metal. Alexi was the first to speak, as if the conversation of the night before had not been interrupted by sleep.

'OK, I agree, it's a human interest story and that's how I'm going to write it. The politicians are not going to reveal anything; I have to talk to the ordinary people whose lives are being changed by what's happening. If the editor doesn't like it, he can lump it.'

'Good for you Alexi. I'll take you to meet my cathedral man. I'm sure he can point you in the right direction from there. I have to meet Schneider this morning. I'll phone you later.'

So we walked into the city centre, along the well-swept streets, past the shining shop windows, a city that bustled and succeeded, while the ragged battalions of the east gathered at its gates. At the entrance to the cathedral the same beggarwoman sat crouched on the steps, holding her plastic card and her collecting tin. We climbed the steps quickly, passed into the relative gloom of the church, and I looked around to find my elderly verger. He was standing by a desk displaying copies of information leaflets in various languages. The church was empty and he came across to greet us.

'Good morning,' he began and then he recognised me from the previous day. 'Ah, I see you have returned for another visit.'

'Not quite,' I replied, 'but my wife is very interested in the German issue and would like to ask you some questions, if that is alright.'

'Of course. I would be delighted,' he said.

'I should tell you,' said Alexi, 'that I'm a journalist doing a piece on the changing face of eastern Europe. If that alters things, please say so.'

'Not at all,' he replied, 'it is a subject I have been studying for years. My name is Dietrich Müller. I was professor of modern history at Bonn University until two years ago. I'm here because I love the cathedral, you know, but it's not my job, only a passion. I would be happy to talk to you.'

Alexi introduced herself to Müller. I saw she was in good hands and made my escape as soon as I could. I left the cathedral, and the beggar at the doors, and made my way to the station square where I knew I could find a taxi. A row of Mercedes and Audis stood in a queue waiting for custom and in no time I was travelling across town to the Government quarter and the Interior Ministry building. As we drove I watched the people on the streets, going about their business, as if this were the reason the world went round. It was one of those moments I had experienced so many times before: the questioning of the point of it all, pursuing the fragment of truth that affects only me, in a world where millions of separate fates persuade their owners they are unique and

273

significant, when in fact they are grains of sand in a desert. These were the black thoughts in the abyss from which Alexi had so often lifted me. Did I really have the drive to see this through? If it hadn't been for the chance meeting with Schneider last night would I still be pursuing it at all? Wasn't it just English politeness that was making me keep my appointment? Looking back on it all now, I realise I could not have thrown up the puzzle I had started. The pieces were being assembled and I was not the guiding hand. I had to let it happen.

Schneider met me at the lift on the third floor. He was dressed half casually, with no tie, his pen stuck in his shirt pocket. I supposed he was the head of the show but he dressed like a junior from the mailroom; last night he had worn a suit and a stiff shirt. It was the Whitehall dress code thrown upside down. He greeted me with a welcoming smile and I waited for him to say what he had to offer me.

'I thought about your problem, Peter, and I wondered if we could help you. You probably think that we in the west have nothing to do with the east but that would be a mistake. For some years now we have been sharing information about missing persons. There has been an exchange of certain files and we have gone some way to creating an archive. The war left thousands with no information about their relatives but it is now possible for people to institute a search, you understand. You could say the DDR wants to begin the process of reconciliation.'

'You mean before the east collapses?'

Schneider paused for a while, thinking carefully about his response.

'If you were a German, I would deny that. When you throw a pebble into a pool, you do not know where the ripples will end. We don't know how this will work out, so we don't want to raise expectations.'

'I understand, but what about my problem?'

'It struck me as you were talking last night that there may be a file on Thomas Engel in our archive, or in the DDR. He would have been a prominent figure, a military colonel, and apparently executed by the Russians. There would have been a trial and a record of it. I could make a search for you, if you like. You never know, it might throw up some information that might help you find your family. Would you like me to proceed?'

My black thoughts began to ebb in the face of his inexplicable kindness. He had nothing to gain from this gesture but he had thought it important, while I, who had everything to gain, had been ready to discard it as worthless.

'I would appreciate that very much, Klaus,' I replied.

'Good. Now let me note down as much as you can tell me,' and he took his pen from his shirt pocket.

Before I left I gave him my telephone number. He would ring me if he found anything but I was warned it could take time.

Later that day I telephoned Alexi. She arranged to meet me at seven at a small restaurant on the corner near our hotel.

'I've had a great day Peter,' she said over the telephone, 'just one more meeting then I'm finished. Tell you all later.'

I could hear the enthusiasm in her voice, so different from the day before, and I was glad for her. At a little after seven she arrived, tired but happy. We ordered a bottle of that gentle white German wine and sat at a simple wooden table in the corner of the panelled room.

'I have a real story at last,' she said. 'Professor Müller took me to meet a group of East German academics at the university, all of them recent emigrants via Czechoslovakia. I've got loads on the collapsing economy and the relaxation of the borders. Then I went with them to meet some real refugees, camping out behind the railway station on some waste land. No one admits it's happening but I got some real-life stories from them all. One was a young army conscript who had served as a border guard. He told me that the guards have made an unwritten agreement not to shoot at anybody any more. It seems the flow of defectors getting across the river is increasing every day. This is how it's going to finish it seems: not with a bang but a whimper. I want to put these points to the Interior Ministry lot tomorrow before we leave.

275

Do you think they'll see me?'

'Schneider knows its happening,' I replied, 'but whether he would confirm or deny your stories when he's on the record, I don't know. You can try him in the morning I suppose. He was very helpful to me.'

'So you got somewhere?'

I told Alexi of my black hole on the way in the taxi and of my fears that I was chasing shadows and wasting my time. Then of Schneider's amazing generosity.

'I felt ashamed Alexi, actually ashamed, that I could make so little effort while a complete stranger would go to those lengths to help me.'

'So are you convinced now about what you're trying to do?' she asked.

'Yes, I am. I guess life is a process, not an end product; it's what you go through rather than what you achieve, if you see what I mean. I still haven't escaped my Catholic education: article two of the catechism asks "Why did God make you?" Answer: "God made me to know him, love him and serve him in this world and to be happy with him forever in the next".

'I don't follow you Peter,' Alexi said, smiling an indulgent smile.

'Well, it says "Don't worry if life is shit. Love God and the reward comes at the end". But life is the reward. There's nothing after it, don't you see.'

'I see,' she said with a laugh, 'and I understand. So let's enjoy life and bugger the end reward. I'm hungry. Let's order something, as long as it doesn't have pig in it.'

'That could be a challenge.'

Early the next morning, Alexi telephoned Schneider and to her surprise he agreed to meet her. A month later her article appeared and the world began to sit up and take notice of the unravelling of the eastern empire. Her editor had bought the human interest side completely and was happy to run with it.

Chapter 5

It was a fine clear day in March. I could feel for the first time since autumn the warm air heralding the changing season. I was walking on the hill with Rosie, now a lively young dog, full of energy. The becks were full from the melting snow on the moors and the early lambs were already taking their first steps in the lowland meadows. But I had heard nothing from Schneider and assumed the trail was cold; I had made no progress in finding anything about Lundquist; and there was no change in the Brock Hall situation. I was feeling low, bordering on depressed. Alexi's life was steaming ahead, and I was pleased for her, but I felt mine had reached the end of the line and I needed to start out in a new direction.

It was mid afternoon when I got back to the cottage. Alexi had set up office in the living room and was busy on her research and drafting for her paper. She had taken to wearing reading glasses, which sat on the bridge of her nose, and she looked over them as I entered, very much like the disapproving headmistress of a girl's school.

'Schneider called half an hour ago,' she said. 'He left a number for you to call back. It's on that bit of paper over there.'

She pointed to the mantelpiece over the fire. My heart took a lurch and I felt the pinpricks in the back of my neck. I knew I had to do this, so I picked up the paper. Surprisingly, it was a London number. I lifted the telephone and dialled. The distinctive voice of an hotel receptionist answered:

'Park Lane Hilton Hotel. May I help you?'

I asked for Dr Schneider and waited while I was put through on the house telephone. Then I heard his cultured tones.

'Klaus, this is Peter Kingsmill speaking. You called

earlier. How are you?'

'I am well, thank you, Peter. I happen to be in London at the moment with my Minister for a conference of interior ministries in the EEC. I have something for you, regarding Thomas Engel. I can't send it but I wondered if you might meet me here. We go back in two days and, as far as I can see, tomorrow evening would be free. Say eight o'clock in the hotel. We could have dinner together perhaps.'

'Of course. I look forward to that,' I replied, hoping the tremor in my voice did not betray my nerves.

'Good, till then. I'm at the Park Lane Hilton. I guess you will know that from your London days.'

I gave it no thought at the time, but I later wondered how he knew about my so-called London days. He had obviously checked me out. It suddenly came to me: Ken Brandon might well be at the same conference with the Home Secretary and they could have met each other, even discussed me. "When you throw a pebble in the pool, you don't know where the ripples will end", Schneider had said. I was beginning to feel the ripples all around me.

I drove into York the next day and left my car in the station car park. I had no Pimlico apartment any more, the agents having disposed of it readily, so I planned to overnight at my club in St James's. I was glad to have the evening taken up by dinner with Schneider, despite my concern over what he might have to tell me, and in the morning I would make a quick exit from London, back to my new life.

By six o'clock I was in London and I took a taxi to the club. I dropped my bag in my room and found a collar and tie for the meeting with Schneider at eight. I had an hour to spare and I was tired. The library of the Oxford and Cambridge club was a welcoming male environment where I could settle down with the newspaper and drink a whisky in peace. It was quiet when I arrived but, after a few minutes, I heard a conversation from the far end of the room. I thought I vaguely recognised the voice and looked up to check. A familiar face was looking in my direction and, after a moment, I recognised it as that of Professor Wotherspoon, the history don and badge collector whom I had met at High Table a few months before. I nodded to him and the gesture obviously confirmed to him that he too had recognised me. He walked across the carpeted floor, clutching a bursting briefcase open at the top, and stopped at my table.

'Yes, I thought it was you,' he said, his floppy grey hair falling down over one eye. 'It's Peter Kingsmead isn't it? We met at hall before Christmas.'

'Kingsmill,' I replied, 'Professor Wotherspoon. How nice to see you again. Can I get you a drink?'

'That would be splendid,' he said, as he slid into the leather armchair next to me. 'A scotch and water, if you please. And tell me, how did you get on with those military photographs I sent you? Did you find the officer you were looking for?'

I was amazed at the clarity of the man's memory over things that interested him, unlike his failure to remember a simple surname.

'Yes, thank you. I did indeed. Your help was most appreciated.'

I called over the steward and ordered our drinks. More out of the need to say something, than a desire for information, I said:

'And what brings you to London away from the peace of Cambridge, Professor Wotherspoon?'

'Well, it is a burden, but I do a little job for the Foreign Office. I sit on a kind of recruitment board. I'm the token outsider, supposedly the bringer of common sense to the meanderings of the officials.'

He said no more than that but, as I looked down to the bulging briefcase on the floor by his chair, I could not help but notice the confidential sticker on the manila files stuffed into his bag. I wondered how many security breaches he had committed by removing the files from the office, let alone exposing them to the eyes of who-knows-who. I knew enough about Civil Service practice to recognise that his work must involve recruitment to the intelligence arm of the Foreign Office as all other posts were filled through the normal Civil

Service Commission channels. And after all, Oxbridge was the recruiting ground for secret agents. Wotherspoon, as a Cambridge don, was in an ideal position to act as a talent spotter as well as an adviser to the secret appointments committee. I took another sideways look at the files and saw the title "Committee C1" on the top cover.

We talked on for twenty minutes or so about politics, Cambridge and the state of English cricket, before he picked up his over-brimming bag and shuffled off to a lonely dinner in the club dining room. I threw on my overcoat and stepped out into the cool London night to walk to the Hilton Hotel. In no time I reached Hyde Park Corner and turned up for a hundred yards. The Hilton was heaving with departing politicians and their side-kicks, the more important of them escorted by overweight security men in suits, all packed into people carriers, making a target that was an open invitation to terrorists. London policeman occasionally padded up and down the pavement, providing a symbolic shield against the unknown. It was the glamour of the power game, the intoxication of being in the public eye, the self-deception of the assumed ability to change the world, that drove these people on.

Inside the glass and steel entrance lobby I gave my name and asked the girl at the desk for Dr Schneider. She telephoned his room.

'Dr Schneider says come up. Room 305. The lift is just over there.'

Away from the bustle of the lobby, the hotel descended into silence. I walked along the corridor on the third floor, silently stepping on the deep carpet, until I found Room 305. After a couple of knocks the door opened and Schneider stood there, Dictaphone in one hand and a bundle of papers in the other. He was in his stocking feet and shirt sleeves.

'Peter, welcome, do come in. You have caught me finishing off my Minister's statement for the plenary session tomorrow. The German proposal for amending border regulations. He knows nothing about it, of course, so I have to make my paragraphs very simple – and in big letters – but you know how it is, don't you?'

I sat down in one of those hotel chairs that promise luxury but offer little but discomfort. The floor was strewn with paperwork and empty coffee cups were everywhere.

'Let's stop this charade, Klaus, what do you know about me? These references are becoming rather tiresome.'

'OK, Peter. I wanted to find out about you before I plunged into this business. I spoke to Ken Brandon yesterday. You might have worked out he would be here, of course. He speaks very highly of you and still doesn't understand why you quit at the top. I wanted to know I could trust you.'

'And can you?' I asked.

He smiled that engaging smile.

'I can finish this later. A glass or two will give me inspiration. Let's go and eat. There's a half decent brasserie downstairs. We don't want to go into the restaurant. It will be full of dull delegates like me.'

He threw on his jacket, grabbed an envelope and put it in his inside pocket, and we headed down to the ground floor. He was right about the masses heading to the restaurant but the brasserie was relatively quiet and we found a table for two out of sight. I waited for him to broach the topic of our meeting but we had ordered and consumed a bottle of burgundy and eaten two courses before he began.

'Peter, I have something for you which may be of interest.'

He took out the envelope from his inside pocket and handed me three sheets of yellowish paper, typed in Cyrillic script.

'There was a trial in which Thomas Engel was one of the accused. It was a sham, a show trial, and this is the trumped up summary the Russians produced. Here is a German translation.'

And he handed me a newly typed set of sheets.

'Our analysts have looked at this carefully and their view is that the execution of Colonel Engel and his officers was a stage-managed affair meant to display to the Soviet peoples and the world that the Russians were punishing the inhumanity of the Nazis. It seems your father's regiment, after the peace, was put to clearing up a concentration camp site in western Poland. After that was done, the officers were executed. Usual Russian way – bullet in the back of the neck. Very gruesome, I'm afraid.'

'But my father spent the war in Norway. He had nothing to do with concentration camps.'

'That's the interesting thing. There was another document in the file the East Germans released which stated that your father was arrested on charges of espionage for the British. I think that was why he was executed. The Russians hate spies of all kinds, except their own, but they couldn't be seen to be executing one working for their British Allies. So they created another excuse for silencing him.'

'Do you know who made the accusation, who supplied the information?'

'No, we don't, but it must have been someone who had working contact with Colonel Engel. That narrows it down.'

'Is there any more on the file?'

'Yes, this note.'

And he handed me another sheet with a name and address on it.

'Two years ago, a request was made, under our freedom of information laws, for the file of Thomas Engel to be released. The person making the request was a certain Renate Stronheim. I don't think it can be a coincidence that she has the same forename as your half sister. I leave that with you for you to do with as you please. She must have written to your mother after the war with the story the Russians had put about. But that was a lie. Thomas Engel was shot because someone exposed him as a British agent. She will have worked that out by now, I think.'

Schneider could see I was moved by all this and paused. Then he said:

'You see now, Peter, why I needed to know a little about you before I showed you this. I'm putting myself on the line here, even more than talking to your delightful Alexi.'

'Klaus, I am grateful to you. How can I thank you?'

'Say no more Peter. We should drink to your future,' he said, and we clinked glasses.

Klaus got up and returned to his drafting and I went out into the London night, my head spinning with the information he had given me. I slept little that night and rose early to catch the train home.

I drank two cups of railway coffee before I could clear my head. The flat fields of eastern England flashed by at a hundred miles an hour and it felt as if my brain was working at a similar speed, processing the information of the last twenty-four hours. Thomas Engel had been exposed as a spy in order to silence him. The only people who could possibly wish to silence him were Jonathan Blake, who had died before the war had ended, shot by his own hand; or Magnus Lundquist, the Swedish diplomat-cum-British agent-cum-whatever-else he might be in his world of style and high society. I dismissed his man Björn but not with total conviction. My mind came back to Lundquist. He seemed to have fingers in many pies and I was not convinced that he might not have reasons to keep in with the Soviets. As for Renate, would she welcome the appearance of an unknown brother? But, on the other hand, did she know more about Thomas Engel than I had learned from Maria's story or the scant East German file? There was no escape; I needed to find Lundquist, if he was still alive, and I would do this before I approached Renate.

Before I realised it, the train was slowing on its approach to York station. I picked up my car and drove home to the cottage. Alexi was pleased to see me and gave me a great hug when I opened the door. The living room was strewn with papers but I could tell by her lightness of demeanour that she had finished her piece.

'Don't you remember the relief of shoving your essay into your tutor's pigeon-hole at eleven o'clock on a Thursday night, having bared your soul all week over the meaning of *Four Quartets*?' she said.

'I do, but I don't remember what the meaning was, if it had one. Wasn't it all just objective correlatives after all? I take it you've finished your piece, and you've sent it off, and you're happy?'

'I am. Let's celebrate tonight Peter. Go somewhere smart and eat proper food. It's so good to have you back.'

'I was only away a day, Alexi, but yes, I know just the place. Get out your best frock and we shall spend some money in the company of sophisticated north country folk! No more of these effete southerners who speak funny!'

We were laughing together, again, at nothing in particular, in the simple pleasure of being together.

'How did your meeting with Schneider go?' she asked, when we had both settled down somewhat.

I handed her the slim file with the flimsy trial report. She read it in two minutes.

'This is a disgrace Peter. Your father was betrayed and murdered. What are you going to do?'

'Find his betrayer and clear my parents' names, if I can. I need to start with Lundquist, you remember, the smooth Swedish diplomat. He may still be alive. I'm sure he knows a lot. Not sure how to set about it though.'

That evening we drove into York to the Majestic Hotel. Suddenly Alexi said: 'Spurling!'

'I beg your pardon. What did you say?'

'Spurling, you remember, that little creep who followed you around last year. What about the outfit he worked for? They seemed to be in the business of tracking people down. Surely a top Swedish diplomat must have left a trail a mile wide.'

'You're right. I might still have his telephone number. I'll check when we get back.'

The Majestic was a grand Victorian building, all pillars and arches, built to meet the tastes of the empire, but with a restaurant run by an upwardly-mobile young chef who had already collected a Michelin star and possessed several so-called signature dishes acclaimed by food critics in the quality sundays. There was a posh version of Rick's Bar serving odd-coloured cocktails in tall glasses and a small dance floor serenaded by a stylish trio of musicians. It was north country chic and totally enjoyable if you managed to believe in it. And, for the time being I did believe in it, sitting next to the most beautiful girl I had ever met, feeling that exquisite frisson of excitement when you know the world has something good to offer you, just around the corner. I was lost in such dreams when I felt a tap on my shoulder and I turned to see the bespectacled face of Skene peering down at me.

'Mr Kingsmill, I thought it was you. How nice to see you. I've just sent you a letter in fact. Thought I'd pop over and give you the good news. Bold Enterprises have agreed to sell Brock Hall Farm and cottages. Quite a change of mind. Come and see me some time and we can talk about next steps.'

I turned to Alexi:

'Good God, how does he do it?'

'Who?'

'Ken Brandon, of course.'

Chapter 6

The following week I set in motion the Brock Hall business. I told Skene to get a valuation and offer Bold Enterprises ten per cent below it to see if we got a response. If necessary we could then increase the offer. I was surprised by the speed of the reply, which came within days. The deal was to be signed and sealed by the beginning of May. Whatever hold Ken Brandon had over Douglas Bold had worked wonders; he couldn't hand over the property fast enough. I telephoned Ken in his office after I heard the deal was on.

'How the hell did you persuade Bold to sell? Do you have some compromising photographs?' I asked.

I heard Ken laughing down the telephone.

'Not at all, Peter. You remember Bold's insatiable appetite for fame and status? I simply gave him a hint – a hint mind you, no more than that – that a senior politician in the Government was interested in acquiring a shooting lodge in north Yorkshire. Then I told a small lie that his name was on the long list for the Birthday Honours, for services to charity, which was half true. I hadn't actually put him up at that point but I hinted that doing a favour to an S of S might be well regarded. So when the approach was made, he jumped at it, hook, line and sinker.'

'He doesn't know I'm the buyer then?'

'He will do unless you conceal the fact. I'd get your man to buy it in Alexi's name, if I were you. I'll defuse the anger when he finds out it's not the Foreign Secretary after all. His name's already gone through the hoops and he'll be Sir Douglas before the end of April. That should shut him up.'

'Ken, you're a genius. You should go far! How can I thank you?'

'No thanks Peter, just enjoy your new life, and think of

me sometime, slogging it out down here.'

'You mean wading through lunches at the Savoy Grill, I suppose. Your name will be in lights Ken, when you're head of the whole show. But thanks.'

I told Alexi the good news when I thought it was safe enough to do so. I did not want to raise false hopes. I could see the joy in her face and I was glad to have taken the step. I knew it was going to be a long slog to make the place habitable. But I had an idea and that evening we crossed the road to the Queen Catherine to celebrate the good news. Bill was his usual welcoming self and, without asking, he pulled me a pint of Marston's and poured Alexi a glass of wine.

'To my favourite people,' he said, 'and what are we celebrating this time?'

'I've just bought a farm, Bill, Alexi's old home, and we are here to celebrate.'

'Well, well,' he said, 'so that was what the question was all about! I wish you both the very best. I trust you'll still treat this as your local.'

'Of course we will,' said Alexi.

'Bill, I need a builder,' I said, 'someone who does all trades. Do you know anyone?'

'I should say I do, young Bobby down the road. Does everything. He comes in here Friday nights. You can get him then. Big job I guess.'

'Big job.'

Next day Alexi drove down to Rievaulx Cottage. I didn't want to be there when she told Andrew what was happening. I wanted her to gauge his reaction, without the pressure my presence would place upon him. It was a wise move. He broke down in tears, she told me, and it was far better for a Yorkshireman to do that in the privacy of his own home and not in front of his son-in-law. Later, Andrew came to see me. He didn't have any words but I knew what he meant. I knew I had changed his life, as Alexi had mine, and I was happy to have been able to do so. We talked about sheep and cattle, not about feelings, and that suited us both very well. So this was one plank of the platform supporting my new life that was put in place, albeit with some nailing still to be achieved.

My mind turned to Spurling. I had found his telephone number in the inside pocket of my jacket, where it lay as a crumpled relic of a comic interlude I had not thought I would ever revisit. I rustled up enough courage to telephone him, fully expecting him to slam the receiver down. But as it turned out, I was mistaken. I heard the receiver being picked up and then a south London voice answered.

'Mr Spurling, this is Peter Kingsmill speaking.'

'Who?'

'Kingsmill. Remember – you were following me last year, until our encounter outside the pub in Osmotherley.'

There was a long pause. I could hear the cogs grinding over.

'What do you want? I said I wasn't going to follow you any more, and I ain't. So what do you want, mate?'

'Just some information. I need to find somebody.'

He interrupted before I could finish.

'Don't do that kind of fing, no more. Too risky.'

'Not that, Mr Spurling. I want to know who you worked for, so I can contact them.'

There was another pause before he answered.

'Bloke called Farquhar, claimed he was ex-army, more likely ex-Scrubs if you ask me. A right farquhar an' all. Got an office in Soho.'

'Have you got his number?'

'Somewhere 'ere,' he replied, and he read out the London number for me. 'Still owes me back pay, 'e does.'

The line went dead before I could say any more and I imagined Spurling sitting back in front of his oversize television in the seedy living room of his Camden council flat. I wasn't sure this was a world I wanted to enter but I could think of no alternative. I telephoned the number he had given me and made an appointment to see the self-styled Major Farquhar the following week. I thought it best not to mention Spurling – it might mucky my ticket.

A week later I was walking down Oxford Street on a fine spring morning. When I turned into Soho Square the birds were singing in the trees and the first signs of green leaves could be seen, weeks ahead of the northern hills. Half way down Frith Street I stopped to examine the name plates at number thirty-six: the name Hugh Farquhar was opposite a button, which I pressed, and the door buzzed open. Three floors up, in a narrow staircase with grubby walls and scratched paintwork, I found his office. In an anteroom a single girl sat at a computer screen and, pointing to the door, told me to go straight in.

Major Hugh Farquhar was the opposite of what his surroundings had suggested he might be. I saw before me a tall straight military figure, fifty years old perhaps, dressed in an immaculately tailored pin-striped suit, white Oxford shirt and a Guards tie. He stepped forward to greet me and shook my hand in an iron grasp.

'Mr Kingsmill, how can I be of service?' he asked as we sat down, he behind his antique desk and I in a carved armchair I took to be of significant age and value. This seemed to be a world away from the one Spurling occupied. It took me by surprise.

'I hope you can help me find a missing person,' I replied. And then I corrected myself by adding: 'That is inaccurate, a person who may still be alive whose whereabouts are unknown to me.'

I felt I had not made a good start.

'Perhaps you had better start from the beginning, Mr Kingsmill, and then I may say if I can help you.'

I told Farquhar the bones of the story relating to Lundquist, giving him dates and places as far as I knew them, and the gist of my reasons for seeking him. After I had finished he lit a cigarette and took a long pull, swivelled on his chair, threw his head back and, looking at the ceiling, exhaled. He said nothing for what seemed eternity.

'My fees are high, Mr Kingsmill, especially when a case involves a foreign element.'

'You mean, you can do it?' I asked.

'Of course. Give me your address and telephone number. Here is a note of my charges,' he said, handing me a typed sheet. 'I will contact you if I need to ask further questions or when I have something for you.'

The interview, such as it was, lasted no more than ten minutes and, as he was showing me out, he said:

'I take it you heard of me through Spurling? Wretched little man.'

And as I descended the staircase I realised that Farquhar knew everything about me. I had not disturbed his icy demeanour in the slightest.

I walked back to King's Cross through Bloomsbury and Russell Square with the sunlight flickering through the branches of the plane trees. I felt I had a breathing space now. It was out of my hands. I simply had to wait.

Bill had promised that Bobby the builder would be in the Queen Catherine on Friday night and that is where I sought him out at the end of the week. At seven o'clock I peered through the blue smoke in the public bar where the usual gang of working men had gathered. Bill shouted across to Bobby who was in the process of throwing darts. He threw his final dart and then walked across to the bar.

'Job for you Bobby,' said Bill. 'Big one at that. This is Mr Kingsmill. Just bought Brock Hall.'

'Mr Kingsmill. What can I do for you?'

Bobby was a short, overweight, ginger-haired Scot with a winning smile.

'I hope you can do quite a lot, Bobby. I don't want to disrupt your evening. I wonder whether you might look at the building with me tomorrow morning.'

'Aye, that would be fine Mr Kingsmill. What time would suit?'

'Say ten at Brock Hall. Is that OK?'

We shook hands. I finished my pint and walked back to the cottage.

'Bobby the builder – sounds like a variation on Postman Pat,' said Alexi.

'Will I have a room of my own at Brock Hall, Peter?' Katie piped up.

'Of course you will,' I replied, 'and you can choose

everything that goes in it.'

I could see the little girl's brain begin to do its calculations. I wondered when the question of a pony would arise. It took precisely thirty seconds and the answer took no longer. Alexi looked across the room at me, smiling. Life was going OK.

The next morning I drove up to Brock Hall through a swathe of fog that wreathed the village before vanishing to reveal a brilliant spring day. Bobby's Transit was already there and he was walking round the farmhouse, examining the walls and the roof. Andrew had discovered a back door key that he had forgotten to hand in when he moved out and I took Bobby inside.

'Not really supposed to do this yet, Bobby, but I just happened to have a key.'

We walked from room to room in silence, Bobby poking skirtings and floorboards with his Leatherman, and examining ominous dark stains in the upstairs ceilings and black mould on the lower walls in the kitchen. At last we emerged into the sunshine and I awaited Bobby's verdict.

'Not too bad, Mr Kingsmill. The back wall needs underpinning – there's a bit of subsidence there. Two corners need brackets and expanding bolts to halt a crack. The roof needs a few new slates and there's rot in the window sills and some rising damp in the kitchen which will have to be lagged. Some pointing up of the walls. We can fix all that. You'll need a couple of rooms stripped out and replastered and a new ceiling in the dining room. If you want central heating, it's going to have to be oil up here but I've a good mate who can put the system in for you.'

'Sounds like a hell of a lot, Bobby.'

'Nothing to worry about. I'll give you a price on Monday. Anything else? I see there are other buildings here.'

'The Grieve's Cottage and one other cottage, to begin with. The rest can wait.'

'OK, let's take a look,' he said.

We did a similar tour of the other buildings with Bobby taking notes as he went. At last we were finished and we sat on the low wall in front of the farmhouse to review the situation.

'I reckon it'll be a couple of weeks' work to make these wind and water tight,' he said. 'It's difficult to give you an accurate quote, because we might find some other things to do. A ball park figure to think about is five grand. I can give you a more detailed breakdown on Monday.'

'That's OK Bobby. Just go ahead. Can you start at the beginning of May?'

'That's no problem, Mr Kingsmill. I'll pencil it in.'

On Monday Alexi, Katie and I drove across to Worsall House. I had last seen it that dismal day after Christmas when I had driven across to tell Mrs Cuthbert I was selling the house. That was in my age of innocence, before I had read the harrowing account Maria had left me, before I knew what my mission was to be, before my future had crystallised into sharpness. We drove into the garden and stopped to talk to Bert who was giving the front lawn a first cut.

'Missus is in the kitchen,' he said.

As usual Mrs Cuthbert was ready for us. The coffee pot was keeping warm on the stove and a batch of cakes had just come out of the oven. Alexi gave her a hug and Mrs Cuthbert handed round the hot cakes.

'I hope you and Bert are keeping well, Mrs Cuthbert,' I said.

'And thanks so much for coming to our wedding,' Alexi added.

'No, pet, thank you for asking us. It was a right good do and you and Katie looked really lovely.'

We were force-fed more cake and poured a second cup of coffee.

'Mrs Cuthbert, the last time I spoke to you I told you I would be selling Worsall House. Well, I still am, but things have moved on a little. I've bought Alexi's old farm, Brock Hall, above Osmotherley.'

'Well, that's really splendid,' she said. 'I'm sure Alexi and Katie will love living there.'

I recognised the kindness in her voice but couldn't help

noticing a tinge of sadness at what she expected me to say next. Before I could speak, Alexi butted in.

'The thing is Mrs Cuthbert, I know it's a big step, but we wondered if you would like to live up there – as housekeeper and gardener that is. There's a cottage going empty that would suit you very well. You could carry on exactly as you are now, except there would be people getting in your way.'

'You could make cakes every day!' laughed Katie.

There was no reply from Mrs Cuthbert but a tear began to appear at the corner of each eye, then the apron went up to her face as her emotions mounted. I stood by, helpless, but Alexi put her arm round her old shoulders.

'I take it that means "yes",' I said.

'Yes, Mr Peter, it does. Wait till I tell Bert.'

'No need. I heard it all,' came a voice from the back door and Bert walked in from the garden. 'I take it you'll have a vegetable garden, and the like.'

'Of course,' said Alexi, 'but you might have to grow Italian vegetables, if my mother gets involved.'

'Don't worry about that Mrs Kingsmill' – showing old-fashioned respect to his new mistress – 'I can grow owt yer like! Now, best be getting on.'

And he pottered off as quietly as he came.

'Always been strange, our Bert,' said Mrs Cuthbert, 'but you've made him very happy, not that you'd notice.'

Chapter 7

The Arlanda Airport Express raced through the flat Swedish countryside. The digital display above the carriage door showed we had reached one hundred and eighty kilometres an hour; then, in English and Swedish, it announced "Next station – Stockholm Central". As I looked out of my window, the bridges flashing overhead, the passing electric gantries pulsing, fields of yellow rape vanishing, I could not help but think over the strange new shape my life had taken since that fateful letter from Skene had landed on my doormat in Pimlico. And here I was again, following another trail from another letter.

It was late April when Hugh Farquhar at last contacted me. I had waited patiently at first but, as time passed, my mind fell to other things, in the almost tacit assumption that my search for Magnus Lundquist would be fruitless. Perhaps he was dead, for he would by now be an old man; perhaps he had vanished to another continent, another world. Then one day the telephone rang and Farquhar delivered his terse message. When he had finished, he said:

'That's it, Mr Kingsmill. I've sent you the details in writing, together with my invoice. If I can be of further assistance, let me know.'

In a few minutes I would be in the centre of the city. I took the letter from my pocket and looked at it again. Magnus Lundquist was still alive and the Swedish Government had smothered him with awards and decorations. He lived in a villa overlooking the Baltic – Farquhar had researched this – on one of the thousands of tiny islands that made up the Stockholm archipelago. I also had his telephone number, which I had yet to call. Looking back, I think I felt I needed to maintain an exit route if, at the final hurdle, I decided to pull out. And as the train slowed as it ploughed through the suburbs, I still had not formulated exactly what I would say to Lundquist; and did I really expect him to tell me anything, a complete unknown to him? I had in my pocket the only photograph I had of Maria, together with the letter Renate had sent her in 1946. I hoped that this would convince him of my authenticity; beyond that, I could only trust to his goodwill, and his memory.

That night I spent in a soulless Stockholm hotel and in the morning ate an equally soulless breakfast from an uninspiring cold buffet, with a hot water machine for do-it-yourself tea and coffee. The hotel dining room looked out over the Baltic and a cruel April wind whipped up the waves, blowing from the east and the Russian steppes. It was still early in the year and I was very far north. My plan for the day was simply to reconnoitre, so I hailed a taxi on the quayside and asked the driver to take me to the address I had on my piece of paper.

'That will be a lot of kronor,' he said.

'Don't worry, just take me there,' I replied.

We headed north-east past the Vasa Museum and then on out beyond the big-dipper and the amusement park at Skansen. Soon the road began to cross bridges and causeways linking small islands, rising over tiny coves and past hamlets of red and white wooden houses. The conifers became thicker by the roadside, closing out the view and the sky, and ten minutes later the driver turned off the smooth asphalt road on to a gravel track, full of pot-holes. He pulled up in a clearing and pointed ahead. I looked out of the car window to see a large yellow and white wooden villa, which would have been in place in a movie of the deep south, except for the granite blocks that made up a jetty jutting out into the Baltic.

'I'll walk from here,' I said and paid him his two hundred kronor.

'You can catch a bus back to town from the main road back there,' he said, as he drove off.

I walked slowly up the track towards the jetty. I wanted, for some reason, to try to catch a glimpse of Lundquist before I approached him. I suppose I had built up a mental picture of him as a ruthless operator, for I had decided he was the one who must have deliberately sent Thomas Engel to his death and condemned Maria to a life of loss. I had in fact persuaded myself to hate him.

The approach to the house was half-concealed by a belt of trees which allowed me to gain a vantage point without revealing my presence. From here I looked across the wide lawns to a long glass conservatory facing the sea. At first I saw no movement but, after a few minutes, a figure appeared, that of a woman, wheeling before her an invalid chair in which an old silver-haired man sat. She turned the chair to face the sea and left the room. So this was Lundquist, the arch-schemer, at the end of his life, looking out to the retreating horizon in a quiet backwater of the Baltic. I pulled my mobile phone from my pocket and dialled the number Farquhar had given me. There was a pause, then the unfamiliar ringing tone of the Swedish exchange, before I heard a woman's voice in Swedish and I recognised the words "Herr Lundquist". I spoke in English, gave my name and asked to speak to Lundquist. Then I heard the receiver picked up and Lundquist was on the line, speaking in immaculate English.

'Who are you, Mr Kingsmill? What do you want?' he said.

'I need to meet you, Mr Lundquist. Maria Bienkowska sent me.'

There was a pause.

'I don't understand you. What do you mean?'

'Or should I say, Camilla Andreassen? Perhaps you remember her better by that name.'

There was a longer pause.

'We'd better talk, Mr Kingsmill. Where are you?'

'Just outside. I can be with you right away,' and I shut off the phone.

I felt a cold sweat on my brow and a prickling sensation at the back of my neck as the nerves set in, but I strode out from behind the trees and up to the front door of the house. It opened before I could ring the bell. The housekeeper led me down a long hall, through a library lined from ceiling to floor with books, and into the sunlit conservatory. There before me, awaiting my arrival, was Lundquist, gripping the wheels of his chair, and smiling gently.

'This is intriguing, Mr Kingsmill,' he said. He was completely at his ease. 'Do sit down.'

I remembered the way Maria had described him, how they had mistrusted him so, and I understood why. I felt at his mercy.

'How can I help you?' he asked.

I was disarmed. I had come full of accusations. But now I knew all I could do was to tell my story of Maria and Thomas as I knew it, which is what I did.

Lundquist listened carefully to what I said, without interruption, gazing fixedly on the sea. When I had finished, he turned to me:

'And so you think I betrayed Thomas Engel and destroyed Maria's life, all because I needed their silence? Is that what you think?'

'That's what I think,' I replied. 'You were the only person alive who knew their secret and to whom it mattered. I ruled out your man Björn from the start.'

'Ah, yes, honest Björn. I had forgotten him. Tell me, Mr Kingsmill, how do you know all this?'

'Maria told me her story – in writing – but I only read it after she died. I learned about Thomas' death from a contact in West Germany. The rest is a process of deduction, which led me to you.'

'So Maria died. I remember her well. Such a bright lively girl but very innocent. And Thomas, the cultured aristocratic man of honour, in the wrong war, fighting for the wrong side. He loved music, I remember, all except Wagner, of course. I heard about his death after the war. It was an outrage. But tell me about Maria. I could have fallen in love with her at the time.'

'I never knew her. I met her just once. She was dying of cancer. She took an overdose the day after we met for the only time as adults. It was her way of freeing me from any responsibilities. I regret very much the way I disregarded her then.'

There was a long silence. We looked out to sea, where low scudding clouds were racing across the distant forests. Then Lundquist turned to look at me, straight in the eyes.

'But why do you think I would betray these two beautiful people? I worked for the British and the Swedes. We were on the same side after all. What had I to gain?'

'There was no one else left,' I said. 'Maria and Thomas themselves did not trust you. Perhaps your versatility went as far as the Russians, as well as the British and the Swedes.'

'You mean I was some kind of international espionage whore?'

He threw back his head and laughed.

'No, no, my dear friend. Your imagination has run ahead of you. Let me tell you, there was one other person alive who needed to silence them both. He succeeded with Engel but could not manipulate the end of Maria. She had become anonymous until it was too late to bother.'

'And who was that?' I asked, looking him straight in his piercing blue eyes.

'It was a dead man, of course. Who else but Jonathan Blake.'

'But he died at Nordmarka Chapel, in your abortive trap with Maria as the bait. He shot himself to avoid capture. Maria saw it with her own eyes.'

'She thought she saw it but it never happened. Yes, it went wrong. He put his gun to his head but, before he pulled the trigger, I shot him myself. Then the lights went out and chaos followed. We got Maria and Thomas away as quickly as possible so they saw nothing. The British special forces carried Blake back to their base and I went with them. We thought he was dead but he was still breathing and we needed him alive. That was the whole aim of the exercise. We patched him up, flew him over the border as quickly as possible, and took him to a military hospital set up for British guerilla fighters wounded in raids. He was there for weeks before he was transferred to Stockholm for interrogation. When the British were finished I expected them to lock him up for the duration of the war and deal with him later. But the strangest thing happened. We received an order from the top – and I mean the very top – to fly him back to London. I heard he was back at his desk before long, with a promotion of course! That was the last I heard of him. After the war, I was posted to Washington and I chose not to remember the dirty deeds I had been involved in. Then the Cold War produced a whole host of new enemies and friends, and Nazi Germany became just a chapter in the sordid history of the world. That's why I never thought of Blake again, until today that is.'

'Why do you think the British took him back, instead of putting him up against a wall?'

'Only one reason, Mr Kingsmill. They did a deal. Everything Blake had on German intelligence – and he knew the people in Berlin, of course – in return for a clean sheet. Remember the war was far from over.'

'So you think Blake was the one who needed to silence Engel and Maria?'

'I think it's very likely. A man with a career, and a new identity no doubt, would not want ghosts from his past to reappear.'

There was a long silence, as I took in the impossible facts Lundquist had offered me. And then I said:

'If what you say is true, I need to find Blake. He needs to pay for what he did.'

'I understand that Mr Kingsmill but, as you see,' he said, looking down at his wheel chair, 'I am no longer the man I was.'

I looked at Lundquist and saw a tired old man. It was time for me to leave. But before I left I had a further question for him.

'Tell me, Mr Lundquist, why you never chose to help Maria after the war? You knew what she had done, after all?'

'It was simply this, Mr Kingsmill. I never knew she needed help. Remember, she disappeared into the city before the war ended and I never heard from her again. Why did she not seek me out? Well, I can only surmise that she thought the evidence that Blake had fabricated against her, that she had gone over to the other side, that she had betrayed her network, would be so powerful as to negate anything else. Particularly since Blake had been taken back into the bosom of the British intelligence service and even given higher status by them, although she did not know that at the time. You see, Blake continued to control her fate. She probably did not have the strength to fight anymore.'

His housekeeper showed me to the door and bade me an icy goodbye. I was happy for the time it took to walk back to the main road along the fir-lined track, and for the wait for the country bus that threaded its way to the city through the harbours and inlets of the archipelago. It was late afternoon when I reached my hotel. I felt sad and alone, all the memories of Maria and her story having been rekindled. And I was not sure what I would do next. Half of me told me to get back to Yorkshire, to my sweet new life, and think only of the future; the other half told me the future only existed from the pieces of the past we carried with us. I could hear Alexi's voice in my head telling me to give up on *Four Quartets* and get on with life but I was not able to do so.

Later that evening, as I cut a solitary figure in a half-empty restaurant by the harbour, my mobile rang. It was a Swedish number.

'I'm sorry to bother you Mr Kingsmill.'

It was Lundquist's voice.

'Your visit today moved me, I must admit. I wondered if I could help after all. So I looked through some papers I have kept from the past. My wife kept a scrapbook of newspaper cuttings and so on. You understand when you are a public figure you are constantly being photographed with important people. Our time in Oslo threw us together with the whole Nazi gang, of course, and I have them all in pictures. I found one from a Christmas Ball at the Grand Hotel. The interesting thing is that Blake was there, all dressed to kill, with his latest girl on his arm. Everybody thought he was one of those entrepreneurs you know, lining his pockets by selling during the war. I can send you the picture if you like. He was very young then, of course.'

This could be the impetus I had needed to keep moving on. I thanked him and gave him my hotel address. The next morning a brown envelope was waiting at reception.

'It came by courier this morning,' the receptionist said.

I opened it over my coffee. In the middle of a group of German officers stood a tall dark-haired man of around thirty, hair sleeked back, in dinner jacket and black tie, with a young girl in a long ball gown next to him. He smiled back at the photographer as if he were the star of a Hollywood premier.

Chapter 8

It was the Easter vacation and the university had gone down. The city had resumed its secular routine, freed from the frenetic surge of undergraduate life. The college quadrangles were quiet, save for the camera-bearing Japanese and American tourists who were beginning to arrive as the spring sunshine coaxed the daffodils from their roots along the grassy Backs by the Cam. The streets were free of bicycles and the voices of young people rushing back to college for evening hall from the lecture rooms on West Road and the aisles of the University Library. I was here again, but this time not by chance, for I needed to see Wotherspoon for a specific purpose. And I needed him to trust me.

My trip to Stockholm had forced me to revise my detective activities and revealed me as the amateur I was, rushing to conclusions and making snap decisions, instead of letting the story piece itself together. I needed to be Isherwood's camera, watching and recording, leaving the pattern of events untouched for fear of changing its meaning and significance. But I was so involved, I began to feel that events were shaping my destiny, more or less, beyond my control. Maria had given me a trail I had to follow; Lundquist had given me a fact I had not believed was possible. And I was in Cambridge again because an open briefcase in the club that evening in Piccadilly had presented me with an opportunity for dealing with that impossible fact.

I had telephoned Alexi from Heathrow.

'I'm going to Cambridge,' I said. 'Lundquist has given me information I didn't think was possible. I need to do some more work. It's to do with Jonathan Blake.'

'The handsome Lothario,' she said. 'I thought there might be something more to be said about him. How long will you be? I miss you, Peter.'

'Two days at most. Give my love to Katie.'

I felt desolate as I put down the telephone. It was as if I could never finally free myself of this terrible fate, always seeking, always finding the horizon receding, like some classical hero set an endless task by a malignant god. I felt desolate too as the train trundled across the flatlands of East Anglia and pulled into the dreary yellow- brick station. I took a taxi to the University Arms and checked in, took a shower and changed, and then strolled down St Andrew Street, past Great St Mary's and down Senate House Passage to the Front Court of Trinity Hall. At the Porter's Lodge I asked for Professor Wotherspoon.

'Just out, Mr Kingsmill,' replied the head porter, to my great surprise having remembered my name from my last visit before Christmas.

But then I recalled the skill of the porters in memorising freshers' names from the group photograph at the start of my first year.

'Shall I leave a message in his pigeon-hole, sir? For when he comes back.'

'Please. Ask him to ring me on this number and say, if possible, I would like to meet him this evening.'

I passed on through Front Court, the mellow sandstone walls beginning to retreat behind the profusion of climbing flowers, and into Latham Court, next to the river. A wide archway opened on to Garret Hostel Lane which led me over the river and on to the footpath heading up river past Clare, then King's and finally Queens'. The daffodils were in full bloom, great wide swathes of yellow, and the willows showed the first fresh green leaves of the season. Before I knew it, I was halfway to Grantchester when my mobile rang. It was Wotherspoon.

'I got your message. Why don't you join me for dinner? In my rooms tonight around seven-thirty. I'll get the college kitchens to send something up.'

'That's very kind of you. I look forward to that.'

'More army hat badges?'

'Not quite, but it's the end of that story, in a way.'

I retraced my steps to Queens'. I suddenly realised I needed to plan what I would say to Wotherspoon, if he was going to take the leap of faith I wanted from him. I began to formulate my story in my head as I turned up towards Parker's Piece and the hotel. The sun was beginning to set as I looked out from my window across the green. I could not say how Wotherspoon would react.

Nothing had changed since my last visit to Q staircase, except that Wotherspoon had begun to remember my name. A drop-leaf Pembroke table stood open in the centre of his study and a college servant was in the process of spreading a white cloth and setting out cutlery. Wotherspoon shook me warmly by the hand and poured me a dry sherry from a ship's decanter. His bright eyes looked out from beneath his bushy grey eyebrows, like a small animal looking out for prey. We sat in the same leather armchairs by the two-bar electric fire. Two more sherries into the evening, dinner arrived on a large tray, under metal covers to keep in the heat on the trip from the kitchens. We took our places at the table and Wotherspoon ladled out soup from a tureen.

'Pretty simple fare, I'm afraid, Kingsmill,' he said, as later he handed over a slice of steak and kidney pie, 'but it beats self-catering when you're a lonely old bachelor like me.'

We had finished a bottle of burgundy by the time the cheese arrived and then the servant brought in coffee, which we took in the leather armchairs, with a large brandy and a cigar. The conversation throughout the evening had ranged widely, in the way that educated Englishmen affect even between total strangers. But I knew it was time to get on with the real business of my visit although Wotherspoon had shown no curiosity so far.

'Professor Wotherspoon, thank you for your hospitality this evening. But you must be wondering why I wanted to see you.'

'Not at all, my young friend, but I see that you wish to tell me,' he replied with a twinkle in his eye.

'The fact is, I'm here to seek your help, in a very sensitive matter.'

'Tell me.'

And I began my story from the beginning, from the discovery of my real mother and her wartime exploits, of her life after the war, of Thomas Engel's betrayal and execution, of Maria's sacrifice of her child and of my regret at my final rejection of her, now that I understood her motives. I told him of the larger-than-life figure of Jonathan Blake and the sophisticated shadow that was Magnus Lundquist.

'And tell me, how do you think I can help you?' he asked, after my long recitative.

'I want to heal the wounds in my life,' I replied. 'There is something I must do in order to achieve that, and I hope that you can help me.'

'Is this a matter of revenge, or of compensating for your sense of guilt?' he asked, with that sharp insightfulness of his analytic brain.

'Neither – I believe. I've thought about this a lot. It seems to me it's about finishing a task I've started. I've been drawn into this, as if I were being led forward by a pattern of events beyond my control. But there's a bit of the pattern where there's a gap. I've a good idea where to find the missing piece and fill the gap. When I look back over my life I can see more clearly now all those times where I stood back on the brink, afraid to commit to the leap forward, because I thought it too irrational or too emotional to do so. Better to hold back, never to make a mistake, never to be wrong through trying too hard. But I've learned the value of doing the opposite – I've seen it in action now – and I can't go back to the old ways. I have to finish this task, fill the gap. I have to bring together the two people in my story – even though they are dead – by giving the world an explanation of their actions. They have been dealt with badly.'

'And this is very important to you. I can see that in your face. But I think what you are about to ask me, may be – shall we say – an invitation to compromise my position?'

'How did you deduce that, Professor?' I asked, amazed at his perceptiveness.

'Shall we say – an educated guess – influenced by the fact that you know I have a role in intelligence? I have been expecting a call from you ever since we met in the club those days ago. You see, I knew you had worked out my role with MI5. I knew you had spotted my security lapse, and I remembered your interest in identifying the British officer in your photograph. It was a fair guess. Something to do with intelligence personnel. But I need to know exactly what you are asking of me Kingsmill.'

I took a sip of brandy then came out with it.

'Can you help me identify Jonathan Blake, Professor? Who is he really? I know that he returned to British intelligence after the Oslo incident but Lundquist could not tell me what became of him. Can you?'

Professor Wotherspoon poured another brandy and swirled it around in his glass as if he were reading tea leaves. Then he put back his head.

'The isle is full of strange noises,' he said, 'but Prospero will help explain them.'

'I don't understand you.'

'We live in a brave new world, Kingsmill. The Security Service database is called Prospero. It is encrypted; only the few can access it. I happen to be one of them. I looked you up the other day, just out of interest. Your tutor – you remember Gordon Stevens, don't you – sent me a note about you in 1966. Possible recruit. It's still on the file but was never acted upon. "A fine intellect but perhaps too scrupulous" were his words, I think. Oh, yes, you could have been one of the few yourself by now. Such strange creatures, we inhabitants of the secret island, which is what I call the intelligence world. You realise what you are asking of me is a criminal offence and that I would be breaking the Official Secrets Act, the very same one to which you pledged allegiance when you joined your own Service?'

'That's certainly true,' I interrupted, 'but Blake was a double agent and a traitor to his country. He should be exposed, regardless of my own personal interests.'

'And you think you can make it stick, all these years

later?'

I could sense he was coming round to my way of thinking.

'Don't you think, wherever he is now, this Jonathan Blake, that he will have surrounded himself with a wall of steel against denunciation, rolled himself up in the thick blanket of respectability, and surrounded himself with friends in high places?'

'I think I can make it stick.'

Wotherspoon stood up and walked slowly around the room, puffing gently at the remains of his cigar, and stopped before the window. The evening light was fading over the Backs, casting a silver sheen on the river. What was it about this place that had led so many into duplicity? Was it the forensic examination of motive and reason in this tight-knit intellectual community which created the restlessness of spirit that pervaded Cambridge, and from which I too had suffered for so many years? The failure to commit whole-heartedly, the triumph of scepticism; I had known it so well. I was roused from my thoughts by the sound of Wotherspoon filling the brandy glasses once more.

'Do you know what he looks like?' he asked.

'I have a photograph from the war, taken with a gang of German officers in Oslo. He was young then. Lundquist gave it to me.'

I took the photograph from my breast pocket and handed it to Wotherspoon. He looked at it carefully and then took it across to his desk to examine it through his magnifying glass.

'A handsome fellow, wasn't he,' he said. 'May I hold on to this?'

'Does this mean you will help?' I asked.

'Of course,' he replied.

Chapter 9

Bobby the builder started work on Brock Hall farmhouse the day after the early May Bank Holiday. A couple of days later I drove up with Alexi and Katie to observe progress. The building stood like a blinded giant, the black holes of the windows gazing across the moors. Scaffolding reached up to the gutters and roof ladders were hooked on to the apex. A ramp of planks led up to a skip which was filling with damp plaster and rotten timber hacked out of the interior. We found Bobby himself with his head down a hatch in the drawing room floor, ample backside hoisted into the air.

'Just checking for signs of rising damp, Mrs Kingsmill,' he said with a grin, sensing the growing panic in Alexi's face as she saw her future home falling into ruin around her, to the sound of shovel and lump hammer.

Two weeks later the building was wind and water tight and the builders moved on to the Grieve's Cottage. Throughout, Alexi was working at her journalism and I tried to take my mind off things by following the building project. But it was small beer to my real thoughts, which lay with Wotherspoon and the mysterious magic island of secrecy that he had evoked that night in Cambridge. One evening, in the cottage, Alexi stood behind me as I sat at the table by the window, gazing out. She leaned down and put her face close to mine.

'You're restless, Peter, aren't you? Have you heard nothing?'

I had told her everything that had happened in Stockholm and with Wotherspoon. She understood the waiting game I had to play.

'I would tell you if I had. This silence is worse than anything. I keep wanting to chuck it up and start living again but I'm always being dragged back. There's no escape. I feel like the little boy in *The Snow Queen*, trying to fit together the pieces of ice to solve the puzzle and earn his freedom from the wicked queen. There's just one piece missing.'

'So that was what you were reading to Katie this evening. She told me about it when I put her to bed. Wasn't it the power of Gerda's love that freed Kai after all? Well, we all love you, Peter, and you will be free of this, I know.'

And Alexi, as usual, proved to be right. The next morning, Bill came across from the Queen Catherine with a message.

'There's a strange old geezer stayed overnight, Peter. Drove up from somewhere south in an old Jag. Asked me at breakfast this morning where you lived. Said he'd lost your phone number but remembered the name of the village. Didn't know whether I should tell 'im or not. Yer not in trouble are yer, like the time before? That Spurling chap.'

'No Bill, I'm not in trouble. I'd better come over and speak to him myself.'

Bill led the way. Breakfast at the pub was served in a section of the lounge bar and when I arrived I recognised instantly the shaggy hair and tweed jacket of Professor Wotherspoon, deeply engaging with his Yorkshire ham and eggs.

'Ah, Kingsmill,' he shouted, 'found you at last. Lost your number but I recalled your mentioning Osmotherley. Knew the name from my medieval history days – you know, Mount Grace Priory and all that. This ham and eggs is really wonderful. Not surprised you live in Yorkshire. Come and join me.'

I sat down at his table and Bill brought me a coffee cup. I knew Wotherspoon had something important to say but I contented myself with drinking coffee and watching him finish his breakfast. Whatever he had to say, he would say in his own way, in his own time. But my heart rate had rocketed. At last he put down his knife and fork, drained his umpteenth cup of coffee, and finished his last slice of toast and marmalade.

'I've got something for you,' he said at last, looking at me through those piercing eyes, 'but I'm not sure what you are going to do with it. Is there somewhere private we can go?'

'Come to my house, Professor. It's just over the road. You can meet my wife. She knows everything that I know about this. It's good of you to drive all this way.'

My mind was dwelling on his comment: I too was not sure what I was going to do. But then, this had been the way throughout my voyage of discovery: my hand had rarely been on the tiller.

As we crossed the road, Alexi was pulling up alongside the passage to the cottage, having just dropped Katie at school. She waited as Wotherspoon and I crossed the road towards her. I introduced them.

'You're a lucky fellow, Kingsmill. You have a beautiful wife and you live in God's Own County,' he said laughing.

Despite his bachelor ways, he still knew how to flirt with young women, a skill I had never begun to understand. I showed the way into the cottage and we settled down in the small front room. Wotherspoon had with him a battered leather briefcase from which he proceeded to extract a number of manila files which he dropped in a pile on the floor by his chair.

'These are photocopies of the real thing,' he began. 'Files going back to the late forties have not yet been computerised, unlike the later ones,' he added by way of explanation. 'I had to – shall we say – borrow them and then copy them.'

'The real thing?' asked Alexi.

'Yes, indeed, the early years of Jonathan Blake – and, yes, I believe he is still alive.'

The name hit me like a bullet. I now knew what Wotherspoon had meant when he said he didn't know what I would do with the information. My target was no longer a literary figure in a story. He was flesh and blood and I had to confront him.

'I drove here, Kingsmill, because I simply could not risk sending these papers to you, as you will understand. The fact that I had lost your telephone number was irrelevant. I'm glad

I found you so easily, otherwise I might have left them in the back of a taxi, in line with an old Whitehall tradition. I'm going to leave these with you for you to use as you wish and then you must destroy them. Can I trust you to do that? I'm sure I can.'

'What persuaded you to take such a risk to help us?' asked Alexi.

'I heard Peter's story, my dear, and I thought: right must be done; let right be seen to be done. I'm not moved by stories of who betrays his country and who doesn't. For the most part this is a kind of game people play. But I could see the hurt that had been done and the hurt that still remained. That's why I did this. And now I will leave you.'

And with that Professor Wotherspoon rose to his feet and gathered up his briefcase. I shook him warmly by the hand.

'Thank you so much, Professor. Thank you.'

'Dear boy, no thanks, please. The next time you are in Cambridge bring your wife to dinner with you. I would be delighted to entertain you. I have a small house by the river at Grantchester, with a lawn running down to the water's edge. The summers are delightful there.'

After he had gone, I sat down and looked at the pile of documents he had left.

'What do we do now,' I said, looking at Alexi.

'How about reading them?' she replied.

Two weeks later we moved into Brock Hall Farm. It was only then that I opened the file that Wotherspoon had left me. I was drawing back the curtain on another's existence and the feeling of trespass and intrusion pervaded my mind as I studied the papers. They had been typed on an old Imperial typewriter, by some matronly secretary in a pre-war Government office that the world never knew existed. I could almost smell the carbon paper and hear the clatter of steel filing cabinets in that secret world. At least, this was what my imagination told me. I felt as if I were about to dissect a cadaver, gained illicitly for nefarious purposes. And for two weeks I had shied away from the task.

I sat in my undecorated new study on the first floor. From

my desk in the window I looked south across the Hambleton Hills and down to the Vale of York. Tiny white clouds scudded north-east against the blue sky and disappeared across the moors to the North Sea. All around me I could feel the burgeoning life of the hills as spring took hold. Below me I heard the bleating of sheep. Andrew had bought a flock of a hundred ewes and was holding them in the paddock. Through the window I watched as he and Katie, aided by the measured manoeuvres of Bess and hindered by the excited yelps of Rosie, corralled them for inspection. I looked at the dull pile of files before me and opened the first cover. I read for two hours, leafing through the pages, backwards and forwards, his background first and then his recruitment, followed by details of his deployment and ultimately his demise. And then the file stopped; it was as if Blake had ceased to exist, or had become another person. It was like hitting a brick wall. As Wotherspoon had suggested: where did I go from here?

I descended the creaking wooden staircase, as yet uncarpeted, and walked out into the wilderness of the front garden. Alexi had started to clear the undergrowth and Bert was digging in a far corner.

'Well?' she asked, as I approached her. 'What have you learned?'

'Plenty,' I replied, 'but the file stops dead. There's no mention of anything after the Nordmarka incident. He just disappears, it seems.'

I told her what I had written down in my notes.

'John Edward Blake was born in Finchley in 1910. Maria referred to him always as "Jonathan" which I suppose was an affectation by Blake, a bit more stylish than plain John. But the date is right: he would have been thirty in 1940, a mature man to a very young girl. In 1921 he started grammar school in north London and won a state scholarship to London University in 1928 to read Modern Languages – French and German. He graduated in 1932, having spent a year in Germany as part of his studies. Perhaps that was where it all had started – his involvement with the Nazis. A year later he was at Lincoln College, Oxford, doing an advanced diploma in Scandinavian languages. There was a letter on file from his tutor there, addressed to personnel division in the Security Service, dated June 1933, which seemed to be a recommendation for recruitment. There was also a letter of appointment from the Civil Service Commission, dated September of that year, and a signed copy of the Official Secrets Act. He was already calling himself Jonathan Blake. A year later he was posted to Oslo, to be attached to the embassy there. These are the bare facts.'

Alexi had read Maria's account carefully and had thought about it as much as I.

'I suppose that was where he began to cultivate his contacts in the upper echelons of the business community so that when the Germans arrived in 1940 they found Blake to be exactly what they wanted: a friendly wheeler and dealer, sympathetic and helpful, fluent in their language, with a foot in every door that needed to be opened.'

'You're right, I'm sure,' I continued, 'and for the British how perfect too: a direct line to the gossip of the German command, feeding back bits and pieces, to flesh out the reports of the network of British agents Blake was handling. It was too good to be true. It was perfect symmetry: Blake the servant of two masters, satisfying the needs of each, while living himself with style and dash, and with a steady supply of impressionable young women. Everybody was happy.'

'But that's not where the file stops, is it?' she asked.

'No, there are two complete files, filled with notes of activities, field reports, code-named operations, in all of which Blake played a role. He was clearly a rising star. But it all went wrong.'

I had left my study with the last file under my arm.

'Take a look at these. It's a collection of photographs,' I said, handing Alexi the file, which she began to examine.

'Blake with Nazis; Blake getting into cars with people; Blake walking on a city street; it goes on and on. What do you reckon these are, Peter?' she said.

'Pretty clearly Blake was under surveillance. The file is packed with photographic evidence. These other people he's with must be known German agents. That's my guess anyway. The British were simply collecting the evidence. It was the backdrop to the Nordmarka trap they were about to spring.'

'Peter, if Lundquist told you the truth, and Blake was reinstated, there must be a record of him on the files that Wotherspoon gave you,' said Alexi.

'Of course there must be, but not in the name of Blake. It's obvious to me that Blake reinvented himself as somebody else. Blake was dead; enter his successor. And all this was done with the approval of the top people in the Security Service, and no record was kept of it.'

'So where do we go from here? Is this the end of the journey?' Alexi asked.

That night Alexi lay in my arms in our new house. The curtains were drawn and through the gap I could watch the seven stars of the Plough move slowly across the inky black sky. My life had changed so much from six months ago and, though the sweetest girl I had ever met lay sleeping beside me, breathing softly against my shoulder, I could not rest. And then I remembered: Wotherspoon had said Blake was still alive. How did he know that? And what did he mean when he said he didn't know what I would do with the information he had given me? There was only one answer: Wotherspoon knew that Blake was still alive because he knew him, in his new identity, but he was not going to reveal him. That must be the case. And the problem of what I would do was not at all about what I would do; it was what would I do given that Blake was who he was? Perhaps Wotherspoon meant that Blake was so powerful, he was untouchable. That could be it.

These thoughts crowded in upon me with such rapidity that my chance of sleep was destroyed. I leapt from my bed and rushed into my study. There on the table by the window lay the pile of files. Lundquist had given me a photograph of Blake with the German officers in Oslo. I looked through the files for something better and then I came across it. Pinned to the last page of the last file was a full-size portrait of Blake, dressed in military khaki, standing by a camel, with a pyramid in the background. Someone had written in ink at the bottom:

"Cairo 1955". So this was the last sighting. I could surely do something with this. He hadn't been in Egypt a year before the Suez war unless he was engaged on some major intelligence activity. I needed to get back to Wotherspoon as soon as possible. I took the photograph from the file, as evidence to push Wotherspoon for more information. By this time Alexi was awake and had found me in my study.

'What on earth are you doing?' she asked.

'Thinking – and looking at this,' I answered, passing her the photograph of Blake.

'Cairo, 1955. What was he doing between 1943 and then?'

'Precisely. He not only gets off scot free from his treachery charge, he thrives and rises to the top. Wotherspoon knows a lot more than he is telling us, Alexi. We're going to Grantchester tomorrow, darling. Tea on the lawn running down to the river.'

'Peter, I never know what is going through your head. Why Grantchester?'

'I thought we might take up the dotty professor's invitation after all.'

'He's not so dotty, is he?' she replied.

'Not dotty at all. I think cunning might be a better word. He knows much more than he pretends.'

Chapter 10

Grantchester in that spring was as Rupert Brooke remembered it from the trenches. The lilacs indeed were in bloom and the poppies blew in the wind along the edge of the herbaceous border leading down to the river. We sat in a sheltered arbour looking south across the Granta. The air was still and the bees were beginning to hover around the blossom on the fruit trees scattered across Wotherspoon's garden.

'I wondered how long it would take for you to get back to me,' said Professor Wotherspoon, as he handed round the tea cups. 'It was the photograph wasn't it? Egypt 1955. I should have cut that out.'

'Not only that, Professor. There is nothing on the file between Nordmarka and Egypt. That's twelve missing years. Blake the traitor thrives. How can that be unless he has friends in high places? Is that what you were warning us of when you doubted our ability to take action?'

I looked him firmly in the eye, across the oh-so-English garden table spread with tea things from the Orchard Cafe up the road. And it was a very English conversation, about treachery and betrayal, not cut-throat, but gentile and polite as befitted the sacred sandstone cloisters of an ancient university. Wotherspoon paused for thought before he spoke.

'My dear boy,' he said, 'I never for a moment doubted that you could take action. The opposite in fact: I knew you could, and that made me afraid. Afraid for what might happen to you. When I looked at the papers I gave you, I came to the same conclusion as you. Whoever decreed that twelve years would be blanked out was in a very high place indeed. Certainly beyond the top level of the Security Service. The decision to round up Blake at Nordmarka must have been taken at director level because it was operational. He was discovered as a spy and the plan was to get as much out of him as possible. The Service would never have had him back. If he squealed, he would have been put out to grass, after the Swedish interrogation. But suddenly to be recalled, without any explanation to Lundquist and his people, and then to disappear for twelve years from Security Service records, before reappearing as a senior military figure, a colonel in fact, in Egypt in 1955, smacks to me of friends political rather than official. Are you really prepared to take on this man, who has so successfully covered his tracks for more than forty years, and who must have been sheltered by very senior political figures at the time? What evidence can you call on, except the memoirs of a woman who was living with a German officer? No, I don't doubt the truth of her story for one minute. But I want to protect you from the pain of public scorn when your accusations are dismissed, as they surely will be. Remember, by denouncing Blake you inevitably denounce his protectors too. Are you ready to face that?'

Before I could answer, Alexi had spoken for me.

'Of course we are. Peter is not alone in this. I know only what I have read but I know that a terrible injustice was meted out to Peter's father, and a lifetime of loss thrust upon his mother. Would you accept that, Professor?'

'When I was your age, Alexi, I suppose I would not. I admire you very much. I have, by the way, read every word you have written. Not all the senior common room were so impressed, I might add.'

Wotherspoon was visibly moved and we fell silent. There was a clinking of teaspoons and the passing of plates before he recovered himself.

'I can see I have failed, as I suspected I would, in persuading you both to take the course of compromise. And why should you, I suppose? You have your lives to live and your battles to fight. If you choose the wrong side now, heaven knows how you live with yourselves. I can't help feeling, Peter, that this piercing morality might have been the reason why we never recruited you to the Service. To be good, one needs to bend a little in the wind, not fight it to the death.'

'Tell us, Professor, who is Jonathan Blake? Whatever happens after that, is my responsibility, mine alone. I promise you.'

'The politicians – Government ministers at the time – who sponsored his return and his triumph are dead, all of them. But their families live on, and the bag-carriers who profited from their connivance with the Russians after the war – yes, they were traitors, you could say – will defend their reputations vigorously. You will have a fight on your hands, make no mistake. The Government that took power after the war contained many who had formed their views at the time when Communism was the ideal and who dealt with the Russians throughout the war. You were right to deduce that Blake betrayed your father to the Russians. Disclosure by a third party would be very difficult to handle and he was about to thrive on his good contacts with the enemy of us all. It was this covert link that brought him into favour with a cabal of socialist interests, and that was how he flourished after the war. Percentages from trade deals, back-handers for information, arranging business deals that were supposed never to happen, opening doors in the west for a rising Soviet oligarchy. Oh, yes, it was all going on. And Blake was at the centre, as the unreported, un-filed, anonymous and ubiquitous link man, raking in the riches.'

'How do you know all this?' I asked.

Wotherspoon looked at Alexi and then me, with a look that in other circumstances might have been that of shame.

'Because, my dears, I was one of that cabal.'

Silence fell like a hammer blow. I looked towards the river where the slender new leaves of the willows fanned gently in the breeze. In the distance, across the water meadows, I could see the pointed roof of King's Chapel. I imagined I could hear the calm tones of the choir, echoing from the vaulted ceiling. I hardly registered what Wotherspoon had said. Then I heard him say:

'Blake is alive. I've written what you need to know on this piece of paper. Please take it and do with it what you will. I wish you the very best. I envy you your clean souls.'

Afterwards, as Alexi drove us home, I said to her:

'You realise what Wotherspoon has just done, don't you?'

'Yes, he's put his fate in our hands. Some trust. What will you do?'

'I think he's done his penance. His sin is absolved. It's not for me to cast the stone. Blake, however, is a different matter.'

We drove on in silence, thinking our own thoughts. I imagined Wotherspoon as a young academic, just out of Cambridge, fired with left-wing ideals, thrust into a political adviser job with a battle-hardened minister, seduced by the power and the influence, sucked into the vortex. How hard to resist! And now, mellowed and liberal, regretful of his youthful zeal but not dismissive of it, following a wiser if less exciting route, and suddenly a figure from the past resurfaces and threatens his composure. I admired his courage; he could have sent me packing. Instead he gave me the chance to destroy him, as well as Blake.

By June the Grieve's Cottage was habitable and Andrew and Angelina moved in. It was as if the pieces of my life's jigsaw were slowly assembling around me: a pastoral idyll but, lurking behind, the inescapable imperative commanded by the name on the piece of paper Wotherspoon had given me. Alexi did not press me, and for that I was grateful, but it was her strength always to let things take their course, and that was what she did for me, in the knowledge that I would act when I was ready. And I was not yet ready. I watched the farm grow around me. Bert Cuthbert had got into the habit of driving up to Brock Hall three days a week, Worsall House no longer satisfying his obsessive gardening habit. Piece by piece the vegetable garden took shape: one day a row of broccoli plants would appear, then a row of lettuce, seed drills in perfect straight lines, winter cabbages, military files of leeks. From the window I watched the earnest discussions between Angelina and Bert as they argued out the way things should be: espalier plums, pears and apples were trained along the stone walls and redcurrant, blackcurrant and gooseberry bushes took root, each in their rigid square yard of ground. Man was shaping nature to his own designs, as he had done since Elizabethan times. On the hill, Andrew's flock of black-faced sheep grazed peacefully, chivvied occasionally by Katie's dog; while in the house Mrs Cuthbert began to make things ship-shape, amid the ladders and paint pots of the decorators. In the paddock a pony had arrived, kept company by Andrew's tup and an old donkey for which his brother needed a home. Alexi was happy to be a quiet part of this activity, writing and researching, glad to be back home after her years of wandering. I could feel the love of Gerda making me whole again. It was time for me to place the final piece in the pattern on the ice.

It was not what I expected. I knew that Blake would have aged, that time would have worn his fine features and slowed his dashing pace, but I was not prepared for what I found. Wotherspoon had provided me with no more than a telephone number. I had no name and no location. All I had was Wotherspoon's word that this was Blake, under whatever name he now travelled, and that he was still alive. And so one afternoon in early June I picked up the telephone and dialled the number. The voice that answered was distant and frail, but with that London slant that reminded me of Maria's description of him: a cross between the public school and a barrow boy. He called himself James Ballantyne. I hoped to God that Wotherspoon had got it right and I was not making an absolute fool of myself. I said my name but there was no response at first. Then after a pause there came an answer.

'I do not know you Mr Kingsmill. What do you want?'

'I would like to meet you. I need to talk to you about the war. Something that happened many years ago,' I said, hoping to entice him.

'The war? What would I have to say about the war? I have nothing to discuss, Mr Kingsmill. Who are you? Why are you bothering me?' came the reply, and I sensed he was about to hang up.

I needed a line to hook him. And then I remembered what Maria had written.

'Camilla would like to meet Mr Rodgers,' I said, slowly and deliberately.

The telephone line went quiet but I could just detect low breathing from the other end. Then after what seemed an age, Blake spoke.

'Where did you hear that?'

And then I knew for certain that this was Jonathan Blake.

'From someone we both know,' I replied, 'Someone close to both of us.'

There was a long pause, during which time I expected the line to go dead. Then, somewhat surprisingly, he took the bait.

'Very well. We had better talk. You had better come and see me. I warn you Mr Kingsmill, I live quietly now, away from it all. The world is too much with us, is it not, getting and spending. And God knows, I have done plenty of that. Where did you get my number?'

'Professor Wotherspoon.'

'Ah yes, of course, Wotherspoon. The only other one left alive from our little coterie. It would have to be him. I wonder why he did that. I thought we had a vow of silence to the grave.'

And I knew he was thinking exactly the same as I had thought previously: why risk his own neck when he could have drifted away into anonymity?

'I'm afraid I live very remotely,' he continued. 'You'd better write this down. Lismore House, Isle of Lismore, in Argyll and Bute.' I heard a dry laugh from the other end: 'Never heard of it, have you?'

'No, but I can find it.'

'Drive to Oban, take the Fort William road and turn off to Port Appin. There's a ferry from the Pierhouse Hotel, foot passengers only. I'll meet you at the other end. Wednesday, ten o'clock.'

The telephone went dead. The meeting was two days away. I was shaking with released tension. I still did not know what I was hoping to achieve from this but I was committed to the final throw. I flung open the window and breathed in the fresh air of the moors, bracken and early heather and the smell of freshly turned earth from the walled garden. In the paddock the pony cantered away, frightened by the movement of a rabbit, in this fresh new world.

After supper that evening I told Alexi what had happened. She knew I was nervous.

'He sounded strange and old. He quoted a Wordsworth sonnet at me. I would never have thought he could have much in common with romantic poetry.'

'Perhaps his road to Damascus ended at Lismore. I think I'll come with you,' she said. 'Sounds exotic. I'll look up the Pierhouse Hotel and book us in for tomorrow night. We can make it in a day, can't we? Have you thought he might be dangerous, Peter? After all, you might be exposing him for what he is.'

'Surely you don't think a seventy-nine-year-old man might pull a service revolver on me when he hears what I have to say? Do you think this is a plot to lure me to my doom on a remote Scottish island? That's too fantastic, Alexi.'

But I knew deep inside me that my trip was still shrouded in confusion: what did I really want to achieve and how would Blake react? Nevertheless, I put on abrave face to Alexi, as if I really knew what I was about.

Next morning we left Katie with Angelina and set off early to drive to the west coast of Scotland. Our journey was a secret between us; no one else knew the story that Maria had told and Alexi's parents assumed we were simply taking a break away from home for a couple of days. We followed the A1 north to Edinburgh. It was a brilliant June day, one of those days when the new leaves shine lime-green in the white light of the northern sun and it seems that this is the best place in the world. We cleared the sprawl of Newcastle and the wilds of Northumberland opened before us. Away to the north-west loomed the massive hulk of the Cheviot and to the east the stark rock of Lindisfarne rose from a mirror sea, topped by the grey stones of the castle.

'You remember Tadeusz?' I said, as we passed the turn-off to Alnmouth.

'Yes, I do,' Alexi replied. 'It seems like a million years ago now. Tadeusz and Stanislaw – that was when it seemed a simple thing, Peter. Do you wish it had stayed that way?'

'No,' I said, after a pause, 'I'm glad I learned about Maria. But I will regret for ever that I rejected her. There is no escape from that.'

'You mustn't blame yourself. How could you have known the real story then?'

And she put her hand across to mine as I drove northward. I felt the pulse of her blood beating next to mine and a lump in my throat rising in that painful way that sentiment has of weakening even the severest of stiff upper lips. I felt my eyes welling up and I could not explain why, except to say that I had learned to love at last and was glad for it.

At Stirling we took the winding road through Callander and on to Crianlarich. The hills rose into mountains, bare and gaunt, mountain ash and birch clinging to barren rock faces. At Tyndrum the road forked: left to Oban and the sea, right to the wilderness of Rannoch Moor, where the stag breeds for the gun, and down the grim chasm of Glencoe.

'Which way?' I said.

'Take the right fork,' came the answer.

The road rose steadily for mile after mile, winding through the contours of the barren moor, still red with winter bracken, past silent lochs of burn water, sprinkled with tiny islets where stunted trees braced themselves against the wind. At last we reached the pass and looked down upon the vast void of Glencoe. The narrow road seemed carved out of the mountain side as we threaded our way downwards, a sheer drop on our left to the valley floor. The grey rocks loomed above us as we descended, past rushing torrents of water from the crags above. Occasionally we passed a deserted cottage or farm building where earlier generations had scraped a living from the barren landscape. Inky clouds had gathered overhead blocking the sun from sight.

'This feels like a descent into hell,' said Alexi, 'or the heart of darkness.'

I did not reply, my mind on the road but, beyond that, on the meeting ahead.

A few miles later we reached Ballachulich and the sea.

The weather cleared as we followed the sea loch south. Another thirty minutes and we saw the sign to Port Appin to the right, and five miles further, along a tortuous single-track road, reached the Pierhouse at the Lismore ferry. It was four in the afternoon, the sea was calm, and the sun hovered above the western horizon in a blaze of light. Lismore lay opposite us, verdant and lush, and somewhere there sat Mr Kirtz himself, Jonathan Blake.

The Pierhouse Hotel was a low building, a strange conjunction of two roundhouses linked by a plain cottage building, all painted in white. It was the gathering point for locals waiting to catch the island ferry, a few intrepid holidaymakers, and a collection of fishermen here for the trout and salmon in the local rivers. But it was homely and comfortable. After dinner, we sat outside in the little courtyard between the roundhouses and watched the sun sink behind the island of Mull. The hills of Morvern faded into rose as the sun descended, like a Turner landscape, losing itself in a wreath of colours and shades. I looked across to Alexi and smiled, without speaking.

'What is it Peter?' she said, after a while.

'I can never get used to this, Alexi. Having you, that is. How did I deserve you?'

'Deserve me? You don't have to do anything to deserve me. I love you. It's as simple as that. I love you for what you are. All you need to do is love me back. You don't earn love, as a payment in return. The people you thought were your parents never showed you love; but you know that Maria could not have loved you more.'

'But I didn't know that, until it was too late,' I replied.

'It's not too late Peter. She's dead but you have her love nevertheless. You always were worth her love, although you were never told that. That's what this is about, isn't it? You're here because you want to repay Maria's love for you by confronting the man who destroyed her happiness.'

'That's it, Alexi. You've said it.'

I woke early the next morning, having slept badly, my mind on the coming encounter. The first ferry of the day had already crossed to Lismore and returned; and I waited on the jetty for the ten o'clock boat to depart. Alexi had said goodbye to me at the hotel and I was alone, apart from a few foot passengers who had already gathered. Five minutes before ten, two young men arrived on bicycles from the village. One began to sell tickets and the other jumped aboard and started the clanking diesel engine, which leapt into life with a dense puff of black smoke. The *Lismore* was a stubby little tub of a boat, half as broad as long, with a tiny inner cabin for wet weather and an open half-deck where islanders transported their children in prams, their dogs on leads or their new purchases in bulky packages. There was ample chatter among the passengers travelling that morning for, with a population of eighty, there were few introductions necessary. Halfway across, the current was strong as the tide ran out across a shallow and we had to fight against it in order to make our landfall, a tiny wooden jetty at the bottom of a steep track leading to the narrow road, which I had seen from the map was the sole link running the length of the island. The crossing had taken no more than ten minutes but, looking back to the mainland, it felt we were in another world. I wondered why Blake had chosen this place, so far away from the world he had inhabited.

The *Lismore* tied up at the jetty and we disembarked, the locals disappearing rapidly into waiting cars. Soon I was left alone. I had no choice but to wait. It was not for long; within five minutes a black car appeared and drew to a halt in the scrubby roadside clearing that passed for a car park. A young man, hair cut short, in jeans and a leather jacket, got out.

'Mr Kingsmill? I'm Jason. I'll take you to James. Hop in.'

We set off along the single track road, skirting the sea, through dense woodlands of ash and birch. After a mile or so the road descended and ran along a shingle beach, then at a fork we turned right, over a hill and up to a grey stone house standing alone on a rise. There was a porch with stripped tree trunks painted green, acting as pillars, in the style of a highland lodge, and a verandah running along the front. A crunching gravel drive swept us round to the side door. This was Lismore House; small, humble and remote.

'This is it,' said Jason, who had remained silent throughout the journey. 'Follow me.'

I had a mental image of what Blake would look like, derived from Maria's description and the photographs Wotherspoon and Lundquist had given me. I had added the years but I still expected to see a tall, silver-haired man, well-dressed, with style and composure, albeit a little bent by the passage of time. What I saw in that room overlooking the sea shocked me. And I suppose my shock was apparent.

'Not what you expected, Mr Kingsmill, am I?' was the greeting. 'Jason, fetch some coffee, will you, there's a good boy.'

I began to understand the relationship.

'Been with me five years, Jason. Good boy, found him in Marrakesh, of all places. Just too corny to be true, isn't it. A lost boy. So I took him in. He cares for me. Do sit down Mr Kingsmill.'

I took the armchair opposite Blake, in the bay window, and studied his appearance. The sharp light from the east caught his face and threw it into relief, every blister, every scar, every deep furrow. It was the face not only of an old man, but of one ravaged by a wasting illness.

'I suppose I caught this somewhere in Africa, maybe Cairo. I can't remember and in any case, who cares? It was in another country and besides the wench is dead – probably – or perhaps it was a boy. Again, does it matter?'

I had no answer to this. I kept my silence. Jason returned with the coffee, then sidled out of the room.

'So tell me, Mr Kingsmill, what exactly do you want from me?' he asked, taking a long cigarette from a packet on the side table next to him.

I watched him as his skeletal shaking hand struggled to open his Zippo lighter. I did not reply immediately but paused and looked at him steadily. I could see he was observing me as I had observed him. He nodded and made a gesture with his hand that seemed to invite me to speak. My head was racing: where to begin?

'There was once a young and beautiful girl, intelligent but innocent and naïve, who found herself involved in fighting for the side of freedom in the war. She didn't really understand at first why she was fighting except that she knew inside that it was the right thing to do. She worked with an older, more worldly-wise man, in a secret occupation. She fell in love with him, as most young women he met seemed to do. She became dependent on him and he led her on, entrusting herself to him. As a team they were so successful and he particularly revelled in the fame and prestige this gave him. He was most ambitious.'

'Is this story going anywhere, Mr Kingsmill? It's beginning to pall,' he said, exhaling theatrically from his cigarette.

'Be patient, please, Mr Ballantyne, or is it Blake?'

I could see his attention suddenly take grip as he heard that name.

'Over the years they built up a team of secret helpers, all of whom depended on the girl and the man for their survival, and for a while all went well. The Government they served thrived on the information they supplied about the enemy. The man was the hero of the whole operation, a star in his own right. But he wanted more: he wanted to achieve the greatest success of all, a brilliant stratagem that would take him to the top of the tree: to place the girl in the very centre of the enemy's camp. And so he did; she became to the outside world the enemy itself, living and working with it, but just to make sure her cover was perfect, the man betrayed her helpers, every one of them, so that the world thought she had become a complete traitor. She could never find a way back, ever. But then she worked out that the man really was working for the enemy all along and he held over her the power to betray her again. She was in his clutches completely.'

I paused and looked at Blake. His face had become stern, devoid of emotion, but he was following my every word.

'Do you know what the girl was called?' I asked.

'Tell me,' he said.

'Maria, Maria Bienkowska.'

He turned his face away and looked out across the sea. I heard a low sigh and a slow intake of breath. Then he spoke.

'Maria, yes. I remember beautiful Maria. She was my best achievement. Do you know her?'

'I met her once. She is dead now. But let me finish my story. She was not alone, hiding away among the enemy. She had a partner, an honourable man, who detested the evil of his country. He was gentle and cultured and they fell in love. When the war was over, they planned to live together as man and wife, but he too was betrayed and killed unjustly. He was betrayed by the man at the centre of everything, with a finger in every pie, the servant of every master, in order to protect his own skin. Am I making sense to you, Mr Blake?'

'What was this honourable man's name?' he asked with a sneer.

'His name was Colonel Thomas Engel. I'm sure you remember that. You should, because you had him killed!'

There was a long silence. Blake lit another cigarette.

'You know, Kingsmill, I have no regrets. They tried to finish me. They set a trap, at Nordmarka Chapel. I would have ended it then, in a blaze of glory, but they shot me in the leg. Comic, is it not?'

'I know. It was to stop you from shooting yourself. That's how fierce your pride was. You'd rather die than be exposed for what you are. You had Engel killed for the same reason, after you'd done a deal and got yourself back in the saddle.'

'Who the hell are you, Kingsmill?' he shouted, suddenly picking up his coffee cup and flinging it across the room, 'and how the hell do you know all this?'

'Just a little more of the story, Blake, then all will be clear. The war ended and Maria waited for Thomas to return from his last posting. But he never did. He couldn't – he was dead. Maria had to live on without him, in a country where she was treated as a traitor. But she had something, she had his child to remember him by, and to give this child a better life, she gave him away to a sister in England. She saw him only once more in her life, the day before she died by her own hand. She lost her son just as she had lost her beloved Thomas; her life was destroyed, just as his. You ask me who I am. I think you know. I am the son of Thomas and Maria. I want you to look at me and think what that means. I want you to tell me why you did this. I want you to tell me the great reason behind all this, your great mission in life!'

Blake dragged himself from his chair, his face white, his hand shaking on his walking stick, and he patrolled the length of the room, before stopping by the fireplace.

'You ask me that, in your cut-glass English public school voice?' he said. 'You who have analysed this whole thing already. Do you really think I have a reason, a justification, that can be found in your scheme of things? Would you understand me, whatever I said? I think we live in different worlds and speak different languages. My world is not a playing field, with rules of decency laid out. I don't subscribe to a moral code that sets out right and wrong in sharp relief. My world is one of survival, getting on, standing on other people to get to the top, smashing them down if need be. And I got to the top, Kingsmill, and I wasn't going to let anyone pull me down. If I was going to fall I would do it myself. Do you understand that? I doubt it.'

So that was it: what Maria took to be his English style was merely a pretence; his assumed veneer of superiority concealing a burning sense of inadequacy. Could such a motive of simple envy have driven this man to destroy with such venom in order to succeed? I feared that it was.

'I understand it well enough, Blake, but I hate your world. It's not one I would want to live in. But strangely, I don't hate you; I pity you.'

It was as if I were standing outside myself; I had never thought I would say these words, but the spiritual vacuum that I saw before me, more than the physical wreck, led me on.

'I pity you Blake because you have never cared about anyone, never loved anyone. You've never known what that means. Your life has been a void, you are an empty shell, and because you have the deepest disgust for yourself – oh yes, you have – you had no hesitation in murdering my father and destroying my mother's life. These actions to you were meaningless. I could expose you for what you have done but, instead, I pity you.'

I stood up and walked to the door. Blake remained leaning on his stick by the fireplace, his eyes towards the floor, as if he were studying the pattern in the carpet.

'You won't hear from me again Blake,' I said as I opened the door.

Jason was standing in the hall, hands in pocket.

'Take me to the ferry please,' I said.

We drove back the way we had come.

'You'll have a few minutes to wait for the eleven-fifteen,' he said.

'That's OK,' I replied.

Then, more by way of conversation than curiosity, I asked him if he got off the island much.

'I come and go as I please. James only leaves once a month though. I take him to the clinic in Oban for his tests and his medication. There's a small car ferry from the other end of the island. But he doesn't live in the world any longer. He sees no one and no one comes here. It's peaceful here but I won't stay – after he dies, that is.'

'Where will you go?'

'Somewhere. Anywhere. I'll find somebody else.'

We had reached the jetty and the ferry stood waiting to depart. I got out of the car and Jason drove off without another word. Across the loch I could see the white walls of the Pierhouse and I thought I caught a glimpse of Alexi standing on the jetty, waiting for me. A few minutes later the *Lismore* swung its stocky hull round into the sea loch and headed back to Port Appin, following its curving course around shallows and fighting the current. I looked back to the island and caught a glimpse of Blake's car moving slowly along the shore road back to Lismore House and its tragic owner. Jason showed no more loyalty to him than his next pay packet. This was not what I had expected: I felt no hatred; I felt no anger; I did not lust for revenge. I felt pity: pity for the lost years of Maria's life; pity for Thomas; pity for the empty person who had executed all this. At the jetty Alexi came forward and took my hand.

'I'm so glad to have you back safe, Peter. I was worried.'

'It's over Alexi. It wasn't a journey to the heart of darkness; more like seeing the picture of Dorian Gray.'

'What do you mean?' she asked.

'He's just an empty shell. He's dying. His life has destroyed him. I feel nothing but pity for him.'

That evening we sat in the courtyard of the hotel once more, watching the sun sink below the western isles. I told Alexi what had happened that day. I fancied I could glimpse the grey stone wall of Lismore House on its island hilltop, the red light of the setting sun glinting from the windows, and from there the wasted frame of Jonathan Blake gazing out across the sea, on nothing, his boy waiting for him to die. But it was my fantasy, simply the image on my mind, like the image burned on to your eyes when you have stared too long at the sun, the passing footprint of a creature long gone.

'We should go home now,' I said. 'I want to breath the fresh air of the moors again. This is over.'

'We'll leave first thing in the morning,' Alexi said. 'I need to go too.'

But the morning brought a dawning we could never have predicted. From the hotel dining room, from a window in one of the roundhouses, we could look out across the loch. This morning a thick belt of fog lay dormant on the windless surface of the sea. Outside a car pulled up, in the distinctive markings of the Strathclyde police, and two officers got out and walked down the jetty. At the same time, a black van, rear windows tinted dark, parked behind the police car. As we watched, the ferry from Lismore slowly took shape out of the fog, first the black hull butting the waves, then the white steering house. I looked at my watch. It was fifteen minutes to nine.

'There shouldn't be a ferry at this time,' I said. 'They leave Lismore at quarter past and are here in ten minutes.'

'Must be an extra sailing,' said Alexi, busy with her coffee and toast.

'No, something's happened. There's a police car parked outside and a couple of policeman are waiting to meet the ferry.'

The *Lismore* slowed as it reached the quay and, as it tied up, two men appeared pushing along the jetty a folding stretcher on wheels which they had unloaded from the black van. The policemen had already boarded the ferry and after a while emerged from the cabin carrying a long black sealed bag which they rapidly placed on the stretcher, covered with a blanket. A third policeman stepped off the boat after them. In a moment the stretcher was loaded into the waiting van and the vehicle disappeared up the road. The two policeman were walking slowly towards their car when I saw a third figure on the jetty, a slim young man dressed in jeans and tee shirt. I recognised him instantly as Jason. I rushed to the door into the courtyard and crossed to where he was standing, waiting to get into the police car.

'Jason, what's happened?' I asked.

'Oh, Mr Kingsmill. I'll be moving on sooner than I planned,' he replied with a wry smile. 'James is dead. The body's on its way to the police mortuary. They need to carry out an autopsy.'

'How did it happen?'

'He killed himself yesterday. Shot himself. Never knew he had a gun. Seems to have been an old pistol he'd kept from the war. Shot himself through the head. The police came over last night to clear up. I'm going with them now. I'm the only one around to identify him, no family or anything.'

With that he walked on towards the car, got in the back seat, and was whisked off up the road. So Blake had managed it at last, I thought to myself. This time there was no one to stop him.

Chapter 11

That summer at Brock Hall Farm was the most glorious of times. The sun seemed to shine every day from the wide blue sky and the purple heather burst into blossom with unusual vigour, painting the hills in garish colour for its brief moment of triumph. The buzz of the honey bees from the hives by the stone wall was a constant counterpoint to the rhythm of our daily lives. Andrew had bought from a farmer friend a Cleveland Bay pony for Katerina, not quite thoroughbred perhaps, and everyday walked her round the paddock, with his granddaughter perched proudly on top. And then she ran wild with the dogs on the hill, patrolling the growing herd of Blackfaces, as Andrew taught Rosie to answer to the commands that Bess knew so well. Bert and Angelina's vegetable garden bloomed, the untouched soil of years rich with goodness: early potatoes, white and round, broad beans in their pods, broccoli and kale, and strange multi-coloured lettuces of which Bert disapproved. Then raspberries, strawberries, followed by later plums and apples. It was a cornucopia of delights into which Angelina dived each day, emerging with glittering dishes which reminded her of home. I felt as if I were living in some Elizabethan allegorical poem, with beneficent nature showering the virtuous with the fruits of heaven. And all the time my love for Alexi, and hers for me, grew stronger. I would often watch her at work at the desk by the window of her little study, mind intent upon the structure of the next sentence of some article she was writing, oblivious of her watcher, her unruly hair falling over her shoulders, until the exquisite pain of her beauty became too much for me and I would kiss her neck gently.

But throughout that summer of calm after the storm, before the first yellow leaves fell from the trees, I knew there was one troubling thought that would never go away until I forced it out. I tried to draw a line under events by writing two letters: one to James McAlister, telling him I had spoken to Marta and that she had wished him well; another to Professor Wotherspoon, to tell him that Blake had killed himself after meeting me.

McAlister did not reply and I thought often of him sitting in his empty house in Norfolk, with no escape from his regrets. Wotherspoon, on the other hand, sent me in reply a breezy postcard from Menton, praising the Mediterranean climate. I could not decide whether this was obtuseness or humour on his part, but I tended towards the latter.

My periods of gloom persisted, when the buoyant mood of my new life sank below the surface for a while, and I stared again at the past and felt once more the regret I had tasted so often. It was deep in one of these black hollows that Alexi found me late one September evening, standing at the French windows in the drawing room, looking wistfully out across the valley.

'What is it Peter, my love?' she asked, 'You must tell me.'

'Can you guess?'

'I think I can.'

'How could I have done that? How could I have walked away? After what she had done for me, all those years of suffering. I need to do something to put that right but I'm not yet clear what that should be.'

'Let it rest for a while, Peter, and then you will know what to do. You'll recognise it when you see it.'

'How can you be so wise, Alexi, always?'

But she was right. I wrote a letter to Marta Pettersen later that month. I told her that I had read Maria's story, that Blake was dead, and that I felt sorrow for the way I had walked away from Maria that day in Oslo. I asked her who had mourned for Maria and where her remains lay. Sooner than I could have hoped I received a reply.

My dear Peter

I was so pleased to hear from you. I was afraid that our brief meeting in Oslo would be the first and the last. You should not be hard on yourself for what happened last year. Maria's intention from the outset was to give you the chance to walk away but I see now that she misjudged. Love is much more than a mathematical equation; the sides are never equal in the way that numbers and symbols can be. I don't think she quite understood the power of what she had to tell you. But that was her way. You must never blame yourself for the way you reacted.

Yes, I attended her funeral, which she had told me not to publicise, so I was the only mourner. A few weeks later the funeral people asked me what to do with the ashes. I took them myself. They stand on the window ledge of the garden shed in my allotment, along with my pots of begonia and pelargonia. They are another kind of flower, in my mind, and are in the best place I could find. You must tell me what you wish to do with them: they are yours by right.
With every good wish
Marta Pettersen

And that is how it came about that the small huddle of figures gathered together one November day – I think it was the twenty-seventh of the month – on a cold clifftop overlooking the city: Alexi, Marta Pettersen, Renate Stronheim and myself. I had written to Renate at the address Schneider had given me, enclosing a copy of Maria's manuscript. I was not sure how she would react, to hear from a half-brother she had never met, or how sympathetic she might prove towards Maria. As for the latter, I remembered that she had written to Maria after the war, to inform her of her father's death, and I expected that she would show understanding now, when the years would have mellowed any lingering resentment. As it turned out, meeting Renate was a bitter-sweet moment for each of us, mingling regret for the lost years and happiness at an unexpected turn in the lives of us both.

We had met at Marta's flat in Oslo and from there we took a taxi to Akershus. It was a bitterly cold day with a biting wind from the north. As the driver pulled up in the courtyard my memory flooded with the images from Maria's manuscript. It was as if I could hear the sounds of jackboots on the cobbled yard, the shouts of soldiers, and the tracks of armoured patrol cars clashing across the stones. Despite the passage of more than forty years, the menace of Maria's and Thomas' sojourn in this place seemed as vivid as ever. Marta led us through an inner courtyard and across another to an enclosed area in the far corner of the castle. I recognised it instantly as the castle garden, so dear to Maria in those harrowing years.

'The authorities gave us permission to be here,' said Marta. 'The grounds are normally closed to the public at this time.'

It was three in the afternoon and the northern day was already turning to night but looking south we could trace the silver-grey water of the fjord as it stretched its way towards the open sea. From our cliff top perch the steep face swept away, tree-lined, down to the sea. Marta handed me the casket and, reaching out across the stone wall, I sprinkled the ashes on to the wind.

'In memory of Maria and Thomas,' I said, 'and their love for each other.'

We watched as the swirling breeze carried the dwindling grey cloud away, across the wooded slope below, and perhaps even as far as the sea itself, to its ceaseless ebb and flow, to the world which had treated them so cruelly, turning relentlessly on its cold axis. Renate stepped forward and gently released a handful of wild flowers on to the cushion of air below, and we watched them disappear into the tree tops, sifting down towards the dark earth. I thought of Maria's girlhood in Poland, the dusty country roads, lined with wild flowers, traced across the flat plains, and I imagined what she might have been in another world, another time. I felt Alexi's hand tighten in mine and then I heard her speak:

'It's over now Peter. Let's go. It's cold and getting dark.'

So we turned away and walked towards the garden gate. As we neared it, I felt a hand touch my arm and turned to see an old man with a deeply lined face standing before me.

'Mr Kingsmill, thank you for what you have done. You

don't know me but I knew Maria. She was beautiful in every way. My name is Björn. I used to be the gardener here.'

'I know you better than you think, Björn,' I replied, and shook his hand. 'Thank you for the kindness you showed her.'

Later in that same week, when we were back home in Yorkshire, I was walking in the paddock, with Katie's pony trotting along beside me, nudging my hand for treats as she was always doing. Alexi had been away in Northallerton and from the paddock edge I caught sight of her Land Rover slowly winding up the hill and coming to a halt before the farmhouse. I walked across to meet her. She seemed happy and strangely coy about something and her happiness proved infectious. We walked together to a rise behind the house, from where we could see the rolling moors stretch out into the horizon, and watch the buzzards circling overhead chivvied by the crows.

'I'm glad to see you so relaxed again, Peter, but I do worry about what you will do now,' she said.

'I'm relaxed because I now have all the pieces assembled. Do you remember the Snow Queen story? I can complete the pattern now. I have everything I need.'

'But what will you do?'

'When I left London, I told Sir Gerald I was going to write. And that's what I shall do. I shall tell their story. The question really is what you will do while I'm busy.'

Alexi looked away and the low afternoon sun threw her face into relief. I had never seen her look so bursting with life. When she turned towards me again her eyes were laughing.

'While you're busy writing, my darling, I shall be having your baby. Or should I say, adding another piece to your jigsaw?'

A year later I had a son and I finished a book about Maria and Thomas, after whom we named our baby. A year after that, to my surprise, I found a publisher and I sent a signed copy to Ken Brandon, thanking him for his help on the way. He was Permanent Secretary at the Foreign Office by then – marching inexorably to the top as I had predicted – and he passed his copy to the Norwegian Ambassador in London.

Some time later, Ken telephoned me in Yorkshire.

'Peter, this story you wrote. Is it all true?' he asked.

'Certainly, Ken, why do you ask?'

'Because Olafssen wants to nominate your parents for some terribly posh medal, or something, but he wants to know if you will accept it first. Their officials have done their research – he mentioned a Swede called Lundquist but I wasn't clear what he had to do with it. They don't like to offer medals that get turned down.'

'Yes, I'll accept it. What's it called?'

'The Norwegian War Cross, I think he said. I guess his people will be in touch.'

I took Alexi with me to Norway to receive the medal. It was a sunny day in May. From the terrace of the palace we looked down the length of Carl Johan Gate, the very stretch of road where the Nazi invaders had paraded in 1940. In the distance I caught a glimpse of the fortress of Akershus, high on a promontory, where Thomas and Maria had passed their few years together, and I wondered if they had ever looked this way as they yearned for peace to come.

'What did he say?' asked Alexi.

'Who?'

'King Harald, of course!'

'Oh, he said I must be proud of what my parents did. That's all.'

I keep the medal on my desk at home in Yorkshire and look at it every day.

Thanks for reading my work. You can contact me directly at
pb_north@btinternet.com
If you have enjoyed it, please write me a review on Amazon.

By the same author available from Amazon:

Girl in the Picture

P B NORTH

WATERMILL CLASSICS

Printed in Great Britain
by Amazon